Waylander II: In the Realm of the Wolf

WAYLANDER II:
In the Realm of the Wolf

David A. Gemmell

LEGEND

LONDON SYDNEY AUCKLAND JOHANNESBURG

The right of David A. Gemmell to be identified as the author
of this work has been asserted by him in accordance with the
Copyright, Designs and Patents Act 1988

First published in Great Britain in 1992 by
Random House UK Limited
20 Vauxhall Bridge Road, London SW1V 2SA

Legend paperback edition 1993

Random House South Africa (Pty) Ltd
PO Box 337, Bergvlei 2012, South Africa

Random House Australia Pty Ltd
20 Alfred Street, Milsons Point, Sydney, NSW 2061
Australia

Random House New Zealand Ltd
PO Box 40–086, Glenfield, Auckland 10
New Zealand

The catalogue data record for this book is available from the
British Library

ISBN 0 09989 502

Phototypeset by Deltatype Ltd, Ellesmere Port
Printed and bound in Great Britain by
Cox & Wyman Ltd, Reading, Berkshire

DEDICATION

This novel is dedicated with great affection to Jennifer Taylor, and her children Simon and Emily, for sharing the joy of the American adventure, and to Ross Lempriere who walked the dark woods once more in search of the elusive Waylander.

ACKNOWLEDGEMENTS

My thanks to my editor Oliver Johnson, to Justine Willett, and to proof readers Jean Maund and Stella Graham, test readers Tom Taylor and Edith Graham, and to Mary Sanderson, Alan Fisher, Stan Nicholls, and Peter Austin.

Prologue

The man called Angel sat quietly in the corner of the tavern, his huge gnarled hands cupped around a goblet of mulled wine, his scarred features hidden by a black hood. Despite the four open windows, the air in the sixty-foot room was stale, and Angel could smell the smoke from the oil-filled lanterns, merging with the combined odours of sweating men, cooked food and sour ale.

Lifting his goblet Angel touched his lips to the rim, taking just a sip of the wine and rolling it around his mouth. The Spiked Owl was full tonight, the drinking area crowded, the dining-hall packed. But no one approached Angel as he nursed his drink. The hooded man did not like company, and such privacy as a man could enjoy in a tavern was accorded to the scarred gladiator.

Just before midnight an argument began between a group of labourers. Angel's flint-coloured eyes focused on the group, scanning their faces. There were five men, and they were arguing over a spilled drink. Angel could see the rush of blood to their faces, and knew that despite the raised voices, none of them was in the mood to fight. When a battle is close the blood runs from the face, leaving it white and ghostly. Then his gaze flickered to a young man at the edge of the group. This one was dangerous! The man's face was pale, his mouth set in a thin line, and his right hand was hidden within the folds of his tunic.

Angel looked back towards Balka, the tavern-owner. The burly former wrestler stood behind the serving shelf, watching the men. Angel relaxed. Balka had seen the danger and was ready.

The row began to die down – but the pale young man said something to one of the others and fists suddenly flew. A knife flashed in the lantern light, and a man shouted in pain.

1

Balka, a short wooden club in his right hand, vaulted the serving shelf and leapt at the white-faced knife-wielder, cracking the club first against the man's wrist, forcing him to drop the blade, then hammering a blow to the temple. He dropped to the sawdust-covered floor as if poleaxed.

'That's it, my lads!' roared Balka. 'The night is done.'

'Oh, one more drink, Balka?' pleaded a regular.

'Tomorrow,' snapped the tavern-keeper. 'Come on, lads. Let's clear away the mess.'

The drinkers downed the last of their ale and wine, and several took hold of the unconscious knifeman, dragging him into the street. The man's victim had been stabbed in the shoulder; the wound was deep, his arm numb. Balka gave him a large tot of brandy before sending him on his way to find a surgeon.

At last the tavern-owner shut the door, dropping the lock-bar into place. His barmen and serving girls began gathering tankards, goblets and plates, and righting tables and chairs knocked over in the brief fight. Balka slipped his club into the wide pocket of his leather apron and strolled to where Angel sat.

'Another quiet evening,' he muttered, pulling up a chair opposite the gladiator. 'Janic!' he called. 'Bring me a jug.'

The young cellar boy emptied a bottle of the finest Lentrian red into a clay jug, sought out a clean pewter goblet, and carried both to the table. Balka looked up at the boy and winked. 'Good lad, Janic,' he said. Janic smiled, cast a nervous glance at Angel and backed away. Balka sighed and leaned back in his chair.

'Why don't you just pour it from the bottle?' asked Angel, his grey eyes staring unblinking at the tavern-keeper.

Balka chuckled. 'It tastes better from clay.'

'Horse dung!' Angel reached across the table, lifting the jug and holding it below his misshapen nose. 'It's Lentrian red . . . at least fifteen years old.'

'Twenty,' said Balka, grinning.

'You don't like people knowing you're rich enough to drink it,' observed Angel. 'It would tarnish the image. Man of the people.'

2

'Rich? I'm just a poor tavern-keeper.'

'And I'm a Ventrian veil-dancer.'

Balka nodded and filled his goblet. 'To you, my friend,' he said, draining the drink in a single swallow, wine overflowing to his forked grey beard. Angel smiled and pushed back his hood, running his hand across his thinning red hair. 'May the gods shower you with luck,' said Balka, pouring a second drink and downing it as swiftly as the first.

'I could do with some.'

'No hunting parties?'

'A few – but no one wants to spend money these days.'

'Times are hard,' agreed Balka. 'The Vagrian Wars bled the treasury dry and now that Karnak's upset the Gothir and the Ventrians I think we can expect fresh battles. A pox on the man!'

'He was right to throw out their ambassadors,' said Angel, eyes narrowing. 'We're not a vassal people. We're the Drenai and we shouldn't bend the knee to lesser races.'

'Lesser races?' Balka raised an eyebrow. 'This may surprise you, Angel, but I understand that non-Drenai people also boast two arms, two legs and a head. Curious, I know.'

'You know what I mean,' snapped Angel.

'I know – I just don't happen to agree with you. Here, enjoy a little quality wine.'

Angel shook his head. 'One drink is all I need.'

'And you never finish that. Why do you come here? You hate people. You don't talk to them and you don't like crowds.'

'I like to listen.'

'What can you hear in a tavern, save drunkards and loud-mouths? There is little philosophy spoken here that I've ever heard.'

Angel shrugged. 'Life. Rumours. I don't know.'

Balka leaned forward, resting his massive forearms on the table. 'You miss it, don't you? The fights, the glory, the cheers.'

'Not a bit,' responded the other.

'Come on, this is Balka you're talking to. I saw you the

3

day you beat Barsellis. He cut you bad – but you won. I saw your face as you raised your sword to Karnak. You were exultant.'

'That was then. I don't miss it. I don't long for it,' Angel sighed, 'but I remember the day, right enough. Good fighter was Barsellis, tall, proud, fast. But they dragged his body across the arena. You remember that? Face-down he was, and his chin made a long, bloody groove in the sand. Could have been me.'

Balka nodded solemnly. 'But it wasn't. You retired undefeated – and you never went back. That's unusual. They all come back. Did you see Caplyn last week? What an embarrassment. He used to be so deadly. He looked like an old man.'

'A dead old man,' grunted Angel. 'A dead old fool.'

'You could still take them all, Angel. And earn a fortune.'

Angel swore and his face darkened. 'I'd bet that's what they told Caplyn.' He sighed. 'It was better when we fought hand to hand, no weapons. Now the crowd just want to see blood and death. Let's talk about something else.'

'What – politics? Religion?'

'Anything. Just make it interesting.'

'Karnak's son was sentenced this morning: one year in exile in Lentria. A man is murdered, his wife falls to her death, and the killer is exiled for a year to a palace by the coast. There's justice for you.'

'At least Karnak put the boy on trial,' said Angel. 'The sentence could have been worse. And don't forget, the murdered man's father pleaded for leniency. Quite a moving speech, I understand – all about high spirits and accidents and forgiveness.'

'Fancy that,' observed Balka drily.

'What is that supposed to mean?'

'Oh, come on, Angel! Six men – all nobles – all drunk, snatch a young married woman and try to rape her. When her husband attempts to rescue her he is cut down. The woman runs and falls over a cliff-edge. High spirits? And as for the murdered man's father, I understand Karnak was so

4

moved by his pleas that he sent a personal gift of two thousand Raq to the man's village, and a huge supply of grain for the winter.'

'Well, there you are,' said Angel. 'He's a good man.'

'I don't believe you sometimes, my friend. Don't you think it odd that the father should suddenly make that plea? Gods, man, he was coerced into it. People who criticise Karnak tend to have *accidents*.'

'I don't believe those stories. Karnak's a hero. He and Egel saved this land.'

'Yes, and look what happened to Egel.'

'I think I've had enough of politics,' snapped Angel, 'and I don't want to talk about religion. What else is happening?'

Balka sat silently for a moment, then he grinned. 'Oh, yes, there's a rumour that a huge sum has been offered for the Guild to hunt down Waylander.'

'For what purpose?' asked Angel, clearly astonished.

Balka shrugged. 'I don't know. But I heard it from Symius, and his brother is the clerk at the Guild. Five thousand Raq for the Guild itself, and a further ten thousand to the man who kills him.'

'Who ordered the hunt?'

'No one knows, but they've offered large rewards for any information on Waylander.'

Angel laughed and shook his head. 'It won't be easy. No one has seen Waylander in . . . what . . . ten years? He could be dead already.'

'Someone obviously doesn't think so.'

'It's madness – and a waste of money and life.'

'The Guild are calling in their best men,' offered Balka. 'They'll find him.'

'They'll wish they hadn't,' said Angel softly.

1

Miriel had been running for slightly more than an hour. In that time she had covered around nine miles from the cabin in the high pasture, down to the stream path, through the valley and the pine woods, up across the crest of Axe Ridge, and back along the old deer trail.

She was tiring now, heartbeat rising, lungs battling to supply oxygen to her weary muscles. But still she pushed on, determined to reach the cabin before the sun climbed to noon high.

The slope was slippery from last night's rain and she stumbled twice, the leather knife-scabbard at her waist digging into her bare thigh. A touch of anger spurred her on. Without the long hunting knife and the throwing-blade strapped to her left wrist she could have made better time. But Father's word was law, and Miriel did not leave the cabin until her weapons were in place.

'There is no one here but us,' she had argued, not for the first time.

'Expect the best – prepare for the worst,' was all he said.

And so she ran with the heavy scabbard slapping against her thigh, the hilt of the throwing-blade chafing the skin of her forearm.

Coming to a bend in the trail she leapt the fallen log, landing lightly and cutting left towards the last rise, her long legs increasing their pace, her bare feet digging into the soft earth. Her slim calves were burning, her lungs hot. But she was exultant, for the sun was at least twenty minutes from noon high and she was but three from the cabin.

A shadow moved to her left – talons and teeth flashing towards her. Instantly Miriel threw herself forward, hitting the ground on her right side and rolling to her feet. The lioness, confused at having missing her victim with the first leap, crouched down, ears flat to her skull, tawny eyes focusing on the tall young woman.

Miriel's mind was racing. *Action and reaction. Take control!*

Her hunting knife slid into her hand and she shouted at the top of her voice. The lioness, shocked by the sound, backed away. Miriel's throat was dry, her heart hammering, but her hand was steady on the blade. She shouted once more and jumped towards the beast. Unnerved by the suddenness of the move the creature slunk back several more paces. Miriel licked her lips. It should have run by now. Fear rose, but she swallowed it down.

Fear is like fire in your belly. Controlled, it warms you and keeps you alive. Unleashed, it burns and destroys you.

Her hazel eyes remained locked to the tawny gaze of the lioness and she noted the beast's ragged condition, the deep angry scar to its right foreleg. No longer fast it could not catch the swift deer, and it was starving. It would not – could not – back away from this fight.

Miriel thought of everything Father had told her about lions: *Ignore the head – the bone is too thick for an arrow to penetrate. Send your shaft in behind the front leg, up and into the lung.* But he had said nothing about fighting such a beast when armed with but a knife.

The sun slid from behind an autumn cloud and light shone from the knife-blade. Instantly Miriel angled the blade, directing the gleam into the eyes of the lioness. The great head twisted, the eyes blinking against the harsh glare. Miriel shouted again.

But instead of fleeing the lioness suddenly charged, leaping high towards the girl.

For an instant only Miriel froze. Then the knife swept up. A black crossbow bolt punched into the creature's neck, just behind the ear, a second slicing into its side. The weight of the lioness struck Miriel, hurling her back, but the hunting knife plunged into the beast's belly.

Miriel lay very still, the lioness upon her, its breath foul upon her face. But the talons did not rake her, nor the fangs close upon her. With a coughing grunt the lioness died.

7

Miriel closed her eyes, took a deep breath, and eased herself from beneath the body. Her legs felt weak and she sat upon the trail, her hands trembling.

A tall man, carrying a small double crossbow of black metal, emerged from the undergrowth and crouched down beside her. 'You did well,' he said, his voice deep.

She looked up into his dark eyes and forced a smile. 'It would have killed me.'

'Perhaps,' he agreed. 'But your blade reached its heart.'

Exhaustion flowed over her like a warm blanket and she lay back, breathing slowly and deeply. Once she would have sensed the lioness long before any danger threatened, but that Talent was lost to her now, as her mother and her sister were lost to her. Danyal killed in an accident five years ago, and Krylla wed and moved away last summer. Pushing such thoughts from her mind she sat up. 'You know,' she whispered, 'I was really tired when I came to the last rise. I was breathing hard, and my limbs felt as if they were made of lead. But when the lioness leapt, all my weariness vanished.' She gazed up at her father.

He smiled and nodded. 'I have experienced that many times. Strength can always be found in the heart of a fighter – and such a heart will rarely let you down.'

She glanced at the dead lioness. 'Never shoot for the head –that's what you told me,' she said, tapping the first bolt jutting from the creature's neck.

He shrugged and grinned. 'I missed.'

'That's not very comforting. I thought you were perfect.'

'I'm getting old. Are you cut?'

'I don't think so . . .' Swiftly she checked her arms and legs, as wounds from a lion's claws or fangs often became poisonous. 'No. I was very lucky.'

'Yes, you were,' he agreed. 'But you made your luck by doing everything right. I'm proud of you.'

'Why were you here?'

'You needed me,' he answered. Rising smoothly to his feet he reached out, drawing her upright. 'Now skin the beast and quarter it. There's nothing quite like lion meat.'

'I don't think I want to eat it,' she said. 'I think I'd like to forget about it.'

'Never forget,' he admonished her. 'This was a victory. And you are stronger for it. I'll see you later.' Retrieving his bolts the tall man cleaned them of blood, returning them to the leather quiver at his side.

'You're going to the waterfall?' she asked him softly.

'For a little while,' he answered, his voice distant. He turned back to her. 'You think I spend too much time there?'

'No,' she told him sadly. 'It's not the time you sit there. Nor the effort you put into tending the grave. It's you. She's been . . . gone . . . now for five years. You should start living again. You need . . . more than this.'

He nodded, but she knew she had not reached him. He smiled and laid his hand on her shoulder. 'One day you'll find a love and then we can talk on equal terms. I do not mean that to sound patronising. You are bright and intelligent. You have courage and wit. But sometimes it is like trying to describe colours to a blind man. Love, as I hope you will find, has great power. Even death cannot destroy it. And I still love her.' Leaning forward he drew her towards him, kissing her brow. 'Now skin that beast. And I'll see you at dusk.'

She watched him walk away, a tall man moving with grace and care, his black and silver hair drawn back into a tightly-tied ponytail, his crossbow hanging from his belt.

And then he was gone – vanished into the shadows.

*

The waterfall was narrow, no more than six feet wide, flowing over white boulders in a glittering cascade to a leaf-shaped bowl thirty feet across and forty-five long. At its most southern point a second fall occurred, the stream surging on to join the river two miles south. Golden leaves swirled on the surface of the water, and with each breath of breeze more spiralled down from the trees.

Around the pool grew many flowers, most of them planted by the man who now knelt by the graveside. He

9

glanced up at the sky. The sun was losing its power now, the cold winds of autumn flowing over the mountains. Waylander sighed. A time of dying. He gazed at the golden leaves floating on the water and remembered sitting here with Danyal and the children, on another autumn day ten lifetimes ago.

Krylla was sitting with her tiny feet in the water, Miriel swimming among the leaves. 'They are like the souls of the departed,' Danyal had told Krylla. 'Floating on the sea of life towards a place of rest.'

He sighed again and returned his attention to the flower-garlanded mound beneath which lay all he had lived for.

'Miriel fought a lion today,' he said. 'She stood and did not panic. You would have been proud of her.' Laying his ebony-handled crossbow to one side he idly dead-headed the geraniums growing by the headstone, removing the faded, dry red blooms. The season was late and it was unlikely they would flower again. Soon he would need to pull them, shaking dry the roots and hanging them in the cabin, ready for planting in the spring.

'But she is still too slow,' he added. 'She does not act with instinct, but with remembered learning. Not like Krylla.' He chuckled. 'You remember how the village boys used to gather around her? She knew how to handle them, the tilt of the head, the sultry smile. She took that from you.'

Reaching out he touched the cold, rectangular marble head-stone, his index finger tracing the carved lines.

> *Danyal, wife of Dakeyras,*
> *the pebble in the moonlight*

The grave was shaded by elms and beech, and there were roses growing close by, huge yellow blooms filling the air with sweet fragrance. He had bought them in Kasyra, seven bushes. Three had died as he journeyed back, but the remainder flourished in the rich clay soil.

'I'm going to have to take her to the city soon,' he said. 'She's eighteen now, and she needs to learn. I'll find a husband for her.' He sighed. 'It means leaving you for a while. I'm not looking forward to that.'

The silence grew, even the wind in the leaves dying down. His dark eyes were distant, his memories solemn. Smoothly he rose and, taking up the clay bowl beside the headstone, he moved to the pool, filled the bowl and began to water the roses. Yesterday's rain had been little more than a shower and the roses liked to drink deep.

*

Kreeg crouched low in the bushes, his crossbow loaded. How easy, he thought, unable to suppress a smile.

Find Waylander and kill him. He had to admit that the prospect of such a hunt had frightened him. After all, Waylander the Slayer was no mean opponent. When his family were slain by raiders, he roamed the land until he had hunted down every one of the killers. Waylander was a legend among the Guild, a capable swordsman, but a brilliant knife-fighter and a crossbowman without peer. More than this he was said to possess mystical abilities, always sensing when danger was near.

Kreeg sighted the crossbow at the tall man's back. Mystical abilities? Pah. In one heartbeat he would be dead.

The man at the graveside picked up a clay bowl and moved towards the pool. Kreeg shifted his aim, but his intended victim crouched down, filling the bowl. Kreeg lowered his bow a fraction, slowly letting out his held breath. Waylander was side-on now, and a sure killing shot would have to be to the head. What was he doing with the water? Kreeg watched the tall man kneel by the roses, tipping the bowl and splashing the contents around the roots. He'll go back to the grave, thought Kreeg. And once there I'll take him.

So much in life depended on luck. When the kill order came to the Guild, Kreeg had been out of money and living off a whore in Kasyra, the gold he had earned from killing the Ventrian merchant long since vanished in the gambling dens of the city's south side. Now Kreeg blessed the bad luck that had dogged him in Kasyra. For all life, he knew, was a circle. And it was in Kasyra that he had heard of the hermit in the mountains, the tall widower with the shy daughter. He thought of the message from the Guild.

Seek out a man named Dakeyras. He has a wife Danyal and a daughter Miriel. The man has black and silver hair, dark eyes, and is tall, close to fifty years of age. He will be carrying a small double crossbow of ebony and bronze. Kill him and bring the crossbow to Drenan as proof of success. Move with care. The man is Waylander. Ten thousand in gold is waiting.

In Kasyra Kreeg had despaired of earning such a fabulous sum. Then – blessed be the gods – he had told the whore of the hunt.

'There's a man with a daughter called Miriel who lives in the mountains to the north,' she said. 'I've not seen him, but I met his daughters years ago at the Priests' School. We learned our letters there.'

'Do you remember the mother's name?'

'I think it was something like Daneel . . . Donalia . . .'

'Danyal?' he whispered, sitting up in bed, the sheet falling from his lean, scarred body.

'That's it,' she said.

Kreeg's mouth had gone dry, his heart palpitating. Ten thousand! But Waylander? What chance would Kreeg have against such an enemy?

For almost a week he toured Kasyra, asking about the mountain man. Fat Sheras the miller saw him about twice a year, and remembered the small crossbow.

'He's very quiet,' said Sheras, 'but I wouldn't like to see his bad side, if you take my meaning. Hard man. Cold eyes. He used to be almost friendly, but then his wife died – five . . . six years ago. Horse fell, rolled on her. There were two daughters, twins. Good-looking girls. One married a boy from the south and moved away. The other is still with him. Shy child. Too thin for my taste.'

Goldin the tavern-keeper, a thin-faced refugee from the Gothir lands, also remembered him. 'When the wife was

12

killed he came here for a while and drank his sorrows away. He didn't say much. One night he just collapsed and I left him lying outside the door. His daughters came and helped him home. They were around twelve then. The city elders were talking of removing them from his care. In the end he paid for places at the Priests' School and they lived there for almost three years.'

Kreeg was uplifted by Goldin's tale. If the great Waylander had taken to drinking heavily then he was no longer to be feared. But his hopes evaporated as the tavern-keeper continued.

'He's never been popular. Keeps to himself too much,' said Goldin. 'But he killed a rogue bear last year, and that pleased people. The bear slaughtered a young farmer and his family Dakeyras hunted it down. Amazing! He used a small crossbow. Taric saw it – the bear charged him and he just stood there, then, right at the last moment, as the bear reared up before him he put two bolts up through its open mouth and into the brain. Taric says he's never seen the like. Cold as ice.'

Kreeg found Taric, a slim blond hostler, working at the Earl's stables.

'We tracked the beast for three days,' he said, sitting back on a bale of hay and drinking deeply from the leather-bound flask of brandy Kreeg offered him. 'Never saw him break sweat – and he's not a young man. And when the bear reared up he just levelled the bow and loosed. Incredible! There's no fear in the man.'

'Why were you with him?'

Taric smiled. 'I was trying to pay court to Miriel, but I got nowhere. Shy, you know. I gave up in the end. And he's a strange one. Not sure I'd want him for a father-in-law. Spends most of his time by his wife's grave.'

Kreeg's spirits had soared anew. This was what he had been hoping for. Hunting a man through a forest was chancy at best. Knowing his victim's habits made the task slightly less hazardous, but to find there was one place the victim always visited . . . that was a gift from the gods. And a graveside at that. Waylander's mind would be occupied, full of sorrow, perhaps, and fond memories.

So it had proved. Kreeg, following Taric's directions, had located the waterfall soon after dawn this morning, and found a hiding place which overlooked the headstone. Now all that was left was the killing shot. Kreeg's gaze flickered to the ebony crossbow, still lying on the grass beside the grave.

Ten thousand in gold! He licked his thin lips and carefully wiped his sweating palm on the leaf-green tunic he wore.

The tall man walked back to the pool, collecting more water, then crossed to the furthest rose bushes, crouching once more by the roots. Kreeg switched his gaze to the headstone. Forty feet away. At that distance the barbed bolt would punch through Waylander's back, ripping through the lungs and exiting through the chest. Even if he missed the heart his victim would die within minutes, choking on his own blood.

Kreeg was anxious for the kill to be over and his eyes sought out the tall man.

He was not in sight.

Kreeg blinked. The clearing was empty.

'You missed your chance,' came a cold voice.

Kreeg swung, trying to bring the crossbow to bear. He had one glimpse of his victim, arm raised, something shining in his hand. The arm swept down. It was as if a bolt of pure sunlight had exploded within Kreeg's skull. There was no pain, no other sensation. He felt the crossbow slipping from his hands, and the world spinning.

His last thought was about luck.

It had not changed at all.

*

Waylander knelt by the body and lifted the ornate crossbow the man had held. The shoulder-stock of ebony had been expertly crafted, and embossed with swirling gold. The bow itself was of steel, most likely Ventrian, for its finish was silky smooth and there was not a blemish to be seen. Putting aside the weapon he returned his scrutiny to the corpse. The man was lean and tough, his face hard, the chin square, the mouth thin. Waylander was sure he had

14

never seen him before. Leaning forward he dragged his knife clear of the man's eye-socket, wiping the blade across the grass. Drying the knife against the dead man's tunic he slipped it once more into the black leather sheath strapped to his left forearm.

A swift search of the man's clothing revealed nothing, save four copper coins and a hidden knife, hanging from a thong at his throat. Taking hold of the leaf-green tunic Waylander hauled the corpse upright, hoisting the body over his right shoulder. Foxes and wolves would fight over the remains, and he wanted no such squabbles near Danyal's grave.

Slowly he made his way to the second waterfall, hurling the body out over the rim and watching it plummet to the rushing stream below. At first the impact wedged the corpse against two boulders, but slowly the pull of the water exerted itself and Kreeg's lifeless form floated away, face-down towards the distant river. Retrieving his own crossbow, and taking up the assassin's weapon, Waylander made his way back to the cabin.

Smoke was lazily drifting up from the stone chimney and he paused at the edge of the trees, staring without pleasure at the home he had crafted for Danyal and himself. Built against the base of a rearing cliff, protected from above by an overhang of rock, the log cabin was sixty feet long, with three large, shuttered windows and one door. The ground before it had been cleared of all trees, bushes and boulders, and no one could approach within a hundred feet without being seen.

The cabin was a fortress, and yet there was beauty also. Danyal had covered the corner joints with mottled stones of red and blue, and planted flowers beneath the windows, roses that climbed and clung to the wooden walls, pink and gold against the harsh, ridged bark.

Waylander scanned the open ground, searching the tree line for any second assassin who might be hidden. But he could see no one. Carefully keeping to cover he circled the cabin, checking for tracks and finding none, save those made by his own moccasins and Miriel's bare feet. Satisfied

15

at last, he crossed to the cabin and stepped inside. Miriel had prepared a meal of hot oats and wild strawberries, the last of the season. She smiled as he entered, but the smile faded as she saw the crossbow he carried.

'Where did you find that?' she asked.

'There was a man hidden near the graveside.'

'A robber?'

'I don't believe so. This bow would cost perhaps a hundred gold pieces. It is a beautifully crafted weapon. I think he was an assassin.'

'Why would he be hunting you?'

Waylander shrugged. 'There was a time when I had a price on my head. Perhaps I still have. Or maybe I killed his brother, or his father. Who knows? One thing is certain, he can't tell me.'

She sat down at the long oak table, watching him. 'You are angry,' she said at last.

'Yes. He shouldn't have got that close. I should have been dead.'

'What happened?'

'He was hidden in the undergrowth some forty paces from the graveside, waiting for the killing shot. When I moved to get water for the roses I saw a bird fly down to land in the tree above him, but it veered off at the last moment.'

'It could have been a fox or any sudden movement,' she pointed out. 'Birds are skittish.'

'Yes, it could have been,' he agreed. 'But it wasn't. And if he'd had enough confidence to try for a head shot I would now be lying beside Danyal.'

'Then we've both been lucky today,' she said.

He nodded, but did not answer, his mind still puzzling over the incident. For ten years they had lived without his past returning to haunt him. In these mountains he was merely the widower Dakeyras. Who, after all this time, would send an assassin after him?

And how many more would come?

*

The sun was hanging over the western peaks, a blazing copper disc of fire casting a last, defiant glare over the mountainside. Miriel squinted against the light.

'It's too bright,' she complained.

But his hand swept up, the wooden chopping board sailing into the sky. Smoothly she brought the crossbow to her shoulder, her fingers pressing the bronze trigger. The bolt leapt from the weapon, missing the arcing wood by little more than a foot. 'I said it was too bright,' she repeated.

'Picture failure and it will happen,' he told her sternly, recovering the wooden board.

'Let me throw it for you, then.'

'I do not need the practice – you do!'

'You couldn't hit it, could you? Admit it!'

He gazed into her sparkling eyes, and noted the sunlight glinting red upon her hair, the bronzed skin of her shoulders. 'You ought to be married,' he said suddenly. 'You are far too beautiful to be stuck on a mountainside with an old man.'

'Don't try to evade the issue,' she scolded, snatching the board from him and walking back ten paces. He chuckled and shook his head, accepting defeat. Carefully he eased back the steel string of the lower bow arm. The spring-loaded hook clicked and he inserted a short black bolt, gently pressing the notch against the string. Repeating the manoeuvre with the upper bow arm, he adjusted the tension in the curved bronze triggers. The weapon had cost him a small fortune in opals many years ago, but it had been crafted by a master and Waylander had never regretted the purchase.

He looked up and was about to ask Miriel to throw when she suddenly hurled the board high. The sunlight seared his eyes but he waited until the spinning board reached its highest point. Extending his arm he pressed the first bronze trigger. The bolt flashed through the air, hammering into the board, half splitting it. As it fell he released the second bolt. The board exploded into shards.

'Horrible man!' she said.

17

He made a low bow. 'You should feel privileged,' he told her, holding back his smile. 'I don't usually perform without payment.'

'Throw again,' she ordered him, restringing the crossbow.

'The wood is broken,' he pointed out.

'Throw the largest piece.'

Retrieving his bolts he hefted the largest chunk of wood. It was no more than four inches across and less than a foot long. 'Are you ready?'

'Just throw!'

With a flick of his wrist he spun the chunk high into the air. The crossbow came up, the bolt sang, plunging into the wood. Waylander applauded the shot. Miriel gave an elaborate bow.

'Women are supposed to curtsey,' he said.

'And they are supposed to wear dresses and learn embroidery,' she retorted.

'True,' he conceded. 'How do you like the assassin's bow?'

'It has good balance, and it is very light.'

'Ventrian ebony, and the stock is hollowed. Are you ready for some swordplay?'

She laughed. 'Is your pride ready for another pounding?'

'No,' he admitted. 'I think we'll have an early night.' She looked disappointed as they gathered their weapons and set off back to the cabin. 'I think you need a better swordmaster than I,' he told her as they walked. 'It is your best weapon and you are truly skilled. I'll think on it.'

'I thought you were the best,' she chided.

'Fathers always seem that way,' he said drily. 'But no. With bow or knife I am superb. With the sword? Only excellent.'

'And so modest. Is there anything at which you do not excel?'

'Yes,' he answered, his smile fading.

Increasing his pace he walked on, his mind lost in painful memories. His first family had been butchered by raiders, his wife, his baby girls and his son. The picture was bright in his mind. He had found the boy lying dead in the flower garden, his little face surrounded by blooms.

And five years before, having found love a second time, he had watched helplessly as Danyal's horse had struck a hidden tree root. The stallion hit the ground hard, rolling, trapping Danyal beneath it and crushing her chest. She had died within minutes, her body racked with pain.

'Is there anything at which you do not excel?'

Only one.

I cannot keep alive those I love.

2

Ralis liked to tell people he had been a tinker since the stars were young, and it was not far from the truth. He could still remember when the old king, Orien, had been but a beardless prince, walking behind his father at the Spring Parade on the first road called the Drenai Way.

Now it was the Avenue of Kings, and much wider, leading through the triumphal arch built to celebrate victory over the Vagrians.

So many changes. Ralis had fond memories of Orien, the first Battle King of the Drenai, wearer of the Armour of Bronze, victor in a hundred battles and a score of wars.

Sometimes, when he was sitting in lonely taverns, resting from his travels, the old tinker would tell people of his meeting with Orien, soon after the Battle at Dros Corteswain. The King had been hunting boar in Skultik Forest and Ralis, young then and dark-bearded, had been carrying his pack towards the fort town of Delnoch.

They had met at a stream. Orien was sitting on a boulder, his bare feet submerged in the cold water, his expensive boots cast aside. Ralis had released the straps of his pack and moved to the water's edge, kneeling to drink.

'The pack looks heavy,' said the golden-haired King.

'Aye, it is,' Ralis had agreed.

'A tinker, are you?'

'Aye.'

'You know who I am?'

'You're the King,' said Ralis.

Orien chuckled. 'You're not impressed? Good for you. I don't suppose you have any ointment in that pack. I have blisters the size of small apples.'

Ralis shook his head and spread his arms apologetically. At that moment a group of young noblemen arrived on the scene, surrounding the King. They were laughing and shouting, bragging of their skills.

Ralis had left unnoticed.

As the years passed he followed the King's exploits, almost as if gathering news of an old friend. Yet he doubted if the memory of their meeting had survived for more than a moment or two with the King himself. It was all different now, he thought, as he hitched his pack for the walk up to the cabin. The country had no king – and that wasn't right. The Source would not look kindly upon a country without a prince.

Ralis was breathing heavily as he topped the last rise and gazed down on the flower-garlanded cabin. The wind died down and a beautiful silence settled over the forest. Ralis took a deep breath. 'You can both step out here,' he said softly. 'I may not be able to see you, but I know you're close by.'

The young woman appeared first. Dressed in leggings of oiled black leather and a tunic of grey wool she rose from the undergrowth and grinned at the old man. 'You're getting sharper, Ralis,' she observed.

He nodded and turned to his right. The man stepped into view. Like Miriel he wore leggings of black leather and a tunic shirt, but he also sported a black, chain-mail shoulder-guard and a baldric, from which hung three throwing knives. Ralis swallowed hard. There was something about this quiet mountain man that always disturbed the ancient tinker, and had done ever since they met on this same mountainside ten years before. He had thought about it often. It was not that Dakeyras was a warrior – Ralis had known many such – nor was it in the wolf-like way that he moved. No, it was some indefinable quality that left Ralis thinking of mortality. To stand close to Dakeyras was somehow to be close to death. He shuddered.

'Good to see you, old man,' said Dakeyras. 'There's meat on the table, and cold spring water. Also some dried fruit – if your teeth can manage it.'

'Nothing wrong with my teeth, boy,' snapped Ralis. 'There may not be so many as once there were, but those that are left can still do their job.'

Dakeyras swung to the girl. 'You take him down. I'll join you presently.'

Ralis watched him move silently back into the trees. 'Expecting trouble, are you?' he asked.

'What makes you ask that?' replied the girl.

'He's always been a careful man – but he's wearing chain mail. Beautifully made, but still heavy. I wouldn't think he'd wear it in these mountains just for show.'

'We've had trouble,' she admitted.

He followed her down to the cabin, leaving his pack by the door and stretching out in a deep horsehair-padded leather chair. 'Getting too old for this life,' he grunted.

She laughed. 'How long have you been saying that?' she asked him.

'About sixty years,' he told her. Leaning back he rested his head against the chair and closed his eyes. I wonder if I'm a hundred yet, he wondered. I'll have to work it out one day – find a point of reference.

'Water or fermented apple juice?' she asked him.

Opening the pouch at his side he removed a small packet, handing it to her. 'Make a tisane of that,' he requested. 'Just pour boiling water on it and leave it for a little while.'

'What is it?' she enquired, lifting the packet to her nose and drawing in the scent.

'A few herbs, dill and the like. Keeps me young,' he added with a wide grin.

She left him then and he sat quietly, drinking in his surroundings. The cabin was well built, the main room long and wide, the hearth and chimney solidly constructed of limestone. The south wall had been timbered, and a bearskin hung there. Ralis smiled. It was neatly done, but he had walked these mountains before Dakeyras was born, and he knew about the cave. Had sheltered there a time or two. But it was a clever idea to build a cabin against a cave mouth, then disguise the entrance. A man should always have an escape route.

'How long should I leave it brewing?' came Miriel's voice from the back room.

'Several minutes,' he replied. 'When the shredded leaves start to sink it'll be ready.'

The weapons rack on the wall caught his eye: two longbows, several swords, a sabre, a Sathuli tulwar and half a dozen knives of various lengths and curves. He sat up. A new crossbow lay upon the table. It was a nice piece and Ralis levered himself from his chair and picked up the weapon, examining the gold embossing.

'It is a good bow,' said Miriel, striding back into the room.

'It's better than the man who owned it,' he told her.

'You knew him?'

'Kreeg. A cross between a snake and a rat. Good Guild member, though. Could have been rich if he wasn't such a bad gambler.'

'He tried to kill my father – we don't know why.'

Ralis said nothing. Miriel moved to the kitchen, returning with his tisane, which he sipped slowly. They ate in comfortable silence, the old man devouring three helpings of lion meat. Dipping a slab of freshly-baked bread into the rich gravy he looked up at Miriel and sighed. 'They don't eat as well as this in the palace at Drenan,' he said.

'You are a flatterer, Ralis,' she chided him. 'But I like it.'

Wandering to his pack he untied the flap and delved deep into the interior, coming up at last with a corked metal flask and three small silver cups. Returning to the table he filled the cups with amber liquid. 'The taste of heaven,' he said, savouring the moment.

Miriel lifted her cup and sipped the spirit. 'It's like swallowing fire,' she said, reddening.

'Yes. Good, isn't it?'

'Tell me about Kreeg.'

'Not much to tell. He was from the south, a farmboy originally. Fought in the Vagrian Wars, and then joined Jonat for the rebellion. When Karnak smashed the rebel army Kreeg spent a year or two in Ventria. Mercenary, I think. He joined the Guild three years ago. Not one of their best, you understand, but good enough.'

'Then someone paid him to kill my father?'

23

'Yes.'

'Why?'

The old man shrugged. 'Let's wait until he gets back.'

'You make it sound like a mystery.'

'I just don't like repeating myself. At my age time is precious. How much do you remember of your childhood?'

'What do you mean?'

'I mean, Dakeyras . . . where did you meet him?' He could see that the question surprised her, and watched her expression change from open and friendly to guarded and wary.

'He's my father,' she said softly.

'No,' he told her. 'Your family were killed in a raid during the Vagrian Wars. And Dakeyras, riding with a man named Dardalion, found you and your sister . . . and a brother, I believe, in the care of a young woman.'

'How do you know this?'

'Because of Kreeg,' he said, refilling his cup.

'I don't understand.'

The voice of Dakeyras cut in from the doorway. 'He means he knows who Kreeg was sent to kill.' The tall man untied the thong of his black leather cloak and draped it over the chair. Taking up the third silver cup he tossed back the contents.

'Fifteen thousand in gold,' said Ralis. 'Five for the Guild, ten for the man who brings your crossbow to the Citadel. There are said to be more than fifty men scouring the country for news of you. Morak the Ventrian is among them, as are Belash, Courail and Senta.'

'I've heard of Morak and Courail,' said Dakeyras.

'Belash is Nadir and a knife-fighter. Senta is a swordsman paid to fight duels. He's very good – old noble family.'

'I expect there is also a large reward for information regarding my whereabouts,' said Dakeyras softly.

'I wouldn't doubt it,' said Ralis, 'but then it would be a brave man who betrayed Waylander the Slayer.'

'Are you a brave man?' The words were spoken gently, but the undercurrent was tense and the old man found his stomach knotting.

24

'More guts than sense,' admitted Ralis, holding the man's dark gaze.

Waylander smiled. 'That's as it should be,' he said, and the moment passed.

'What will we do?' asked Miriel.

'Prepare for a long winter,' said Waylander.

*

Ralis was a light sleeper, and he heard the creaking of leather hinges as the main door opened. The old man yawned and swung his legs from the bed. Although it was almost dawn thin shafts of moonlight were still seeping through the cracks in the shutters of the window. He rose and stretched. The air was cool and fresh with the threat of approaching winter. Ralis shivered and pulled on his warm woollen leggings and tunic.

Opening his bedroom door he stepped into the main room and saw that someone had fanned the embers of last night's fire, laying fresh kindling on the hungry flames. Waylander was a courteous host, for there would not normally have been a fire this early on an autumn day. Moving to the shuttered window he lifted the latch and pushed at the wooden frame. Outside the moon was fading in a greying sky, the stars retreating, the pale pink of the dawn showing above the eastern peaks.

Movement caught his eye and Ralis squinted, trying to focus. On the mountainside, at least a quarter of a mile distant, he thought he saw a man running. Ralis yawned and returned to the fire, easing himself down into the deep leather chair. The kindling was burning well and he added two seasoned logs from a stack beside the hearth.

So, he thought, the mystery is solved at last. What was surprising was that he felt in such low spirits now. For years he had known Dakeyras and his family, the beautiful wife, the twin girls. And always he had sensed there was more to the mountain man. And the mystery had occupied his mind, perhaps even helping to keep him active at an age when most – if not all – of his youthful contemporaries were dead.

A fugitive, a nobleman having turned his back on wealth and privilege, a refugee from Gothir tyranny . . . all these he had considered as backgrounds for Dakeyras. And more. But the speculation was now over. Dakeyras was the legendary Waylander – the man who killed King Orien's son, Niallad. But he was also the hero who had found the hidden Armour of Bronze, returning it to the Drenai people, freeing them from the murderous excesses of the invading Vagrians.

The old man sighed. What fresh mysteries could he find now to exercise his mind, and blot out the passing of time and the inevitable approach of death?

He heard Miriel rise from her bed in the far room. She wandered in, tall and slim and naked. 'Good morning,' she said brightly. 'Did you sleep well?'

'Well enough, girl. You should put some clothes on.' His voice was gruff, the words said in a sharper tone than he had intended. It wasn't that her nakedness aroused him; it was the opposite, he realised. Her youth and her beauty only made him feel the weight of his years, looming behind him like a mountain. She returned to her room and he leaned back in his chair. When had arousal died? He thought back. It was in Melega that he had first noticed it, some fifteen years before. He had hired a whore, a buxom wench, but had been unable to perform despite all her expert ministrations.

At last she had shrugged. 'Dead birds cannot rise from the nest,' she told him cruelly.

Miriel returned, dressed now in grey leggings and a shirt of creamy white wool. 'Is that more to your liking, sir tinker?'

He forced a smile. 'Everything about you, my dear, is to my liking. But naked you remind me of all that there once was. Can you understand that?'

'Yes,' she said, but he knew she was humouring him. What did the young ever understand? Pulling a tall chair to the fireside she reversed it and sat astride it opposite him, her elbows resting on the high back. 'You mentioned some of the men who are hunting my father,' she said. 'Can you tell me of them?'

'They are all dangerous men – and there will be those among them I do not know. But I know Morak the Ventrian. He's deadly, truly deadly. I believe he is insane.'

'What weapons does he favour?' she asked.

'Sabre and knife, but he is a very skilled bowman. And he has great speed – like a striking snake. He'll kill anyone – man, woman, child, babe in arms. He has a gift for death.'

'What does he look like?'

'Medium height, slim. He tends to wear green, and he has a ring of heavy gold, set with a green stone. It matches his eyes, cold and hard.'

'I will watch out for him.'

'If you see him – kill him,' snapped Ralis. 'But you won't see him.'

'You don't think he'll come here?'

'That's not what I said. You would both be best advised to leave here. Even Waylander cannot defeat all who are coming against him.'

'Don't underestimate him, tinker,' she warned.

'I don't,' he replied. 'But I am an old man, and I know how time makes dotards of us all. Once I was young, fast and strong. But slowly, like water eating at stone, time removes our speed and our strength. Waylander is not a young man. Those hunting him are in their prime.'

She nodded and looked away. 'So you advise us to run?'

'Another place, under another name. Yes.'

'Tell me of the others,' she said.

And he did, relating all he had heard of Belash, Courail, Senta and many more. She listened, mostly in silence, but occasionally interrupting him with pertinent questions. At last satisfied she had drained his knowledge, she stood.

'I will prepare you some breakfast,' she said. 'I think you have earned it.'

'What did you gain from my stories?' he asked her.

'It is important to know your enemy,' she answered him. 'Only with knowledge can you ensure victory.'

Ralis said nothing.

*

Waylander sat quietly on the rough-hewn platform, high in the oak, staring out to the west, over the rolling plains towards the distant towers of Kasyra. Some four miles to his left he could see the Corn Road, a ribbon of a trail leading from the Sentran Plain south towards Drenan. There were few wagons now, the corn having been gathered and stored, or shipped to markets in Mashrapur or Ventria. He saw several horsemen on the road, all riding towards Kasyra and the surrounding villages.

A cool breeze rustled the leaves around him and he settled back, his mind drifting through the libraries of memory, sifting, seeking. His early training as a soldier in the Sathuli Wars told him that a static enemy was one facing defeat. The forest and mountains of Skeln boasted many caves and hiding places, but a persistent enemy would find him, for a man had to hunt to eat, and in hunting he left tracks. No, the soldier he had been knew only one way to win – attack!

But how? And where? *And against whom?*

The hunt-geld had been placed in the Guild. Even if he were to find the man who had ordered the kill, and slay him, the hunt would go on.

The wind picked up, and Waylander pulled his fur-lined cloak more tightly around his frame. The run had been hard, his ageing muscles complaining at the severity of the exercise, his lungs on fire, his heartbeat a pounding drum. Stretching out his right leg he rubbed at the still-burning muscles of his calf, and thought of all he knew of the Guild.

Fifteen years ago the Guild had approached Waylander, offering to broker his contracts. He had refused them, preferring to work alone. In those days the Guild had been a mysterious, shadowy organisation, operating in secret. Its rules were simple. Firstly, all killings were to be accomplished with blade, shaft or knotted rope. Murder by poison or fire was not allowed – the Guild wished for no innocent victims to be slain. Secondly, all monies were paid direct to the Guild and a signed document was placed with the Patriarch, giving reasons for the contract. Such reasons could not include matters of the heart, or religious quarrels.

In theory a cuckolded husband could not hire an assassin to murder his wife, her lover, or both. In practice, of course, such niceties never applied. As long as the contractor declared his reasons as being business or political, no questions were asked. Under Karnak the trade had become – if not morally acceptable –at least more legitimate. Waylander smiled. By allowing the Guild to operate openly, the financially-beleaguered Karnak had found yet one more source of taxable income. And in times of war such income was vital to pay soldiers, armourers, merchants, ship-builders, masons . . . the list was endless.

Waylander stood and stretched his aching back. How many would come against him? The Guild would have other contracts to meet. They could not afford to send all their fighters scouring the country for news of him. Seven? Ten? The best would not come first. They would sit back and watch, while lesser men began the hunt, men like Kreeg.

And were they already here, hidden, waiting?

He thought of Miriel and his stomach tightened. She was strong and lithe, skilled with all weapons. But she was young, and had never fought warriors, blade to blade.

Removing his cloak Waylander rolled it and looped it over his shoulder, tying it to his knife-belt. The cold wind bit into his naked chest, but he ignored it as he climbed down the tree. His eyes scanned the undergrowth, but there was nothing to be seen. Swiftly he leapt from the lowest branch, landing lightly on the moss-covered earth.

The first move would have to be left to the enemy. The fact galled him but having accepted it, he pushed it from his mind. All he could do now was prepare himself. You have fought men and beasts, demons and Joinings, he told himself. And you are still alive while your enemies are dust.

I was younger then, came a small voice from his heart.

Spinning on his heel he swept a throwing blade from its forearm sheath and sent it flashing through the air, to plunge home into the narrow trunk of a nearby elm.

Young or old, I am still Waylander.

*

Miriel watched the old man make his way slowly towards the north-west and the distant fortress of Dros Delnoch. His pack was high on his shoulders, his white hair and beard billowing in the breeze. He stopped at the top of a rise, turned and waved. Then he was gone. Miriel wandered back through the trees, listening to the birdsong, enjoying the leaf-broken sunlight dappling the path. The mountains were beautiful in the autumn, leaves of burnished gold, the last fading blooms of summer, the mountainsides glowing green and purple; all seemingly created just for her pleasure.

Coming to the brow of a hill she paused, her eyes scanning the trees and the paths wending down to the Sentran Plain. A figure moved into sight, a tall man, wearing a cloak of green. The cold of a remembered winter touched her skin, making her shiver, her hand moving to the hilt of the shortsword at her side. The green cloak identified him as the assassin Morak. Well, this was one killer who would not live to attack her father.

Miriel stepped into sight and stood waiting as the man slowly climbed towards her. As he approached she studied his face – his broad, flat cheekbones and scarred and hairless brows, a nose flattened and broken, a harsh gash of a mouth. The chin was square and strong, the neck bulging with muscle.

He paused before her. 'The path is narrow,' he said, politely enough. 'Would you be so kind as to move aside?'

'Not for the likes of you,' she hissed, surprised that her voice remained steady, her fear disguised.

'Is it customary in these parts to insult strangers, girl? Or is it that you rely on gallantry to protect you?'

'I need nothing to protect me,' she said, stepping back and drawing her sword.

'Nice blade,' he said. 'Now put it away – lest I take it from you and spank you for your impudence.'

Her eyes narrowed, anger replacing fear, and she smiled.

'Draw your sword – and we'll see who suffers,' she told him.

'I do not fight girls,' he replied. 'I am seeking a man.'

'I know whom you seek, and why. But to get to him you must first pass me. And that will not be easy with your entrails hanging to your ankles.' Suddenly she leapt forward, the point of her blade stabbing towards his belly. He swayed aside, his arm flashing up and across, the back of his hand cannoning against her cheek. Miriel stumbled and fell, then rolled to her feet, her face burning from the slap.

The man moved to the right, slipping the thong from his green cloak and laying the garment over a fallen tree. 'Who taught you to lunge like that?' he asked. 'A farmer, perhaps? Or a herdsman? That is not a hoe you are holding. The thrust should always be disguised, and used following a riposte or counter.' He drew his own sword and advanced on her. Miriel did not wait for his attack, but moved in to meet him, thrusting again, this time at his face. He blocked the blow and spun on his heel, his shoulder thudding into her chest, hurling her from her feet.

She sprang up and rushed in, slashing the blade towards his neck. His own sword swept up, blocking the blow, but this time she spun and leapt, her booted foot cracking against his chin. She expected him to fall but he merely staggered, righted himself, and spat blood from his mouth. 'Good,' he said softly. 'Very good. Swift and in perfect balance. Perhaps there is something to you after all.'

'You'll never know,' she told him, launching an attack of blistering speed, aiming cuts and thrusts to face and body. Each one he blocked, and never once made the riposte. At last she fell back, confused and dismayed. She could not breach his defences, but what was more galling was that he made no attempt to breach hers.

'Why will you not fight me?' she asked him.

'Why should I?'

'I mean to kill you.'

'Do you have a reason for this hostility?' he enquired, the ugly gash of a mouth breaking into a smile.

31

'I know you, Morak. I know why you are here. That should be enough.'

'It would . . .' he started to say, but she attacked again, and this time he wasn't quite fast enough, her blade slicing past his face and cutting his earlobe. His fist lashed out and up, thundering against her chin. Half-stunned, Miriel lost her grip on her sword and fell to her knees. The newcomer's blade touched her neck. 'Enough of this nonsense,' he said, moving away from her and picking up his cloak.

Gathering her sword she faced him again. 'I will not let you pass,' she said grimly.

'You couldn't stop me,' he told her, 'but it was a game effort. Now where is Waylander?' She advanced again. 'Wait,' he said, sheathing his sword. 'I am not Morak. You understand me? I am not from the Guild.'

'I don't believe you,' she said, her blade now resting on his throat.

'Then believe this: had I wished to kill you I would have. You know that is true.'

'Who are you?'

'My name is Angel,' he answered, 'and a long time ago I was a friend to your family.'

'You are here to help us?'

'I don't fight other men's battles, girl. I came to warn him. I see now it was unnecessary.'

Slowly she lowered her sword. 'Why are they hunting him? He has harmed no one.'

He shrugged. 'Not for many a year, I'll grant you that, but he has many enemies. It is one of the drawbacks of an assassin's life. Did he teach you to use a sword?'

'Yes.'

'He ought to be ashamed of himself. Swordfighting is heart and mind in perfect harmony,' he said sternly. 'Did he not tell you that?'

'Yes he did,' she snapped.

'Ah, but like most women you only listen when it suits you. Yes, I can see that. Well, can you cook?'

Holding back her temper she gave her sweetest smile. 'I

can. I can also embroider, knit, sew, and what else? Ah yes . . .' Her fist cracked against his chin. Standing alongside the fallen tree he had no time to move his feet and steady himself, and a second blow sent him sprawling across the trunk to land in a mud-patch on the other side. 'I almost forgot,' she said. 'He taught me to fight with my fists.'

Angel pushed himself to his knees and slowly rose. 'My first wife was like you,' he said, rubbing his chin. 'A dreadful woman, soft as goosedown on the outside, baked leather and iron inside. But I'll say this, girl – he did a better job of teaching you to punch than he did to thrust. Can we have a truce now?'

Miriel chuckled. 'Truce,' she agreed.

*

Angel rubbed his swollen jaw as he walked behind the tall mountain woman. A kick like an angry horse and a punch almost as powerful. He smiled ruefully, his eyes watching the way she moved, graceful and yet economical. She fought well, he conceded, but with too much head and too little instinct. Even the punches she had thrown had been ill-disguised, but Angel had allowed them to land, sensing she needed some outlet for frustration at having been so easily defeated.

A proud woman. And attractive, he decided, somewhat to his surprise. Angel had always favoured big-breasted women, buxom and comfortable, warm between the sheets. Miriel was a mite thin for his taste and her legs, though long and beautifully proportioned, were just a little too muscular. Still, as the saying went, she was a woman to walk the mountains with.

He chuckled suddenly, and she turned. 'Something is amusing you?' she asked, her expression frosty.

'Not at all, Miriel. I was just remembering the last time I walked these mountains. You and your sister would have been around eight, maybe nine. I was thinking that life goes by with bewildering speed.'

'I don't remember you,' she said.

'I looked different then. This squashed nose was

aquiline, and my brows boasted hair. It was long before the mailed gloves of other fist-fighters cut and slashed at the skin. My mouth too was fuller. And I had long red hair that hung to my shoulders.'

She leaned in close, peering at him. 'You were not called Angel then,' she announced.

'No. I was Caridris.'

'I remember now. You brought me a dress – a yellow dress, and a green one for Krylla. But you were . . .'

'Handsome? Yes, I was. And now I am ugly.'

'I did not mean . . .'

'No matter, girl. All beauty passes. I chose a rough occupation.'

'I don't understand how any man would wish to pursue such a way of life. Causing pain, being hurt, risking death – and for what? So that a crowd of fat-bellied merchants can see blood flow.'

'I used to think there was more to it,' he said softly, 'but now I will not argue with you. It was brutal and barbaric, and mostly I loved it.'

They walked on to the cabin. After he had eaten Angel sat down by the dying fire and pulled off his boots. He glanced at the hearth. 'A little early for fires, isn't it?'

'We had a guest – an old man,' said Miriel, seating herself opposite him. 'He feels the cold.'

'Old Ralis?' he enquired.

'Yes. You know him?'

'He's been plying his trade between Drenan and Delnoch for years – decades. He used to make knives the like of which I've never seen since. Your father has several.'

'I'm sorry I struck you,' she said suddenly. 'I don't know why I did it.'

'I've been struck before,' he answered, with a shrug. 'And you were angry.'

'I am not usually so . . . short-tempered. But I think I am a little afraid.'

'That is a good way to be. I've always been careful around fearless men – or women. They have a tendency to

34

get you killed. But take some advice, young Miriel. When the hunters come don't challenge them with the blade. Shoot them from a distance.'

'I thought I was good with a sword. My father always tells me I am better than him.'

'In practice, maybe, but in combat I would doubt it. You think out your moves and that robs you of speed. Swordplay requires subtle skills and a direct link between hand and mind. I'll show you.' Leaning to his right he lifted a long twig from the tinderbox and stood. 'Stand opposite me,' he ordered her. Then, holding the stick between his index fingers he said: 'Put your hand over the stick and, when I release it, catch it. Can you do that?'

'Of course, it is . . .' As she was answering him he opened his fingers. The twig dropped sharply. Miriel's hand flashed down, her fingers closing on air, and the twig landed at her feet. 'I wasn't ready,' she argued.

'Then try again.'

Twice more she missed the falling twig. 'What does it prove?' she snapped.

'Reaction time, Miriel. The hand should move as soon as the eye sees the twig fall – but yours doesn't. You see the twig. You send a message to your hand. Then you move. By this time the twig is falling away from you.'

'How else can anyone catch it?' she asked him. 'You have to tell your hand to move.'

He shook his head. 'You will see.'

'Show me,' she demanded.

'Show her what?' asked Waylander from the doorway.

'She wants to learn to catch twigs,' said Angel, turning slowly.

'It's been a long time, Caridris. How are you?' asked the mountain man, the small crossbow pointing at Angel's heart.

'Not here looking for a kill, my friend. I don't work for the Guild. I came to warn you.'

Waylander nodded. 'I heard you retired from the arena. What do you do now?'

'I sold hunting weapons. I had a place in the market square, but it was sequestered against my debts.'

'Ten thousand gold pieces would buy it back for you,' said Waylander coldly.

'Indeed it would – five times over. But as I have already told you, I do not work for the Guild. And do not even think of calling me a liar!'

Waylander pulled the bolts clear of the weapon then released the strings. Dropping the bow to the table he turned back to the scarred fighter. 'You are no liar,' he said. 'But why would you warn me? We were never close.'

Angel shrugged. 'I was thinking of Danyal. I didn't want to see her widowed. Where is she?'

Waylander did not reply, but Angel saw the colour fade from his face, and a look of anguish that was swiftly masked. 'You may stay the night,' said Waylander. 'And I thank you for your warning.' With that he took up his crossbow and left the cabin.

'My mother died,' whispered Miriel. 'Five years ago.' Angel sighed and sank back in his chair. 'You knew her well?' she asked.

'Well enough to be a little in love with her. How did she die?'

'She was riding. The horse fell and rolled on her.'

'After all she'd been through . . . battles and wars . . .' He shook his head. 'There's no sense to such things, none at all. Unless it be that the gods have a grim sense of humour. Five years, you say. Gods! He must have adored her to stay alone this long.'

'He did. He still does, spending too much time by her grave, talking to her as if she can still hear him. He does that here sometimes.'

'I see it now,' said Angel softly.

'What do you see?'

'Isn't it obvious, Miriel? The killers are gathering – assassins, hunters, stalkers of the night. He cannot kill them all, he knows that. So why is he still here?'

'You tell me.'

'He's like the old stag hunted by wolves. It takes to the high ground, knowing it is finished, and then it turns and waits, facing the enemy for one last battle.'

'But he's not like that stag. He's not old! He's not! And he's not finished, either.'

'That's not how he sees it. Danyal was what he lived for. Perhaps he thinks that in death they will be reunited, I don't know. What I *do* know – and so does he – is that to stay here means death.'

'You are wrong,' said Miriel, but her words carried no conviction.

3

Floating on a sea of pain Ralis knew he was dying; his arms were tied behind him, the skin of his chest was seared and cut, his legs broken. All his dignity had been stripped from him in the screams of anguish the knives and hot irons had torn from his soul. There was nothing of the man left, save one small flickering spark of pride.

He had told them nothing. Cold water drenched him, easing the pain of the burns and he opened his one remaining eye. Morak knelt before him, an easy smile on his handsome face.

'I can free you from this pain, old man,' he said. Ralis said nothing. 'What is he to you? A son? A nephew? Why do you suffer this for him? You have walked these mountains for what . . . fifty, sixty years? He's here and you know where he is. We will find him anyway, eventually.'

'He . . . will . . . kill you . . . all,' whispered Ralis.

Morak laughed, the others following his lead. Ralis smelt the burning of his flesh moments before the pain seared into his skull. But his throat was hoarse and bleeding from screaming and he could only utter a short, broken groan.

And suddenly, wonderfully, the pain passed, and Ralis heard a voice calling to him.

He rose from his bonds and flew towards the voice. 'I did not tell them, Father,' he shouted triumphantly. 'I did not tell them!'

*

'Old fool,' said Morak, as he stared at the corpse sagging against the ropes. 'Let's go!'

'Tough old man,' put in Belash as they left the glade. Morak rounded on the stocky Nadir tribesman.

'He made us waste half a day – and for what? Had he told

us at the start, he would have walked off with ten, maybe twenty gold pieces. Now he's dead meat for the foxes and the carrion birds. Yes, he was tough. But he was also stupid!'

Belash's jet-black eyes stared up into Morak's face. 'He died with honour,' muttered the Nadir. 'And great will be his welcome in the Hall of Heroes.'

Morak's laughter welled out. 'The Hall of Heroes, eh? They must be getting short of men if they need to rely on elderly tinkers. What stories will he tell around the great table? How I sold a knife for twice its worth, or how I mended a broken cookpot? I can see there'll be some merry evenings ahead for all of them.'

'Most men mock what they can never aspire to,' said Belash, striding on ahead, his hand on his sword-hilt.

The words cut through Morak's good humour, and his hatred of the little Nadir welled anew. The Ventrian swung to face the nine men who followed him. 'Kreeg came to these mountains because he had information that Waylander was here. We'll split up and quarter the area. In three days we'll meet at the foot of that peak to the north, where the stream forks. Baris, you go into Kasyra. Ask about Kreeg, who he stayed with, where he drank. Find out where he got his information.'

'Why me?' asked the tall, sandy-haired young man. 'And what happens if you find him while I'm gone? Do I still get a share?'

'We all get a share,' promised Morak. 'If we find him and kill him before you get back I will see that the gold is held for you in Drenan. Can I be fairer than that?'

The man seemed unconvinced, but he nodded and walked away. Morak cast his eyes over the remaining eight men. All were woodsmen and proven warriors, men he had used before, tough and unhindered by morals. He despised them all, but was careful to keep his thoughts to himself. No man needed to be wakened by a saw-edged blade rasping across his jugular. But Belash was the only one he hated. The tribesman was fearless and a superb killer with knife or bow. He was worth ten men on a hunt such as this.

One day, though, Morak thought with grim relish, one day I will kill you. I will slide a blade into that flat belly, and rip out your entrails.

Organising the men in pairs he issued his instructions. 'If you come upon any dwellings, ask about a tall man and a young daughter. He may not be using the name Dakeyras, so seek out any widower who fits the description. And if you find him make no move. Wait until we are all together. You understand?'

The men nodded solemnly, then departed.

Ten thousand Raq in gold was waiting for the man who killed Waylander, but the money meant little to Morak. He had ten times that amount hidden away with merchants in Mashrapur and Ventria. What mattered was the hunt and the kill – to be the man who slew a legend.

He felt the sharp rise of anticipated pleasure, as he considered all he might do to fill Waylander's last hours with exquisite pain. There was the girl, of course. He could rape and kill her before Waylander's eyes. Or torture her. Or give her to the men, to use and abuse. Be calm, he told himself. Let the anticipation build. First you have to find him.

Swinging his leaf-green cloak about his shoulders he walked off in pursuit of Belash. The Nadir had made camp in a sheltered hollow and was kneeling upon his blanket, hands clasped in prayer, several old fingerbones, yellowed and porous, lying before him. Morak sat down on the other side of the fire. What a disgusting practice, he thought, carrying the bones of your father in a bag. Barbarians! Who would ever understand them? Belash finished his prayer and returned the bones to the pouch at his side.

'Your father have anything interesting to tell you?' asked Morak, his green eyes alight with amusement.

Belash shook his head. 'I do not speak with my father,' he said. 'He is gone. I speak to the Mountains of the Moon.'

'Ah yes, the mountains. Do they know where Waylander dwells?'

'They know only where each Nadir warrior rests.'

'Lucky them,' observed Morak.

40

'There are some matters you should not mock,' warned Belash. 'The mountains house the souls of all Nadir, past and future. And through them, if I am valiant, I will find the home of the man who killed my father. I shall bury my father's bones in that man's grave, resting on his chest. And he will serve my father for all time.'

'Interesting thought,' said Morak, keeping his voice neutral.

'You *kol-isha* think you know everything. You think the world was created for your pleasure, but you do not understand the land. You, you sit there and you breathe air and feel the cold earth beneath you, and you notice nothing. And why? Because you live your lives in cities of stone, building walls to keep at bay the spirit of the land. You see nothing. You hear nothing. You feel nothing.'

I can see the boil starting on your neck, you ignorant savage, thought Morak. And I can smell the stench from your armpits. Aloud he said: 'And what is the spirit of this land?'

'It is female,' answered Belash. 'Like a mother. She nourishes those who respond to her, giving them strength and pride. Like the old man you killed.'

'And she talks to you?'

'No, for I am the enemy of this land. But she lets me know she is there and watching me. And she does not hate me. But she hates you.'

'Why would that be true?' asked Morak, suddenly uncomfortable. 'Women have always liked me.'

'She reads your soul, Morak. And she knows it is full of dark light.'

'Superstition!' snapped Morak. 'There is no woman. There is no force in the world save that which is held in ten thousand sharp swords. Look at Karnak. He ordered the assassination of the great hero Egel, and now he rules in his place, revered, even loved. He is the force in the Drenai world. Does the lady love him?'

Belash shrugged. 'Karnak is a great man – for all his faults – and he fights for the land, so maybe she does. And no man truly knows whether Karnak ordered Egel's killing.'

I know, thought Morak, remembering the moment when he stood over the great man's bed and plunged the dagger into his right eye.

Oh yes, I know.

*

It was close to midnight when Waylander returned. Angel was sitting beside the fire, Miriel was asleep in the back room. Waylander lifted the lock-bar into place on the iron brackets of the door then unclipped the quiver from his belt, laying it on the table beside his ebony crossbow. Angel glanced up. The only light in the room came from the flickering fire, and in its glow Waylander seemed an eldritch figure surrounded by dancing demon shadows.

Silently, Waylander lifted clear his black leather baldric, with its three throwing knives, then untied the two forearm sheaths, placing the weapons upon the table. Two more knives came from hidden scabbards in his knee-length moccasins. At last he walked to the fire and sat down opposite the former gladiator.

Angel sat back, his pale eyes watching the warrior, observing his tension.

'I see you fought Miriel,' said Waylander.

'Not for long.'

'No. How many times did you knock her down?'

'Twice.'

Waylander nodded. 'The tracks were not easy to read. Your footprints were deeper than hers, but they overlaid one another.'

'How did you know I knocked her down?'

'The ground was soft, and I found where her elbow struck the earth. You beat her easily.'

'I defeated thirty-seven opponents in the arena. You think a girl should best me?'

Waylander said nothing for a moment. Then: 'How good was she?'

Angel shrugged. 'She would survive against an unskilled swordsman, but the likes of Morak, or Senta? She'd be dead within seconds.'

'She's better than me,' said Waylander. 'And I would survive against them for longer than that.'

'She's better than you when you *practise*,' replied Angel. 'You and I both know the difference between that and the reality of combat. She is too tense. Danyal once told me of the test you set her. You recall?'

'How could I forget?'

'Well, were you to try it with Miriel she would fail. You know that, don't you?'

'Perhaps,' admitted Waylander. 'How can I help her?'

'You can't.'

'But you could.'

'Yes. But why would I?'

Waylander threw a fresh chunk of wood to the coals, remaining silent as the first yellow flames licked at the bark. His dark gaze swung to Angel. 'I am a rich man, Caridris. I will pay ten thousand in gold.'

'I notice you don't live in a palace,' remarked Angel.

'I choose to live here. I have merchants looking after my investments. I will give you a letter to one of them in Drenan. He will pay you.'

'Even after you are dead?'

'Even then.'

'I don't intend to fight for you,' said Angel. 'Understand? I will be a tutor to your daughter, but that is all.'

'I need no one to fight for me,' snapped Waylander. 'Not now. Not ever.'

Angel nodded. 'I accept your offer. I will stay and teach her, but only so long as I believe she is learning. When the day comes – as it will – when I can teach her no more, or she cannot learn, then I leave. Is that agreeable?'

'It is.' Waylander rose and moved to the rear wall. Angel watched him press his palm against a flat stone, then reach inside a hidden compartment. Waylander turned and tossed a heavy pouch across the room. Angel caught it, and heard the chink of metal within. 'There is a part-payment,' said Waylander.

'How much?'

'Fifty gold Raq.'

'I'd have undertaken the task for this alone. Why pay so much more?'

'You tell me?' countered Waylander.

'You set the price at the same level as the hunt-geld upon you. You are removing temptation from my path.'

'That is true, Caridris. But not the whole truth.'

'And what is the whole truth?'

'Danyal was fond of you,' replied Waylander, rising to his feet. 'And I wouldn't want to kill you. Now I'll bid you goodnight.'

*

Waylander found sleep elusive, but he lay still, eyes closed, resting his body. Tomorrow he would run again, building his strength and stamina, preparing for the day when the assassins would come.

He was pleased Angel had chosen to stay. He would be good for Miriel, and when the killers finally tracked him down he would ask the gladiator to take the girl to Drenan. Once there she would inherit all his wealth, choose a husband and enjoy a life free from peril.

Slowly he relaxed and faded into dreams.

Danyal was beside him. They were riding by a lakeside, and the sun was bright in a clear blue sky.

'I'll race you to the meadow,' she shouted, digging her heels into the grey mare's flanks.

'No!' he shouted, his panic growing. But she rode away. He saw the horse stumble and fall, watched as it rolled across Danyal, the pommel of the saddle crushing her chest. 'No!' he screamed again, waking, his body bathed in sweat.

All was silent. He shivered. His hands were trembling and he rose from the bed and poured himself a goblet of water. Together he and Danyal had crossed a war-torn land, enemies all around them. Werebeasts had hunted them, Nadir warriors had tracked them. But they had survived. Yet in peace-time, beside a still lake, Danyal had died.

Forcing back the memories he focused instead upon the

dangers he faced, and how best to tackle them. Fear settled upon him. He knew of Morak. The man was a torturer who revelled in the pain of others – unhinged, perhaps even insane, yet he never failed. Belash was unknown to him, but he was Nadir, and that meant he would be a fearless fighter. A warrior race, the Nadir had little time for weaklings. Constantly at war the tribesmen fought one another with pitiless ferocity, and only the very strong survived to manhood.

Senta, Courail, Morak, Belash . . . how many more? And who had paid them? The last question he pushed aside. It didn't matter. Once you have killed the hunters you can find out, he told himself.

Once you have killed the hunters . . .

A great weariness of spirit settled upon him. Taking up his tinder-box he lifted a bronze lantern from the hook on the wall above his bed and struck a flame, holding it to the wick. A golden light flickered. Rehanging the lantern, Waylander sat down upon the bed and gazed at his hands.

Hands of death. The hands of the Slayer.

As a young soldier he had fought for the Drenai against Sathuli raiders, protecting the farmer and the settlers of the Sentran Plain. But he hadn't protected them well enough, for a small band of killers had crossed the mountains to raid and pillage. On the return journey they stopped at his farmhouse, raped and murdered his wife and killed his children.

On that day Dakeyras changed. The young soldier resigned his commission and set out in pursuit of the killers. Coming upon their camp he had slain two of them, the rest fleeing. But he tracked them and, one by one, hunted them down. Each man he caught he tortured, forcing information on the names and likely destinations of the remaining raiders. It took years, and on the endless journey the young officer named Dakeyras died, to be replaced by the empty killing-machine known as Waylander.

By then, death and suffering meant nothing to the silent hunter and, one night in Mashrapur, his money gone, he had been approached by a merchant seeking revenge on a

45

business rival. For forty silver pieces Waylander undertook his first assassination. He did not try to justify his actions, not even to himself. The hunt was everything, and to find the killers he needed money. Cold and heartless he moved on, a man apart, feared, avoided, telling himself that when the quest was over he would become Dakeyras again.

But when the last of the raiders had died screaming, staked out across a campfire, Waylander knew Dakeyras was gone forever. And he had continued his bloody trade, the road to Hell carrying him forward until the day he killed the Drenai King.

The enormity of the deed, and its terrible consequences, haunted him still. The land had been plunged into war, with thousands slain, widowed, orphaned.

The golden lantern light flickered on the far wall and Waylander sighed. He had tried to redeem himself, but could a man ever earn forgiveness for such crimes? He doubted it. And even if the Source granted him absolution it would mean nothing. For he could not forgive himself. Maybe that's why Danyal died, he thought, not for the first time. Perhaps he was always to be burdened by sorrow.

Pouring himself a goblet of water he drained it and returned to his bed. The gentle priest Dardalion had guided him from the road to perdition, and Danyal had found the tiny spark of Dakeyras that remained, fanning it to life, bringing him back from the dead.

But now she too was gone. Only Miriel remained. Would he have to watch her die?

Miriel would fail the test. That's what Angel had said, and he was right. Dakeyras recalled the day he himself had tested Danyal. Deep in Nadir territory assassins had come upon him, and he had slain them. Danyal asked him how it was that he killed with such ease.

He walked away from her and stooped to lift a pebble. 'Catch this,' he said, flicking the stone towards her. Her hand snaked out and she caught the pebble deftly. 'That was easy, was it not?'

'Yes,' she admitted.

'Now if I had Krylla and Miriel here, and two men had

46

knives at their throats, and you were told that if you missed the pebble they would die, would it still be easy to catch? The onset of fear makes the simplest of actions complex and difficult. I am what I am because, whatever the consequences, the pebble remains a pebble.'

'Can you teach me?'

'I don't have the time.' She had argued, and finally he said, 'What do you fear most at this moment?'

'I fear losing you.'

He moved away from her and lifted a second pebble. Clouds partly obscured the moonlight and she strained to see his hand. 'I am going to throw this to you,' he said. 'If you catch it, you stay and I train you. If you miss it you return to Skarta.'

'No, that's not fair! The light is poor.'

'Life is not fair, Danyal. If you do not agree, then I ride away alone.'

'Then I agree.'

Without another word he flicked the stone towards her – a bad throw, moving fast and to her left. Her hand flashed out and the pebble bounced against her palm. Even as it fell her fingers snaked around it, clutching it like a prize.

She laughed. 'Why so pleased?' he asked her.

'I won!'

'No, tell me what you did.'

'I conquered my fear.'

'No.'

'Well, what then? I don't understand.'

'You must if you wish to learn.'

Suddenly she smiled. 'I understand the mystery, Waylander.'

'Then tell me what you did.'

'I caught a pebble in the moonlight.'

Waylander sighed. The room was cold, but his memories were warm. Outside a wolf howled at the moon, a lonely sound, haunting and primal. And Waylander slept.

*

'You move with all the grace of a sick cow,' stormed Angel,

as Miriel pushed herself to her knees, fighting to draw air into her tired lungs. Angry now she surged to her feet, the sword-blade lunging at Angel's belly. Sidestepping swiftly he parried the thrust, the flat of his left hand striking her just behind the ear. Miriel hit the ground on her face.

'No, no, no!' said Angel. 'Anger must be controlled. Rest now for a while.' He walked away from her and stopped at the well, hauling up the copper-bound bucket and splashing water to his face.

Miriel rose wearily, her spirits low. For months now she had believed her sword skills to be high, better than most men, her father had said. Now she was faced with the odious truth. A sick cow, indeed! Slowly she made her way to where Angel sat on the wall of the well. He was stripped to the waist now and she saw the host of scars on the ridged muscles of his chest and belly, on his thick forearms and his powerful shoulders.

'You have suffered many wounds,' she said.

'It shows how many skilful swordsmen there are,' he answered gruffly.

'Why are you angry?'

He was silent for a moment. Then he took a deep breath. 'In the city there are many clerks, administrators, organisers. Without them Drenan would cease to run. They are valued men. But place them in these mountains and they would starve to death while surrounded by game and edible roots. You understand? The degree of a man's skill is relative to his surroundings, or the challenges he faces. Against most men you would be considered highly talented. You are fast and you have courage. But the men hunting your father are warriors. Belash would kill you in two . . . three . . . heartbeats. Morak would not take much longer. Senta and Courail both learned their skills in the arena.'

'Can I be as good?'

He shook his head. 'I don't think so. Much as I hate to admit it I think there is an evil in men like them . . . men like me. We are natural killers, and though we may not talk of our feelings yet each of us knows the bitter truth. We

48

enjoy fighting. We enjoy killing. I don't think you will. Indeed, I don't think you should.'

'You think my father enjoys killing?'

'He's a mystery,' admitted Angel. 'I remember talking to Danyal about that. She said he was two men, the one kind, the other a demon. There are gates in the soul which should never be unlocked. He found a key.'

'He has always been kind to me, and to my sister.'

'I don't doubt that. What happened to Krylla?'

'She married and moved away.'

'When I knew you as children you had a . . . power, a Talent. You and she could talk to each other without speaking. You could see things far off. Can you still do it?'

'No,' she said, turning away.

'When did it fail?'

'I don't want to talk about it. Are you ready to teach me?'

'Of course,' he answered. 'That is why I am being paid. Stand still.' Rising he moved to stand before her, his hands running over her shoulders and arms, fingers pressing into the muscles, tracing the lines of her biceps and triceps, up over the deltoids and the joints of her shoulders.

She felt herself reddening. 'What are you doing?' she asked, forcing herself to meet his eyes.

'Your arms are not strong enough,' he told her, 'especially at the back here,' he added, squeezing her triceps. 'All your power is in your legs and lungs. And your balance is wrong. Give me your hand.' Even as he spoke he took hold of her wrist, lifting her arm and staring down at her fingers. 'Long,' he said, almost to himself. 'Too long. It means you cannot get a good grip on the sword-hilt. We'll cut more leather for it tonight. Follow!'

He strode to the edge of the tree line and walked from trunk to trunk, examining the branches. At last satisfied he stood beneath a spreading elm, a thick limb sprouting just out of reach above him. 'I want you to jump and catch hold of that branch and then slowly pull yourself up until your chin touches the bark. Then – and still slowly, mind –

lower yourself until the arms are almost straight. Understand?'

'Of course I understand,' she snapped. 'It was hardly the most complex of instructions.'

'Then do it!'

'How many times?'

'As many as you can. I want to see the limits of your strength.'

She leapt upwards, her fingers hooking over the branch, and hung for a moment adjusting her grip. Then slowly she hauled herself up.

'How does it feel?' he asked.

'Easy,' she answered, lowering herself.

'Again!'

At three she began to feel her biceps stretching. At five they began to burn. At seven her arms trembled and gave way and she dropped to the ground. 'Pathetic,' said Angel. 'But it is a start. Tomorrow morning you will begin your day with seven, eight if you can. Then you can run. When you return you will do another seven. In three days I will expect you to complete twelve.'

'How many could you do?'

'At least a hundred,' he replied. 'Follow!'

'Will you stop saying *follow!* It makes me feel like a dog.'

But he was moving even as she spoke and Miriel followed him back across the clearing. 'Wait here,' he ordered, then walked to the side of the cabin where the winter wood was stored. Selecting two large chunks he carried them back to where Miriel was waiting and laid them on the ground twenty feet apart. 'I want you to run from one to the other,' he said.

'You want me to run twenty feet? Why?'

His hand snaked out, rapping against her cheek. 'Stop asking stupid questions and do as you are told.'

'You whoreson!' she stormed. 'Touch me again and I'll kill you!'

He laughed and shook his head. 'Not yet. But do as I tell you – and maybe you'll have the skill to do just that. Now move to the first piece of wood.'

Still seething she walked to the first chunk, his voice following her. 'Run to the second and stoop down, touching the wood with your right hand. Turn instantly and run back to the first, touching it with your left hand. Am I going too fast for you?'

Miriel bit back an angry retort and started to run. But she covered the distance in only a few steps and had to chop her stride. Feeling both ungainly and uncomfortable she ducked down, slapped her fingers against the wood then turned and ran back. 'I think you have the idea,' he said. 'Now do it twenty times. And a little faster.'

For three hours he ordered her through a series of gruelling exercises, running, jumping, sword-work, endless repetition of thrusts and cuts. Not once did she complain, but nor did she speak to him. Grimly she pushed herself through all of his exercises until he called a break at midday. Tired now, Miriel strode back to the cabin, her limbs trembling. She was used to running, inured to the pain of oxygen-starved calves and burning lungs. In truth she even enjoyed the sensations, the sense of freedom, of speed, of power. But the weariness and aches she felt now were all in unaccustomed places. Her hips and waist felt bruised and tender, her arms leaden, her back aching.

To Miriel strength was everything, and her faith in her own skills had been strong. Now Angel had undermined her confidence, first with the consummate ease of his victory in the forest, and now with the punishing routines that exposed her every weakness. She had been awake when Waylander made his offer to the former gladiator, and had heard his response. Miriel believed she knew what Angel was trying to do, force her to refuse his training, humiliate her into quitting. Then he would claim his fortune from her father. And, because Dakeyras was a man of pride and honour, he would pay the ten thousand.

You will not find it easy, Angel, she promised. No, you will have to work for your money, you ugly whoreson!

*

Angel was well satisfied with the day's training. Miriel had performed above his expectations, fuelled no doubt by anger at the slap. But Angel cared nothing for the motivation. It was enough that the girl had proved to be a fighter. At least he would have something to work with. Given the time, of course.

Waylander had left just after dawn. 'I will be back in four days. Perhaps five. Make good use of the time.'

'You can trust me,' Angel told him.

Waylander smiled thinly. 'Try to stop her attacking anyone else. She should be safe then. The Guild has a rule about innocent victims.'

Morak follows no rules, thought Angel, but he said nothing as the tall warrior loped away towards the north.

An hour before dusk Angel called a halt to the work, but was surprised when Miriel announced she was going for a short run. Was it bravado, he wondered? 'Carry a sword,' he told her.

'I have my knives,' she answered.

'That's not what I meant. I want you to *carry* a sword. To hold it in your hand.'

'I need this run to loosen my muscles, stretch them out. The sword will hamper me.'

'I know. Do it anyway.'

She accepted without further argument. Angel returned to the cabin and pulled off his boots. He too was tired, but would be damned before letting the girl know. Two years out of the arena had seen his stamina drain away. He poured himself a drink of water and slumped down in front of the dead fire.

Given a month, possibly two, he could make something of the girl. Increase her speed, lower her reaction time. The side sprints would help with balance, and the work to build her arms and shoulders add power to her lunges and cuts. But the real problem lay within her heart. When angry she was fast but wild, easy meat for the skilled swordsman. When cool her movements were stilted, her attacks easy to read and counter. The end result of any combat, therefore, would be the same.

She had been gone perhaps an hour when he heard her

light footfalls on the hard-packed clay of the clearing. He looked up as she entered, her tunic drenched in perspiration, her face red, her long hair damp. The sword was still in her hand.

'Did you carry it all the way?' he asked softly.

'Yes. That's what you told me.'

'You did not drop it on the trail and pick it up on your return?'

'No!' she answered, offended.

He believed her, and swore inwardly. 'Do you always do as you are told?' he snapped.

'Yes,' she told him, simply.

'Why?'

Throwing the sword to the table top she stood before him, hands on hips. 'Are you now criticising me for obeying you? What do you want from me?'

He sighed. 'Merely your best – and you gave that today. Rest now. I will prepare supper.'

'Nonsense,' she said sweetly. 'You are an old man, and you look weary. You sit there and I'll bring you some food.'

'I thought we had a truce,' he said, following her to the kitchen, where she took down a large ham and began to slice it.

'That was yesterday. That was before you set out to cheat my father.'

His face darkened. 'I have never cheated anyone in my life.'

She swung on him. 'No? What would you call ten thousand in gold for a few days' work?'

'I did not ask for the sum – he offered it. And if you were eavesdropping – a womanly skill, I've found – then you will have heard me tell him I'd do it for fifty.'

'You want cheese with this ham?' she asked.

'Yes, and bread. Did you hear what I said?'

'I heard you, but I don't believe you. You were trying to force me to fail. Admit it!'

'Yes, I admit it.'

'Then that's all there is to say. There's your food. When you have finished it, clean your plate. And then do me the

53

kindness of spending the evening in your room. I've had enough of your company today.'

'The training doesn't stop just because the sun's gone down,' he said softly. 'Today we worked your body. This evening we work your mind. And I will go to my room when it pleases me. What are you going to eat?'

'The same as you.'

'Do you have any honey?'

'No.'

'Dried fruit?'

'Yes – why?'

'Eat some. I learnt a long time ago that sweetmeats and cakes sit more easily on a tired stomach. You'll sleep better and wake more refreshed. And drink a lot of water.'

'Anything else?'

'If I think of anything I'll tell you. Now let us finish this meal and start to work.'

*

Having finished his meal Angel cleared away the ash of the previous night's fire, laid fresh kindling, and struck a spark to the tinder. Miriel had eaten in the kitchen, and had then walked through the cabin and out into the night. Angel was angry with himself. You are no teacher, he thought. And the girl was right –he wanted her to quit. But not for the reasons she believed. He sighed and leaned back on his haunches, watching the tiny flames devouring the kindling, feeling the first soft waves of heat from the fire.

He had tried to train the boy, Ranuld, showing him the moves and defences he would need in his new career, but Ranuld had died from a disembowelling cut in his first fight. Then there was Sorrin, tall and athletic, fearless and fast. He had lasted for seven fights – had even become a favourite with the crowd. Senta had killed him – heelspin and reverse thrust to the throat. Good move, beautifully executed. Sorrin was dead before he knew it.

That was the day Angel retired. He had fought a dull Vagrian, whose name he couldn't recall. The man was tough, but slowed by a recent wound. Even so he had almost taken Angel, cutting him twice. After the battle Angel had sat in the arena surgery, the doctor stitching his wounds, while on the table opposite lay Sorrin's bloody corpse. Beside it sat Senta, a bandage soaked in honey and wine being applied to a shallow cut in his shoulder.

'You trained him well,' said Senta. 'He almost took me.'

'Not well enough,' answered Angel.

'I look forward to meeting the master.'

Angel had looked into the young man's eager eyes, seeing the mocking expression on the handsome face, the smile that was almost a sneer. 'It won't happen, boy,' he had said, the words tasting like acid in his mouth. 'I'm too old and slow. This is your day. Enjoy it.'

'You are leaving the arena?' whispered Senta, astonished.

'Yes. That was my last fight.'

The young man nodded, then cursed as the orderly tied the knot in the bandage on his shoulder. 'You dolt!' snapped Senta.

'I'm sorry, sir!' said the man, moving back, his face twisted in fear.

Senta returned his gaze to Angel. 'I think you are wise, old man, but for myself I am disappointed. You are a favourite with the crowds. I could have made my fortune by defeating you.'

Angel added wood to the fire and stood. Senta had only fought for one more year, then he had joined the Guild, earning far more as an assassin than a gladiator.

The door opened behind him, and he felt a cold draught. Turning he saw Miriel walking towards her room. She was naked and carrying her clothes, her body wet from a bath in the stream. His gaze took in her narrow back and waist, the long muscular legs and firm, rounded buttocks. Arousal touched him and he swung back to the fire.

After a few minutes Miriel joined him, her body clothed in a loose woollen robe of grey wool. 'What work did you have in mind?' she asked him, seating herself in the chair opposite.

'You know why I slapped you?'

55

'You wanted to dominate me.'

'No. I wanted to see you angry. I needed to know how you reacted when your blood was high.' Idly he stabbed at the fire with an iron poker. 'Listen to me, girl, I am not a teacher. I have only trained two people – young men I loved. Both died. I am . . . was . . . a fine fighter, but just because I have a skill does not mean I can pass it on. You understand?' She remained silent, her large eyes staring at him, expressionless. 'I was a little in love with Danyal, I think, and I have respect for your father. I came here to warn him, so that he would leave the area, travel to Ventria or Gothir. And yes, I could use the gold. But that's not why I came, nor is it why I agreed to stay. If you choose not to believe me then I will leave in the morning – and I will not claim the fortune.'

Still she said nothing.

'I don't know what else I can say to you.' He shrugged and sat back.

'You told me we were going to work,' she said softly. 'On my mind. What did you mean?'

He spread his hands and stared into the fire. 'Did your father ever tell you about the test he set Danyal?'

'No. But I heard you say I would fail it.'

'Yes, you would.' And Angel told her of the pebble in the moonlight, and talked on of the warrior's heart, the willingness to risk everything, but the confidence to believe the risk was calculated.

'How do I achieve this?' she asked.

'I don't know,' he admitted.

'The two men you trained – did they have it?'

'Ranuld believed he did, but he tied up in his first fight, his muscles tense, his movements halting. Sorrin had it, I think, but he met a better man. It comes from an ability to close off that part of the imagination that is fuelled by fear. You know, the part that pictures terrible wounds and gangrene, pumping blood and the darkness of death. But at the same time the mind must continue to function, seeing the opponent's weaknesses, planning ways through his defences. You have seen my scars. I have been cut many times – but always I won. And I beat better men, faster men, stronger men. I beat them because I was too obstinate to give up. And their confidence would begin to fail, and the windows of their minds would creep open. Their imagination would seep out, and they would begin to doubt, to fear. And from that moment it did not matter that they were better, or faster or stronger. For I would grow before their eyes and they would shrink before mine.'

'I will learn,' she promised.

'I doubt it can be learned. Your father became Waylander because his first family were butchered by raiders, but I don't believe the atrocity *created* Waylander. He was always there, beneath the surface of Dakeyras. The real question is, what lies beneath the surface of Miriel?'

'We will see,' she said.

'Then you wish me to stay?'

'Yes. I wish you to stay. But answer me one question honestly.'

'Ask.'

'What is it *you* fear?'

'Why would you think I fear anything?' he hedged.

'I know that you did not want to stay, and I sense you are torn between your desire to help me and a need to leave. So what is it?'

'The question is a fair one. Let us leave it that you are right. There *is* something I fear, but I am not prepared to talk about it. As you are not prepared to speak of the loss of your Talent.'

She nodded. 'There is one – or more – among the assassins that you do not wish to meet. Am I close?'

'We must thicken the grip on your sword,' he said. 'Cut some strips of leather – thin, no wider than a finger's width. You have glue?'

'Yes. Father makes it from fishbones and hide.'

'First bind the hilt until the size feels comfortable. When curled around it your longest finger should just touch the flesh below your thumb. When you are satisfied, glue the strips into place.'

'You did not answer me,' she said.

'No,' he replied. 'Cut and bind the strips tonight. It will give the glue time to dry. I will see you in the morning.' He rose and strode across the room.

'Angel!'

His hand was on the door latch. 'Yes.'

'Sleep well.'

4

Dardalion swung away from the window and faced the two priests standing before his desk.

'The argument,' he said, 'is of intellectual interest only. It is of no real importance.'

'How can that be, Father Abbot?' asked Magnic. 'Surely it is central to our beliefs?'

'In this I must agree with my brother,' put in the forked-bearded Vishna, his dark eyes staring unblinking at the Abbot. Dardalion beckoned them to be seated and leaned back in his wide leather chair. Magnic looked so young against Vishna, he thought, his pale face, soft-featured and unlined, his blond, unruly hair giving him the appearance of a youth some years from twenty. Vishna, tall and stern, his black forked beard carefully combed and oiled, looked old enough to be Magnic's father. Yet both were barely twenty-four.

'The debate is of worth only because it makes us consider the Source,' said Dardalion at last. 'The pantheistic view that God exists in everything, every stone and every tree, is an interesting one. We believe the Universe was created by the Source in a single moment of blinding energy. From Nothing came Something. What could that Something be, save the body of the Source? That is the argument of the pantheists. Your view, Magnic, that the Source is separate from the world, and that only the Chaos Spirit rules here, is also widely held. The Source, in a terrible War against His own rebellious angels, sent them hurtling to the earth, there to rule, as He rules in Heaven. This argument makes Hell of our world. And I would agree that there is strong evidence to suggest that sometimes it is.

'But in all these debates we are trying to imagine the unimaginable, and therein lies a great danger. The Source of All Things is beyond us. His actions are timeless, and so

59

far above our understanding as to make them meaningless to us. Yet still we try to force our minds to comprehend. We struggle to encompass His greatness, to draw Him in and place Him in acceptable compartments. This leads to dispute and disruption, discord and disharmony. And these are the weapons of the Chaos Spirit.' Dardalion rose and walked around the oak desk to stand beside the two priests, laying a hand on each of them. 'The important point is to know that He exists, and to trust His judgement. You see, you could both be right, and both be wrong. We are dealing here with the Cause of All Causes, the one great truth in a universe of lies. How can we judge? From what perspective? How does the ant perceive the elephant? All the ant sees is part of the foot. Is that the elephant? It is to the ant. Be patient. When the Day of Glory arrives all will be revealed. We will find the Source together – as we have planned.'

'That day is not far off,' said Vishna quietly.

'Not far,' agreed Dardalion. 'How is the training progressing?'

'We are strong,' said Vishna, 'but we have problems still with Ekodas.'

Dardalion nodded. 'Send him to me this evening, after meditation.'

'You will not talk him round, Father Abbot,' ventured Magnic diffidently. 'He will leave us rather than fight. He cannot overcome his cowardice.'

'He is not a coward,' said Dardalion, masking his annoyance. 'I know this. I once walked the same road, believed the same dreams. Evil can sometimes be countered with love. Indeed, that is the best way. But sometimes evil must be faced with steel and a strong arm, yet do not call him a coward for holding to high ideals. It lessens you as much as it insults him.'

The blond priest blushed furiously. 'I am sorry, Father Abbot.'

'And now I am expecting a visitor,' said Dardalion. 'Vishna, wait for him at the front gate and bring him straight to my study. Magnic, go to the cellar and fetch a bottle of wine and some bread and cheese.' Both priests stood. 'One more thing,' said Dardalion, his voice little more than a whisper. 'Do not shake hands with the man, or touch him. And do not try to read his thoughts.'

'Is he evil, then?' asked Vishna.

'No, but his memories would burn you. Now go and wait for him.'

Dardalion returned to the window. The sun was high, shining down on the distant Delnoch peaks, and from this high window the Abbot could just see the faint grey line of the first wall of the Delnoch fortress. His eyes tracked along the colossal peaks of the mountains, traversing west to east towards the distant sea. Low clouds blocked the view, but Dardalion pictured the fortress of Dros Purdol, saw again the dreadful siege, heard the screams of the dying. He sighed. The might of Vagria was humbled before the walls of Purdol, and the history of the world changed in those awful months of warfare. Good men had died, iron spears ripping into their bodies . . .

The first Thirty had been slaughtered there, battling against the demonic powers of the Brotherhood. Dardalion alone had survived. He shivered, as he relived the pain of the spear plunging into his back, and the loneliness as the souls of his friends flew from him, hurtling towards the eternal serenity of the Source. The Thirty had fought on the astral plane alone, refusing to bear weapons in the world of flesh. How wrong they had been!

The door opened behind him, and he stiffened, his mouth suddenly dry. Swiftly he closed the gates of his Talent, shutting out the swelling violence emanating from his visitor. Slowly he turned. His guest was tall, wide-shouldered and yet lean, dark-eyed and stern of appearance. He was dressed all in black and even the chain-mail shoulder-guard was stained with dark dye. Dardalion's eyes were drawn to the many weapons, the three knives sheathed to the man's baldric, the throwing blades in scabbards strapped to his forearms, the short sabre and crossbow bolt quiver at his side. Two more knives were hidden, he knew, in the man's knee-length moccasins. But the weapon of death that drew his gaze was the small ebony crossbow the man held in his right hand.

'Good day, Dakeyras,' said Dardalion, and there was no welcome in his voice.

'And to you, Dardalion. You are looking well.'

'That will be all, Vishna,' said the Abbot, and the tall, white-robed priest bowed and departed. 'Sit you down,' Dardalion told his visitor, but the man remained standing, his dark eyes scanning the room, the shelves packed with ancient tomes, the open cupboards bursting with manuscripts and scrolls, the dust-covered rugs and the decaying velvet hangings at the high, arched window. 'I study here,' said Dardalion.

The door opened and Magnic entered, bearing a tray on which stood a bottle of wine, two loaves of black bread and a hunk of blue-veined cheese. Placing them on the desk the blond priest bowed and departed.

'They are nervous of me,' said Waylander. 'What have you told them?'

'I told them not to touch you.'

Waylander chuckled. 'You don't change, do you? Still the same priggish, pompous priest.' He shrugged. 'Well, that is your affair. I did not come here to criticise you. I came for information.'

'I can offer you none.'

'You don't know yet what I am going to ask. Or do you?'

'You want to know who hired the assassins and why.'

'That's part of it.'

'What else?' asked Dardalion, filling two goblets with wine and offering one to his guest. Waylander accepted it, taking the drink with his left hand, politely sipping the contents and then replacing the goblet on the desk top, there to be forgotten. The sound of clashing sword-blades rose up from the courtyard below. Waylander moved to the window and leaned out.

'Teaching your priests to fight? You do surprise me, Dardalion. I thought you were against such violence.'

'I am against the violence of evil. What else did you want to know?'

62

'I have not heard from Krylla since she moved away. You could . . . use your Talent and tell me if she is well.'

'No.'

'That is it? A simple *no* – not a word of explanation?'

'I owe you no explanations. I owe you nothing.'

'That's true,' said Waylander coldly. 'I saved your life, not once but many times, but you owe me nothing. So be it, priest. You are a fine example of religion in action.'

Dardalion reddened. 'Everything you did was for your own ends. I used all my powers to protect you. I watched my disciples die while I protected you. And yes, for once in your life you did the decent deed. Good for you! You don't need me, Waylander. You never did. Everything I believe in is mocked by your life. Can you understand that? Your soul is like a blazing torch of dark light, and I need to steel myself to stand in the same room as you, closing off my Talent lest your light corrupt me.'

'You sound like a windy pig, and your words smell about as fine,' snapped Waylander. 'Corrupt you? You think I haven't seen what you are doing here? You had armour made in Kasyra, and helms bearing runic numbers. Knives, bows, swords. Warrior priests: isn't that a contradiction, Dardalion? At least my violence is honest. I fight to stay alive. I no longer kill for hire. I have a daughter I am trying to protect. What is your excuse for teaching priests to kill?'

'You wouldn't understand!' hissed the Abbot, aware that his heartbeat was rising and that anger was threatening to engulf him.

'You are right again, Dardalion. I don't understand. But then I am not a religious man. I served the Source once, but then He discarded me. Not content with that He killed my wife. Now I see His . . . Abbot, isn't it? . . . playing at soldiers. No, I don't understand. But I understand friendship. I would die for those I love, and if I had a Talent like yours I would not deny it to them. Gods, man, I would not even deny it to a man I disliked.' Without another word the black-garbed warrior strode from the room.

Dardalion slumped back in his chair, fighting for calm. For some time he prayed. Then he meditated before praying again. At last he opened his eyes. 'I wish I could have told you, my friend,' he whispered. 'But it would have been too painful for you.'

Dardalion closed his eyes once more and let his spirit free. Passing through flesh and bone as if his body had become water he rose like a swimmer seeking air. High now above the Temple he gazed down on the grey castle and the tall hill upon which it stood, and he saw the town spread out around the foot of the hill, the narrow streets, the wide market square and the bear-pit beyond it, stained with blood. But his spirit eyes sought out the man who had been his friend. He was moving easily down the winding path towards the trees and Dardalion felt his sorrow, and his anger.

And the freedom of the sky could not mask the sadness which swept through the Abbot.

'You could have told him,' whispered the voice of Vishna in his mind.

'The balance is too delicate.'

'Is he so important, then?'

'Of himself? No,' answered Dardalion, 'but his actions now will change the future of nations – that I know. And I must not – will not – attempt to guide him.'

'What will he do when he finds out the truth?'

Dardalion shrugged. 'What he always does, Vishna. He will look for someone to kill. It is his way – a law made of iron. He is not evil, you know, but there is no compromise in him. Kings believe it is their will that guides history. They are wrong. In all great events there are men like Waylander. History may not recall them, but they are there.' He smiled. 'Ask any child who won the Vagrian War and they will tell you it was Karnak. But Waylander recovered the Armour of Bronze. Waylander slew the enemy general Kaem.'

'He is a man of power,' agreed Vishna. 'I could feel that.'

'He is the deadliest man I ever met. Those hunting him will find the truth of that, I fear.'

*

Waylander found his anger hard to control as he followed the winding hill path that led down to the forest. He paused and sat at the edge of the path. Anger blinds, he told himself. Anger dulls the senses! He took a deep, slow breath.

What did you expect of him?

More than I received.

It was galling, for he had loved the priest. And admired him – the gentleness of his soul, the bottomless well of forgiveness and understanding he could bring to bear. What changed you, Dardalion, he wondered. But he knew the answer, and it lay upon his heart with all the weight only guilt can muster.

Ten years ago he had found the young Dardalion being tortured by robbers. Against his better judgement he had rescued him, and in so doing had been drawn into the Vagrian War, helping Danyal and the children, finding the Armour of Bronze, fighting were-beasts and demonic warriors. The priest had changed his life. Dardalion had been pure then, a follower of the Source, unable to fight, even in order to survive, unwilling to eat meat. He could not even hate the men who tortured him, nor the vile enemy that swept across the land bringing blood and death to thousands.

Waylander had changed him. With the priest in a trance, his spirit hunted across the Void, Waylander had cut his own arm, holding it above Dardalion's face. And the blood had splashed to the priest's cheek, staining his skin and lips, flowing into his mouth. The unconscious Dardalion had reacted violently, his body arching in an almost epileptic spasm.

And he killed the demon spirit hunting him.

To save Dardalion's life, Waylander had sullied the priest's soul.

'You sullied me too,' whispered Waylander. 'You touched me with your purity. You shone a light on the dark places.' Wearily he pushed himself to his feet. From here he could see the town below, the small church a stone's throw from the bloodstained bear-pit, the timber-built

65

homes and stables. He had no wish to journey there. South lay his home; south was where Danyal waited, silent among the flowers and the glittering falls.

Once under cover of the trees he relaxed a little, feeling the slow, eternal heartbeat of the forest all around him. What did these trees care for the hopes of Man? Their spirits were everlasting, born into the leaf, carried back to the ground, merging with the earth, feeding the tree, becoming leaves. An endless passive cycle of birth and rebirth through the eons. No murders here, no guilt. He felt the weight of his weapons, and wished he could cast them all aside and walk naked in the forest, the soft earth beneath his feet, the warm sun upon his back.

A shout of pain came from some way to his left, followed by the sound of cursing. Stepping swiftly, knife in hand, he pushed back a screen of bushes and saw four men standing close to the mouth of a shallow cave some fifty paces away, at the foot of a gentle slope. Three were carrying wooden clubs, the fourth a shortsword which, even at this distance, Waylander could see was part-rusted.

'Bastard damn near took my arm off,' complained a burly balding man, blood dripping from a shallow wound in his forearm.

'We need a bow, or spears,' said another.

'Leave the beast. It's a demon,' said a third, backing away, 'and it's dying anyway.'

One by one they moved back from the cave mouth, but the last man stopped and threw a large stone into the dark recesses of the cave. A deep growl was heard and a huge hound appeared in the entrance, blood on its fangs. The men suddenly panicked and ran back up the slope. The first of them, the balding fat man with the injured arm, saw Waylander standing there and paused.

'Don't go down there, friend,' he said. 'The dog is a killer.'

'Rabid?' queried Waylander.

'Nah. It was one of the pit dogs. There was a bear-fight this morning, damn fine one at that. But one of Jezel's hounds got loose. Worst of them too, part-wolf. We thought the bear had killed it and we were hauling the bodies out, but it wasn't dead. Bastard reared up and tore Jezel's throat away. Terrible thing. Terrible. Then it ran. The gods alone know how it managed it. Ripped up by the bear and all.'

'Not many dogs would turn on their owners that way,' observed Waylander.

'Pit dogs will,' said a second man, tall and skeletally thin. 'It's the training you see, the beatings and the starving and the like. Jezel is . . . was . . . a damn fine trainer. The best.'

'Thanks for the warning,' said Waylander.

'Not at all,' replied the thin man. 'You looking for lodgings for the night? I own the inn. We've a good room.'

'Thank you, no. I have no coin.'

The man's interest died instantly; with a swift smile he moved past Waylander and, followed by the others, strode off in the direction of the town. Waylander transferred his gaze to the hound, which had slumped exhausted to the grass and was now lying on its right side breathing hoarsely, its blood-covered flanks heaving.

Waylander moved slowly down the slope, halting some ten feet from the injured animal. From here he could see that its wounds were many, and its grey flanks carried other, older scars from claw and fang and whip. The hound gazed at him through baleful eyes, but its strength was gone, and when Waylander rose and moved to its side it managed only a weary growl.

'You can stop that,' said Waylander, gently stroking the hound's huge grey head. From the gashes and cuts he could see the dog had attacked the bear at least three times. There was blood seeping from four parallel rips in the hide, the skin peeled back exposing muscle and bone. Judging by the size of the clawmarks, the bear must have been large indeed. Sheathing his knife Waylander examined the injuries. There were muscle tears, but no broken bones that he could find.

Another low growl came from the hound as Waylander eased a flap of skin back into place, and the beast struggled to turn its head, baring its fangs. 'Lie still,' ordered the man. 'We'll see what can be done.' From a leather pouch at his belt Waylander removed a long needle and a thin length of twine, stitching the largest of the wounds, seeking to stem the flow of blood. At last satisfied he moved to the head, stroking the beast's ears. 'You must try to rise,' he said, keeping his voice low, soothing. 'I need to see your left side. Come on. Up, boy!' The hound struggled, but sank back to the earth, tongue lolling from its gaping jaws.

Waylander rose and moved outside to a fallen tree, cutting from it a long strip of bark, which he twisted into a shallow bowl. Nearby was a slender stream and he filled the bowl, carrying it back to the stricken hound, and holding it beneath the creature's mouth. The hound's nostrils quivered, and once more it struggled to rise. Waylander pushed his hands beneath the huge shoulders, helping it to its feet. The head drooped, the tongue slowly lapping at the water. 'Good,' said Waylander. 'Good. Finish it now.' There were four more jagged cuts on the hound's left side, but these were matted with dirt and clay, which had at least stopped the flow of blood.

Having finished drinking the exhausted hound sank back to the earth, its great head resting on its huge paws. Waylander sat beside the beast, which gazed up at him unblinking, and noted the many scars, old and new, which crisscrossed its flanks and head. The right ear had been ripped away some years before and there was a long, thick scar which ran from the hound's shoulder to the first joint of its right leg. 'By the gods, you're a fighter, boy,' said the man admiringly. 'And you're no youngster. What would you be? Eight? Ten? Well, those cowards made a mistake. You're not going to die, are you? You won't give them the satisfaction, will you?'

Reaching into his shirt the man pulled clear a wedge of smoked meat, wrapped in linen. 'This was to have lasted me another two days,' said Waylander, 'but I can live without a meal for a while. I'm not sure that you can.' Unfolding the linen he took his knife and cut a section of meat which he laid before the hound. The dog merely sniffed at it, then returned its brown gaze to the man. 'Eat, idiot,' said Waylander, lifting the meat and touching it to the hound's long canines. Its tongue snaked out and the man watched as the dog chewed wearily. Slowly, as the hours passed, he fed the rest of the meat to the injured hound. Then, with the light fading, he took a last look at the wounds. They were mostly sealed, though a thin trickle of blood was seeping from the deepest cut on the rear right flank.

'That's all I can do for you, boy,' said Waylander, rising. 'Good luck to you. Were I you, I wouldn't stay here too long. Those oafs may decide to come back for some sport – and they could bring a bowman.' Without a backward glance the man left the hound and made his way back into the forest.

The moon was high when he found a place to camp, a sheltered cave where his fire could not be seen, and he sat long into the night, wrapped in his cloak. He had done what he could for the dog, but there was little chance it would survive. It would have to scavenge for food, and in its wounded state it would not be able to move far. If it had been stronger he would have encouraged it to follow him, taken it to the cabin. Miriel would have loved it. He recalled the orphaned fox cub she had mothered as a child. What was the name she gave it? Blue. That was it. It stayed near the cabin for almost a year. Then, one day, it just loped off and never returned. Miriel had been twelve then. It was just before . . .

The memory of the horse falling, rolling, the terrible scream . . .

Waylander closed his eyes, forcing the memories back, concentrating on a picture of little Miriel feeding the fox cub with bread dipped in warm milk.

Just before dawn he heard something moving at the cave entrance. Rolling to his feet he drew his sword. The grey wolfhound limped inside and settled down at his feet. Waylander chuckled and sheathed his sword. Squatting down he reached out to stroke the beast. The dog gave a low, warning growl and bared its fangs.

'By Heaven, I like you, dog,' said Waylander. 'You remind me of me.'

Miriel watched the ugly warrior as he trained, his powerful hands clasped to the branch, his upper body bathed in sweat. 'You see,' he said, hauling himself smoothly up, 'the movement must be fluid, feet together. Touch your chin to the wood and then lower – not too fast, mind. No strain. Let your mind relax.' His voice was even, no hint of effort in his actions.

He was more powerfully built than her father, his shoulders and arms ridged with massive bands of muscle, and her eyes caught a trickle of sweat flowing over his shoulder and down his side. Like a tiny stream over the hills and valleys of his body. Sunlight gleamed on his bronzed skin, and the white scars shone like ivory on his chest and arms. Her gaze moved to his face, the smashed nose, the gashed, deformed lips, the swollen damaged ears. The contrast was chilling. His body was so beautiful.

But his face . . .

He dropped to the ground and grinned. 'Was a time I could have completed a hundred. But fifty's not bad. What are you thinking?'

Caught offguard she blushed. 'You make it look so simple,' she said, averting her gaze.

In the three days she had been practising she had once struggled to fifteen. He shrugged. 'You are getting there, Miriel. You just need more work.' Moving past her he picked up a towel and draped it over his neck.

'What happened to your wife?' she asked suddenly.

'Which one?'

'How many have you had?'

'Three.'

'That's a little excessive, isn't it?' she snapped.

He chuckled. 'Seems that way now,' he agreed.

'What about the first one?'

He sighed. 'Hell-cat. By Heaven she could fight. Half-demon –and that was the gentle half. The gods alone know where the other half came from. She swore her father was

70

Drenai – I didn't believe it for a moment. Had some good times, though. Rare good times.'

'Did she die?'

He nodded. 'Plague. She fought it, mind. All the swellings had gone, the discolouration. She'd even begun to get her hair back. Then she caught a chill and had no strength left to battle it. Died in the night. Peaceful.'

'Were you a gladiator then?'

'No. I was a merchant's book-keeper.'

'I don't believe it! How did you meet her?'

'She danced in a tavern. One night someone reached up and grabbed her leg. She kicked him in the mouth. He drew a dagger. I stopped him.'

'Just like that? A book-keeper?'

'Do not make the mistake of judging a man's physical courage, or his skills, by the work he is forced to do,' he said. 'I knew a doctor once who could put an arrow through a gold ring at forty paces. And a street cleaner in Drenan who once held off twenty Sathuli warriors, killing three, before he carried his injured officer back to camp. Judge a man by his actions, not his occupation. Now let's get back to work.'

'What about the other wives?'

'Don't want to work yet, eh? All right. Let's see, what can I tell you about Kalla? She was another dancer. Worked in the south quarter in Drenan. Ventrian girl. Sweet – but she had a weakness. Loved men. Couldn't say no. That marriage lasted eight months. She ran off with a merchant from Mashrapur. And lastly there was Voria. Older than me, but not much. I was a young fighter then, and she was the patron of the Sixth Arena. She took a fancy to me, showered me with gifts. Married her for her money, have to admit it, but I learned to love her, in my own way.'

'And she died, too?'

'No. She caught me with two serving maids and threw me out. Made my life Hell. For three years she kept trying to have me killed in the arena. Spiked my special wine with a sleeping-draught once. I was almost dead on my feet when I went out to fight. Then she hired two assassins. I had to leave Drenan for a while. I fought in Vagria, Gothir, even Mashrapur.'

'Does she still hate you?'

He shook his head. 'She married a young nobleman, then died suddenly leaving him all her money. Fell from a window – accident, they said, but I spoke to a servant who said he'd heard her having a terrible row with her husband just before she fell.'

'You think he killed her?'

'Sure of it.'

'And now he lives fat off her wealth?'

'No. Curiously he fell from the same window two nights later. His neck was broken in the fall.'

'And you wouldn't have had anything to do with that?'

'Me? How could you think it? And now let's work, if you please. Swords, I think.'

But just as Miriel was drawing her sword she saw movement in the undergrowth to the north of the cabin. At first she thought it was her father returning, for the first man who came into sight was dressed all in black. But he carried a longbow and was darkly bearded. He was followed by a shorter, stockier man in a tan leather jerkin.

'Follow my lead,' whispered Angel. 'And say nothing, even if they speak to you.'

He turned and waited as the men approached. 'Good day,' said the black-garbed bowman.

'And to you, friend. Hunting?'

'Aye. Thought we might find a stag.'

'Plenty south of here. Boar too, if you like the meat.'

'Nice cabin. Yours?'

'Yes,' said Angel. The man nodded.

'You'd be Dakeyras then?'

'That's right. This is my daughter, Moriae. How do you know of us?'

'Met some people in the mountains. They said you had a cabin here.'

'So you came to visit?'

'Not exactly. Thought you might be an old friend of

72

mine. His name was Dakeyras, but he was taller than you and darker.'

'It's not an uncommon name,' said Angel. 'If you kill a stag I'll buy some of the meat. Game will be pretty scarce once winter comes.'

'I'll bear that in mind,' said the bowman.

The two men walked off towards the south. Angel watched them until they were out of sight.

'Assassins?' asked Miriel.

'Trackers, huntsmen. They'll be in the employ of Senta or Morak.'

'You took a risk claiming to be Dakeyras.'

'Not really,' he said. 'They were likely to have been given a description of Waylander – and I certainly don't fit it.'

'But what if they hadn't? What if they had merely attacked you?'

'I'd have killed them. Now, let's work.'

*

Kesa Khan stared gloomily into the green flames, his jet-black eyes unblinking. He hawked and spat into the fire, his expression impassive, his heart beating wildly.

'What do you see, shaman?' asked Anshi Chen. The wizened shaman waved a hand, demanding silence, and the stocky chieftain obeyed. Three hundred swords he could call upon, but he feared the little man as he feared nothing else in life, not even the prospect of death.

Kesa Khan had seen all he needed to, but still his slanted eyes remained locked to the dancing flames. Reaching a skeletal hand into one of the four clay pots before him he took a pinch of yellow powder and flicked it into the fire. The blaze flared up, orange and red, shadows leaping to the cave wall and cavorting like demons. Anshi Chen cleared his throat and sniffed loudly, his dark Nadir eyes flickering nervously left and right.

Kesa gave a thin smile. 'I have seen the dragon in the dream,' he said, his voice a sibilant whisper.

The colour fled from Anshi's face. 'Is it over, then? We are all dead?'

73

'Perhaps,' agreed Kesa, enjoying the fear he felt emanating from the warrior.

'What can we do?'

'What the Nadir have always done. We will fight.'

'The Gothir have thousands of warriors, fine armour, swords of steel that do not dull. Archers. Lancers. How can we fight them?'

Kesa shook his head. 'I am not the Warlord of the Wolves, you are.'

'But you can read the hearts of our enemies! You could send demons to rip open their bellies. Or is Zhu Chao mightier than Kesa Khan?' For a moment there was silence then Anshi Chen leaned forward, bowing his head. 'Forgive me, Kesa. I spoke in anger.'

The shaman nodded sagely. 'I know. But there is truth in your fear. Zhu Chao *is* mightier. He can call upon the blood of many souls. The Emperor has a thousand slaves and many hearts have been laid upon the altar of the Dark God. And what do I have?' The little man twisted his body and pointed at the three dead chickens. He gave a dry laugh. 'I command few demons with those, Anshi Chen.'

'We could raid the Green Monkeys, steal some children,' offered Anshi.

'No! I will not sacrifice Nadir young.'

'But they are the enemy.'

'This day they are the enemy, but one day all Nadir will unite – this is written. This is the message Zhu Chao has carried to the Emperor. This is why the dragon is in the dream.'

'You cannot help us, then?'

'Do not be a fool, Anshi Chen. I am helping you now! Soon the Gothir will come against us. We must prepare for that day. Our winter camp must be close to the Mountains of the Moon, and we must be ready to flee there.'

'The Mountains?' whispered Anshi. 'But the demons . . .'

'It is that, or die. Your wives and your children, and the children of your children.'

'Why not flee south? We could ride hundreds of leagues

74

from Gulgothir. We could merge with other tribes. How would they find us?'

'Zhu Chao would find you,' said Kesa. 'Be strong, warlord. From one among us will come the leader the Nadir have longed for. Can you understand that? The Uniter! He will end Gothir rule. He will give us the world.'

'I will live to see this?'

Kesa shook his head. 'But neither will I,' he told the chieftain.

'It will be as you say,' pledged Anshi. 'We will move our camp.'

'And send for Belash.'

'I don't know where he is.'

'South of the new Drenai fortress, in the mountains they call Skeln. Send Shia to bring him.'

'Belash has no love for me, shaman. You know this.'

'I know many things, Anshi. I know that in the coming days we will rely on your steady judgement, and your calm skills. You are known and respected, as the Wily Fox. But I know we will need the power of Belash, the White Tiger in the Night. And he will bring another: he will give us the Dragon Shadow.'

*

Ekodas paused outside the Abbot's study, composing his thoughts. He loved life at the temple, its calm and camaraderie, the hours of study and meditation, even the physical exercises, running, archery and sword skills. In every way he felt a part of The Thirty.

Bar one.

He tapped at the door then pushed the latch. The room was lit by the golden light of three glass-sided lanterns and he saw Dardalion sitting at his desk, poring over a goatskin map. The Abbot looked up. In this gentle light he seemed younger, the silver highlights in his hair gleaming gold.

'Welcome, my boy. Come in and sit.' Ekodas bowed then strode to a chair. 'Shall we share thoughts, or would you like to speak out loud?' asked Dardalion.

'To speak, sir.'

'Very well. Vishna and Magnic tell me you are still troubled.'

'I am not troubled, Father. I know what I know.'

'You do not see this as arrogance?'

'No. My beliefs are only those that you enjoyed before your adventures with the killer, Waylander. Were you wrong then?'

'I do not believe that I was,' replied Dardalion. 'But then I no longer believe that there is only one road to the Source. Egel was a man of vision, and a believer. Three times a day he prayed for guidance. Yet he was also a soldier, and through him – aye, and Karnak – the lands of the Drenai were saved from the foe. He is dead now. Do you think the Source refused to take his soul to paradise?'

'I do not know the answer to that question,' said the young man, 'but what I do know is that I have been taught, by you and others, that love is the greatest gift of the Source. Love for all life, for all His Creation. Now you are saying that you expect me to lift a sword and take life. That cannot be right.'

Dardalion leaned forward, resting his elbows on the desktop, his hands clasped together as if in prayer. 'Do you accept that the Source created the lion?'

'Of course.'

'And the deer?'

'Yes – and the lion slays the deer. I know this. I do not understand it, but I accept it.'

'I feel the need of flight,' said Dardalion. 'Join me.'

The Abbot closed his eyes. Ekodas settled himself more comfortably in the chair, resting his arms upon the padded wings then took a deep breath. The release of spirit seemed effortless to Dardalion, but Ekodas mostly found it extraordinarily difficult, as if his soul had many hooks into the flesh. He followed the lessons he had learned for the last ten years, repeating the mantras, cleansing the mind.

The dove in the temple, the opening door, the circle of gold upon the field of blue, the spreading of wings in a gilded cage, the loosing of chains on the temple floor.

76

He felt the first loosening of his hold upon his body, as if he was floating in the warm waters of the womb. He was safe here, content. Feeling drifted back to him, his spine against the hard wood of the chair, his sandalled feet on the cold floor. No, no, he chided himself. You are losing it! His concentration deepened once more. But he could not soar.

Dardalion's voice whispered into his mind, 'Take my hand, Ekodas.'

A light shone golden and warming and Ekodas accepted the merging. The release was instant and his spirit broke clear of the temple of his body, soaring up through the second temple of stone to float high in the night sky above the land of Drenai.

'Why is it so difficult for me?' he asked the Abbot.

Dardalion, young again, his face unlined, reached out and touched his pupil's shoulder. 'Doubts are fears, my boy. And dreams of the flesh. Small guilts, meaningless but worrisome.'

'Where are we going, Father?'

'Follow and observe.' East they flew, across the glittering, star-dappled Ventrian Sea. A storm raged here, and far below a tiny trireme battled the elements, great waves washing over her flat decks. Ekodas saw a sailor swept overboard, watched him fall below the waves, saw the gleaming spark of his soul float up and vanish.

The land appeared dark below them, the mountains and plains of Ventria stretching to the east, while here on the coast, brightly-lit towns and ports shone like jewels on a cloak of black. Dardalion flew down, down . . . The two priests hovered some hundred feet in the air and Ekodas saw the scores of ships harboured here, heard the pounding of the armourers' hammers in the town.

'The Ventrian battle fleet,' said Dardalion. 'It will sail within the week. They will attack Purdol, Erekban and Lentrum, landing armies to invade Drenai. War and devastation.'

He flew on, crossing the high mountains and swooping down over a city of marble, its houses laid out in a grid pattern of wide avenues and cluttered streets. There was a palace upon the highest hill, surrounded by high walls manned by many sentries in gold-embossed armour of white and silver. Dardalion flew into the palace, through the walls and drapes of silk and velvet, coming at last to a bedchamber where a dark-bearded man lay sleeping. Above the man hovered his spirit, formless and vague, unaware and unknowing.

'We could stop the war now,' said Dardalion, a silver sword appearing in his hand. 'I could slay this man's soul. Then thousands of Drenai farmers and soldiers, women and children, would be safe.'

'No!' exclaimed Ekodas, swiftly moving between the Abbot and the formless spirit of the Ventrian king.

'Did you think I would?' asked Dardalion, sadly.

'I . . . I am sorry, Father. I saw the sword and . . .' his voice tailed away.

'I am no murderer, Ekodas. And I do not know the complete Will of the Source. No man does. No man ever will, though there are many who claim such knowledge. Take my hand, my son.' The walls of the palace vanished and with bewildering speed the two spirits crossed the sea once more, this time heading north-east. Colours flashed before Ekodas' eyes and, if not for the firm grip of Dardalion's hand, he would have been lost in the swirling lights. Their speed slowed and Ekodas blinked, trying to adjust his mind.

Below him was another city with more palaces of marble. A huge amphitheatre to the west and a massive stadium for chariot races at the centre marked it as Gulgothir, the capital of the Gothir empire.

'What are we here to see, Father?' asked Ekodas.

'Two men,' answered Dardalion. 'We have crossed the gates of time to be here. The scene you are about to witness happened five days ago.'

Still holding to the young priest's hand Dardalion floated down over the high palace walls and into a narrow room behind the throne hall. The Gothir Emperor was seated on a silk-covered divan. He was a young man, no more than twenty, with large protruding eyes and a receding chin, which was partly hidden by a wispy beard. Before him, seated on a low stool, was a second man, dressed in long dark robes of shining silk, embroidered with silver. His hair was dark and waxed flat to his skull, the sideburns unnaturally long and braided, hanging to his shoulders. His eyes were slanted beneath high flared brows, his mouth a thin line.

'You say the empire is in danger, Zhu Chao,' spoke the Emperor, his voice deep, resonant and strong, belying the weakness of his appearance.

'It is, sire. Unless you take action your descendants will be overthrown, your cities vanquished. I have read the omens. The Nadir wait only for the day of the Uniter. And he is coming, from among the Wolfshead.'

'And how can I change this?'

'If wolves are killing one's sheep, one kills the wolves.'

'You are talking of an entire tribe among the Nadir.'

'Indeed, sire. Eight hundred and forty-four savages. They are not people as you and I understand the term. Their lives are meaningless, but their future sons could see an end to Gothir civilisation.'

The Emperor nodded. 'It will take time to gather sufficient men for the task. As you know, the Ventrians are about to invade the lands of the Drenai and I have plans of my own.'

'I understand that, sire. You will wish to reclaim the Sentran Plain as part of Gothir, which is only just and right, but that will take no more than ten thousand men. You have ten times that many under your command.'

'And I need them, wizard. There are always those who seek the overthrow of monarchs. I can spare you five thousand for this small task. In one month you will have the massacre you desire.'

'You misjudge me, sire,' put in Zhu Chao, bowing deeply and spreading his hands like a supplicant. 'I am thinking only of the future good of Gothir.'

'Oh, I believe in the prophecy, wizard. I have had other sorcerors and several shamen telling me similar stories, though none named a single tribe. But you have other

79

reasons for wanting the Wolves destroyed, otherwise you would have traced the line of this Uniter back to one named man. Then the task would have been made so much more simple: one knife in the night. Never take me for a fool, Zhu Chao. You want them all dead for your own reasons.'

'You are all-wise, sire, and all-knowing,' whispered the wizard, falling to his knees and touching his forehead to the floor.

'No, I am not. And knowing that is my strength. But I will give you the deaths you desire. You have been a good servant to me, and never played me false. And as you say, they are only Nadir. It will sharpen the troops, give a cutting edge to the soldiers before the invasion of Drenan. I take it you will send your Brotherhood knights into the fray?'

'Of course, sire. They will be needed to combat the evil powers of Kesa Khan.'

The scene faded and Ekodas felt again the warm prison of his body. He opened his eyes to find Dardalion staring at him. 'Am I supposed to have learned something, Father Abbot? I saw only evil men, proud and ruthless. The world is full of such.'

'Yes, it is,' agreed Dardalion. 'And were we to spend our lives travelling the earth and slaying such men there would still be more of them at the end of our journey than there were at the beginning.'

'But surely that is *my* argument, Lord Abbot,' said Ekodas, surprised.

'Exactly. That is what you must consider. I appreciate your argument, and accept the premise on which it is made, and yet I still believe in the cause of The Thirty. I still believe we must be a Temple of Swords. What I would like you to do, Ekodas, is to lead the debate tomorrow evening. I will present your arguments as if they were my own. You will deliver mine.'

'But . . . that makes no sense, Father. I do not even begin to understand your cause.'

'Do the best that you can. I will make this debate an open vote. The future of The Thirty will depend upon the outcome. I will do my utmost to sway our brothers to your argument. You must do no less. If I win then the swords and armour will be returned to the storerooms and we will continue as an order of prayer. If you win we will await the guidance of the Source and ride to our destiny.'

'Why can I not argue my own beliefs?'

'You believe I will do them less than justice?'

'No, of course not, but . . .'

'Then it is settled.'

5

Morak listened to the reports as the hunters came in, his irritation growing. Nowhere was there any sign of Waylander, and the man Dakeyras had proved to be a balding redhead with a face that looked as if it had seen a stampede of oxen from underneath.

I hate forests, thought Morak, sitting with his back to the trunk of a willow, his green cloak wrapped tightly around him. I hate the smell of mould, the cold winds, the mud and the slime. He glanced at Belash, sitting apart from the others sharpening his knife with long sweeping strokes. The grating noise of the whetstone added to Morak's ill-humour.

'Well, somebody killed Kreeg,' he said at last. 'Somebody put a knife or an arrow through his eye.' No one spoke. They had found the body the previous day, wedged in the reeds of the River Earis.

'Could have been robbers,' said Wardal, a tall, thin bowman from the Forest of Graven, far to the south.

'Robbers?' sneered Morak. 'Hell's teeth! I've had lice with more brains than you! If it was robbers don't you think a fighter like Kreeg would have had more wounds? Don't you think there would have been a fight? Someone very skilful sent a missile through his eyeball. A man with rare talent is killed – that suggests to me he was slain by someone with *more* talent. Is my reasoning getting through to you?'

'You think it was Waylander,' muttered Wardal.

'A giant leap of the imagination. Many congratulations. The question is, where in Hell's name is he?'

'Why should he be easy to find?' asked Belash, suddenly. 'He knows we are here.'

'And what mighty spark of logic leads you to that conclusion?'

'He killed Kreeg. He knows.'

Morak felt a chill breeze blowing and shivered. 'Wardal, you and Tharic take the first watch.'

'What are we watching for?' enquired Tharic.

Morak closed his eyes and took a deep breath. 'Well,' he said at last, 'you could be watching for enormous elephants that will trample all over our supplies. But were I you, I would be alert for a tall man, dressed in black, who is rather good at sending sharp objects through eyeballs.' At that moment a tall figure stepped from the undergrowth. Morak's heart missed a beat, but then he recognised Baris. 'The normal procedure is to shout "Hallo the camp",' he observed. 'You took your time.'

The blond forester settled down by the fire. 'Kasyra is not a small place, but I found the whore Kreeg was living with. She told him about a man called Dakeyras who lives near here. I've got directions.'

'Wrong man,' said Morak. 'Wardal and Tharic already met him. What else did you find?'

'Little of interest,' answered Baris, pulling the remains of a loaf of bread from the pouch at his side. 'By the way, how long has Angel been a member of the Guild?'

'Angel? I've not heard that he is,' said Morak. 'Why?'

'He was in Kasyra a week or so back. Tavern-keeper recognised him. Senta is there, too. He said to tell you that when he finds your body he'll be sure to give it a fine burial.'

But Morak wasn't listening. He laughed and shook his head. 'Wardal, have you ever been to the arena?'

'Aye. Saw Senta fight there. Beat a Vagrian called . . . called . . .'

'Never mind! Did you ever see Angel fight?'

'Oh yes. Tough. Won some money on him once.'

'Would you remember his face at all?'

'Red hair, wasn't it?' answered Wardal.

'Correct, numbskull. Red hair. And a face his mother would disown. I wonder if the tiniest thought is trying to make its way through that mass of bone that houses your brain? If it is, do share it with us.'

Wardal sniffed loudly. 'The man at the cabin!'

'The man who said he was Dakeyras, yes,' said Morak.
'It was the right cabin, just the wrong man. Tomorrow you
can return there. Take Baris and Tharic. No, that might not
be enough. Jonas and Seeris as well. Kill Angel and bring
the girl here.'

'He's a gladiator,' objected Jonas, a stout balding
warrior with a forked beard.

'I didn't say fight him,' whispered Morak. 'I said kill him.'

'Wasn't nothing about no gladiators,' persisted Jonas.
'Tracking, you said. Find this Dakeyras. I've seen Angel
fight as well. Don't stop, does he? Stick him, cut him, hit
him . . . still keeps going.'

'Yes, yes, yes! I am sure he would be delighted to know
you are among his greatest admirers. But he's older now.
He retired. Just walk in, engage him in conversation, then
kill him. If that sounds a little too difficult for you, then
head for Kasyra – and kiss goodbye to any thought of a
share in ten thousand gold pieces.'

'Why don't *you* kill him?' asked Jonas. 'You're the
swordsman here.'

'Are you suggesting that I am frightened of him?'
countered Morak, his voice ominously low.

'No, not at all,' answered Jonas, reddening. 'We all
know how . . . skilled you are. I just wondered, that's all.'

'Have you ever seen the nobles hunt, Jonas?'

'Of course.'

'Have you noticed how, when chasing boar, they take
hounds with them?'

The man nodded glumly. 'Good,' said Morak. 'Then
take this thought into that pebble-sized brain: I am a
hunting noble and you are my dogs. Is that clear? I am not
being paid to kill Angel. I am paying you.'

'We could always shoot him from a distance, I suppose,'
said Jonas. 'Wardal's very good with that bow.'

'Fine,' muttered Morak. 'Just so long as it is done. But
bring the girl to me, safe and hearty. You understand? She
is the key to Waylander.'

'That is against Guild rules,' said Belash. 'No innocents
may be used . . .'

'I know the Guild rules!' snapped Morak. 'And when I want lessons in proper conduct I shall be sure to call on you. After all, the Nadir are well known for their rigid observance of civilised behaviour.'

'I know what you want from the girl,' said Belash. 'And it is not this key to her father.'

'A man is entitled to certain pleasures, Belash. They are what make living worthwhile.'

The Nadir nodded. 'I have known some men who share the same . . . pleasures . . . as you. When we catch them among the Nadir we cut off their hands and feet and stake them out over anthills. But then, as you say, we do not understand you civilised people.'

*

The face was huge and white as a fish belly, the eye sockets empty, the lids shaped like fangs, clacking as they closed. The mouth was lipless, the tongue enormous and cratered with tiny mouths.

Miriel took Krylla's hand, and the children tried to flee – but the demon was faster, stronger. One scaled hand closed on Miriel's arm, the touch burning.

'Bring them to me!' came a soft voice, and Miriel saw a man standing close by, his face also pale, his skin scaled like a beautiful albino snake. But there was nothing beautiful about the man. Krylla began to cry.

The monstrous creature that held them leaned over the children, touching the cavernous mouth to Miriel's face. She felt pain then, terrible pain. And she screamed.

And screamed . . .

'Wake up, girl,' said the demon, his hand once more on her shoulder. Her fingers snaked out, clawing at his face, but he grabbed her wrist. 'Stop this. It is me, Angel!'

Her eyes flared open and she saw the rafters of the cabin, the light of the moon seeping through the knife-thin gaps in the shutters, felt the rough wool of the blankets on her naked frame. She shuddered and fell back. He stroked her brow, pushing back the sweat-drenched hair. 'Just a

85

dream, girl. Just a dream,' he whispered. She said nothing for a moment, trying to gather her thoughts. Her mouth was dry and she sat up, reaching for the goblet of water by her bedside.

'It was a nightmare. Always the same one,' she said, between sips. 'Krylla and I were being hunted across a dark place, an evil place. Valleys without trees, a sky without sun or moon, grey, soulless.' She shivered. 'Demons caught us, and terrible men . . .'

'It's over,' he assured her. 'You are awake now.'

'It's never over. It's a dream now – but it wasn't then.' She shivered again, and he reached out, drawing her to him, his arms upon her back, his hand patting her. Lowering her head to his shoulder she felt better. The remembered cold of the Void was strong in her mind, and the warmth of his skin pushed it back.

'Tell me about it,' he said.

'It was after Mother died. We were frightened, Krylla and me. Father was acting strangely, shouting and weeping. We knew nothing about drunken men. And to see Father stumbling and falling was terrifying. Krylla and I used to sit in our room, holding hands. We used to soar our spirits high into the sky. We were free then. Safe – so we thought. But one night, as we played beneath the stars we realised we were not alone. There were other spirits in the sky with us. They tried to catch us, and we fled. We flew so fast, and with such terror in our hearts that we had no idea where we were. But the sky was grey, the land desolate. Then the demons came. Summoned by the men.'

'But you escaped from them.'

'Yes. No. Another man appeared, in silver armour. We knew him. He fought the demons, killing them, and brought us home. He was our friend. But he does not appear in my dreams now.'

'Lie back,' said Angel. 'Have a little gentle sleep.'

'No. I don't want the dream again.'

Pulling back the woollen blanket Angel slid in beside her, resting her head on his shoulder. 'No demons, Miriel. I shall be here to bring you back if there are.' Pulling the

86

blanket up around them both he lay still. She could feel the slow, rhythmic beat of his heart and closed her eyes.

She slept for a little over an hour and awoke refreshed. Angel was sleeping soundlessly beside her. In the faint light of pre-dawn his ugliness was softened, and she tried to picture him as he had been all those years ago when he had brought her the dress. It was almost impossible. Her arm was draped across his chest and she slowly drew it back, feeling the softness of his skin and the contrasting ridges of hard muscle across his belly. He did not wake, and Miriel felt a powerful awareness of her own nakedness. Her hand slid down, the tips of her fingers brushing over the pelt of tightly curled hair below his navel. He stirred. She halted all movement, aware now of her increased heartbeat. Fear touched her, but it was a delicious fear. There had been village boys who had filled her with longing, left her dreaming of forbidden trysts. But never had she felt like this, the onset of fear synchronised to her passion. Never had she been so aware of her desires. Her needs. His breathing deepened again. Her hand slid down, fingers caressing him, circling him, feeling him quicken and swell.

Doubt followed by panic suddenly flared within her. What if he opened his eyes? He could be angry at her boldness, might think her a whore. Which I am, she thought, with a burst of self-disgust. Releasing him she rolled from the bed. She had bathed the previous night, but somehow the thought of ice-cold water on her skin seemed not only pleasurable, but necessary. Moving carefully to avoid waking him she eased open the bedroom door and crossed the cabin floor.

Lifting the bar from its brackets she opened the main door and stepped out into the sunlit clearing before the cabin. The bushes and trees were still silvered with dew, the autumn sunlight weak upon her skin. How could she have acted so, she wondered as she strolled to the stream. Miriel had often dreamed of lovers, but never in her fantasies had they been ugly. Never had they been so old. And she knew she was not in love with the former gladiator. No, she realised, that's what makes you a whore. You just wanted to rut like an animal.

Reaching the stream she sat down on the grass, her feet dangling in the water. Flowing from the high mountains there were small rafts of ice on the surface, like frozen lilies. And it was cold.

She heard a movement behind her but, lost in thought, she was not swift enough, and as she rolled to her feet a man's hands caught her shoulder, hurling her to the grass. Ramming her elbow sharply back she connected with his belly. He grunted in pain and sagged across her. The smell of woodsmoke, greasy leather and stale sweat filled her nostrils and a bearded face fell against her cheek. Twisting she slammed the heel of her hand against the man's nose, snapping his head back. Scrambling to her feet she tried to run, but the man grabbed her ankle, and a second man leapt from hiding. Miriel's fist cracked against the newcomer's chin, but his weight carried him forward and she was knocked to the ground, her arms pinned beneath her.

'A real Hellcat,' grunted the second man, a tall blond forester. 'Are you all right, Jonas?' The first man struggled to his feet, blood seeping from his nose and streaming into his black beard.

'Hold her still, Baris. I've just the weapon to bring her to heel.' The balding warrior began to unfasten the thongs of his leggings, moving forward to stand over Miriel.

'You heard what Morak said. Unharmed,' objected Baris.

'I've never known a woman harmed by it yet,' responded Jonas.

Miriel, her arms and shoulders pinned, arched her back then sent her right foot slamming up between the forester's legs. Jonas grunted and slumped to his knees. Baris slapped her face, grabbed her hair and hauled her to her feet. 'Don't give up, do you?' he snarled, slapping her again, this time with the back of his hand. Miriel sagged against him.

'That's better,' he said. Her head came up sharply, cannoning against his chin. He stumbled back, then drew his knife, his arm arcing back for the throw. Miriel, still half-stunned, threw herself to her right, rolling to her knees. Then she was up and running.

Another man jumped into her path, but she swerved round him, and almost made the clearing before a stone from a sling ricocheted from her temple. Falling to her knees she tried to crawl into the undergrowth, but the sound of running feet behind her told her she was finished. Her head ached, and her senses swam. Then she heard Angel's voice.

'Time to die, my boys.'

*

Miriel awoke in her own bed, a water-soaked cloth on her brow, her head throbbing painfully. She tried to sit up, but felt giddy then sick. 'Lie still,' said Angel. 'That was a nasty strike. You've a lump the size of a goose egg.'

'Did you kill them?' she whispered weakly.

'No. Never seen men run so fast. They sent up a cloud of dust. I have a feeling they knew me – it was very gratifying.'

Miriel closed her eyes. 'Don't tell my father I went out without weapons.'

'I won't. But it was stupid. What were you thinking of – the dream?'

'No, not the dream. I just . . . I was just stupid, as you say.'

'The man who never made a mistake never made anything,' he said.

'I'm not a man!'

'I'd noticed. But I'm sure it holds true for women. Two of the men were bleeding, so I'd guess you caused them some pain before they downed you. Well done, Miriel.'

'That's the first time you've praised me. Be careful. It might go to my head.'

He patted her hand. 'I can be a mean whoreson, I know that. But you're a fine girl – tough, strong, willing. I don't want to see your spirit broken – but I don't want to see your body broken, either. And I know only one way to teach. I'm not even sure I know that very well.'

She tried to smile, but the pain was growing and she felt herself slipping into sleep.

'Thank you,' she managed to say. 'Thank you for being there.'

*

From his high study window Dardalion saw the troop of lancers slowly climbing the winding path, twenty-five men in silver armour, cloaked in crimson, riding jet-black horses, their flanks armoured in chain-mail. At their head rode a man Dardalion knew well. Against the sleek, martial perfection of his men Karnak should have looked comical; overweight and dressed in clothes of clashing colours – red cloak, orange shirt, green trews tied with blue leggings and below them black riding boots, edged with a silver trim. But no one laughed at his eccentric dress. For this was the hero of Dros Purdol, the saviour of the Drenai.

Karnak the One-eyed.

The man's physical strength was legendary, but it paled against the colossal power of his personality. With one speech he could turn a motley group of farmers into sword-wielding heroes who would defy an army. Dardalion's smile faded. Aye, and they would die for him, *had* died for him – in their thousands. They would go on dying for him.

Vishna entered the study, his spirit voice whispering into Dardalion's mind, 'Will their arrival delay the Debate, Father?'

'No.'

'Was it wise to instruct Ekodas to argue the cause of right?'

'Is it the cause of right?' countered Dardalion, speaking aloud and swinging to face the dark-bearded Gothir nobleman.

'You have always taught me so.'

'We shall see, my boy. Now go down and escort the Lord Karnak to me. And see that his men are fed, the horses groomed. They have ridden far.'

'Yes, Father.'

Dardalion returned to the window, but he did not see the distant mountains, nor the storm clouds looming in the north. He saw again the cabin on the mountainside, the two frightened children, and the two men who had come to kill them. And he felt the weight of the weapon of death in his hands. He sighed. The cause of right? Only the Source knew.

He heard the sound of booming laughter from the winding stairs beyond his room, and felt the immense physical presence of Karnak even before the man crossed the threshold.

'Gods, but it is good to see you, old lad!' boomed Karnak, striding across the room and clasping a huge hand to Dardalion's shoulder. The man's smile was wide and genuine, and Dardalion returned it.

'And you, my lord. I see your dress sense is as colourful as ever.'

'Like it? The cloak is from Mashrapur, the shirt from a little weavery in Drenan.'

'They suit you well.'

'By Heaven you are a terrible liar, Dardalion. I expect your soul will burn in Hellfire. Now sit you down and let us talk of more important matters.' The Drenai leader moved round the desk to take Dardalion's chair, leaving the slender Abbot to sit opposite him. Karnak unbuckled his sword-belt, laying it on the floor beside him, then eased his great bulk into the seat. 'Damned uncomfortable furniture,' he said. 'Now, where were we? Ah, yes! What can you tell me about the Ventrians?'

'They will sail within the week, landing at Purdol, Erekban and the Earis estuary,' answered Dardalion.

'How many ships?'

'More than four hundred.'

'That many, eh? I don't suppose you'd consider whipping up a storm to sink the bastards?'

'Even if I could – which I can't – I would refuse such a request.'

'Of course,' said Karnak, with a wide grin. 'Love, peace, the Source, morality and so on. But there are some who could, yes?'

'So it is said,' agreed Dardalion, 'among the Nadir and the Chiatze. But the Ventrians have their own wizards, sir, and I don't doubt they'll be making sacrifices and casting spells to ensure good weather.'

'Never mind their problems,' snapped Karnak. 'Could you locate a demon conjurer for me?'

Now it was Dardalion who laughed. 'You are a wonder, my lord. And I shall do you the kindness of treating that request as a jest.'

'Which of course it wasn't,' said Karnak. 'Still, you've made your point. Now, what of the Gothir?'

'They have reached agreement with the Sathuli tribes, who will allow an invading force to pass unopposed to occupy the Sentran Plain once the Ventrians have landed. Around ten thousand men.'

'I knew it!' snapped Karnak, his irritation growing. 'Which legions?'

'The First, Second and Fifth. Plus two mercenary legions made up of Vagrian refugees.'

'Wonderful. The Second and the Fifth are not a worry to me – our spies say they are mostly raw recruits with little discipline. But the First are the Emperor's finest, and the Vagrians fight like pain-maddened tigers. Still, I have a week, you say. Much can happen in that time. We'll see. Tell me of the Sathuli leader.'

For more than an hour Karnak questioned Dardalion until, satisfied at last, he rose to leave. Dardalion raised his hand. 'There is another matter to be discussed, my lord.'

'There is?'

'Yes. Waylander.'

Karnak's face darkened. 'That is none of your affair, priest. I don't want you spying on me.'

'He is my friend, Karnak. And you have ordered his killing.'

'These are affairs of state, Dardalion. Damn it all, man, he killed the King. There has been a price on his head for years.'

'But that is not why you hired the Guild, my lord. I know the reason, and it is folly. Worse folly than you know.'

'Is that so? Explain it to me.'

'Two years ago, with the army treasury empty, and a rebellion on your hands, you received a donation from a merchant in Mashrapur, a man named Gamalian. One hundred thousand in gold. It saved you. Correct?'

'What of it?'

'The money came from Waylander. Just as this year's donation of eighty thousand Raq from the merchant, Perlisis, came from Waylander. He has been supporting you for years. Without him you would have been finished.'

Karnak swore and slumped back into his seat, rubbing a massive hand across his face. 'I have no choice, Dardalion. Can you not see that? You think I want to see the man killed? You think there is any satisfaction in it for me?'

'I am sure there is not. But in having him hunted you have unleashed a terrible force. He was living quietly in the mountains, mourning his wife. He was no longer Waylander the Slayer, no longer the man to be feared, but day by day he is becoming Waylander again. And soon he will consider hunting down the man who set the price.'

'I'd sooner he tried that, than the other alternative,' said Karnak, wearily. 'But I hear what you say, priest, and I will think on it.'

'Call them off, Karnak,' pleaded Dardalion. 'Waylander is a force like no other, almost elemental, like a storm. He may be only one man, but he will not be stopped.'

'Death can stop any man,' argued Karnak.

'Remember that, my lord,' advised Dardalion.

*

It was the dog that found the remains of the old tinker. Waylander had been moving warily through the forest when the hound's head had lifted, its great black nostrils quivering. Then it had loped off to the left. Waylander followed and found the animal tearing rotting meat from the old man's leg.

The dog was not the first to find the body and the corpse was badly mauled.

Waylander made no attempt to call the dog away. There

93

was a time when such a scene would have revolted him, but he had seen too much death since then: his memories were littered with corpses. He recalled his father walking him through the woods near their home in the valley, and they had come across a dead hawk. The child he had been was saddened by the sight. 'That is not the bird,' said his father. 'That is merely the cloak he wore.' The man pointed up to the sky. 'That is where the hawk is, Dakeyras. Flying towards the sun.'

Old Ralis had gone. What was left was merely food for scavengers, but cold anger flared in Waylander neverthe- less. The tinker had been harmless, and always travelled unarmed. There was no need for such senseless torture. But that was Morak's way. The man loved to inflict pain.

The tracks were easy to read and Waylander left the dog to feed and set off in pursuit of the killers. As he walked he studied the spoor. There were eleven men in the group, but they had soon split up. He knelt and examined the trail. There had been a meeting. One man – Morak? – had addressed the group, and they had paired and moved off. A single set of prints headed east, perhaps towards Kasyra. The others moved in different directions. They were quartering the forest, and that meant they did not know of the cabin. The old man had told them nothing.

Identifying the track of Morak, narrow-toed boots with deep heels, he decided to follow the Ventrian. Morak would not be wandering the forest in the search. He would find a place to wait. Waylander set off once more, moving with care, stopping often to scan the trees and the lines of the hills, keeping always to cover.

Towards dusk he halted and loaded his crossbow. Ahead of him was a narrow path, wending up a gentle rise. The wind had changed and he smelt woodsmoke coming from the south-west. Squatting by a huge, gnarled oak he waited for the sun to go down, his thoughts sombre. These men had come into the forest to kill him. That he understood; this was their chosen occupation. But the torture and murder of the old man had lit a cold fire in Waylander's heart.

They would pay for that deed.

And they would pay in kind.

A barn owl soared into the night seeking rodent prey and a grey fox padded across the path directly in front of the waiting man. But Waylander did not move, and the fox ignored him. Slowly the sun set, and night changed the personality of the forest. The whispering wind became the sibilant, ghostly hiss of a serpent's breath, the gentle trees stood stark and forbidding, and the moon rose, quarter full and curved like a Sathuli tulwar. A killer's moon.

Waylander eased himself to his feet and removed his cloak, folding it and laying it over a boulder. Then he moved silently up the slope, crossbow in hand. There was a sentry sitting beneath a tall pine. As a safeguard against being surprised he had scattered dry twigs in a wide circle around the base of the tree, and was now sitting on a fallen log, sword in hand. His hair was pale, almost silver in the moonlight.

Waylander laid his crossbow on the ground and moved out behind the seated man, his moccasined feet gently brushing aside the twigs. His left hand seized the man's hair, dragging back his head, his right swept out and across, the black blade slicing jugular and vocal chords. The sentry's feet thrashed out, but blood was gouting from his throat and within seconds all movement had ceased. Waylander eased the body to the ground and walked back to where his crossbow lay. The campfire was some thirty paces to the north and he could see a group of men sitting around it. Moving closer he counted them. Seven. Three were unaccounted for. Silently he circled the camp, finding two more of the assassins standing guard. Both died before they were even aware of danger.

Closer to the fire now Waylander puzzled over the missing man. Was it the one sent towards Kasyra? Or was there a sentry he had not located? He scanned the group by the fire. There was Morak, sitting on the far side, wrapped in a green cloak. But who was missing? Belash! The Nadir knife-fighter.

Keeping low to the ground Waylander moved into the

deeper shadows of the forest, stopping only once to smear his face with mud. His clothes were black, and he merged into the darkness. Where in Hell's name was the Nadir? He closed his eyes, letting the soft sounds of the forest sweep over him. Nothing.

Then he smiled. Why worry about what you cannot control, he thought. Let Belash worry about me! He slid out from his hiding place and angled in towards the camp. A little confusion was called for.

There was a screen of low bushes to the north of the campsite. Dropping to all fours Waylander edged closer then rose, crossbow pointed. The first bolt crashed through a man's temple, the second plunged into the heart of a bearded warrior as he leapt to his feet.

Ducking, Waylander ran to the south then traversed a slope and moved north once more, coming up to the camp from the opposite side. It was, as he had expected, deserted now, save for the two corpses. Reloading the crossbow he squatted down in the shadows and waited. Before long he heard movement to his right. He grinned and dropped to his belly.

'Any sign of him?' whispered Waylander.

'No,' came the reply from close by. Waylander sent two bolts in the direction of the voice. The thudding of the impacting bolts was followed by a grunt and the sound of a falling body.

Fool! thought Waylander, easing himself back into the undergrowth.

The moon disappeared behind a thick bank of cloud. Total darkness descended on the forest. Waylander crouched low, waiting, listening. Taking two bolts from his small quiver he waited for the night breeze to rustle the leaves above him before pulling back the strings and loading the weapon, the forest sounds covering the slight noise of the bolts slipping into place. The wounded man he had shot cried out in pain, begging for help. But no one came.

Waylander crept deeper into the forest. Had they run, or were they hunting him? The Nadir would not run. Morak? Who knew what thoughts filled the mind of a torturer.

To his left was an ancient beech, its trunk split. Waylander looked at the sky. The moon was still hidden, but the clouds were breaking. Stepping up to the trunk he reached up with his left hand and swiftly hauled himself to the lowest branch, climbing some twenty feet up into the tree.

The moon shone bright, and he ducked down. Below him the forest was lit by eldritch light. He scanned the undergrowth. One man was crouched behind a section of gorse. A second was close by. This one carried a short Vagrian hunting bow, a barbed arrow notched to the string. Laying down the crossbow Waylander traversed the trunk and sought out the others. But no one else could be seen.

Returning to his original position, he watched the two hidden men for some time. Neither moved, save to glance around fearfully. And neither made any attempt to communicate with the other. Waylander wondered if each knew of the other's presence so close by.

Reaching into his pouch he pulled clear a large triangular copper coin, and this he threw into the screen of bushes close to the first assassin. The man swore and lunged up. Immediately the second man spun round and loosed an arrow which tore into the first man's shoulder.

'You puking idiot!' shouted the wounded man.

'I'm sorry!' answered the bowman, dropping the bow and moving forward to his comrade's side. 'Is it bad?'

Waylander dropped quietly to the ground on the other side of the tree.

'You damn near killed me!' complained the first man.

'Wrong,' said Waylander. 'He has killed you.'

A bolt punched through the man's skull just above his nose. The bowman leapt to his right, diving for cover, but Waylander's second bolt lanced through his neck. An arrow flashed by Waylander's face, burying itself in the trunk of the ancient beech. Ducking he ran for cover, hurling himself over a fallen tree and scrambling up a short steep bank into dense undergrowth.

Three left.

And one of these was the Nadir!

Sword in hand Morak hid behind a large boulder, listening for any signs of movement. He was alone, and filled with the fear of death.

How many were dead already?

The man was a demon! The hilt of his sword was greasy with sweat, and he wiped it on his cloak. His clothes were filthy, his hands mud-streaked. This was no place for a nobleman to die, surrounded by filth and worms and rotted leaves. He had fought men before, blade to blade, and knew he was no coward, but the dark of the forest, the hissing of the wind, the sibilant rustling of the leaves and the knowledge that Waylander was moving towards him like Death's shadow, almost unmanned him.

A movement from behind caused his heart to palpitate. He swung, trying to bring up his sword, but Belash's powerful hand gripped his wrist. 'Follow me,' whispered the Nadir, easing back into the undergrowth. Morak was more than willing to obey and the two men crept towards the south, Belash leading the way down the slope to where Waylander's cloak lay upon a boulder.

'He will come back here,' said Belash, keeping his voice low.

Morak saw that the Nadir was carrying a short hunting bow of Vagrian horn, a quiver of arrows slung across his broad shoulders. 'What about the others?' he asked.

'Dead – all except Jonas. He loosed a shaft at Waylander, but it missed. Jonas dropped his bow and ran.'

'Cowardly scum!'

Belash grinned. 'Bigger share for us, yes?'

'I didn't think you were interested in coin. I thought this was just an exercise in valiant behaviour. You know, Father's bones and all that.'

'No time for talk, Morak. You sit here and rest. I will be close by.'

'Sit here? He'll see me.'

'Of course. It is a small crossbow – he will come in close. Then I'll kill him.'

Morak uttered a foul curse. 'What if he just creeps up and lets fly before you see him?'

'Then you die,' said Belash.

'Quaint sense of humour you have. Why don't you sit here? I'll take the bow.'

'As you wish,' answered Belash contemptuously, his dark eyes gleaming with amusement. He handed Morak the weapon then folded his arms and sat, staring towards the south. Morak faded back into the undergrowth and notched an arrow to the string.

The moonlight cast spectral shadows on the small clearing where Belash waited and Morak shivered. What if Waylander were to come from a different direction? What if, even now, he was creeping silently through the forest behind him? Morak swung his head, but could see nothing untoward. But then who could see anything in this cursed gloom!

The Nadir's plan was a simple one, born of a simple mind. But they were not dealing with a simpleton. If he stayed here he could die. There was no certainty to the plan. Yet if he left the Nadir behind, then Belash would feel betrayed. And if he survived, the Nadir would then hunt him down. Morak toyed with the thought of taking the risk, of slipping away quietly, but Belash was a woodsman of almost mystical skill. He would hear him – and give chase immediately. An arrow then – straight through the back. No. The Nadir was strong. What if it failed to kill immediately? Morak knew he could best Belash sword to sword, but the Nadir's immense strength might bring him in close enough to use that wicked dagger . . . That was a thought he didn't enjoy.

Think, man!

Dropping the bow, Morak felt around the soft earth until his fingers closed on a large stone the size of his fist. This was the answer. Standing, he walked back out into the clearing. Belash glanced round.

'What is wrong?'

'I have another plan,' he said.

'Yes?'

'Is that him?' hissed Morak, pointing to the north. Belash's head jerked round.

'Where?'

The stone cracked against the back of the Nadir's neck. Belash fell forward. Morak hit him again. Then again. The Nadir slumped to the ground. Morak dropped the stone and drew his dagger. Always best to make sure. Then he heard movement in the undergrowth. Backing away from the sound, Morak turned and ran, sprinting down the track.

And did not see the ugly hound that emerged from the bushes.

*

Belash floated up from the darkness to a painful awakening. Soft earth was against his face and his head pounded. He tried to rise, but nausea swamped him. Reaching up he touched the back of his neck. The blood was beginning to congeal. His hand moved down to his belt. The knife was still in its sheath. For a while he struggled to remember what had happened. Had Waylander come upon them?

No. I would now be dead.

His mouth was dry. Something cold pushed against his face. He turned his head and found himself staring into the baleful eyes of a huge, scarred hound. Belash lay perfectly still, save for his hand which inched slowly towards his knife.

'That would not be wise,' said a cold voice.

At first he thought it was the hound that had spoken to him. A devil dog come to claim his soul?

'Here, dog!' came the voice again. The hound padded away. Belash forced himself to his knees, and saw the black-garbed figure sitting on the boulder. The man's crossbow was now hanging from his belt, his knives sheathed.

'How did you surprise me?' asked Belash.

'I didn't. Your friend – Morak? – struck you from behind.'

Belash tried to stand, but his legs were too weak and he

100

slumped back. Slowly he rolled to his back then, taking hold of the jutting branch of a fallen tree he pulled himself to a sitting position. 'Why am I still alive?' he asked.

'You intrigue me,' the man told him.

Truly the ways of the southerners are mysterious, thought Belash, leaning his head against the rough bark of the tree trunk. 'You left me my weapons. Why?'

'I saw no reason to remove them.'

'You think I am so poor an opponent that you need not fear me?'

The man chuckled. 'I never yet met a Nadir who could be described as a poor opponent, but I have seen many head wounds – and yours will leave you weak for several days, if not longer.'

Belash did not reply. Bracing his legs beneath him he rose unsteadily and then sat back upon the tree. His head was spinning, but he preferred to be on his feet. He was only some three paces from Waylander, and he wondered if he could draw the knife and catch the man unawares. It was unlikely, but it was the only chance he had to stay alive.

'Don't even think of it,' said Waylander softly.

'You read thoughts?'

'I don't need any special skill to understand a Nadir mind, not when it comes to battle. But you wouldn't make it – trust me on that. Are you Notas?'

Belash was surprised. Few southerners understood the complex structures governing the Nadir tribes and their compositions. Notas meant no tribe, an outcast. 'No. I am of the Wolves.'

'You are a long way from the Mountains of the Moon.'

'You have walked among the Tent-people?'

'Many times. Both as friend and enemy.'

'What was the name the Nadir gave you?' enquired Belash.

The man smiled thinly. 'They called me the Soul Stealer. And an old Notas leader once gave me the name Oxskull.'

Belash nodded. 'You rode with the giant, Ice-eyes. There are songs about you – dark songs, of dark deeds.'

'And they are true,' admitted the man.

'What happens now?'

'I haven't decided. I will take you to my home. You can rest there.'

'Why do you think I would not kill you, once my strength has returned?'

'The Guild allows no Nadir members. Therefore you were to be paid by Morak. Judging by the lumps on your skull I would say that Morak has terminated your employment. What would you gain by killing me?'

'Nothing,' agreed Belash. Except the honour of being the man who slew the Soul Stealer. And surely the Mountains would look kindly upon the man who avenged the theft of the treasure? Surely they would then grant him the vengeance he sought.

Waylander moved forward. 'Can you walk?'

'Yes.'

'Then follow me.' The tall man strode away, his broad back an inviting target.

Not yet, thought Belash. First let me find my strength.

6

The table was forty feet long and three feet wide, and had once been covered by fine linens and decorated with golden plates and goblets. The finest of foods had graced the plates, and nobles had carved their meats with knives of gold. Now there was no fine linen, and the plates were of pewter, the goblets of clay. Bread and cheese lay upon the plates, cool spring water in the goblets. At the table sat twenty-eight priests in white robes. Behind each priest, glittering in the lantern light, was a suit of armour, a bright silver helm, a shining cuirass and a scabbarded sword. And against each suit of armour rested a long wooden staff.

Ekodas sat at the head of the table, Dardalion beside him.

'Let me present my own arguments,' pleaded Ekodas.

'No, my son. But I will do them justice, I promise you.'

'I did not doubt that, sir. But I cannot do justice to yours.'

'Do your best, Ekodas. No man can ever ask for more than that.' Dardalion lifted a finger to his lips, then closed his eyes. All heads bowed instantly and the union began. Ekodas felt himself floating. There was no sight, no sound, no feeling. Just warmth. He sensed Vishna, and Magnic, Palista, Seres . . . all the others flowing all around him.

'We are One,' pulsed Dardalion.

'We are One,' echoed the Thirty.

And the prayer-song began, the great hymn to the Source, mind-sung in a tongue unknown to any of them, even Dardalion. The words were unfathomable, but the sensations created by the sounds produced a sweet magic, filling the soul with light.

Ekodas was transported back to his childhood, to see again the tall, gangling dark-haired youth with the violet eyes, working behind his father in the fields, planting the seed, gathering the harvest. Those were good days, though he did not know it at the time. Shunned by the other youths of the village he had no friends, and no one to share his small joys, his discoveries. But now, as he soared within the hymn he saw the love his parents gave him, despite their fears at his Talent. He felt the warm hugs from his mother, and his father's calloused hand ruffling his hair.

And such was the power of the hymn he could even see, without hate, the Vagrian soldiers attacking his home, watch the axe that dashed his father's brains to the floor, the plunging knife that snatched his mother from life. He had been in the barn when the Vagrians rode in. His parents had been slain within the first minute of the raid. Ekodas had leapt from the high hay-stall and run towards the soldiers. One turned and lashed out with a sword. It cut the boy's shoulder and neck, glancing up to slash across his brow.

When he awoke he was the only living Drenai for miles around. The Vagrians had even butchered the farm animals. All the buildings were burning, and a great pall of smoke hung over the land. He walked the two miles to the village on the third day after the raid. Bodies lay every-where, and though the smoke was gone now, great flocks of crows circled in the sky. He gathered what food remained – a half-charred side of ham, a small sack of dried oats –and found a shovel which he carried back to his home, digging a deep grave for his parents.

For a year he had lived alone, gathering grain, edible roots and flowers that could be made into soups. And in that year he saw no one. In the day he would work. At night he would dream, dream of flying through the night sky, of soaring above the mountains in the clean light of the stars. Such dreams!

One night as he circled and soared a dark shape had materialised before him. It was a man's face, black hair waxed close to the skull, high slanted eyes, long braided sideburns that hung far below the chin.

'Where are you from, boy?' asked the man.

Ekodas had been frightened. He backed away, but the

face swelled and a body appeared, long arms reaching out for him. The hands were scaled and taloned, and Ekodas fled. Other dark shapes appeared, like the crows above the village, and they called out to him. Far below he saw the little shelter he had created for himself from the unburnt timber of the barn. Down, down he flew, merging with his body and snapping awake, his heart beating wildly. In the heartbeat between dream and awakening he was sure he had heard triumphant laughter.

Two days later a traveller came by, a slender man with a gentle face. He walked slowly, and when he sat he winced with pain, for there was a stitched wound in his back.

'Good morning Ekodas,' he had said. 'I am Dardalion – and you must leave this place.'

'Why? It is my home.'

'I think you know why. Zhu Chao has seen your spirit soaring. He will send men to bring you to him.'

'Why should I trust you?'

The man smiled and reached out his hand. 'You have the Talent, the gift of the Source. Touch me. Find, if you can, a spark of evil.'

Ekodas gripped the hand, and in an instant Dardalion's memories flowed through him, the great Siege of Purdol, the battles with the Brotherhood, the journey with Waylander, the terrible memories of bloodshed and death.

'I will come with you, sir.'

'You will not be alone, my boy. There are nine like you so far. There will be more.'

'How many more?'

'We will be Thirty.'

The prayer-hymn ended. Ekodas felt the coldness of separation, and the awareness of flesh and sinew, the cold breeze from the open window blowing against his bare legs. He shivered and opened his eyes.

Dardalion stood. Ekodas glanced up at the Abbot's slender, ascetic face.

'My brothers,' said Dardalion, 'behind you stands the armour of the Thirty. Beside it is the staff of the Source priest. Tonight we will decide where our destiny lies. Do we wear the armour and find the Source in a battle to the death against the forces of evil, or do we go our separate ways in peace and harmony? Tonight I speak for the latter. Ekodas will argue the former. At evening's end you will each stand and make your decisions. You will either take up the staff or the sword. May the Source guide us in our deliberations.'

He was silent then for several moments, and then he began to speak of the binding power of love, and the changes it wrought in the hearts of men. He spoke of the evil of hatred and greed and lust, pointing out, with great force, the folly of believing that swords and lances could eradicate evil. He spoke of rage and the demons that lay waiting within every human soul; demons with whips of fire that could impel a good man to rape and murder. Ekodas listened with growing astonishment. All his own arguments, and more, flowed from the Abbot.

'Yes love,' continued Dardalion, 'can heal the wounds of hatred. Love can eradicate lust and greed. Through love a man of evil can come to repentance and find redemption. For the Source abandons no man.

'Each of us here has been blessed by the Source. We have Talents. We can read minds, we can soar. Some can heal wounds with a touch. We are gifted. We could walk from here and spread our message of love throughout the realm.

'Many years ago I found myself in a terrible predicament. The Dark Brotherhood were reforming, seeking out gifted children, drawing them into their evil ways. Those who resisted were sacrificed to the forces of darkness. I decided then that I too would seek out those with talent, training them, building a new Thirty to stand against evil. While doing so I came upon two sisters, children of tragedy. They lived with a widower, a strong man, fearless and deadly. But they were lost in the soulless grey of the Void, hunted by demonic powers and by two of the Brotherhood. I fought them off and saved the spirits of these children, bringing them to their home. And then I returned to my body and I rode for their cabin.

The Brotherhood killers knew where to find them, and I sought to warn their father.

'But when I arrived he was unconscious, having filled his belly with strong wine, trying to erase his grief at the death of his wife. The children were alone. While at the cabin I sensed the imminent arrival of the two men. I could feel their lust for violence and death travelling before them like a red mist. There was nowhere to run. Nowhere to hide.

'I did something then that I have always regretted. I took a small double crossbow from the unconscious man, and I loaded it. Then I stepped out to wait for the killers. During the Vagrian Wars I had killed with the sword, but I had sworn never to take another human life. As I waited I prayed they would be turned back by the very threat of the bow.

'But they came on, and they laughed at me, for I was known to them. I was a Source priest, a preacher of love. They mocked me and drew their swords. This bow I held had killed many men and it had power, dread power, in its ebony stock. The men advanced. My arm came up. And the first bolt flew. The first man died. The second man turned to run. Without thinking I shot him through the back of the neck. I felt like leaping into the air with joy. I had saved the children. Then the enormity of the deed came home to me, and I fell to my knees, hurling the crossbow from me.

'At Dros Purdol the first Thirty had fought against demons and the spirits of evil. But none of them – save myself – had ever lifted a sword against a human foe. And they died unresisting when the enemy breached the walls. Yet I, in one moment, had betrayed all we stood for.

'I had not only taken human life, I had robbed two men of any chance of redemption.

'I went back in to the children and I took them in my arms. My spirit went into both of them, closing the doorways to their Talent, robbing them of their Source-given gift so that the Brotherhood would not find them again. I put them in their bed and soothed them to sleep.

107

Then I dragged the bodies from the clearing, burying them in a shallow grave.

'I have been haunted by that day, and not an hour of my life has passed without my thinking of it. I want none of you to face those regrets. And the surest way I know of avoiding such pain would be if each of you takes up the Source staff.' Dardalion sat down and Ekodas saw that the Abbot's hands were trembling.

The young priest took a deep breath and rose. 'Brothers, there is not a word spoken by the Abbot with which I disagree. But that alone does not make his argument true. He spoke of love generating love, and hatred breeding more hatred. We all agree with that – and if that was all there was to discuss, there would be no need for me to speak. But it is infinitely more complex. I have been asked to present an argument with which I fundamentally disagree. Is Ekodas right and his argument wrong? Is the argument a good one and Ekodas' judgement flawed? How can I know? How can any of us know? So let us examine a broader picture.

'We sit here safe, within a circle of swords held by other men. Recruits at Delnoch, lancers at the Skeln Pass, infantry at Erekban; all preparing to fight and perhaps to die to protect their families, their land and, yes, all of us. Are they evil? Will the Source deny them the gift of eternity? I would hope not. This world was created by the Source, every animal, every insect, plant and tree. But for one to live another usually dies. It is the way of all things. When the rose rises up it blocks the light that feeds the smaller plants, smothering them. For the lion to prosper the deer must die. All the world is in combat.

'Yes we sit safe. And why? Because we allow the responsibility – aye and the sin – to sit with other men.' He paused and stared at the listening priests, proud Vishna, the former Gothir nobleman, the fiery Magnic, whose eyes registered his surprise at the apparent change in the speaker, the slender, witty Palista, who was watching with a look of wry amusement.

Ekodas smiled. 'Ah, my brothers, if the argument were

purely that we become warrior priests it would be the more easy to raise moral objections. But that is not the reality. We were gathered here because the Dark Brotherhood is abroad in the world, ready to bring chaos and despair to these and other lands. And we know, through the memories of our Father Abbot, what these men are capable of. We know that ordinary warriors cannot stand against their vile powers.'

He paused again and sipped water from his goblet of clay. 'The Lord Abbot talked of slaying the men who came for the children –but what was the alternative? To allow two innocent babes to be sacrificed? Whose purpose would that have served? As for the men and their redemption, who is to say where their souls travelled, and what hopes of redemption lie there?

'No, the Abbot has cause to regret only one aspect of that terrible day – the joy he felt at the killings. For that is the central point to this argument. As warrior priests we must fight – if fight we must – without hatred. We must be defenders of the Light.

'This Source-made world is in delicate balance, and when the scales of evil outweigh those of the good, what should we do? We were given gifts by the Source, gifts which enable us to stand against the Brotherhood. Do we deny those gifts? Many are the men who could take up the staff. Many are the priests who could –and will – journey the world with their gospels of love.

'But where are the Warriors of Light who can stand against the Brotherhood? Where are the Source Knights who can turn aside the spells of evil?' He spread his hands. 'Where, save for here? Not one of us can say with certainty that the path we choose is the right one. But we judge a rose by its bloom and by its fragrance. The Brotherhood seeks to rule, and by so doing, to usher in a new age of blood. We seek to see men living in peace and harmony, free to love, free to father their sons and daughters, free to sit in the evenings and watch the glory of the sunset, content that evil is far from them.

'We know where evil lies and, with pure hearts, we

should stand against it. If it can be turned aside by love, so be it! But if it comes seeking slaughter and pain, then we should meet it with sword and shield. For that is our purpose. For we are the Thirty!' He sat down and closed his eyes, his emotions surging, his thoughts suddenly confused.

'Let us pray,' said Dardalion, 'and then let each man choose his path.'

For some minutes there was silence, then Ekodas saw Vishna rise and draw his silver sword, laying it on the table before him. Magnic followed, the grating rasp of steel blade on steel scabbard sawing through the silence. One by one the priests drew the swords, until only Dardalion and Ekodas were left. Dardalion waited and Ekodas smiled thinly. He stood, his eyes locked to the Abbot's level gaze.

'Did you trick me, Father?' pulsed Ekodas.

'No, my son. Did you convince yourself?'

'No, Dardalion. I still believe that to fight evil with its own weapons is folly and will lead merely to more hatred, more death.'

'Then why did you present the argument with such power?'

'Because you asked me to. And I owe you everything.'

'Then take up the staff, my son.'

'It is too late for that, Father.' Ekodas reached out and curled his fingers around the hilt of the silver longsword. The blade hissed into the air, catching the light from the many lanterns.

'*We are One!*' shouted Vishna.

And thirty swords were raised high, glittering like torches.

*

Karnak strode through the cheering troops, smiling and waving. Three times he stopped to exchange a few words with individual soldiers whose names he remembered. It was this common touch that endeared him to the men, and he knew it.

Behind him walked two officers of his general staff. Gan

Asten, a former low-ranking officer promoted by Karnak during the civil war, was now one of the most powerful commanders in the Drenai army. Beside him was Dun Galen, nominally Karnak's aide, but in reality the man whose network of spies kept Karnak's hand on the reins of power.

Karnak reached the end of the line and stooped to enter the tent. Asten and Galen followed him. The two guards extended their lances across the opening, signalling that the Lord Protector was not to be disturbed, and the soldiers drifted back to their campfires.

Inside Karnak's smile vanished. 'Where in the devil's name is he?' he snapped.

The skeletally thin Galen shrugged. 'He was in the palace and reportedly told his guards he would be visiting friends. That was the last they saw of him. Later, when his room was searched they found he had taken several changes of clothing and had also stolen gold from Varachek's vault – some two hundred Raq. Since then there has been no sign.'

'He was living in fear of Waylander,' said Asten. 'Every sound in the night, every banging shutter.'

'Waylander is a dead man!' roared Karnak. 'Could he not trust me with that? By Shemak's balls, he's one man. One!'

'And still alive,' pointed out Asten.

'Don't say it!' stormed Karnak. 'I know you advised me against bringing in the Guild, but how in the name of all that's holy did we arrive at this mess? One girl dies – an accident. And yet it has cost me damn near twenty thousand in gold – money I can ill-afford to lose – and seen my son scurrying away like a frightened rabbit!'

'There is a troop of lancers hunting him even as we speak, sir,' said the black-garbed Galen. 'They will bring him in.'

'I'll believe that, old lad, when I see it,' grunted Karnak.

'The Guild has proved a disappointment,' pointed out Asten, quietly.

Karnak grinned. 'Well, when the war is over I'll close

them down and get the money back. One of the advantages of power.' The smile faded. 'Three wives, scores of willing women, and what do I get? Bodalen. What did I do to deserve such a son, eh, Asten?'

Wisely Gan Asten chose not to reply, but Galen stepped in swiftly. 'He has many talents, sir. He is highly thought of. He is just young and headstrong. I'm sure he didn't intend the girl to die. It was just sport, young men chasing a filly.'

'Until she fell and broke her neck,' grunted Asten, his florid face expressionless.

'An accident!' responded Galen, flashing a murderous glance at the general.

'It wasn't an accident when they killed her husband.'

'The man ran at them with a sword. They defended themselves. What else would you expect from Drenai noblemen?'

'I would not know of the ways of noblemen, Galen. My father was a farmer. But I expect you are correct. When drunken young nobles set off on a quest for rape one should not be surprised when they turn to murder.'

'Enough of this,' said Karnak. 'What's past is past. I'd cut off my right arm to bring the girl back – but she's dead. And her former guardian is alive. Neither of you know Waylander. I do. You would not want him hunting you – or your sons.'

'As you said yourself, sir, he is only one man,' said Galen, his voice softening, but still sibilant. 'And Bodalen is not even in the realm.'

Karnak sat down on a canvas-covered stool. 'I liked Waylander, you know,' he said quietly. 'He stood up to me.' He chuckled. 'He went into Nadir lands and fought off tribesmen, demonic beasts and the Vagrian Brotherhood. Amazing!' He glanced up at Galen. 'But he has to die. I can't let him slay my son.'

'You can rely on me, sir,' answered Galen, bowing deeply.

Karnak swung to Asten. 'What happened with the witch woman, Hewla?'

'She would not use her powers against Waylander,' answered the general.

'Why?'

'She didn't tell me, sir. But she did say she would consider raising a storm against the Ventrian fleet. I told her no.'

'No?' raged Karnak, lurching from his seat. '*No?* There'd better be a damn good reason, Asten.'

'She wanted a hundred children sacrificed. Something about paying the price for demonic assistance.'

Karnak swore. 'If we lose there'll be a lot more than a hundred children suffering. More like ten thousand.'

'You want me to go back to her?'

'Of course I don't want you to go back to her! Damn it, why does the enemy always have more power at his command? I'll wager the Ventrian King wouldn't think twice about a few scrawny brats.'

'We could use captured Sathuli children,' offered Galen. 'Make a swift raid into the mountains. After all, they have allied with Gothir against us.'

Karnak shook his head. 'Such an action would sully my reputation, turn the people against me. There's no way it could be kept secret. No, my friends, I think we'll have to rely on stout hearts and sharp swords. And luck, let's not forget that! But in the meantime, find Bodalen.'

'He probably believes he's safer in hiding,' said Asten.

'Find him and convince him otherwise,' ordered Karnak.

*

Waylander banked up the fire and settled back against the boulder, watching the sleeping Nadir. Belash had tried to keep up, but had fallen several times, vomiting beside the trail. The blows to the head had weakened the warrior and Waylander had helped him to a sheltered hollow.

'Your skull may be cracked,' said Waylander, as the man lay shivering beside the fire.

'No.'

'It's not made of stone, Belash.'

'Tomorrow I will be strong,' promised the Nadir. In the dying light of the sun his face was grey, dark streaks colouring the skin beneath his slanted eyes.

Waylander touched the man's throat. The pulse was strong, but erratic. 'Sleep,' he said, covering the man with his cloak. The flames licked hungrily at the dry wood and Waylander reached out his hands, enjoying the warmth. The hound lay at his side, huge head on massive paws. Idly Waylander stroked the beast's ruined ears. A low rumbling growl came from its throat. 'Quiet,' said Waylander, smiling. 'You know you enjoy it, so stop complaining.'

He gazed at the sleeping Nadir. I should have killed you, he thought idly, but he did not regret allowing the man to live. There was something about Belash that struck a chord in him. A shadow flickered at the edge of his vision. Waylander glanced to his left. Sitting by the fire was a hooded old woman, her face a remarkable picture of ancient decay and ugliness, her teeth rotten, her nose swollen and blue-veined, her eyes rheumy and yellow.

'You move silently, Hewla,' whispered Waylander.

'No, I don't. I move like an old crone with my joints cracking like dry twigs.'

'I did not hear you.'

'That's because I'm not here, child,' she told him, reaching out her hand and thrusting it into the flames, which danced and flickered through suddenly transparent skin and bone. 'I am sitting by my own fire, in my own cabin.'

'What do you require of me?'

Her eyes glinted with amusement, her mouth forming the parody of a smile. 'Not impressed with my magic? How dull. You have no inkling of the concentration needed to produce this image. But do your eyes widen in wonder? Do you sit there jaw agape in amazement? No. You ask what I require. What makes you think I require anything, child? Perhaps I felt in need of company.'

'Unlikely,' he said, with a wry smile. 'But you are welcome whatever. Are you well?'

'When you are four hundred and eleven years old the question is irrelevant. I haven't been well since the old King's grandfather was a child. I'm just too stubborn to die.' She glanced at the sleeping Nadir. 'He dreams of killing you,' she said.

He shrugged. 'His dreams are his own affair.'

'You arc a strange man, Waylander. Still, the dog likes you.'

He chuckled. 'He'll make a better friend than most men.'

'Aye.' The old woman fell silent, but her gaze remained on the black-garbed warrior. 'I always liked you, child,' she said softly. 'You never feared me. I was sorry to hear of the death of your lady.'

He looked away. 'Life moves on,' he said.

'Indeed it does. Morak will come again. He is no coward, but he likes to be sure. And Senta is even now approaching your cabin. What will you do?'

'What do you think?' he countered.

'You'll fight them until they kill you. Not the most subtle of plans, is it?'

'I never was a man suited to subtlety.'

'Nonsense. It's just that you have always been a little in love with death. Perhaps it would help to know why they are hunting you?'

'Does it matter?'

'You won't know unless I tell you!' she snapped.

'Then tell me.'

'Karnak has a son, Bodalen. He is allied to the Brotherhood. He and some friends were riding near a village, south of Drenan. They saw a young woman gathering herbs. The men had been drinking, and she aroused their lust. They chased her. She turned and fought, breaking one man's jaw. Then she ran. Bodalen followed her. As she fled she glanced back, lost her footing, and fell. She tumbled over the edge of a rock-face. Her neck was broken in the fall. Her husband came upon the scene. He was unarmed. The men killed him, leaving him by her body. You hear what I am saying?'

'I hear, but I don't know what it has to do with me,' he answered.

'They were seen riding from the area and Bodalen was brought to trial. He was sentenced to a year in exile, and

Karnak paid a fortune in blood-geld to the dead man's father.'

Waylander's mouth was dry. 'Where was the village?'

'Adderbridge.'

'Are you saying he killed my Krylla!' hissed Waylander.

'Yes. Karnak found out that you were her guardian. He fears you will seek Bodalen. That is why the Guild hunt you.'

Waylander's mind was reeling and his unfocused eyes stared into the darkness, memories flooding him with echoes of the past, Krylla and Miriel splashing in the stream by the cabin, laughing and squealing in the sunshine, Krylla's tears when the pet goose died, her happiness when Nualin had proposed, the gaiety of the wedding and the dance that followed it. He saw her smiling face, the twin of Miriel, but with a mouth that smiled more easily and a manner that won over every heart. With great effort he forced the memories back and turned his now cold eyes on the witch woman's image.

'Why did you come here, Hewla?' he asked icily.

'I told you. I like you. Always have.'

'That may or may not be true. But I ask again, why did you come?'

'Hmm, I do so admire you, child. There is no fooling you, is there?' Her malevolent eyes gleamed in the firelight. 'Yes, there is more to this than just Bodalen.'

'I did not doubt it.'

'Have you heard of Zhu Chao?'

Waylander shook his head. 'Nadir?'

'No. Chiatze. He is a practitioner of the Dark Arts. No more than that, though he would no doubt describe himself as a wizard. He is young – not yet sixty, and still has the strength to summon demons to his bidding. He has rebuilt the Brotherhood, and – nominally, mark you! – serves the Gothir Emperor.'

'And Bodalen?'

'Karnak's son reveres him. The Brotherhood is behind the coming wars. They have infiltrated many of the noble houses of Ventria, Gothir and Drenai. They seek to rule, and perhaps they will succeed – who knows?'

116

'And you want me to kill Zhu Chao.'

'Very astute. Yes, I want him dead.'

'I am no longer an assassin, Hewla. If the man was threatening you then I would deal with him. But I will not hunt him down for you.'

'But you will hunt Bodalen,' she whispered.

'Oh, yes. I will find him. And he will know justice.'

'Good. You will find him with Zhu Chao,' she said. 'And if the little wizard should happen to step into the path of one of your bolts, so be it.'

'He is in Gulgothir?'

'Indeed he is. I think he feels safer there. Well, I shall leave you now. It is difficult at my age to hold such a spell.' He said nothing. She shook her head. 'Not even a thank you for old Hewla?'

'Why should I thank you?' he answered. 'You have brought me only pain.'

'No, no, child. I have saved your life. Look inside yourself. You no longer wish to wait here and die alongside your lovely Danyal. No. The wolf is back. Waylander lives again.'

Angry words rose in his throat. But Hewla had vanished.

Miriel's head was aching, but the acute pain of the night before had faded to a dull ache as she rose and dressed, making her way through the cabin to the clearing where Angel was chopping logs. Stripped to the waist he was swinging the long-handled axe with practised ease, splitting the wood expertly.

He stopped as he saw her and thudded the axe into a log, then took up his shirt and strolled towards her. 'How are you feeling today?' he asked.

'I'm ready,' she told him.

He shook his head. 'I think you should rest this morning. Your colour is not good.'

There was a chill in the air and she shivered. 'They will come back,' she said.

He shrugged. 'There's not a blessed thing we can do about that, Miriel.'

'Except wait?'

'Exactly.'

'You don't seem concerned.'

'Oh, but I am. It is just that I learned long ago that there is little point in worrying about matters over which you have no control. We could flee, I suppose, but to where? We don't know where they are, and could run straight into them. At least here we have the advantage of home ground. And this is where your father expects to find us. Therefore we wait.'

'I could track them,' she offered.

He shook his head. 'Morak wasn't with them, nor was Belash. I wouldn't want to track either of them. They would have sentries watching from the high hills, or trees. They would see us coming. No, we wait for Waylander.'

'I don't like the thought of just sitting,' she said.

'I know,' he told her, stepping forward and laying his

118

hand on her shoulder. 'It is always the hardest part. I was the same when I was waiting for the call into the arena. I could hear the clash of swords outside, smell the sand and the sawdust. I always felt ill.'

Miriel's eyes narrowed. 'There's someone coming,' she said.

He swung, but there was no one in sight. 'Where?' She pointed to the south, where a flock of doves had flown up from a tall pine. 'It could be your father.'

'It could,' she agreed, spinning on her heel and walking back into the cabin. Angel stood where he was, one hand on the porch-rail, the other resting on the leather-bound hilt of his shortsword. Miriel rejoined him, a sword belted to her waist, a baldric of throwing-knives hanging from her shoulder.

A tall man appeared at the edge of the clearing, saw them, and walked down the slope, sunlight glinting in the gold of his hair. He moved with animal grace, arrogantly, like a lord in his domain, thought Miriel, anger flaring. The newcomer was dressed in expensive buckskin, heavily fringed at the shoulders. He wore two swords, short sabres in black leather scabbards adorned with silver. His leggings were dark brown and tucked into thigh-length tan cavalry boots that had been folded down, exposing the lining of cream-coloured silk.

Coming closer he bowed to Miriel, his arm sweeping out in courtly style. 'Good morning, Miriel.'

'Do I know you?'

'Not yet, and the loss is entirely mine.' He smiled as he spoke and Miriel found herself blushing. 'Ah, Angel,' said the newcomer, as if noticing the gladiator for the first time. 'The princess and the troll . . . I feel as if I have stepped into a fable.'

'Really?' countered Angel. 'Seeing you makes me feel I have stepped into something altogether less pleasant.'

The man chuckled with genuine humour. 'I have missed you, old man. Nothing was the same once you left the arena. How is your . . . shop?'

'Gone, but then you knew that.'

'Yes, come to think of it someone did mention that to me. I was distressed to hear of it, of course. Well, is no one going to offer breakfast? It's a long walk from Kasyra.'

'Who is this . . . this popinjay?' asked Miriel.

'Oh yes, do introduce us, Angel, there's a good fellow.'

'This is Senta, one of the hired killers sent to murder your father.'

'Delicately put,' said Senta. 'But it should be pointed out that I am not a bowman, nor am I the kind of assassin who kills from hiding. I am a swordsman, lady, probably the best in the land.'

Miriel's fingers closed around the hilt of her sword, but Angel caught her arm. 'He may be conceited, and self-obsessed, but he is quite right,' said Angel, his eyes holding to Senta's gaze. 'He *is* a fine bladesman. So let us stay calm, eh? Prepare some food, Miriel.'

'For him? No!'

'Trust me,' he said softly, 'and do as I say.'

Miriel looked into his flint-coloured eyes. 'Is this what you want?'

'Yes,' he said simply.

Her hands were trembling as she carved the cold meat. She felt confused, uncertain. Angel's strength was prodigious, and she knew he was no coward. So why was he pandering to this man? Was he frightened?

The two men were sitting at the table when she returned. Senta stood as she entered. 'You really are a vision!' he said. Her reply was short and obscene. Senta's eyes widened. 'Such language from a lady?'

Furious and embarrassed, Miriel laid down the tray of food and bit back an angry retort.

'Seen anything of Morak?' asked Angel, breaking the bread and passing a section to Senta.

'Not yet – but I sent him a message. He's got Belash with him, did you know?'

'It doesn't surprise me. What does is that you and Morak do not travel together,' said Angel. 'You are two of a kind – the same easy smiles, the same sly wit.'

'And there the resemblance ends,' said Senta. 'His heart

is rotten, Angel, and his desires are vile. It hurts me that you would link us so.' He glanced at Miriel. 'This is very fine bread. My compliments.'

Miriel ignored him, but he seemed not to notice. 'Lovely area this,' he went on. 'Close to the sea, and not yet plagued by people and their filth. One day I must find myself such a home in the mountains.' He looked around him. 'Well-built, too. A lot of love and effort.' His eyes were drawn to the weapons on the wall. 'That's Kreeg's crossbow, isn't it? Well, well! His whore was missing him in Kasyra. Something tells me he won't be going back to her.'

'He was like you,' said Miriel softly. 'He thought it would be easy, but when you face Waylander the only easy part is the dying.'

Senta laughed. 'Everyone dies, beauty. Everyone. And if he is useful with a sword it might be me.'

Now it was Angel who chuckled. 'You are a strange man, Senta. What on earth makes you think Waylander will face you blade to blade? You won't even see him. All you'll feel is the bolt that cleaves into your heart. And you won't feel that for very long.'

'Well, that wouldn't be very sporting, would it?' countered Senta, his smile fading.

'I don't think he regards this as sport,' said Angel.

'How disappointing. Perhaps I misjudged him. From all I've heard he doesn't seem to be a coward.' He shrugged. 'But then these stories do tend to become exaggerated, don't they?'

'You have a curious sense of what denotes cowardice,' said Miriel. 'When a snake comes into the house a man does not lie down on his belly to fight it fang to fang. He just stamps on its head, then throws the useless carcass out into the night. One does not deal with vermin in the way one deals with men!'

Senta clapped his hands, slowly and theatrically, but anger showed in his blue eyes.

'Finish your breakfast,' said Angel softly.

'And then I am to leave, I suppose?' Senta responded,

slicing a section of meat then lancing it with his knife and raising it towards his mouth.

'No, Senta, then you will die.'

The knife froze. Senta shook his head. 'I'm not being paid to kill you, old man.'

'Just as well,' said Angel. 'You wouldn't be there to collect it. I'll wait for you outside.'

The former gladiator stood and left the room. Senta glanced up at Miriel. 'It's a good breakfast. May I stay on for supper?'

'Don't kill him!'

'What?' Senta seemed genuinely surprised. 'I have no choice, beauty. He has challenged me.' He stared at her. 'Are you and he . . .? No, surely not.' He stood. 'I'm sorry. Truly. I quite like the old boy.'

'He's not that old.'

'He's twice my age, Miriel, and as a swordsman that makes him older than the mountains.'

'If you kill him you'll have to kill me. I'll come for you. I swear it.'

Senta sighed, then bowed. There was no hint of mockery in his eyes. Swinging on his heel the assassin stepped out into the light. Angel was standing some thirty feet from the door, sword in hand.

'Arena rules?' called Senta.

'As you like.'

'Are you sure about this, Angel? There is no need for us to fight. And you know well enough you will lose.'

'Don't tell me, boy, show me!'

Senta drew his sabre and advanced.

*

Waylander emerged from the trees and saw the two swordsmen circling one another.

'Ho Angel!' he called. The two warriors paused, glancing up towards him as he made his way down the slope, the stocky Nadir following. From Ralis' description Waylander guessed the swordsman was Senta.

'Leave him to me!' said Angel, as the gap closed.

'No one fights for me,' replied Waylander, his eyes fixed on Senta, noting the man's balance and his condescending smile. There was no fear here, only a cold confidence bordering on the arrogant. Waylander came closer. Still he had not drawn a weapon and he saw Senta's eyes glance down at the scabbarded sword. 'You are hunting me?' asked Waylander, moving ever closer. Only a few paces separated them.

'I have a commission from the Guild,' replied Senta, taking a step back.

Waylander kept moving. Senta was tense now, for Waylander had halted immediately before him. 'Arena rules?' enquired the assassin.

Waylander smiled. His head snapped forward, butting the blond swordsman on the bridge of the nose. Senta staggered back. Waylander stepped in and hammered his elbow into the man's jaw. Senta hit the ground hard, his sword falling from his fingers. Waylander grabbed the man's long golden hair, hauling him to his knees. 'I don't duel,' he said, drawing a razor-sharp knife from his baldric.

'Don't kill him!' shouted Angel.

'As you wish,' answered Waylander, releasing his hold on the half-conscious swordsman. Senta slumped back to the ground. Waylander sheathed his knife and walked into the cabin.

'Welcome back, Father,' said Miriel, stepping into his embrace. His arms swept round her, stroking her back, his face pressed against her hair.

'We have to leave,' he whispered, his voice trembling. 'We're going north.'

'What has happened?' she asked him.

He shook his head. 'We'll talk later. Prepare two packs – food for three days, winter clothing. You know what is needed.' She nodded and looked past him. He glanced back to see the Nadir warrior standing in the doorway. 'We met in the mountains,' said Waylander. 'This is Belash.'

'But he's . . .'

'Yes, he was. But Morak betrayed him. Left him to die.' Waylander waved the man forward. 'This is my daughter,

123

Miriel.' Belash's face showed no expression, but his eyes were drawn to the weapons she wore. The Nadir said nothing, but walked into the kitchen where he helped himself to a hunk of bread and some cheese.

'Can you trust him?' whispered Miriel.

Waylander's smile was broad. 'Of course not. But he will be valuable where we are going.'

'Into Gothir?'

'Yes.'

'What changed your mind?'

'There's a man there I must find. Now prepare the packs.'

She half-turned, then looked back at him. 'Why did you spare Senta?'

He shrugged. 'Angel asked me to.'

'Hardly a good reason.'

'It's as good as any other.'

Miriel walked away. Waylander moved to the dead fire and sat down in the broad leather chair. Angel entered, half-carrying Senta. Blood was streaming from the man's broken nose, and his eyes were swollen half-shut. Angel lowered him to the bench-seat at the table. Senta sagged forward, blood dripping to the wood. Angel found a cloth, which he passed to the man. Senta held it to his face.

Angel moved in close to Waylander and whispered, 'Why is Belash still among the living?'

'A whim,' answered Waylander.

'Whims like that can kill you. They're not like people, they're savages spawned by demons. I think you have made a bad mistake.'

'I've made mistakes before. Time will tell about this one.' He stepped alongside Senta. 'Lie back along the bench,' he ordered. 'The blood will stop faster that way.'

'I thank you for your concern,' muttered the swordsman thickly.

Waylander sat beside him. 'Be advised. Do not come against me again.'

Senta dropped the blood-covered cloth and sniffed

loudly. 'You taught me a valuable lesson,' he said, forcing a smile. 'I shall not forget it.'

Waylander stood and strode from the cabin. Angel followed him. 'You have not asked me why I wanted him alive.'

'I don't care,' replied Waylander, kneeling and patting the hound, which had stretched out in the shade. The dog gave a low growl and arched its neck. Waylander rubbed its muzzle. 'It is not important, Angel.'

'It is to me. I am in your debt.'

'How is Miriel progressing?'

'Better than she was. And I don't want your ten thousand.'

Waylander shrugged. 'Take it. I won't miss it.'

'That's not the point, damn you!'

'Why so angry?'

'Where are you going from here?' countered Angel.

'North.'

'May I come with you?'

'Why?' asked Waylander, genuinely surprised.

'I have nowhere else to go. And I can still train Miriel.'

Waylander nodded, and was silent for several moments. 'Did anything happen while I was away – between the two of you, I mean?'

Angel reddened. 'Nothing! Gods, man, my boots are older than her!'

'She could do worse, Angel. And I must find her a husband.'

'That won't take long. She's a lovely girl, and I guess it will be good to know she's safe like her sister.'

'Her sister is dead,' said Waylander, fighting to remain calm, his voice barely above a whisper. Once more Krylla's face came back to him, and he felt a cold, berserk rage building. 'That's why they are hunting me,' he went on. 'Karnak's son killed her. The Lord Protector paid the assassins because he fears I'll hunt down the boy.'

'Gods of Mercy! I didn't know it was Krylla,' said Angel. 'There was a trial, but the victim was not even named. Bodalen was exiled for a year.'

'A harsh punishment indeed.'

'But you're not going after him?'

Waylander took a deep calming breath. 'I am heading north,' he answered. 'Travelling to Gothir.'

'It's probably wise,' agreed Angel. 'You cannot go against the whole Drenai army. But you do surprise me – I thought you would have put vengeance above everything else.'

'Perhaps age is making me mellow.'

Angel grinned. 'You didn't look too mellow when you downed Senta. And where in Hell's name did you find that dog? It's the ugliest beast I've ever seen. Look at those scars!'

'Bear-fighter,' said Waylander. 'Retired – just like you.'

Senta, his nose swollen, his nostrils stained with blood, moved out into the sunlight, just as Angel knelt to pet the dog.

'You know, Angel,' said the swordsman, 'the resemblance is striking. If your own mother were to appear in our midst she wouldn't know which of you to call in for dinner.'

'The nose is an improvement – and it's bleeding again,' replied Angel, turning away and reaching out to the hound. Its fangs showed and a low snarl sounded. Angel drew back and stood.

Senta sniffed and spat blood to the dust, then walked past the two men and retrieved the sabre that was still lying in the dust. With the weapon in his hand he strolled back to Waylander. 'Mercy is a rare beast,' he said. 'You think it was wise to let me live?'

'If it proves a mistake I'll kill you,' Waylander told him.

'You are an unusual man. How did you know I wouldn't gut you as soon as you closed in on me?'

Waylander shrugged. 'I didn't.'

The swordsman nodded. 'I think I will travel with you,' he said. 'I heard you tell Angel you were heading north. I've always wanted to return to Gothir. I had some fine times there.'

'I may not want your company,' said Waylander.

'I can see that might be so. But there was something else you told Angel that interested me greatly.'

'I'm listening.'

'You're looking for a husband for Miriel.'

'You know where I might find one?'

'Very droll. I am a rich man, and not – despite your efforts –unhandsome. And my father continues to berate me for not supplying him with a grandson. I'll take her off your hands.'

'Shemak's balls, but you've got nerve!' stormed Angel.

'I like a man with nerve,' said Waylander. 'I'll think on it.'

'You're not serious!' exclaimed Angel. 'A few minutes ago this man was trying to kill you for money. He's an assassin.'

'Which of course puts me lower on the social scale than an arena-killer,' observed Senta.

'Madness!' muttered Angel, stalking back into the cabin.

Senta sheathed his sabre. 'Why are we heading north?' he asked.

'There's someone I must find in Gulgothir.'

*

Miriel carried a bowl of heated water and a clean cloth to where Senta sat. She had not heard his conversation with her father, but she saw he now had his sabre once more. The blond warrior looked up through swollen eyes. He smiled. 'Merciful care for the fallen hero?'

'You are not a hero,' she told him, dipping the cloth in the water and gently sponging away the blood staining Senta's face. Reaching up he took hold of her wrist.

'He stamped on my head, but he did not throw the useless carcass out into the forest.'

'Be grateful for that,' she said, pulling her hand free.

'Interesting man. He read me well. He knew I wouldn't kill him before he'd drawn a weapon.'

'What will you do now?' she asked.

He grinned, then winced as pain flared through his

127

broken nose. 'I shall enter a monastery and devote my life to good works.'

'It was a serious question.'

'And you are a serious woman, beauty. Too serious. Do you laugh much? Do you dance? Do you make assignations with young men?'

'What I do is none of your affair! And stop calling me beauty. I don't like it.'

'Yes, you do. But it makes you uncomfortable.'

'Do you still plan to kill my father?'

'No.'

'Am I expected to believe that?'

'You are free to believe or disbelieve, beauty. How old are you?'

'I will be eighteen next summer.'

'Are you a virgin?'

'You'll never know!' she told him. Taking up the bowl, she walked back to the kitchen where Belash was still eating. Most of the ham had gone, and half of the cheese. 'Is this your first meal in a month?' she snapped.

The Nadir looked up, his dark eyes expressionless. 'Fetch me water,' he ordered.

'Fetch it yourself, bowel-brain!' His face darkened and he rose from his seat. Miriel's dagger swept up. 'One wrong move, you Nadir dog-eater, and the breakfast you've just eaten will be all over the floor.' Belash grinned and walked to the water jug, filling a clay goblet. 'What is so amusing?' she demanded.

'You *kol-isha*,' answered Belash, drawing his own knife and cutting the last slice of ham from the bone. He shook his head and chuckled.

'What about us?' persisted Miriel.

'Where are your babies?' countered Belash. 'Where is your man? Why are you garbed for war? Knives and swords – such foolishness.'

'You think a woman cannot use these weapons?'

'Of course they can. You should see my Shia – knife, sword, handaxe. But it is not natural. War is for men, for honour and glory.'

'And death,' she pointed out.

'Of course death. That is why women must be protected. Many babies must be born to replace the dead warriors.'

'It might be better just to stop the wars.'

'Pah! It is always useless to talk to women. They have no understanding.'

Miriel took a deep breath, but refrained from further argument. Leaving the Nadir to his endless breakfast she walked to her room and began to pack.

8

Hewla eased her frame up from the wicker chair and winced as pain flared in her arthritic hip. The fire was dying down and she slowly bent to lift a log on to the glowing coals. There was a time when her fires needed no fuel, when she had not been forced to walk the forest gathering twigs and sticks.

'Curse you, Zhu Chao,' she whispered. But the words only made her the more angry, for once such a curse would have been accompanied by the beating of demon wings and the harsh raucous cries of the Vanshii as they flew to their victim.

How could you have been so stupid? she asked herself.

I was lonely.

Yes, but now you are still lonely, and the *grimoires* are gone.

She shivered and added another thick stick to the fire, which hungrily devoured it. It was small consolation that the Books of Spellfire would be virtually useless to Zhu Chao. For the spells contained in them had given Hewla life, long after her skin should have turned to dust, had held at bay the mortal pain of her inflamed joints. The six books of Moray Sen. Priceless. She remembered the day she had shown them to him, opening the secret compartment behind the firestone. She had believed in him then, the young Chiatze. Loved him. She shuddered. Old fool.

He had taken the *grimoires* she had schemed for, killed for, sold her soul for.

Now the Void beckoned.

Waylander will kill him, she thought with grim relish.

The room was becoming warmer and Hewla was at last feeling some comfort from the heat. But then an icy blast of freezing air touched her back. The old woman turned. The far wall was shimmering and a cold, cold wind was blowing

130

through it, scattering scrolls and papers. A clay goblet on the table trembled and fell, rolling to the floor, shattering. The wind grew stronger. Hewla's shawl flew back, falling across the fire, and the old woman stumbled against the power of the demon wind.

A dark shape appeared by the wall, silhouetted against icy flames.

Hewla's hand came up and a bright light blazed from her fingers, surrounding the demon. The wind died down, but she felt the creature's elemental power pushing back against the light. A taloned hand clawed through. Flames burst around it and it withdrew.

A flickering figure appeared to her left, and she saw Zhu Chao's image forming.

'I have brought an old friend to see you, Hewla,' he said.

'Rot in Hell,' she hissed.

He laughed at her. 'I see you retain some vestiges of power. Tell me, hag, how long do you think you can hold him from you?'

'What do you want from me?'

'I cannot master the first of the Five Spells. Something is missing from the *grimoires*. Tell me and you shall live.'

Once again the taloned hand tore through the light. Flames seared it, but not as powerfully as before. Fear swelled in Hewla's heart and, had she believed Zhu Chao's promise, she might have told him. But she did not.

'What is missing is something you will never find – courage!' she said. 'You will grow older, your powers fading. And when you die your soul will be carried screaming to the Void.'

'You foolish old crone,' he whispered. 'All the books speak of the Mountains of the Moon. The answers lie there. I shall find them.'

Talons ripped at the light, and it parted like a torn curtain. The dark shape loomed in the room. As swiftly as she could, Hewla drew the small curved dagger from the sheath at her waist.

'I will wait for you in the Void,' she promised.

Holding the dagger blade beneath her left breast she plunged it home.

*

Senta sat quietly on the wall of the well, watching Waylander and Miriel some distance away. The man had his hand on the girl's shoulder. Her head was bowed. Senta did not need to guess at the subject of their conversation. He had heard Waylander telling Angel of the death of Miriel's sister.

Senta looked away. His broken nose was sending shafts of pain behind his eyes and he felt sick. In his four years in the arena he had not felt pain like this. Minor cuts, and once a twisted ankle, were all the swordsman had suffered. But then those fights had been governed by rules. With a man like Waylander there were no rules. Only survival.

Despite his pain Senta felt relieved. He had no doubt that he would have killed the older man in a duel, though if he had, there would still have been Angel to face. And it would have saddened him to slay the old gladiator. But, more than that, it would have wrecked any chance with Miriel.

Miriel . . .

His first sight of her had shocked him, and he still didn't know why. The noblewoman, Gilaray, had a more beautiful face. Nexiar was infinitely more shapely. Suri's golden hair and flashing eyes were far more provocative. Yet there was something about this mountain girl that had fired his senses. But what?

And why marriage? He could hardly believe he'd made the offer. How would she take to life in the city? He focused on her once more, picturing her in a gown of silver satin, pearls laced through her dark hair. And chuckled.

'What is amusing you?' asked Angel, strolling to where he sat.

'I was thinking of Miriel at the Lord Protector's Ball, in a flowing dress and with her knives strapped to her forearms.'

'She's too good for the likes of you, Senta. Far too good.'

'That's a matter of opinion. Would you sooner see her standing behind a plough, old before her time, her breasts flat, like two hanged men?'

'No,' admitted Angel, 'but I'd like to see her with a man who loved her. She's not like Nexiar, or any of the others. She's like a colt – fast, sleek, unbroken.'

Senta nodded. 'I think you are right.' He glanced up at the gladiator. 'How very perceptive of you, my friend. You do surprise me.'

'I surprise myself sometimes. Like asking Waylander not to kill you. I'm regretting it already.'

'No, you're not,' said Senta, with an easy smile.

Angel grunted a short obscenity and sat beside the swordsman. 'Why did you have to talk of marriage?'

'You think I'd have been better advised to suggest rutting with her under a bush?'

'It would have been more honest.'

'I don't think it would,' said Senta softly. He became aware of Angel staring at him and felt himself blushing.

'Well, well,' said Angel. 'That I should live to see the great Senta smitten. What would they say in Drenan?'

Senta grinned. 'They'd say nothing. The entire city would be swept away under an ocean of tears.'

'I thought you were going to marry Nexiar. Or was it Suri?'

'Beautiful girls,' agreed Senta.

'Nexiar would have killed you. She damn near did for me.'

'I heard the two of you were close once. Is it true that she was so repulsed by your ugliness that, when in bed, she insisted you wore your helmet?'

Angel laughed. 'Close. She had a velvet mask made for me.'

'Ah, but I like you, Angel. Always did. Why did you ask him to spare me?'

'Why didn't you kill him when he approached you?' countered Angel.

Senta shrugged. 'My great-grandfather was a congenital idiot. My father was convinced I took after him. I think he was right.'

'Answer the question, damn you!'

'He had no weapon in his hand. I have never killed an unarmed man. It's not in me. Does that satisfy you?'

'Aye, it does,' admitted Angel. His head came up, nostrils flaring. Without a word he strode back to the cabin, emerging moments later with his sword strapped to his waist. The sound of walking horses came to Senta and he loosened his sabres in their scabbards, but remained where he was at the well. Belash came into sight, stepping from the cabin doorway, knife in his right hand, whetstone in his left. Waylander said something to Miriel, and she vanished into the cabin, then the black-garbed warrior lifted his double crossbow from the hook on his belt, swiftly drawing back the strings and notching two bolts into place.

The first of the horsemen came into view. He wore a full-faced helm of gleaming black metal, a black breast-plate and a blood-red cloak. Behind him came seven identical warriors, each riding black geldings, none less than sixteen hands high. Senta stood and strolled to where Waylander and the others were standing.

The horsemen reined in before the cabin, the horses forming a semi-circle around the the waiting men. No one spoke and Senta felt his skin crawl as he scanned the black knights. Only their eyes could be seen, through thin rectangular slits in the black helms. The expressions were all the same – cold, expectant, confident.

Finally one of them spoke. Senta could not tell which one, for the voice was muffled by the helm.

'Which of you is the wolfshead Dakeyras?'

'I am,' replied Waylander, addressing the rider directly before him.

'The Master has sentenced you to death. There is no appeal.'

The knight reached a black gauntleted hand to his sword-hilt, drawing the blade slowly. Waylander started to lift the crossbow –but his hand froze, the weapon still pointing at the ground. Senta looked at him, surprised, and saw the muscles of his jaw clench, his face redden with effort.

Senta drew the first of his sabres and prepared to attack the horsemen, but even as the blade came clear he saw one of the horsemen glance towards him, felt the man's cold stare touch him like icy water. Senta's limbs froze, a terrible pressure bearing down on him. The sabre sagged in his hand.

The black knights dismounted and Senta heard the whispering of steel swords being drawn from scabbards. Something bounced at his feet, rolling past him. It was the whetstone Belash had been carrying.

He struggled to move, but his arms felt as if they were made of stone.

And he saw a black sword rising towards his throat.

*

Inside the cabin Miriel lifted Kreeg's crossbow from the wall, flicking open the winding arms and swiftly rotating them, drawing the string back to the bronze notch. Selecting a bolt she pressed it home and swung back towards the door.

A tall knight stepped into the doorway, blocking out the light. For a moment only she froze. Then the bow came up.

'No,' whispered a sibilant voice in her mind.

A terrible lethargy flowed into her limbs and she felt as if a stream of warm, dark water was seeping through the corridors of her mind, drawing out her soul, emptying her memories. It was almost welcome, a cessation of fear and concern, a longing for the emptiness of death. Then a bright light flared, deep within her thoughts, holding back the black tidal wave of warm despair. And she saw, silhouetted against the light, the silver warrior who had rescued her as a child.

'Fight them!' he ordered. 'Fight them, Miriel! I have opened the doorways to your Talent. Seek it! And live!'

She blinked, and tried to aim the crossbow, but it was so heavy, so terribly heavy . . .

The black knight walked further into the room. 'Give me the weapon,' he said, his voice muffled by the helm. 'And I will give you joys you have not yet even dreamed of.' As he

135

approached Miriel saw Waylander on his knees in the dust of the clearing, a black bladed sword raised above his head.

'*No!*' she shouted. The crossbow tilted to the right. She squeezed the bronze trigger. The bolt slashed through the air, plunging into the black helm and disappearing up to the flights. The black knight toppled forward.

Outside, Waylander, suddenly free of the spell, threw himself to the left as the sword hissed down. Hitting the ground on his shoulder he rolled and let fly the first of his bolts. It took the swordsman under the right armpit, cleaving through to the lungs.

A dark shadow fell across him. Waylander rolled again – but not swiftly enough! A black sword flashed for his face. The hound sprang across the fallen man, its great fangs closing on the swordsman's wrist. Belash took one running step then launched himself feet-first at the knight, cannoning the man from his feet. The Nadir landed lightly and hurled himself on the assailant, driving his knife under the chinstrap of the black helmet and up into the man's brain.

The hound's angry growling panicked the horses. They reared, and – save for one gelding – bolted.

Free of the spell, Senta brought up his sabre, barely blocking the blade thrusting for his throat. He parried a second cut and, twisting his wrist, sent a vicious return that clanged against the knight's neck gorget of reinforced chain mail. Senta shoulder-charged the warrior, spinning him from his feet. A second man attacked, but this time Senta swayed aside from the killing thrust and rammed his sabre up under the man's helmet, the point slicing through the soft skin beneath the chin, and on up through his mouth. The knight fell back. Senta lost hold of the sabre and drew his second blade.

Angel, his back to the cabin wall, was battling against two knights, the former gladiator desperately blocking and parrying. Waylander sent a bolt through the thigh of the first assailant. The man grunted in pain and half-turned. Angel's sword smashed against the knight's helm, cutting through the chinstrap. The helm fell loose. Waylander's sword clove through the man's skull. Angel sidestepped a lunge from the second knight, grabbed the man's arm and hauled him, head-first, into the wall. Dropping to the man's back Angel took hold of the helm, dragging it back and sharply to the left. The knight's neck snapped with a stomach-wrenching crack.

'Look out!' yelled Senta. Waylander dropped to one knee. A sword-blade sliced the air above him. Waylander flung himself backwards, hammering into his attacker and hurling the man from his feet. Senta leapt at the man. His opponent reared to his feet, then lunged. Senta swayed aside, ramming his elbow into the man's helm. The knight staggered. Senta leaned back and kicked out, his booted foot cracking against the knight's knee. The joint gave way. The knight screamed in pain as he fell. Belash threw himself on the fallen warrior, pulling back the neck-guard and driving his knife deep into the knight's throat.

Miriel, the crossbow loaded once more, stepped from the cabin. The last knight ran to the one horse that had not bolted and leapt for the saddle, grabbing the pommel. The horse reared and began to run, dragging the knight with it. The hound bounded after it. Miriel brought the crossbow to her shoulder and sighted the weapon. The bolt sang clear and flashed across the clearing to punch home into the knight's helm. For several seconds he clung to the pommel, but as the horse reached the rise the man's fingers loosened and he fell to the earth. Instantly the dog was upon him, fangs ripping at the dead man's throat, but unable to pierce the chain mail. Waylander called to the hound and it loped back across the clearing, standing close, its flanks pressing against Waylander's leg.

Slowly the swirling dust in the clearing settled back to the earth.

One knight moaned, but Belash sprang upon him, ripping the man's helmet clear and cutting his throat. Another – the first to attack Senta – reared up and ran for the trees. The hound set off in pursuit, but Waylander called out to it and it paused, staring back at its master.

Miriel slowly turned the winding arms of the crossbow

then, with the weapon strung, walked back into the cabin to fetch a bolt.

'He's getting away!' shouted Senta.

'I don't think so,' said Waylander softly.

Miriel reappeared and offered the bow to Waylander. He shook his head. The knight had reached the rise and was scrambling up the slope.

'Allow for the fact that you are shooting uphill,' advised Waylander.

Miriel nodded. The bow came up and, apparently without sighting, she loosed the bolt. It took the knight low in the back. He arched up, then tumbled down the slope. Belash, his bloody knife in hand, ran across to the fallen man, wrenching off the helm and preparing for the killing thrust.

'Dead!' he called back.

'Nicely done,' said Waylander.

'What in Hell's name were they?' asked Angel.

'The Brotherhood,' Waylander told him. 'They have hunted me before. Sorceror knights.'

Belash strolled back to where the others stood. He glanced at Miriel. 'One damn fine archer,' he said. 'For a *kol-isha*,' he added, after a pause. 'I'll fetch the horses.' Sheathing his knife he strolled away to the south.

Miriel dropped the crossbow and rubbed her eyes. All around her she could hear the buzzing of angry insects, but she could see nothing. She tried to concentrate on the sounds, separating them.

'. . . *do that . . . witch . . . powers . . . Brotherhood . . . Kai . . . pain . . . escape . . . Durmast . . . Danyal . . .*'
And she realised she was hearing the fragmented thoughts of the men around her. Belash thought her possessed, Waylander was reliving his last battle with the Brotherhood when the giant Durmast had died to save him. Senta was staring at her, his passion aroused.

She felt Angel move behind her, and a wave of emotion swept over her, warm and protective, strong, enduring. His hand touched her shoulder.

'Do not concern yourself. I am not injured,' she said. She

138

felt his confusion, and turned towards him. 'You remember my Talent, Angel?'

'Yes.'

'It is back!'

*

'You have very powerful enemies,' said Senta, as Waylander retrieved his bolts from the two dead knights.

'I'm still alive,' Waylander pointed out, moving past him and into the cabin, where he slumped down in the wide leather chair. His head was pounding and he rubbed at his eyes. There was no relief. Miriel joined him.

'Let me help you,' she said softly. Her hand touched his neck. Instantly all pain flowed away from him. He sighed, his dark eyes looking up to meet her gaze.

'You saved us. You destroyed their spell.'

'It broke their concentration when I killed the leader,' she said. Miriel knelt before him, her hands resting on his knees. 'Why did you lie to me?' she asked him.

'What lie?' he replied, averting his eyes.

'You said we were going north to escape the assassins.'

'And we are.'

'No. You are seeking Bodalen. Hewla told you where to find him.'

'What else do you know?' he asked wearily.

'Too much,' she answered.

He sighed. 'You found your Talent. I thought it was gone forever.'

'It was given back to me by the man who stole it. You remember when Mother died and you began to drink strong wine? And how you woke up one morning and there were bloodstains in the clearing, and a shallow grave with two corpses? You thought you'd killed them while drunk. You couldn't remember. You asked Krylla and me about them. We said we didn't know. And we didn't. It was your friend, Dardalion. The men were coming to capture us, perhaps to kill us, because we had the Talent. Dardalion stopped them – killed them with your crossbow.'

'He swore never to kill again,' whispered Waylander.

'He had no choice. You were drunk and unconscious, and the weapon carried so much death and violence that it swamped him.' Waylander hung his head, wishing to hear no more, but unwilling to stop her. 'He closed off our Talent. And he took away the memories of the demons and the man who tried to capture our souls. He did it to protect us.'

'But now you remember it all?'

'Yes.'

'I did my best, Miriel . . . Do not read my thoughts . . . my life.'

'It is too late.'

He nodded and stood. 'Then do not hold me in too great a contempt.'

'Oh, Father!' Stepping forward she embraced him. 'How could I hold you in contempt? I love you. I always have.'

Relief washed over him, and he closed his eyes as he held her. 'I wanted you to be happy – like Krylla. I wanted a good life for you.'

'I have had a good life. And I have been happy,' she told him. She drew back from him and smiled, lifting her hand to stroke his cheek. 'The packs are ready, and we should move.' She closed her eyes. 'Belash has found the horses and will be here soon.'

Taking hold of her shoulders he drew her in to him once more. 'You could head south with Angel,' he said. 'I have money in Drenan.'

She shook her head. 'You need me.'

'I do not want to see you . . . hurt.'

'Everyone dies, Father,' she said. 'But this is no longer just a private war between you and Karnak. I wonder if it ever was.'

'What is it, then?'

'I don't know yet, but Karnak did not send the Brotherhood. When I killed the last man he had an image in his mind. He was thinking of a tall man, with black hair, greased to his skull. Slanted eyes, long robes of dark purple. He it was who sent them. And he is the same man who tried to hurt Krylla and me; the man who summoned the demons.'

'From where did the Dark Knights come?'

'Dros Delnoch, and before that Gulgothir.'

'Then that is where the answers lie,' he said.

'Yes,' she agreed, sadly.

*

Angel watched the Nadir leading the five horses across the clearing. Disgusting little savage, he thought! Everything about Belash sickened him, the slanted, soulless eyes, the cruel mouth, the man's barbaric method of killing. It made Angel's skin crawl. He glanced north at the distant mountains. Beyond these the Nadir bred like lice, living their short, violent lives engaged in one bloody war after another. There had never been a Nadir poet, nor an artist nor a sculptor. And never would be! What a vile people, thought Angel.

'Uses that knife well,' observed Senta.

'Bastard Nadir,' grunted Angel.

'I thought your first wife was part-Nadir?'

'She was not!' snapped Angel. 'She was . . . Chiatze. They're different. The Nadir are not human. Devils, all of them.'

'Canny fighters, though.'

'Talk about something else!' demanded Angel.

Senta chuckled. 'How did you know they were coming? You walked away and fetched your sword from the cabin.'

Angel frowned, then smiled, his mood clearing. 'I smelt horse dung – the breeze was blowing from the south. I thought they might be more assassins. I wish they had been. Shemak's balls, but I was frightened when that spell fell upon me. I'm still not over it. To just stand, unable to move, while a swordsman approached me . . .' He shuddered. 'It was like my worst nightmare.'

'Not something I'd like to repeat,' agreed Senta. 'Waylander said they were the Brotherhood. I thought they were wiped out in the Vagrian Wars.'

Angel's pale eyes scanned the bodies. 'Well, they obviously weren't.'

'What do you know of them?'

'Precious little. There are legends of a sorceror who founded the order, but I can't remember his name, nor where they began. Ventria, I think. Or was it further east? They were called the Blood Knights at one time, because of the sacrifices. Or was it the Crimson Knights?'

'Forget it, Angel. I think "precious little" covered it.'

'I never was much of a history student.'

Belash approached them. 'They are the Knights of Blood,' he said. 'The first of their temples was built in Chiatze three hundred years ago, founded by a wizard named Zhi Zhen. They became very powerful and tried to overthrow the Emperor. Zhi Zhen was captured after many battles and impaled on a golden spike. But the Order did not die out. It spread west. The Vagrian General Kaem used Brotherhood priests at the Siege of Purdol. Now they have reformed in Gothir, under a wizard named Zhu Chao.'

'You are well-informed,' said Senta.

'One of them killed my father.'

'Well, they can't be all bad,' said Angel.

Belash stood for a moment, his flat features expressionless, his dark eyes locked to Angel's face. Then he nodded slowly and walked away.

'That shouldn't have been said,' chided Senta.

'I don't like him.'

'That's no excuse for bad manners, Angel. Insult the living, not the dead.'

'I speak my mind,' muttered Angel, but he knew Senta was right, and the insult left a bad taste in his mouth.

'Why do you hate them so?'

'I witnessed a massacre. Sixty miles north of the Delnoch Pass. My father and I were travelling from Namib. We were in the hills, and we saw the Nadir attack a convoy of wagons. I'll never forget it. The torture went on long into the night. We slipped away, but the screams followed us. They follow me still.'

'I lived in Gulgothir for a while,' said Senta. 'I have relatives there, and we used to ride to the hunt. One day, high summer it was, the hunting party spotted three Nadir boys, walking beside a stream. The huntmaster shouted something and the riders broke into a gallop, spearing two of the boys as they stood there. The third ran. He was chased and cut a score of times, not enough to bring him down, but enough to keep him running. Finally he fell to the ground, exhausted and, I would guess, dying. The huntsmen, Gothir nobles all, leapt from their horses and hacked him to pieces. Then they cut off his ears for trophies.'

'There is a point to this tale?' enquired Angel.

'Savagery breeds savagery,' said Senta.

'That's today's sermon, is it?'

'By Heaven but you are in a foul mood, Angel. I think I'll leave you to enjoy it alone.'

Angel remained silent as Senta moved back into the cabin.

Soon they would be heading north. Into Nadir country. Angel's mouth felt dry and the flames of fear grew in his belly.

9

Ekodas loved the forest, the majestic trees living in quiet brotherhood, the plants and flowers cloaking the earth, and the serenity born of eternal life. When the world was young, the earth still warm, the first trees had grown here, living, breathing. And their descendants were still here, endlessly watching the small, fleeting lives of men.

The young priest, his white robes now stained with mud, moved alongside a huge oak, reaching out to lay his hand upon the rough bark. He closed his eyes. The tree had no heart to hear, yet there was still the pulsing beat of life within the trunk, the slow flowing of sap through the capillaries, the stretching of growth in new wood.

Ekodas was at peace here.

He walked on, his mind open to the sounds of the forest, the late birdsong, the skittering of small animals in the undergrowth. He sensed the heartbeat of a fox close by, and smelt the musky fur of an old badger. He stopped. And smiled. The fox and the badger were sharing a burrow.

An owl hooted. Ekodas glanced up. The light was fading, the sun dipping into the western sea.

He turned and began the long climb towards the temple. The debate came back to him then and he sighed, regretting the weakness which had driven him to betray his principles. Deep down he knew that Dardalion himself was now unsure of the path on which they stood. The Abbot had *almost* wanted to be free of the destiny he had planned for so long. Almost.

Yet if love had won the day then everything Dardalion had striven for would have seemed as nothing. A tragic waste of life and Talent. I could not do that to you, Dardalion, thought Ekodas. I could not make a mockery of your life.

The young priest drew in a deep breath, seeking to feel

once more the calm of the forest. Instead there came a sharp, jagged stab in his mind. Anger. Fear. Arousal. Lust. Focusing his Talent, he scanned the trees. And sensed two men . . . and . . . yes, a woman.

Pushing his way through the bushes at the side of the track, he traversed the hill until he came to a deer-trail leading down into a deep gulley. He heard the sound of a man's voice.

'Be sensible, woman. We're not going to hurt you. We'll even pay!'

Another voice cut in, harsh and deep. 'Enough talk! Take the bitch!'

Ekodas rounded the final bend and saw the two men, foresters by their garb, standing with knives drawn and facing a young Nadir woman. She also held a knife and was waiting, poised, her back to a rock-face.

'Good evening, friends,' said Ekodas. The first of the men, tall and slim, wearing a green tunic of homespun wool and brown leather leggings and boots, swung towards him. He was a young man, with sandy hair tied in a pony-tail.

'This is no place for a priest,' he said.

Ekodas walked on, halting immediately before the man. 'The forest is a wonderful place for meditation, brother.' He sensed the man's confusion. There was little that was evil in him, but his lusts were aroused and they had clouded his reason. He wanted the woman, and his mind was seething with erotic thoughts and images.

The second man pushed forward. He was shorter and stockier, his eyes small and round. 'Go back where you came from!' he ordered. 'I'll not be turned aside by the likes of you!'

'What you are planning is evil,' said Ekodas softly. 'I cannot permit it. If you continue along this gulley you will find the road to Estri. It is a small village and there is, I understand, a woman there who has a special smile for men with coin.'

'I know where Estri is,' hissed the second man. 'And when I want your pigging advice I'll ask for it. You know

145

what this is?' The knife-blade came up, hovering before Ekodas' face.

'I know what it is, brother. What is your purpose in showing it to me?'

'Are you a halfwit?'

The first man took hold of his friend's arm. 'Leave it, Caan. It doesn't matter.'

'Matters to me. I want that woman.'

'You can't kill a priest!'

'Pigging watch me!' The knife swept up. Ekodas swayed aside, caught the man's wrist and twisted the arm up and back. His foot snaked out, hooking behind the knifeman's knee. The forester fell back. Ekodas released his grip and the man tumbled to the earth.

'I have no wish to cause you pain,' said Ekodas. The man scrambled up and charged. Ekodas brushed aside the knife-arm and sent his elbow crashing into the man's chin. He dropped as if poleaxed. Ekodas turned to the first man. 'Take your friend to Estri,' he advised. 'And once there bid him goodbye. He brings out the worst in you.' Stepping past the man he approached the Nadir woman. 'Greetings, sister. If you will follow me I can take you to lodgings for the night. It is a temple, and the beds are hard, but you will sleep soundly and without fear.'

'I sleep without fear wherever I am,' she said. 'But I will follow you.'

Her eyes were dark and beautiful, her skin both pale and yet touched with gold. Her lips were full, the mouth wide and Ekodas found himself remembering the images in the forester's mind. He reddened and began the long climb.

'You fight well,' she said, drawing alongside him, her knife now sheathed in a goatskin scabbard, a small pack slung across her shoulders.

'Have you travelled far, sister?'

'I am not your sister,' she pointed out.

'All women are my sisters. All men my brothers. I am a Source priest.'

'Your brother down there has a broken jaw.'

'I regret that.'

146

'I don't. I would have killed him.'

'My name is Ekodas,' he said, offering his hand. She ignored it and walked on ahead.

'I am Shia.' They reached the winding path to the temple and she gazed up at the high stone walls. 'This is a fortress,' she said.

'It was once. Now it is a place of prayer.'

'It is still a fortress.'

The gates were open and Ekodas led her inside. Vishna and several of the other priests were drawing water from the well. Shia stopped and stared at them. 'You have no women for this work?' she asked Ekodas.

'There are no women here. I told you, we are priests.'

'And priests have no women?'

'Exactly so.'

'Only sisters?'

'Yes.'

'Your little tribe won't last long,' she said, with a deep throaty chuckle.

*

The screams died down and a hoarse, choking death-rattle came from the slave. His arms relaxed, sagging into the chains and his legs spasmed. Zhu Chao slashed the knife into the ribcage, sawing through the arteries of the heart and ripping the organ clear. He carried it to the centre of the circle, stepping carefully over the chalk lines that marked the stones, zig-zagging between the candles and the wires of gold that linked the chalice and the crystal. Laying the heart in the chalice he drew back, placing his feet within the twin circles of Shemak.

The Fourth Grimoire lay open on a bronze lectern and he turned the page and began to read aloud in a language lost to the world of men for a hundred millennia.

The air around him crackled, and fire ran along the wires of gold, circling the chalice in rings of flame. The heart bubbled, dark smoke oozing from it, billowing up to form a shape. Massive rounded shoulders appeared, and a huge head with a cavernous mouth. Eyes flickered open, yellow

147

and slitted. Long arms, bulging with muscle, sprouted from the shoulders.

Zhu Chao began to tremble, and felt his courage waning. The creature of smoke threw back its head and a sibilant hissing filled the room.

'What do you want of me?' it said.

'A death,' answered Zhu Chao.

'Kesa Khan?'

'Exactly so.'

A sound issued from the creature of smoke – slow, volcanic hissing that Zhu Chao took to be laughter. 'He wants your death also,' said the demon.

'Can he pay in blood and pain?' countered Zhu Chao, aware that sweat was trickling down his face and that his hands were trembling.

'He has served my master well.'

'As have I.'

'Indeed. But I will not grant your request.'

'Why?'

'Look to the lines of your life, Zhu Chao.'

The smoke dispersed, as if a clean wind had swept through the room. The chalice was empty, the heart vanished without trace. Zhu Chao turned to where, moments before, the body of the young slave had hung in chains. It too was gone.

The sorceror stumbled from the circle, uncaring now about the lines of chalk which his sandalled feet smeared and scattered. Taking up the Third Grimoire he carried it to a leather-topped desk and searched through the pages. The spell he needed was a small one, needing no blood. He spoke the words then traced a pattern in the air. Where his finger passed a shining line appeared, a spider's web forming. At last satisfied he pointed to various inter-sections. Small spheres sprang into being at each spot, some blue, others green, one gold, two black. Zhu Chao drew in a deep breath, focusing his concentration. The web began to shift and move, the spheres spinning, circling the golden globe at the centre. The sorceror took up a quill pen, dipping it into a small well of ink. He found a large sheet of papyrus and began to write, occasionally glancing up at the swirling pattern in the air.

After an hour he had filled the page with symbols. Tired, he rubbed his eyes and stretched his back. The swirling web disappeared. Taking the sheet he walked back to the chalice, said the Six Words of Power and dropped the papyrus into the golden bowl.

It burst into flames, which reared up forming a burning sphere, a great globe which rose from the chalice, hanging in the air before his face. The sphere stretched and flattened, the flames dying down, and Zhu Chao saw a man dressed in black moving along the high walls of his palace. In the man's hand was a small crossbow.

The scene flickered and changed. There was an ancient fortress, with high twisted walls and tilted turrets. An army was gathered there, scaling-ladders and ropes at the ready. Upon the wall, on the highest turret, stood Kesa Khan. Beside him was a woman, also dressed in black.

The vision shimmered and Zhu Chao saw a dragon high in the sky, circling above the fortress. But then it turned and flew straight towards Gulgothir, passing over the quiet homes and flying like an arrow towards Zhu Chao's own palace. Its shadow swept over the land, like a black demon, flowing over the palace walls and into the courtyard. There the shadow froze on the flagstones, blacker than night, rising up and becoming a man.

The same man, carrying the crossbow.

Faint now, the image swirled once more and Zhu Chao found himself gazing at a cabin in the mountains. The man was there again – as were the bodies of the nine knights. The sorceror was shocked. How had Waylander overcome his knights? He knew no spells. Fear flickered in Zhu Chao's heart. The dragon in the dream had flown to his palace, promising death and despair.

Not mine, thought Zhu Chao, fighting down the beginnings of panic. No, not mine.

His weariness was forgotten as he moved up the winding stair to the upper rooms. Bodalen was there, lounging on a couch, his booted feet upon a silver-topped table.

'What is there that you have not told me about Waylander?' demanded the sorceror.

Bodalen rolled to his feet. He was a tall man, wide-shouldered, lantern-jawed, his eyes blue beneath thick brows, his mouth large and full-lipped. He was the image of the younger Karnak and his voice had the same resonant power. 'Nothing, my lord. He is an assassin – that is all.'

'The assassin has slain nine of my knights. You understand? Men of great power.'

Bodalen licked his lips. 'I can't explain it, my lord. My father talked of him often. He said nothing about magic.'

Zhu Chao fell silent. What reason would Waylander have for coming to his palace, save to kill Bodalen? If Karnak's son were no longer here . . . He smiled at the young Drenai. 'He will not thwart us,' he said. 'Now there is something you can do for me, my boy.'

'Gladly, my lord.'

'I want you to ride into the Mountains of the Moon. I will give you a map to follow. There is a fortress of great antiquity there, a curious place. There are many tunnels below it, and chambers filled with gold and jewels, so it is said. Take ten men, and plentiful supplies, and move into the fortress. Find a hiding place in the underground caverns. Within the next few weeks Kesa Khan will journey there. When he does, you can emerge and kill him.'

'There will be many Nadir warriors with him,' objected the younger man.

Zhu Chao smiled thinly. 'Life offers many dangers, Bodalen, and a brave man can overcome them all. It would please me if you agreed to undertake this small quest.'

'You know I would give my life for the cause, my lord. It is just . . .'

'Yes, yes,' snapped Zhu Chao, 'I understand. You were born with the looks of your father and none of his courage. Well, know this, Bodalen: at his side you were of great use to me. Here, as a runaway, you are valueless. Do not make the mistake of displeasing me.'

Bodalen paled. 'Of course not, my lord. I . . . I would be happy to . . . a map, you say?'

'You shall have a map, and ten trustworthy men. Very trustworthy. And if you do this successfully, Bodalen, you will be rewarded beyond your desires. You will become King over all the Drenai.'

Bodalen nodded and smiled. 'I will serve you well, my lord. And you are wrong: I do not lack courage. I will prove it to you.'

'Of course, my boy. Forgive me, I spoke in anger. Now go and prepare for the journey.'

*

Ekodas led Shia through the dining-hall and up through the second and third levels to where Dardalion sat in his study. The young priest tapped at the door.

'Enter,' called the Abbot. Ekodas opened the door, ushering the young Nadir woman into the room.

Dardalion rose and bowed. 'Welcome, my dear. I am sorry that your visit to Drenai lands should have had so unsettling a beginning.'

'Did I say it was unsettling?' countered Shia, walking forward and scanning the study, her mocking gaze drifting over the burdened shelves and open cupboards stacked with scrolls, parchments and books.

'Do you read?' asked Dardalion.

She shook her head. 'What would be the purpose?'

'To understand our own needs and desires we must first understand the needs and desires of our ancestors.'

'I do not see that as true,' she answered. 'The desires of our ancestors were obvious – that is why we are here. And those desires do not change, which is why we have children.'

'You think that history can teach us nothing?' asked Ekodas.

'History can,' she admitted, 'but these are not history, they are merely writings. Are you the leader here?' she asked, turning to Dardalion.

'I am the Abbot. The priests you have seen are my disciples.'

'He fights well,' she said, smiling and pointing at Ekodas. 'He should not be here among prayer-men.'

'You use the term as an insult,' accused Ekodas, blushing.

'If you feel insulted by it, then that is what it must be,' she told him.

Dardalion chuckled and moved around his desk. 'You are welcome here, Shia, daughter of Nosta Vren. And in the morning we will direct you to your brother, Belash.'

Her dark eyes sparkled and she laughed. 'Your powers do not surprise me, Silver-hair. I knew you were a mystic.'

'How?' enquired Ekodas.

Dardalion moved alongside the bewildered priest, laying a hand on the younger man's arm. 'How else would I know about the . . . unsettling, did I say? . . . attack,' Dardalion told him. 'You have a keen mind, Shia. And you are a brave woman.'

She shrugged. 'I do not need you to tell me what I am. But it pleases me to hear the compliment. I would like to sleep now. The fighting prayer-man offered me a bed.'

'Ekodas, take our guest to the western wing. I have had a fire prepared in the south-facing dormitory.' Swinging back to Shia he bowed again. 'May your dreams be pleasant, young lady.'

'They will or they won't,' she answered, her eyes still faintly mocking. 'Is your man allowed to sleep with me?'

'I fear not,' Dardalion told her. 'We are celibate here.'

She shook her head in disbelief. 'Why do men play such games?' she asked. 'Lack of good lovemaking causes diseases of the belly and back. And bad headaches.'

'But set against that,' said Dardalion, barely suppressing a smile, 'is that it frees the spiritual mind to heights rarely found in more earthly pleasures.'

'Do you know that for certain, or is it only in writings?' she countered.

'It is only in writings,' he agreed. 'But faith is an integral part of our life here. Sleep well.'

Ekodas, his face burning, led the Nadir woman along the western corridor, his discomfiture increased by the sound of the Abbot's laughter echoing behind them.

The room was small, but a bright fire was burning in the hearth and fresh blankets had been laid on the narrow bed.

'I hope you will be comfortable here,' he said stiffly. 'I will wake you in the morning with a little breakfast – bread and cheese and the juice of summer apples.'

'Do you dream, prayer-man?'

'Yes. Often.'

'Dream of me,' she said.

10

They were camped in a sheltered hollow within a wood, and a small fire flickered in a circle of stones. Senta, Angel and Belash were sleeping, Waylander taking the third watch. He was sitting on the hilltop, his back to a tree, his black clothing merging him into the night shadows. Beside him lay the hound, which he had named Scar.

Miriel lay wrapped in her cloak, her back to the fire, her shoulders warm, her feet cold. Autumn was fading fast, and the smell of snow was in the air. She could not sleep. The ride from the cabin had been made in near silence, but Miriel had linked into the thoughts of the riders. Belash was thinking of home and vengeance, and whenever his thoughts turned to Waylander he pictured a bright knife. Angel was confused. He did not want to travel north, yet he did not want to leave them. His thoughts of Miriel were equally contrasting. He was fond of her, by turns paternal and yet aroused by her. Senta suffered no confusion. His thoughts were filled with erotic images which both stimulated and frightened the young mountain girl.

Waylander she left alone, fearing the new-found darkness within him.

Sitting up, she added several sticks to the fire, then shifted her position so that her legs and feet could bathe in the warmth of the small blaze. A voice whispered into her mind, so faint she thought at first she had imagined it. It came again, but she could make no sense of the words. Concentrating her Talent she focused all her power on the whispers. Still nothing. It was galling. Lying down she closed her eyes, her spirit drifting up from her body. Now the whisper was clearer, but still seeming to come from an impossible distance.

'Who are you?' she called.

'Trust me!'

'No.'

'Many lives depend on your trust. Women, children, old ones.'

'Show yourself!' she commanded.

'I cannot – the distance is too great, my power stretched.'

'Then what would you have me do?'

'Return to the flesh and awake Belash. Tell him to hold his left hand over the fire and cut his palm. Let the blood fall into the flames. Tell him Kesa Khan commands this.'

'And then what?'

'And then I will come to you and we will talk.'

'Whose lives depend on this?' she asked. Immediately she sensed his agitation.

'I can talk no more. Do this swiftly or the link will be broken. I am nearing exhaustion.'

Miriel returned to her body and rose, moving to Belash. As she neared the Nadir warrior he rolled to his feet knife in hand, his eyes wary. She told him the message she had received from Kesa Khan and expected him to question her, or express his doubts. But the Nadir instantly moved to the fire, slicing his knife-blade across his open palm. Blood spilled instantly from the wound, splashing into the flames.

The voice of Kesa Khan boomed inside her mind, causing her to reel back. 'Now you may come to me,' he said.

'Can I trust this Kesa Khan?' she asked Belash.

'Does he say that you can?' he answered.

'Yes.'

'Then obey him,' advised the Nadir. Miriel did not rely on the words, but read the images beyond them. Belash feared Kesa Khan, but there was no doubt that he also admired him, and would trust him with his life.

Miriel lay back and let her spirit drift clear. Instantly she was swept into a bewildering maze of light and colour. Her senses reeled and she lost control of her flight, spinning wildly through a thousand bright rainbows and into a darkness deeper than death. But before fear could turn to panic the darkness lifted, and she found herself sitting by a lakeside village. There were houses here, rough-crafted but secure against the winter wind and snow. Children were playing at the water's edge, and she recognised herself and Krylla. Sitting beside them on an upturned boat was a man, tall and slim, with wide staring eyes and tightly curled hair.

Miriel's heart leapt, and for the first time in twelve years she remembered her real father's face. This was the winter just before the Vagrians had invaded, just before her parents and all her friends had been butchered. It was a peaceful time, full of quiet joy.

'Are you comfortable with this illusion?' asked the wizened old man sitting beside her.

'Yes,' she told him. 'Very.' She turned her attention to him. He was no more than four and a half feet tall, bird-boned ribs pressing against the taut skin of his chest. His head was too large for his body and his wispy hair hung lank to his shoulders. His two front teeth were missing and his words were sibilant as a result. He was wearing ragged leggings and knee-length moccasins tied with strips of black leather.

'I am Kesa Khan.'

'That means nothing to me.'

'It will,' he assured her. 'We share the same enemy. Zhu Chao.' He almost spat the name.

'I do not know this man.'

'He sent the Dark Knights to kill your father, just as he sends the Gothir army to wipe out my people. And you do know him, Miriel. Look.' The scene flickered, the village disappearing. Now they sat on a high wall overlooking a flower garden. A man sat there, his robes dark, his hair waxed to his head, his sideburns braided and hanging to his chin. Miriel tensed. This was the scaled hunter who had tried to capture her and Krylla five years ago, before the silver knight rescued them. But here he had no scales. He was merely a man sitting in a garden.

'Do not be misled,' warned Kesa Khan. 'You are gazing upon evil.'

'Why does he seek to kill my . . . father?' She hesitated as she spoke, the image of her real father strong in her mind.

'Bodalen serves him. He thought it would be a simple matter to hunt down Waylander and slay him. Then he could have returned Bodalen to the Drenai, awaiting the moment the son betrayed the father.' The old man chuckled, the sound dry and unpleasant. 'He should have known Waylander as I knew him. Ha! I tried to hunt him down once. I sent six great merged beasts to destroy him, and twenty hunters of rare skill. None survived. He has a gift for death.'

'You are my father's enemy?'

'Not now!' he assured her. 'Now I wish him for a friend.'

'Why?'

'Because my people are in peril. You can have no conception of what it is to live under the Gothir yoke. We have no rights under their laws. We can be hunted down like vermin. No one will raise a hand to object – that is bad enough. But now Zhu Chao has convinced the Emperor that my tribe – the oldest of the Tent-people – needs to be eradicated. Exterminated! Soon the soldiers will march against us.'

'How can my father help you? He is only one man.'

'He is the Dragon Shadow, the hope of my people. And he has with him the White Tiger in the Night and old Hard-to-kill. Also there is Senta. And, more importantly perhaps, there is you.'

'That is still only five. We are not an army.'

'We shall see. Ask Waylander to come to the Mountains of the Moon. Ask him to help us.'

'Why should he? You are a man who tried to kill him.'

'Tell him we are outnumbered ten to one. Tell him we are doomed. Tell him we have more than two hundred children who will be slaughtered.'

'You don't understand . . . these are not his children. You are asking him to risk his life for people he does not know. Why would he even consider it?'

'I cannot answer that, Miriel. Just tell him what I have said.'

The colours swirled once more and Miriel felt a sickening lurch as her spirit was united with her body. Waylander was beside her, and the sun was high in the sky.

Waylander felt a surge of relief as Miriel opened her eyes. He stroked her hair. 'What happened?' he asked.

Taking hold of his arm she eased herself into a sitting position. Her head was throbbing with dull pain, her mouth dry. 'A little water,' she croaked. Pulling free the cork, Angel passed her a leather-bound canteen and she drank greedily. 'We need to speak,' she told Waylander. 'Alone.'

Angel, Belash and Senta withdrew and she recounted her meeting with Kesa Khan. Waylander listened in silence until she had finished.

'You believed him?'

'Yes. He did not tell me all he knew, but what he said was true. Or at least he believed it to be true. His people face annihilation.'

'What did he mean by calling me the Dragon Shadow?'

'I don't know. Will you go?'

He smiled. 'You think I should?'

She looked away. 'When we were young Krylla and I used to love the stories that Mother . . . Danyal . . . told. You know, of heroes crossing seas of fire to rescue princesses.' She smiled. 'We felt like princesses because you had rescued us. You were the man who helped save the Drenai. We loved you for that.'

'It wasn't for the Drenai,' he said. 'It was for me.'

'I know that now,' she told him. 'And I don't want to sway you. I know you would die for me, as you would have risked all for Mother or Krylla. And I know why you are heading north. You want vengeance.'

'I am what I am, Miriel.'

'You were always better than you knew,' she said, reaching up and stroking his lean face. 'And whatever choice you make I will not condemn you.'

He nodded. 'Where do you wish to go?'

'With you,' she answered simply.

'Tell me what he said again.' She repeated the words of Kesa Khan. 'A cunning old man,' said Waylander.

'I agree. But what makes you say so?'

'The children. He wanted me to know about the children. He knows me too well. By heaven I hate sorcerors!' Waylander took a long, deep breath. And saw again the flowers in bloom around the dead face of his son. How old would he have been now? A little older than Senta, perhaps?

He thought of Bodalen. And Karnak.

Senta, Belash and Angel were standing by the tethered horses. Summoning them to him he asked Miriel to tell the story for a third time.

'He must think we are insane,' said Angel, as Miriel concluded her tale.

'No,' said Senta softly, 'he knows us better than that.'

'What's that supposed to mean?'

'Oh come on, Angel, don't you just love the thought of impossible odds?' asked Senta, grinning.

'No, I don't. I leave that sort of idiocy for young men like you. Talk sense to him, Dakeyras.'

'You are free to ride where you please,' said Waylander. 'There is nothing holding you here.'

'But you are not going to go to the Mountains?'

'Indeed I am,' said Waylander.

'How will you stop the killing? Will you ride out on a tall horse and face the Gothir army? Tell them you're Waylander the Slayer and you're not going to allow them to butcher a few Nadir?'

'As I said, you are free to go where you will,' repeated Waylander.

'What about Miriel?' asked Angel.

'She can speak for herself,' said Miriel. 'And I shall ride to the Mountains of the Moon.'

'Just tell me why,' pleaded Angel. 'Why are you all doing this?'

Waylander was silent for a moment. Then he shrugged. 'I don't like massacres,' he said.

*

Vishna's voice was calm, but Dardalion could sense the tension in the priest as he spoke. 'I do not see how we can

159

be sure that the woman is sent by the Source. We have all agreed to risk our lives in the battle against evil. I have no qualms concerning that decision. To stand upon the walls of Purdol against the Ventrians would help Karnak maintain the defence of the Drenai, as would offering our assistance to the General at Delnoch. But to ride into the steppes and risk our lives for a small Nadir tribe . . .?' He shook his head. 'What purpose would it serve, Father?'

Dardalion did not answer, but turned to the others, the blond Magnic, the slender Palista and the silent, reserved Ekodas. 'What is your view, brother?' he asked Magnic.

'I agree with Vishna. What do the Nadir offer the world? Nothing. They have no culture, no philosophy, save that of war. To die for them would be meaningless.' The young priest shrugged. 'But I will follow your orders, Father Abbot.'

Dardalion nodded towards Palista. 'And you, my boy?'

'It is a difficult question,' answered Palista, his voice deep, incongruously so, issuing as it did from his small slender frame. 'It seems to me the answer depends on how we view the arrival of the woman. If the Source directed her to us then our way is clear. If not . . .' he spread his hands.

Ekodas spoke. 'I agree with Palista. The woman's arrival is the central issue. For, although I respect Vishna and Magnic, I believe the argument they use is flawed. Who granted us the right to judge the worth or otherwise of the Nadir? If our actions should save a single life, only the Source can know what that life is worth. The saved one could be a future Nadir prophet, or his son may become one, or his grandson. How can we know? But is the woman directed by the Source? She has asked us for nothing. Surely that is the key?'

'I see,' said Dardalion. 'You believe that she should have received wisdom in a dream perhaps, and approached us directly for help?'

'There are many examples of such happenings,' said Ekodas.

'If such was the case here, where would faith begin?' countered the Abbot.

160

'I do not understand, Father.'

'My dear Ekodas, we are talking about faith. Where is the need for faith, if we have proof?'

'Surely another flawed argument,' put in Palista. 'By this token anyone who came and said they were sent by the Source would have to be disbelieved.'

Dardalion laughed aloud. 'Excellent, my dear Palista! But this moves us from one extreme to another. What I am saying is that there must always be an element of faith. Not proof, but faith. If she had come and claimed to be Source-directed we would have read her thoughts and known the truth. Then there would have been no faith. We would have acted thereafter in sure knowledge. Instead, we have prayed for a sign. Where should the Thirty ride? And what was our answer? Ekodas rescued a Nadir woman. Why is she here? To find her brother and bring him home to help face a terrible enemy. Who is that enemy? None other than Zhu Chao, the man whose evil led me to gather the Thirty together. Do these facts not speak to you? Can you not feel the threads of destiny drawing together?'

'This is difficult for me,' said Vishna, with a sigh. 'I am the only Gothir present among the Thirty. My family and friends are high in the council of the Emperor. It is likely that old friends will be riding against these same Nadir. It does not make me feel comfortable to know that I may have to draw a sword against these men.'

'I understand that,' said Dardalion. 'But it is my belief that Shia is sent to us, and that the Mountains of the Moon beckon. What else can I say?'

'I think we all need more prayer – and more guidance,' observed Ekodas. The others nodded in agreement.

'Faith is essential,' added Vishna. 'But there must be another sign.'

'It is unlikely to come with letters of fire in the sky,' said Dardalion softly.

'Even so,' put in Ekodas, 'if it is our destiny to die in Nadir lands then the Source will lead us there.'

Dardalion looked to each of the young men before him,

then he rose. 'Very well, my brothers, we will wait. And we will pray.'

*

Ekodas slept fitfully, Shia's words haunting him like a curse. And he did dream of her, and woke often, his body tense with suppressed passion. He tried prayer, and when that failed he repeated the longest, most complex meditation mantras. For a while his concentration held. Then he would picture her ivory skin, tinged with gold, her dark almond-shaped eyes . . .

He rose silently from his bed in the hour before dawn, moving with care so as not to awaken the five brothers who shared the small dormitory. Taking a clean white robe from the chest beneath his bed he dressed swiftly and made his way down to the kitchens.

Fat Merlon was already there, removing the rough linen from several large rounds of cheese. In the far corner Glendrin was supervising the baking, and the smell of fresh bread filled the room.

'You are awake early,' said Merlon, as Ekodas entered.

'I couldn't sleep,' he admitted.

'I would dearly love another hour, brother,' said Merlon expectantly.

'Of course,' Ekodas told him. 'I will take your duty.'

'I will say ten blessings for you, Ekodas,' beamed Merlon, embracing the smaller man and patting his back. Merlon was a large man, balding already at twenty-six, and his strength was prodigious. The other priests gently mocked him for his vast appetite, but in truth there was little fat upon him, save for his belly, and Ekodas felt himself being crushed by the man.

'Enough, Merlon!' he gasped.

'I'll see you at breakfast,' yawned Merlon, ambling away towards the sleeping area.

Glendrin glanced back. 'Fetch me the tray and pole, Ekodas,' he called, flicking the latch on the oven doors. The two-pronged pole was hanging upon hooks on the far wall. Ekodas lifted it clear, attached the prongs to a ridged metal plate and passed the implement to Glendrin. Using a cloth to protect his hands Glendrin opened wide the oven doors then pushed the pole inside, the plate sliding under three golden crusted loaves. These he withdrew and Ekodas, slipping on gloves of white wool, removed the bread, placing it on the long kitchen table. There were twelve loaves in all and the smell made Ekodas feel as if he had not eaten for a week.

'Merlon churned the butter,' said Glendrin, sitting down at the table. 'But I'll wager he ate half of it.'

'You have flour in your beard,' Ekodas pointed out. 'It makes you look older than time.'

Glendrin grinned and rubbed his hand across the red trident beard. 'You think the woman was sent?' he asked.

Ekodas shrugged. 'If she was she came to haunt me,' he answered.

Glendrin chuckled. 'You'll need those ten blessings Merlon promised you,' he said, wagging a finger at his friend. 'Carnal thoughts are a sin!'

'How do you deal with them?' asked Ekodas.

Glendrin's smile faded. 'I don't,' he admitted. 'Now let us get on.'

Together they prepared the cheese, drew fresh water from the well, and carried the food through to the dining-hall, setting out the plates and cutlery, jugs and goblets.

Then Ekodas prepared a tray of bread and cheese for Shia, feeling his excitement rise at the prospect of seeing her once more. 'I cannot find the apple juice,' he told Glendrin.

'We finished it yesterday.'

'But I promised her some.'

Glendrin shook his head. 'Then I would imagine she will despise you for the rest of your life,' said the red-headed priest.

'Fool!' replied Ekodas, placing a jug of water and a clay goblet upon the tray.

'Do not be too long with her,' advised Glendrin. Ekodas did not reply.

Leaving the heat of the kitchen he climbed the cold stone stairwell and made his way to Shia's room. Balancing the tray on his left arm he opened the door. The Nadir woman was asleep on the floor before the dead fire, her head resting on her elbow, her legs drawn up, her body bathed in the last of the moonlight.

'Good morning,' said Ekodas. She gave a low groan, stretched, then sat. Her hair was unbraided now, hanging dark and lustrous to her shoulders. 'I have some breakfast for you.'

'Did you dream of me?' she asked, her voice husky from sleep.

'There is no apple juice,' he told her. 'But the water is fresh and cold.'

'Then you did, prayer-man. Were they good dreams?'

'You should not speak this way to a priest,' he admonished her.

She laughed at him, and his face reddened. 'You *kol-isha* are a strange people.' Rising smoothly she walked to the bed, sitting cross-legged upon it. Taking the loaf she tore off a chunk and tasted it. 'Needs salt,' she said. He poured her a goblet of water and passed it to her. Her hand reached out, her fingers stroking his skin. 'Soft hands,' she whispered. 'Soft skin. Like a child.' Then she took the goblet and sipped the water.

'Why did you come here?' he asked.

'You brought me,' she told him, dipping her finger into the bowl of butter and licking it.

'Were you sent?'

'Yes. By my shaman, Kesa Khan. To fetch my brother home. But you know this.'

'Yes, but I just wondered . . .'

'Wondered what?'

'Ah, it does not matter. Enjoy your breakfast. The Abbot will see you before you leave. He will tell you where to find Belash.'

'There is still time, prayer-man,' she whispered, reaching out and taking his hand. He snatched it back.

'Please do not speak like this,' he pleaded. 'I find you . . . very unsettling.'

'You desire me.' It was a statement, accompanied by a smile.

Ekodas closed his eyes for a moment, struggling to compose his thoughts. 'Yes. But that in itself is not a sin, I believe.'

'Sin?'

'A wrong action . . . like a crime.'

'Like stealing the pony of your brother?' she enquired.

'Yes, exactly. That would be a sin. Indeed any theft, or lie, or malicious action is a sin.'

She nodded slowly. 'Why then is lovemaking a sin? Where is the theft? The lie? Or the malice?'

'It does not have to be just these actions,' he said, his voice close to a stammer. 'It is also the breaking of rules, or oaths. Each of us here made a promise to the Source. It would be breaking that promise.'

'Did your god ask you to make this promise?'

'No, but . . .'

'Then who did?'

He spread his hands. 'It is a part of our tradition. You understand? Rules made by holy men many centuries ago.'

'Ah, it is in the writings, then.'

'Exactly so.'

'We have no writings,' she said brightly. 'So we live and laugh, we make love and we fight. No diseases of the belly, no head pains, no bad dreams. Our god speaks to us from the land, not in writings.'

'It is the same god,' he assured her.

She shook her head. 'No, prayer-man, I don't think so. Our god is strong.'

'Will he save your people from the Gothir?' snapped Ekodas, before he could stop himself. 'I'm sorry! It was a thoughtless question. Please forgive me.'

'There is nothing to forgive, for you do not understand, Ekodas. Our god *is* the land, and the land makes us strong. We will fight. And we will either conquer or die. It does not matter to the land whether we win or lose, for alive or dead we are at one with it. The Nadir *are* the land.'

'Can you win?' he asked softly.

'Will you be sorry when I am dead?' she countered.

'Yes,' he told her, without hesitation.

Smoothly she rolled to her feet and moved in close to him, her arm circling his neck. Her lips brushed his cheek. 'Foolish Ekodas,' she whispered. Then she released him.

'Why am I foolish?' he asked.

'Take me to the Abbot. I wish to leave now.'

*

Waylander reined in the black gelding and dismounted, walking the last few paces to the crest of the hill where he bellied down and studied the line of mountains stretching from west to east across the great Sentran Plain. The hound Scar padded up the hill, stretching out alongside him.

There were three routes to the north, but which one should they take? North-east lay the Delnoch Pass, with its new six-walled fortress. That was the direct road to Gulgothir and the Mountains of the Moon, but would the commanding officer have been warned to watch for Waylander?

He sighed and swung his gaze to the north and the high lonely passes inhabited by Sathuli tribesmen, long-time enemies of the Drenai. No wagons passed through their lands, no convoys, no travellers. Ferocious fighters, the Sathuli lived their lives in isolation from the civilisations of both Gothir and Drenai.

Lastly there was Dros Purdol, the harbour fortress, far to the east. But beyond that was the great desert of Namib. Waylander had crossed it before. Twice. He had no wish to see it again.

No. He would have to risk Delnoch.

Just as he was about to push back from the skyline he caught a glint of light to the east. Remaining where he was he waited, eyes focused on the distant tree line. A column of riders appeared, lances held to the vertical, sunlight gleaming from the polished iron helms and weapons. There were some thirty lancers, moving slowly, conserving the strength of their mounts.

Waylander eased back from the crest then rose and walked to where the others waited. Scar followed, keeping close to Waylander's side. 'We'll wait here for an hour,' he said, 'then we'll make for Delnoch.'

'You see anything?' asked Angel.

'Lancers. They are riding for the fortress.'

'You think they might be looking for us?' put in Senta.

Waylander shrugged. 'Who knows? Karnak is anxious to see me dead. By now my description could be with every army unit within fifty miles.'

Miriel rose and strolled to the hilltop, crouching behind a screen of gorse to gaze down on the lancers. For some minutes she remained motionless, then returned to the group. 'The officer is Dun Egan,' she told Waylander. 'He is tired and hungry, and thinking about a woman he knows in a tavern by Wall Two. And yes, he has your description. Twenty of his men are behind us, to the south-west. They have orders to apprehend you.'

'What now?' asked Angel.

Waylander's expression was grim. 'Across the mountains,' he said at last.

'The Sathuli are fine fighters, and they don't like strangers,' Senta pointed out.

'I've been through before. To kill me they have to catch me.'

'You intend going alone?' asked Miriel softly.

'It is best,' he replied. 'You and the others make for Delnoch. I will find you beyond the mountains.'

'No. We should be together. My Talents can keep us safe.'

'There's truth in that,' Angel observed.

'Perhaps there is,' agreed Waylander, 'but against that, five riders raise more dust than one. Five horses make more noise than one. The high passes exaggerate every sound. A falling stone can sometimes be heard half a mile away. No. I go alone.' Miriel started to speak, but he touched a finger to her lips. 'No more argument, Miriel,' he said with a smile. 'I have hunted alone for more than half my life. I am at my strongest alone. Go to Delnoch, and once through the fortress head due north. I will find you.'

'I will be with you,' she whispered, leaning in close and kissing his cheek.

'Always,' he agreed.

Moving to his mount, Waylander swung into the saddle and touched heels to the gelding's side. The hound loped alongside as the black-garbed rider crested the hill. The lancers were tiny dots in the distance now and Waylander gave them not a moment of thought as he angled towards the rearing Delnoch peaks.

Alone.

His spirits soared. Much as he loved Miriel he felt a great release, a sense of freedom from the burdens of company. Glancing down at the hound he chuckled. 'Not entirely alone, eh Scar?' The dog cocked its head to one side and ran on, sniffing at the ground, seeking rabbit spoor. Waylander drew in a deep breath. The air was fresh and cold, blowing down from the snow-topped peaks. The Sathuli would be building their winter stores now, their thoughts far from raiding and war. With skill, and a little luck, he should be able to ride the high passes and the echo-haunted canyons without their knowledge.

A little luck? He thought of the route ahead – the narrow, ice-covered trails, the treacherous slopes, the frozen streams, the realms of the wolf, the bear and the mountain lion.

Fear touched him – and he laughed aloud. For with the onset of fear he felt the pounding of his heart, the rushing of blood in vein and muscle, the strength in his arms and torso. Right or wrong he knew this was what he had been born for, the lonely ride into danger, enemies all around. For what was fear if not the wine of life, and the taste of it thrilled him anew.

I have been dead these last five years, he realised. A walking corpse, though I did not know it. He thought of Danyal, and found himself remembering the joys of their life, without the sharp, jagged bitterness at her passing. The mountains loomed, grey and threatening.

And the man rode on.

*

Miriel sat silently in the garden of the tavern staring down over the colossal walls of Dros Delnoch. The journey to the

fortress had passed without incident, save for the bicker-
ing between Angel and Belash. At first Miriel found it
hard to understand the hatred festering within the
gladiator, then she used her Talent. She shivered at the
memory, and switched her line of thought. Her father
would now be travelling through the lands of the Sathuli.
A fiercely independent people, they had crossed the sea
from the deserts of Ventria three hundred years before,
settling in the Delnoch mountains. She knew little of their
history, save that they believed in the words of an ancient
prophet, and were persecuted for their beliefs in their
home country. They were a solitary race, hardy and
ferocious in battle, and permanently at war with the
Drenai.

She sighed. Waylander would not cross their lands
without a fight, she knew, and she prayed he would come
through safely.

Behind the three tavern buildings, the ancient keep
reared between the narrows of the Delnoch Pass. Impressive and strong, the keep was dwarfed by the new fortress
which now filled the valley. Miriel scanned the immense
structure, with its crenellated battlements of reinforced
granite, its massive gate-towers and turrets.

'They call it Egel's Folly,' said Angel, moving alongside
her and handing her a goblet of watered wine. Senta and
Belash followed him from the tavern and sat on the grass
with Miriel. 'Each of the walls is more than sixty feet high,
and the barracks can accommodate thirty thousand men.
Some of them have never been used. Never will be.'

'I have never seen anything like it,' she whispered. 'The
sentries on the first wall seem as small as insects from
here.'

'A magnificent waste of money,' said Senta. 'Twenty
thousand labourers, a thousand stone-masons, fifty
architects, hundreds of carpenters. And all built for a
dream.'

'A dream?' inquired Miriel.

Senta chuckled and turned to Belash. 'Yes. Egel said he
saw a vision of Belash and a few of his brothers – a

169

veritable ocean of warriors gathering against the Drenai. Hence this monstrosity.'

'It was built to keep out the Nadir?' asked Miriel, disbelieving.

'Indeed it was, Miriel,' said Senta. 'Six walls and a keep. The largest fortress in the world, to thwart the smallest enemy. For not one Nadir tribe numbers more than a thousand warriors.'

'But there are more than a thousand tribes,' pointed out Belash. 'The Uniter will bring them all together. One people. One king.'

'Such are the dreams of all poor peoples,' said Senta. 'The Nadir will never unite. They hate each other as much – if not more – than they hate us. They are always at war. And they take no prisoners.'

'That's not true,' hissed Angel. 'They do take prisoners – and then they torture them to death. Men, women and children. They are the most despicable race.'

'No true Nadir would torture children,' said Belash, his dark eyes angry. 'They are killed swiftly.'

'I know what I saw!' snapped Angel. 'And do not think to call me a liar!'

Belash's hand moved to his knife. Angel's fingers curled around the hilt of his sword. Miriel stepped between them. 'We will not fight amongst ourselves,' she said, laying her hand on Angel's arm. 'There is evil in all races, but only a foolish man condemns an entire people.'

'You did not see what I saw!' he told her.

'But I have seen it,' she said softly. 'The overturned wagons, the looting and the deaths. And I can see your father with his arm around you, holding his cloak before your eyes. It was an evil day, Angel, but you must let it go. The memory is poisoning you.'

'Stay out of my head!' he roared suddenly, pulling back from her and striding towards the tavern.

'He carries demons in his soul,' said Belash.

'We all carry them,' added Senta.

Miriel sighed. 'He was only nine years old when he saw the attack, and the screams have been with him ever since.

But he no longer sees the truth – perhaps he never did. His father's cloak blocked the most savage of the sights, and he does not remember that there were others in the attack who were not Nadir. They wore dark cloaks, and their weapons were of blackened steel.'

'Knights of Blood,' said Belash.

Miriel nodded. 'I believe so.'

Belash rose. 'I shall stroll and look at this fortress. I wish to see these walls my people inspired.'

He wandered away and Senta moved alongside Miriel. 'It is nice to be alone,' he said.

'You are picturing me on a bed covered with sheets of satin. It does not please me.'

He grinned. 'It is not courteous to read a man's thoughts.'

'It does not concern you that I know what you are thinking?'

'Not at all. There is nothing to shame me. You are a beautiful woman. No man could sit with you for long without thinking of satin sheets, or soft grass, or summer hay.'

'There is more to life than rutting!' she told him, aware that she was blushing.

'How would you know, beauty? You have no experience of such things.'

'I'll never marry you.'

'You cut me to the quick, beauty. How can you make that judgement? You don't know me yet.'

'I know enough.'

'Nonsense. Take my hand for a moment.' Reaching out he gently clasped her wrist, his fingers sliding down over hers. 'Never mind my thoughts. Feel my touch. Is it not gentle? Is it not pleasing?'

She snatched back her hand. 'No, it is not!'

'Ah ha! Now you lie, beauty. I may not have your Talents, but I know what you felt. And it was far from unpleasant.'

'Your arrogance is as colossal as these walls,' she raged.

'Yes, it is,' he agreed. 'And with good reason. I am a very talented fellow.'

171

'You are conceited and see no further than your own desires. So tell me, Senta, what is it that you offer me? And please, no boasts about the bed-chamber.'

'You say my name so beautifully.'

'Answer my question, damn you. And do remember that I shall know if you are lying.'

He smiled at her. 'You are for me,' he said softly, 'as I am for you. What would I offer you? Everything I have, beauty,' he whispered, his eyes holding to hers. 'And everything I will ever have.'

For a moment she was silent. 'I know that you believe the words as you say them,' she said. 'But I do not believe you have the strength to live by them.'

'That may be true,' he admitted.

'And you were prepared to kill Angel and my father. You think I can forgive that?'

'I hope so,' he told her. And in that moment she saw within his thoughts a flickering image, a remembrance that he was struggling to keep hidden. It shocked her.

'You weren't planning to kill Angel! You were ready to die.'

His smile faded and he shrugged. 'You asked me to spare him, beauty. I thought perhaps you loved him.'

'You didn't even know me – you don't know me now. How could you be prepared to lay down your life in that way?'

'Do not be too impressed. I like the old man. And I would have tried to disarm him, wound him maybe.'

'He would have killed you.'

'Would you have been sorry?'

'No – not then.'

'But you would be now?'

'I don't know . . . yes. But not because I love you. You have had many women – and you have told them all that you loved them. Would you have died for them?'

'Perhaps. I have always been a romantic. But with you it is different. I know that.'

'I do not believe love can strike that swiftly,' she said.

'Love is a strange beast, Miriel. Sometimes it leaps from

172

hiding and strikes like a sudden spear. At other times it can creep up on you, slowly, skilfully.'

'Like an assassin?'

'Indeed so,' he agreed with a bright smile.

11

Jahunda notched an arrow to his bowstring and waited for the rider to emerge from the trees. His fingers were cold, but his blood ran hot with the hunt. The Drenai had chosen his route with care, avoiding the wide, much-used paths, and holding to the narrow deer-trails. But even so Jahunda had spotted him, for the Lord Sathuli had ordered him to watch the south from Chasica Peak, and no one could enter Sathuli lands from the Sentran Plain without being observed from Chasica. It was a great honour to be so trusted – especially for a fourteen-year-old with no blood kills to his name. But the Lord Sathuli knows I will be a great warrior and hunter, thought Jahunda. And he chose me for this task.

Jahunda had sent up a signal smoke then clambered down from the peak, making his way carefully to the first ambush site. But the Drenai had cut to the right, angling up into the high pass. Hooking his bow over his shoulder Jahunda ran to the second site, overlooking the deer-trail. The Drenai must emerge here. He chose his arrow with care, and hoped he could make the kill before the others arrived. Then the horse would be his by right, and a fine beast it looked. He closed his eyes and listened for the soft clopping of hooves in the snow. Sweat was seeping from under his white burnoose and fear made his mouth dry. The Drenai was no merchant. This one was a careful man who knew where he was riding and the danger he was in. That he travelled here at all spoke well of his bravery, and his confidence. Jahunda was anxious that the first shaft should strike a mortal blow.

There was no sound from the snow-shrouded trees and Jahunda risked a glance around the boulder.

Nothing.

But the man had to be close. There was no other route.

174

Jahunda inched his way to the left and leaned out. Still nothing. Perhaps the rider had doubled back. Maybe he should have waited by the first site. Indecision rippled through him. The Drenai could be relieving himself against a tree, he told himself. Give it time! His heart was beating fast and he tried to calm himself. But the horse was magnificent! He could sell it and buy Shora a shawl of silk, and one of those bangles with the blue stones that Zaris sold at ridiculously high prices. Oh, how Shora would love him if he arrived at her father's house bearing such gifts. He would be an acclaimed warrior, a hunter, a defender of the land. It would hardly matter then that he could not yet grow a beard.

He heard the clop of hooves and swallowed hard. Wait! Be patient. He drew back on the string and glanced up at the sun. It would cast a shadow from high and to the right of the rider and from his hiding place behind the boulder Jahunda could time his attack perfectly. He licked his lips and watched for the shadow of the horse. As it drew alongside the boulder he stepped out, bow raised.

The saddle was empty. There was no rider.

Jahunda blinked. Something hard struck the back of his head and he fell to his knees, his bow falling from his fingers. 'I am dying!' he thought. And his last thoughts were of beautiful Shora.

He felt rough hands shaking him and slowly came to consciousness.

'What happened, boy?' asked Jitsan, the Lord Sathuli's chief scout.

He tried to explain, but one of the other hunters came up, tapping Jitsan's shoulder. 'The Drenai sent his horse foward then moved around behind the boy and clubbed him. He is heading for Senac Pass.'

'Can you walk?' Jitsan asked Jahunda.

'I think so.'

'Then go home, child.'

'I am ashamed,' said Jahunda, hanging his head.

'You are alive,' pointed out Jitsan, rising and moving off swiftly, the six hunters following him.

There would be no horse for the young Sathuli warrior now. No bangle. No shawl for Shora.

He sighed and gathered up his bow.

*

Waylander dismounted, leading the gelding up the steep slope. Scar padded alongside him, not liking the cold snow under his paws. 'There's worse to come,' said the man.

He had seen the signal smoke and watched, with grim amusement, the antics of the young Sathuli sentry. The boy could not have been more than fourteen. Callow and inexperienced, he had run too swiftly for the ambush site, leaving footprints easily seen leading to the boulder behind which he hid. There was a time Waylander would have killed him. 'You're getting soft,' he scolded himself. But he did not regret the action.

At the top of the slope he halted, shading his eyes from the snow glare and seeking out the route to Senac Pass. It was twelve years since he had come this way, and that had been summer-time, the slopes of the mountains green and verdant. The wind was biting through his jerkin and he untied his fur-lined cloak from behind his saddle and unrolled it, fastening it into place with a brooch of bronze and a leather thong.

He studied the trail behind him then walked on, leading the gelding. The trail was narrow, wending its way down a snow-covered slope of scree and on to a long, twisting ledge no more than four feet wide. To the right was the mountain, to the left a dizzying drop into the valley some four hundred feet below. In summer the journey across the ledge had been fraught enough but now, ice-covered and treacherous . . .

You must be insane, he told himself. He started to walk, but the gelding held back. The wind was whistling across the mountain face and the horse wanted no part of such a venture.

'Come on, boy!' urged Waylander, tugging on the reins. But the gelding would not move. Behind the horse Scar let out a deep, menacing growl. The gelding leapt forward, almost sending Waylander over the edge. He swayed on the brink, but his hold on the reins saved him and he pulled himself back to safety. The ledge wound on around the mountain face for almost a quarter of a mile until, just beyond a bend, it was split by a steep scree slope leading down into the valley.

Waylander took a deep breath, and was just about to step on to the scree, when Scar growled again. The horse lurched forward, pulling the reins from Waylander's hand. The beast hit the scree head-first, and tumbled down the slope. An arrow flashed past Waylander's head. Spinning, he drew two knives. Scar leapt to attack the first Sathuli to come into sight around the bend behind them. The hound's great jaws snapped at the archer's face. Dropping his bow the warrior threw himself back, cannoning into a second man, who fell from the ledge, his scream echoing away. Scar hurled himself upon the first man, fangs locking to the man's forearm.

Waylander moved closer to the rock-face as a third Sathuli edged into sight. The warrior raised his tulwar over the hound. Waylander's arm snapped forward, the black-bladed knife slicing between the man's ribs. With a grunt he dropped the tulwar and fell to his knees, before toppling to his face in the snow.

'Here, Scar!' shouted Waylander. For a moment only the dog continued to rip and tear at the first Sathuli, but when Waylander called again it released its grip and backed away. Unhooking the small crossbow from his belt Waylander loaded it and waited. The man with the injured arm was lying on the brink of the precipice, breathing hoarsely. The other warrior was dead.

'Who is leader here?' called Waylander, in halting Sathuli.

'Jitsan,' came the reply. 'And I speak your tongue better than you do mine.'

'Do you like to wager?'

'On what?'

'On how long your friend there lives if you do not come for him and bind his wounds.'

'Speak plainly, Drenai!'

'I am passing through. I am no danger to the Sathuli. Nor am I a soldier. Give me your word the hunt will cease and I will leave here now. You can rescue your friend. If not, I wait. We fight. He dies.'

'If you wait you die,' shouted Jitsan.

'Even so,' answered Waylander. The injured man groaned and tried to roll himself from the ledge to certain death on the rocks below. It was a brave move, and Waylander found himself admiring the warrior. Jitsan called out to him in Sathuli and the man ceased his struggle.

'Very well, Drenai, you have my word.' Jitsan stepped into sight, his sword sheathed.

Waylander flicked the bolts from the crossbow and loosed the strings. 'Let's go, dog,' he said, and leapt to the scree, sliding down the slope on his haunches. Scar followed him instantly, tumbling and rolling past his master.

But Waylander had misjudged the speed of the descent and he lost his grip on the crossbow as he struck a hidden rock which catapulted him into the air, spinning and cartwheeling. Relaxing his muscles he rolled himself into a ball and prayed he would not strike a tree or a boulder.

At last the dizzying fall slowed and he came to a stop in a deep drift of snow. His body was bruised and aching, and two of his knives had fallen from their sheaths. Curiously his sword was still in its scabbard. He sat up. His head was spinning, and he felt a rush of nausea. After it had passed he pushed himself to his knees. As well as the two knives, his crossbow quiver was empty, his leggings were torn and his right thigh was gashed and bleeding.

To his right lay the gelding, its neck broken in the fall. Waylander took a long, deep breath, his fingers probing at his bruised ribs. Nothing seemed broken. Scar padded over to him, licking his face. The stitches on the dog's side had opened and a thin trickle of blood was oozing from the wound.

'Well, we made it, boy,' said Waylander. Slowly and with great care he stood. Several of his crossbow bolts and one of his knives lay nearby, close to the dead gelding. Gathering the weapons he searched around the snow for his knife, but could not find it. Scar ran back up the slope and returned with the crossbow in his jaws.

A second search left Waylander with twelve bolts and one knife recovered. The gash in his leg was not deep, requiring no stitches, but he bound the wound with a bandage taken from his saddlebag and then sat on a jutting rock and shared some dried meat with the hound.

High above him he saw the signal smoke. Reaching down he stroked Scar's huge head. 'You just can't trust the Sathuli,' he said. The hound twisted its head and licked the man's hand.

Waylander stood and surveyed the valley. The snow was deep here, but the way to Senac Pass lay open.

Lifting the food sack from the dead horse he set off towards the north.

*

Slowly the six hundred black-cloaked warriors filed into the huge hall, forming twenty ranks before the dais on which stood Zhu Chao and his six captains. Red lanterns glowed with crimson light and shadows flickered across the great curving beams of the high ceiling.

All was silent. Zhu Chao spread wide his arms, his caped gown arching down from his shoulders like the wings of a demon. 'The day is here, comrades!' he shouted. 'Tomorrow the Ventrians attack Purdol and the pass at Skeln. Gothir troops will then march on the Sentran Plain. And five thousand soldiers will obliterate the Nadir wolves, bringing us the treasures of Kar-Barzac.

'Within the month all three great nations will be ruled by the Brotherhood. And we will have the power our strength and our faith deserves.

'The Days of Blood are here! The days when, for us, the only law will be to do as we will, wherever we choose.' A thunderous roar rose up from the ranks, but he quelled it with a swift wave of his hand. 'We are talking about power, comrades. The Elder Races did not understand the power

179

they held. The oceans drank their cities, and their culture is all but lost to us.

'But there is one great centre of their might, named in all the *grimoires*. In the Mountains of the Moon lies the citadel of Kar-Barzac. The arcane strength of the Elders still flows there, and with it we will find not only the instruments to maintain our rule, but the secret of immortality. Win this war and we will live forever, our dreams made true, our lusts sated, our desires fulfilled.' This time he let the cheering mount, and stood arms folded, drinking in the adulation. Gradually the sound died away. Zhu Chao spoke again.

'To those who are chosen to ride against the Wolves I say this: kill them all, and their whores and their brats. Leave nothing alive. Burn their bodies and grind their bones to powder. Consign their dreams to the ashes of history!'

As the renewed cheering died down he strode from the dais, exiting the hall through a small side door. Followed by his captains he made his way to a suite of rooms in the western wing of the palace. Here he stretched himself out on a couch and bade his officers sit around him.

'The plans are all set?' he asked the first of his officers, Innicas, a wide-shouldered albino in his mid-forties, with a forked white beard and a jagged scar across his brow. His long hair was braided and his pink eyes, unblinking, shone with a cold light.

'Yes, lord. Galen will see Karnak delivered to us. He has convinced him to meet with the Sathuli chieftain. He will be captured and delivered alive to Gulgothir. But tell me, lord, why do we need him? Why not just slit his throat and be done with it?'

Zhu Chao smiled. 'Men like Karnak are rare indeed. They have power, deep elemental strength. He will be a worthy gift to Shemak, as will the Emperor. Two lords beneath the sacrificial knife. When has our master known such a sacrifice? And I shall enjoy watching both men beg for their lives.'

'And the Source priests?' enquired a second officer, a slim man with thinning, shoulder-length grey hair.

'Dardalion and his comical troop?' Zhu Chao gave a dry laugh. 'Tonight, Casta. Use sixty men. Destroy their souls as they sleep.'

'I am concerned, lord,' said Innicas, 'about the man, Waylander. Was he not allied with Dardalion many years ago?'

'He is a killer. No more, no less. He has no understanding of the mystic arts.'

'He slew nine of our warriors,' pointed out Casta.

'He has a step-daughter, Miriel. It is she who has Talent. And with him were two arena warriors named Senta and Angel. Also there was the renegade Belash. The timing of the attack was unfortunate, but they will not survive a second assault – that I promise you.'

'I mean no disrespect, sir, but this Waylander does seem to show a spectacular talent for survival,' said Innicas. 'Do we know where he is?'

'At this moment he is being pursued through Sathuli lands. He is wounded, alone   save for a mangy hound – and has little food and no water. The hunters are closing in. We shall see how far his talent for survival can be stretched.'

'And the girl?' asked the grey-haired Casta.

'At Dros Delnoch. But she will join Kesa Khan. She will be at Kar-Barzac.'

'You want her taken alive?' asked Melchidak.

'It matters not to me,' answered Zhu Chao, 'but if she is then give her to the men. Let them amuse themselves. When they are done, sacrifice her to the master.'

'You spoke, lord, of the power of the Elders and immortality,' said Casta. 'What awaits us at Kar-Barzac?'

Zhu Chao smiled. 'One day at a time, Casta. When the Nadir wolves are dead I will show you the Crystal Chamber.'

*

Ekodas lay in his pallet bed listening to the sounds of the night, the flapping of bats' wings beyond the open window, the sibilant sighing of the winds of winter. It was cold, and the single blanket did little to retain body heat.

In the next bed Duris was snoring. Ekodas lay awake, ignoring the cold, his thoughts focused on the Nadir woman, Shia. He wondered where she was, and whether she had found her brother. He sighed and opened his eyes. Moonlight was casting deep shadows from the rafters of the rough-wrought ceiling and a winter moth was flitting between the beams.

Closing his eyes once more Ekodas sought the freedom of flight. As usual this proved difficult, but at last he soared free of his body and floated alongside the moth, gazing down on his sleeping comrades. The moon was shining in a cloudless sky as he flew from the temple, and the country-side was bathed in spectral light.

'Are you restless, brother?' asked Magnic, appearing alongside him.

'Yes,' he answered.

'As am I. But it is silent here, and we are free of the flesh.' It was true and Ekodas acknowledged it. The world was a different place when viewed through spirit eyes, tranquil and beautiful, eternal and almost sentient. 'You spoke well, Ekodas. You surprised me.'

'I surprised myself,' he admitted. 'Though, as I am sure you are aware, I am not totally convinced – even by my own arguments.'

'I think none of us are truly sure,' said Magnic softly, 'but there must be balance. Without it harmony cannot be found. I fear the Brotherhood, and I loathe and despise all they stand for. You know why?'

'Tell me.'

'Because I long for such pleasures myself. Deep in me I can see the attraction of evil, Ekodas. We are stronger than normal men. Our Talents could earn us fame, riches and all the pleasures known to man. And in my quiet moments I know that I lust for these things.'

'You are not responsible for your desires,' said Ekodas. 'They are primal, a part of being human. Only if we act upon them do we sin.'

'I know that, but it is why I could not take up the staff. I could never be a priest of love, never. At some time in the future I would succumb to my desires. This is why the Thirty is for me. I have no future, save with the Source. You are different, my friend. You are strong. Like Dardalion once was.'

'You thought me a coward,' pointed out Ekodas.

Magnic smiled. 'Yes, but I was seeing only my own lack of courage. Transferring it to you.' He sighed. 'Now that our way is set I see everything differently. And now I must continue my watch.' Magnic vanished and Ekodas floated alone in the night sky. The temple below was grey and forbidding, its turrets rearing against the sky like upraised fists.

'It is still a fortress,' Shia had said. And so it was. Just like us, Ekodas realised. Prayer within, might without. There was comfort in the thought, for a fortress, no matter how many spears, swords and arrows were contained within it, could never be an offensive weapon.

He soared higher and to the north, through thin, misty clouds that were forming above the mountains. Below him now the mighty fortress of Dros Delnoch spanned the pass.

He floated down. On the last wall he saw a tall, dark-haired woman, sitting beside a handsome golden-haired man. The man reached out to take the woman's hand, but she drew back, turning her head to gaze up at Ekodas.

'Who are you?' she asked him, her spirit voice loud as thunder within him. Ekodas was astonished and suddenly disconcerted. Swiftly he flew high and away from the fortress. Such power! His mind reeled.

Just then a terrible scream filled his ears. Brief, agonising, and then terminated. He sped for the temple.

A man appeared alongside him, a blade of fire in his hand. Ekodas twisted in the air, the sword hissing by him. He reacted without conscious thought, the long years of his training and Dardalion's endlessly patient tuition, coming together in an instant to save his life. 'In spirit form,' Dardalion had told them, 'we are naked and unarmed. But I will teach you to craft armour from faith, swords from courage and shields made from belief. Then you will stand against the demons of the dark, and the men who aspire to be like them.'

Ekodas armoured himself with a shining breastplate of silver, a glimmering shield appearing on his left forearm. He parried the next blow with his own sword of silver light.

His opponent was protected by black armour and a full-faced helm. Ekodas blocked a thrust then sent his own blade cleaving into the man's neck. The sword of light flashed through the dark armour like sunlight piercing a storm cloud. There was no blood. No scream of pain. His assailant merely disappeared without a sound. But Ekodas knew that wherever the man's body lay the heart had stopped beating, and only a silent, unmarked corpse would lie witness to the battle beneath the stars.

Ekodas flew on to the temple. 'Dardalion!' he pulsed, using all his power. '*Dardalion!*'

Three opponents appeared around him. The first he slew with a slashing cut across the belly, the silver sword slicing through the dark armour with terrible ease. The second he killed with a riposte to the head. The third loomed behind him, blade raised.

Vishna appeared, lancing his sword through the man's back. More warriors appeared above the temple, and the Thirty gathered, silver against black, swords of light against blades of fire.

Ekodas fought on, his sword forming glittering arcs of white light as it clove into the enemy. Beside him Vishna battled with controlled fury. All around them the battle raged in an awful silence.

And then it was over.

Weary beyond anything he had ever experienced, Ekodas returned to his body and sat up. He reached over to Duris, but the man was dead. So too was Branic in the far bed.

Ekodas stumbled from the room, down to the hall. One by one the members of the Thirty gathered there. Twenty-three priests had survived the attack, and Ekodas looked from face to face, seeking out those to whom he was closest. Glendrin was alive. And Vishna. But Magnic was gone. It seemed only moments before he had been talking with the blond priest about life and desire. Now there was only a body to be buried, and they would never, in this world, speak again.

The full weight of sorrow descended upon Ekodas and he sank to the bench-seat, resting his elbows on the table. Vishna moved alongside him, placing a hand on his shoulder.

'Your warning saved us, Ekodas,' he said.

'My warning?'

'You woke Dardalion. He made the Gather.'

Before Ekodas could respond Dardalion spoke up from the far end of the hall. 'My brothers, it is time to pray for the souls of our departed friends.' One by one he named them and many tears were shed as he talked of them. 'They are with the Source now, and are blessed. But we remain. Some days ago we asked for another sign. I think that we have just seen it. The Brotherhood are preparing to ride against the Nadir. It is my belief that we should be in the Mountains of the Moon to receive them. But that is only my view. What is the view of the Thirty?'

Ekodas rose. 'The Mountains of the Moon,' he said.

Vishna echoed the words, as did Glendrin, Palista, fat Merlon and all the surviving priests.

'Tomorrow then,' said Dardalion. 'And now let us prepare the bodies of our friends for burial.'

12

Angel's head was pounding, and his anger flowed unabated as Miriel paid the fine to the master-at-arms.

'We don't like troublemakers here,' the man told Miriel. 'Only his reputation prevented him from receiving the flogging he deserves.'

'We are leaving Delnoch today,' she said, smiling sweetly as the man counted out the twenty silver coins.

'I mean, who does he think he is?' the soldier persisted.

'Why not ask me, you arrogant whoreson?' stormed Angel, his hands gripping the bars of the cell door.

'You see?' said the man, shaking his head.

'He is not usually quarrelsome,' replied Miriel, casting a warning glance at the former gladiator.

'I think he should have been flogged,' put in Senta, with a broad grin. 'What a mess. The tavern looks as though a tidal wave flowed through it. Disgraceful behaviour.'

Angel merely glared. The master-at-arms slowly rose and lifted a huge ring of keys from a hook by the door. 'He is to be taken straight from Delnoch. No stopping. Are your horses outside?'

'They are,' said Miriel.

'Good.' He unlocked the cell door and the glowering Angel stepped into the room. One eye was blackened and half-closed, and his lower lip was split.

'I'd say it was an improvement,' said Senta.

Angel pushed past him, striding out into the sunlight. Belash was waiting, his dark eyes inscrutable.

'Don't say a word!' warned Angel, snatching the reins of his mount from the tethering post and climbing into the saddle. Miriel and Senta emerged into the sunlight, the master-at-arms behind them.

'Straight out, no stopping,' repeated the soldier.

Miriel swung into the saddle and led the group down to

the gate-tunnel below the fifth wall. Sentries examined the passes Miriel had obtained and waved them through, across the open ground to the next tunnel, and the next. At last they rode out into the pass itself.

Senta moved his horse alongside Angel's mount. 'How are you feeling?' he asked.

'Why don't you go . . .' He closed his mouth on the words as Miriel reined back, swinging her horse alongside.

'What happened, Angel?' she asked.

'Why don't you read my mind and find out?' he snapped.

'No,' she said. 'You and Senta are right – it *is* bad manners. I'll not do it again, I promise. So tell me how the fight started.'

'It was just a fight,' he answered with a shrug. 'Nothing to tell.'

Miriel turned to Belash. 'You were there?'

The Nadir nodded. 'A man asked old Hard-to-Kill what it is like to have a face that a cow has trampled on.'

'Yes? And then?'

'He said, "Like this!" Then he broke the man's nose.' Belash mimicked the blow, a straight left.

Senta's laughter pealed out, echoing in the pass. 'It is not something to laugh at,' insisted Miriel. 'One man with a broken nose and jaw, two others with broken arms. One even fractured his leg.'

'That was the man he threw out of the window,' said Belash. 'And it was not even open.'

'Why were you so angry?' Miriel asked Angel. 'Back at the cabin you were always so . . . so controlled.'

He relaxed and sat slumped in the saddle. 'That was then,' he told her, touching his heels to the gelding and riding ahead.

Senta glanced at Miriel. 'You don't see a great deal without your Talent, do you?' he observed, urging his horse into a canter and coming alongside Angel once more.

'What now?' asked the gladiator.

'You took out six men with your bare hands. That's impressive, Angel.'

'Is there a joke coming?'

187

'No. I'm sorry I missed the fight.'

'It wasn't much. A bunch of town-dwellers. Not a single muscle in sight.'

'I'm glad you decided to stay with us. I'd have missed your company.'

'I'd not miss yours, boy.'

'Oh yes, you would. Tell me, how long have you been in love with her?'

'What kind of a stupid question is that?' stormed Angel. 'I'm not in love. Shemak's balls, Senta, look at me! I'm almost as old as her father and my face would curdle milk. No, she'll be better off with a younger man. Even you, may my tongue turn black for saying it.'

Senta was about to speak when he saw a rider emerging from the rocks to the left. It was a young Nadir woman with jet-black hair, wearing a goatskin tunic and tan leggings. Belash galloped past them and leapt from the saddle. The woman dismounted and embraced him. Miriel, Senta and Angel sat their mounts quietly as the two Nadir conversed in their own tongue. Then Belash led the girl to the waiting trio.

'This is Shia, my sister. She was sent to find me,' he told them.

'It is good to meet you,' said Senta.

'Why? You do not know me.'

'It is a traditional greeting,' he explained.

'Ah. What is the traditional response?'

'That depends on the circumstances,' said Senta. 'And this is Miriel.' Shia glanced at the tall mountain woman, seeing the knives on the black baldric and the sabre at her side.

'What a strange people,' she said. 'Men who live like women and women who arm themselves like men. Truly it is beyond understanding.'

'And this is Angel.'

'Yes,' she said. 'Old Hard-to-Kill. It-is-good-to-meet-you.' Angel shook his head and grunted. Tugging his reins he moved off down the pass. 'Was the greeting incorrect?' Shia asked Senta.

188

'He's having a bad day,' observed the swordsman.

*

Bodalen tried to blame his trembling on the cold wind hissing down from the high passes of the Mountains of the Moon, but he knew better. Seven days from Gulgothir, and deep into Nadir territory his fear was almost uncontrollable. The eleven riders had skirted three small tent villages and encountered no hostile action, but Bodalen's mind was filled with images of torture and mutilation. He had heard many stories of the Nadir, and the thought that the tribesmen were close was unmanning him.

What am I doing here, he asked himself. Riding into a hostile land with scum like Gracus and his men. It's your fault, Father. Always pushing, cajoling, forcing! I'm not like you. I never was, nor would I wish to be! But you made me what I am.

He recalled the day Galen had first approached him, bringing with him the refined Lorassium leaf, and remembered with pleasure the taste of it upon his tongue, bitter and numbing. And with it the exquisite thrill that ran through his veins. All his fears vanished, all his dreams grew. Joy beyond reckoning flooded his senses. Oh, yes. The memories of the orgies that had followed aroused him even now, as his horse slowly trudged along the mountain trail. Passion, and the daring excitement of pain inflicted on willing – aye and unwilling – partners, the slender whips, the begging screams.

Then Galen had introduced him to the Lord Zhu Chao. And the promises began. When Karnak – that bloated, self-obsessed tyrant – was dead it would be Bodalen who would rule the Drenai. And he could fill his palace with concubines and slaves. A lifetime of pleasure, free from restraint. What price those promises now?

He shivered and swung to see the dark, hawk-like Gracus riding just behind him, the other riders following in a silent line. 'Almost there, Lord Bodalen,' said Gracus, unsmiling.

Bodalen nodded, but did not reply. He knew he lacked

his father's physical courage, but he lacked nothing of his intelligence. Zhu Chao no longer saw him as a person of value. He was being used as an assassin.

Where had it all gone wrong? He licked his lips. That was easy to answer. When that damned girl had died.

Waylander's daughter.

What a cursed trick of fate!

His horse reached the crest of the trail and Bodalen gazed down on a green valley, with sparkling streams. It was some two miles across and perhaps four deep, and at the centre reared an ancient fortress with four turrets and a portcullis gate. Bodalen blinked and rubbed his eyes. The turrets were leaning and twisted, the walls uneven, as if the earth had reared up below the structure. And yet it still stood.

Gracus drew alongside. 'Kar-Barzac,' he said.

'It looks like something fashioned by a drunken man,' said Bodalen.

Gracus shrugged, unconcerned. 'We can shelter there,' he answered.

Slowly the eleven riders filed down into the valley. Bodalen could not take his eyes from the citadel. The windows, archers' slits, were not straight but crooked, each a different height, some canted, others stretched. 'It couldn't have been built like that, surely?' he asked Gracus. One of the towers leaned out at an impossible angle, and yet there were no cracks in the great stones. As they grew closer Bodalen remembered a visit to an armoury when he was a child. Karnak had showed him a great furnace. They had thrown an iron helm into the fire and the boy had watched as it slowly melted. Kar-Barzac was like that helm.

They rode across the valley and Gracus pointed at a nearby tree. The trunk was split and had curled around itself, forming a weird knot. And the leaves were sharp and long, five-pronged and red as blood. Bodalen had never seen a tree like it.

As they neared the citadel they saw the half-eaten carcass of a bighorn sheep. Gracus angled his mount to ride close to the body. Bodalen followed him. The sheep's eyes were gone, but the head remained, mouth wide open.

'By the blood of Missael!' whispered Bodalen. The sheep had short, pointed fangs.

'This valley is bewitched!' said one of the men.

'Be silent!' roared Gracus, dismounting. He knelt by the carcass. 'It looks as if it has been chewed by rats,' he said. 'The bite-marks are small.' He stood and swung into the saddle.

Bodalen felt his unease growing. Everything in this valley seemed unnatural. Sweat rolled down his back. He glanced at Gracus, noting the beads of perspiration on his brow. 'Is it just fear, or is it hotter here?' he asked the warrior.

'It's hotter,' answered Gracus. 'But that's often the way with mountain valleys.'

'Not this hot, surely?'

'Let's get to the castle,' said Gracus.

A horse screamed and reared, unseating the rider. Instantly a host of rat-like creatures swarmed from the long grass, leaping on the man, covering him in a blanket of grey striped fur. Blood spouted from a score of wounds. Gracus swore and kicked his horse into a gallop, Bodalen following him.

No one even looked back.

The ruined gates of the castle loomed before them and the ten remaining riders galloped into the courtyard beyond. This too was uneven, but showed no cracks, nor breaks in the marble. Bodalen swung down from the saddle and ran to a rampart stair, climbing swiftly to the crooked battlements. Out on the valley floor all was still, save for the writhing, grey fur mounds where once had been horse and man.

'We can't stay here!' said Bodalen, as Gracus joined him at the battlements.

'The master has ordered it. That is an end to the matter.'

'What were those things?'

'I don't know. Some kind of small cat, perhaps.'

'Cats don't hunt like that,' insisted Bodalen.

'Rats! Cats! What difference does it make? The master says to hide here and kill Kesa Khan. That we will do.'

'But what if there are creatures like that living below the castle? What then, Gracus?'

'We will die,' answered the warrior, with a grim smile. 'So let us hope there are none.'

*

Waylander lay flat, he and Scar part-covered by his cloak, reversed now so that the sheepskin lining merged with the snow around him. His right arm was stretched out over the dog and he stroked the broad head.

'Stay silent, boy,' he whispered. 'Our lives depend on it.'

No more than sixty paces back down the trail seven Sathuli warriors were examining tracks in the snow. The gash in Waylander's leg was healing fast, but the wound in his upper left arm nagged at him. They had almost surprised him two days before, laying an ambush in a narrow pass. Four Sathuli had died in the attack, a fifth left mortally wounded, his lifeblood gushing from a tear in the great artery at the groin. Scar had killed two, but had it not been for a sudden change in the direction of the wind which alerted the hound, Waylander would now be dead. As it was his arm ached, the wound constantly leaking blood. It was too far back for him to stitch the tear, and too close to the shoulder joint to bandage. A low rumbling growl began in Scar's throat, but he patted the dog, whispering soothing words.

The seven Sathuli were trying to make sense of the tracks leading up the hill. Waylander knew what they were thinking. The human footprints were leading north, but the tracks of the hound went both up and down the hill. The Sathuli were confused. At the top of the slope the trail narrowed, a huge boulder by the trees making an ideal hiding-place. Not one of the warriors wanted to walk that slope, fearing a hidden crossbowman. Waylander could not hear their arguments, but he saw two of them gesticulating, pointing to the east. Waylander had taken a chance, moving carefully up the slope, then retracing his steps, walking backwards, placing his feet in the tracks he had made during the climb. Then he had lifted Scar, hurling the yelping hound into a snow drift to the left of the trail. A long branch overhung the slope here and Waylander had leapt to grasp it, moving hand over hand until he dropped to the ground by the trunk. Then, the huge hound beside him, he had hunkered down to wait for the Sathuli.

He was cold and wet. Reversing the cloak made him almost invisible in the snow, but it also countered the heat-retaining qualities of the sheepskin and he began to shiver.

The Sathuli concluded their discussions. Three men moved up the slope, two heading to the right of the trail and two to the left.

Waylander winced as he pulled his crossbow into position, the wound in his arm seeping fresh blood. Silently he eased himself back, moving behind a snow-covered screen of bushes, then traversing the slope and climbing to where several fallen trees had created a latticed wall on the hillside. Scar padded behind him, tongue lolling from his massive jaws.

The two Sathuli came in sight. Both carried short hunting bows, arrows notched. Waylander laid his hand on Scar's shoulder, gently pushing him down. 'Quiet now!'

The white-robed warriors drew alongside the tree wall. Waylander rose, arm extended. The first bolt flew, punching through the leading warrior's temple. He dropped without a sound. The second swung, dropped his bow and drew his tulwar.

'Face me like a man, blade to blade!' he demanded.

'No,' replied Waylander. The second bolt slashed through the man's robe, cleaving into his heart. His mouth opened. The tulwar dropped from his hand. He took two tottering steps towards Waylander, then pitched to his face in the snow.

Retrieving his bolts Waylander stripped the white robes from the first corpse and the burnoose from the second. Within moments he became a Sathuli warrior. Scar padded out and stood before him, head cocked to one side, nostrils quivering. 'It is still me,' said the man, kneeling down and extending his hand. Scar edged cautiously forward, sniffing at the outstretched fingers. Satisfied, the hound sat back on its haunches. Waylander patted its head.

'Time to move,' said the man. Reloading the crossbow he carefully traversed the slope.

By now the other hunters would have found where the tracks stopped, and they would be regrouping, rethinking their strategy. Then it would become apparent that two of their number were missing, and they would know Waylander was behind them. They would have two choices: wait for him to come to them, or continue the hunt.

Waylander had fought the Sathuli before, both as a soldier leading troops, and as a lone traveller. They were a patient people, yet also ruthless and courageous. But he did not think they would wait for him. Trusting in the advantage of numbers they would set out to find their missing companions and then follow his tracks. Therefore, since he could not disguise his trail, he would have to render it useless to them.

Reaching the top of the slope he moved silently into the snow-shrouded pine wood. There were few sounds here, the gentle sighing of the mountain breeze, the occasional groaning of a branch weighed down with snow. Drawing in a deep breath he let it out slowly then rose, moving back towards the east in a wide circle until he came to the high point of the slope above where he had earlier lain in wait for the two Sathuli. Kneeling behind a boulder he gazed down to where the bodies lay. The corpses were still there, but had been turned to their backs, arms folded across their chest, their tulwars in their hands.

'Wait here, Scar,' he told the dog and moved to the edge of the slope. The hound trotted after him. Twice more he tried to make the dog obey. At last he gave up. 'You need training, you ugly whoreson!'

Carefully Waylander made his way down to the tree wall until he came to the tracks he had made not an hour before. They were overlaid now by the footprints of the hunters. Waylander smiled. The tracks now formed a great ring, with no beginning and no end. Calling the hound to him he knelt and, with a groan, lifted Scar to his shoulder. 'You are a troublesome ally, boy!' he said. Hauling himself to the tree wall he inched his way back along it, clambering down by the base of the largest fallen tree, where the snow-covered roots clawed uselessly at the sky. Here, his tracks hidden by thick bushes, he climbed back to the crest of the slope and settled down to wait.

It was nearing dusk when the first of the trackers came into sight. Waylander hunkered down behind a boulder and waited until he heard the men slithering down the slope. At the bottom, by the bodies, they began to argue among themselves. He could not follow the debate, but at least one of the men used the Sathuli word for circle. They were angry and tired, and one sat down on the tree wall, flinging down his bow.

Waylander watched them dispassionately. Once more they had two choices: either continue to follow the circle towards the south, or retrace their steps back up the slope. If they moved south he would chance the open valleys to Gothir lands.

If north he would have to kill them.

They talked on for almost an hour. The light was beginning to fail. The warrior who had flung down his bow cleared away a section of snow and built a fire. The others hunkered down around it. Once the flames were high they added wet pine needles to the blaze, a thick, oily smoke rising to the darkening sky.

Waylander cursed and eased back from the crest. 'They're calling for more help,' he told the uncomprehending hound. 'But from where – north or south? Or both?' Scar cocked his head and licked at Waylander's hand. 'We'll have to run for it, boy, and take our chances.'

Rising, he moved silently towards the south, the hound beside him.

*

'It makes no sense,' said Asten, his voice trembling despite his attempts to remain calm.

Karnak chuckled and thumped the angry General on the

195

shoulder. 'You worry too much, old lad. Look, the Gothir are ready to invade as soon as the Ventrians land. They are not going to risk attacking Delnoch – they've made a deal with the Sathuli Lord. Well, I can make deals too. And if we stop the Gothir then we can use all our forces against the Ventrians and crush them in a single battle.'

'That's all well and good, Karnak, but why does it have to be you that rides into Sathuli lands? It's madness!'

'Galen assures me we have safe conduct.'

'Pah!' sneered Asten. 'I wouldn't believe that walking snake if he told me the sun shines in the summer-time. Why can't you see it?'

'See what?' countered Karnak. 'See that you and he are not exactly bosom friends? It matters nothing. You are a fine leader of men, while his talent for duplicity and deceit is invaluable. I don't need my officers to like one another, Asten, but you carry your dislike to extremes that affect your judgement.'

Asten reddened, but took a deep breath before he replied. 'As you say, I am a good leader – no false modesty – but I am not, and never will be, a charismatic leader. I cannot raise morale to the heights you can. You are vital to us, and now you are planning to ride into Sathuli lands with a mere twenty men! They hate us, Karnak – you most of all. Before the Vagrian War you led two legions into their territory and crushed their army. Kashti's teeth, man, you killed the present lord's father!'

'Ancient history!' snapped Karnak. 'They are a warrior race. They understand the nature of battle.'

'The risk is too great,' said Asten wearily, knowing he had lost.

Karnak grinned. 'Risk? Gods, man, that's what I live for! To look into the eye of the beast, to feel its breath upon my face. What are we if we face no dangers? Frail flesh and bone to live and age and die. I'll ride into those mountains with my twenty men, I'll beard the Sathuli lord in his own den, *and* I'll win him over. The Gothir will not reach the Sentran Plain, and the Drenai will be secure. Isn't that a risk worth taking?'

'Aye,' stormed Asten. 'It's a risk I would willingly take. But then the Drenai can afford to lose old Asten, the farmer's son. There are many capable officers who could take *his* place. But who will take yours when the Sathuli betray you and nail your head to a palace post?'

Karnak was silent for a moment. 'If I do . . . die,' he said softly, 'you'll win for us, Asten. You're a survivor, old lad. The men know that.'

'Then know this, Karnak. If for any reason Galen comes back without you, I intend to cut his throat.'

Karnak chuckled. 'You do that,' he said, the smile fading. 'You do exactly that!'

13

Black and grey vultures, their bellies distended, hobbled on the plain. Some still squabbled over the carcasses that lay around the ruined tents. Crows had also gathered, and these darted in among the vultures, their sharp beaks pecking at unresisting flesh. Smoke spiralled lazily from the burning tents, creating a grey pall that hung over the scene of the massacre.

Angel guided his horse down on to the plain. The glutted vultures closest to the horsemen waddled away, the others ignoring the newcomers.

Belash and Shia rode alongside Angel. 'These were Green Monkey tribe,' said Belash. 'Not Wolves.' Vaulting from the saddle he moved among the bodies.

Angel did not dismount. To his left was a small circle of bodies, the men on the outside, women and children within. Obviously the last of the warriors had died defending their families. One woman had covered her baby's body with her own, but the broken lance that jutted from her back had thrust through the infant she shielded.

'Must be more than a hundred dead,' said Senta. Angel nodded. To his right the bodies of five infants lay where they had been thrown against a wagon, their heads crushed. Blood stained the rim of the wagon-wheel, and it was all too obvious how the babes had been killed.

Belash walked back to where Angel sat his mount. 'More than a thousand soldiers,' he said. 'Heading for the mountains.'

'Wanton slaughter,' whispered Angel.

'Yes,' agreed Belash. 'So they can't be all bad, eh?'

Angel felt a piercing stab of shame as he heard his own words repeated back to him, but he said nothing and tugged on the reins, galloping his horse back up the hillside to where Miriel waited.

Her face was the colour of wood-ash and she was gripping the pommel of her saddle, her knuckles bone-white. 'I can feel their pain,' she said. 'I can feel it, Angel. I can't close it out!'

'Then don't try,' he told her.

She let out a shuddering sigh, and huge tears formed, spilling to her cheeks. Dismounting, Angel lifted her from the saddle, holding her close as wracking sobs shuddered her frame. 'It is all in the land,' she said. 'All the memories. Soaked in blood. The land knows.'

He rubbed her back and stroked her hair. 'It's seen blood before, Miriel. And they can't be hurt any more.'

'What kind of men could do this?' she stormed, anger replacing her sorrow.

Angel had no answer. To kill a man in battle he understood, but to lift a baby by its heels and . . . he shuddered. It passed all understanding.

Belash, Shia and Senta rode up the hill. Miriel wiped her eyes and looked up at Belash. 'The soldiers are between us and the mountains,' she said. 'This is your land. What do you advise?'

'There are paths they will not know,' he told her. 'I will lead you – if you still wish to go on.'

'Why would I not?' she countered.

'There will be no time for tears, woman, where we shall ride. Only swords and true hearts.'

She smiled at him then, a cold smile, and mounted her horse. 'You lead, Belash. We will follow.'

'Why are you doing this?' asked Shia. 'We are not your people, and old Hard-to-Kill hates the Nadir. So tell me why.'

'Because Kesa Khan asked me,' said Miriel.

'I will accept that,' the girl said, after a moment. 'But what of you?' She turned her gaze to Angel and Senta.

Senta chuckled and drew his sword. 'This blade,' he said, 'was specially made for me by a master armourer. It was a gift, lovely. He came to me one day and presented it. No man has ever bested me with a sword. I'm rather proud of that. But, you know, I didn't ask the armourer about the quality of the steel, or the amount of care that went into its crafting. I just accepted the gift and thanked him for it. You understand?'

'No,' she answered. 'What has that to do with my question?'

'Like trying to teach mathematics to a fish,' said Senta, shaking his head.

Angel edged his horse forward and leaned close to Shia. 'Let's put it this way, lady. He and I are the finest swordsmen you'll ever see, but our reasons for being here are none of your damned business!'

Shia nodded solemnly. 'That is true,' she admitted, no trace of rancour in her voice.

Senta laughed aloud. 'You should have been a diplomat, Angel.' The gladiator merely grunted.

Belash led the way to the east and the distant mountains, Miriel riding behind with Shia, Angel alongside Senta bringing up the rear. Dark clouds loomed above the peaks and lightning flashed like a jagged spear from earth to sky. The sound of thunder followed almost instantly.

'The mountains are angry,' Belash told Miriel.

'So am I,' she replied. A howling easterly wind blew sheets of rain across the barren, featureless land, and soon the riders travelled hunched in their saddles, drenched through.

For several hours they rode, until at last the sheer walls of the Mountains of the Moon loomed above them. The rain died down and Belash rode on ahead, angling back towards the south, scanning the forbidding peaks and the open steppes to the north. They had seen no soldiers, but now, with the clouds clearing, the smoke of many campfires could be seen in the distance, drifting up to merge with the grey sky.

'This is the secret path,' said Belash, pointing to the mountain face.

'There's no way through,' said Angel, gazing up at the black, basaltic wall of rock. But Belash rode up a short scree slope – and vanished. Angel blinked. 'Shemak's balls!' he whispered.

Miriel urged her mount up the slope, the others following. Virtually invisible from the outside there was a wide crack in the face, some four feet wide, leading to a shining tunnel. Miriel rode in, Angel behind her. There was scarcely a finger's breadth of space between thigh and wall on both sides, and several times the riders had to lift their legs up on to the saddle in order for their mounts to squeeze through. The walls loomed around them and Angel felt his heartbeat quickening. Above them huge boulders were clustered, having fallen and wedged together precariously.

Senta spoke. 'If a butterfly were to land on that mass it would all come tumbling down.' His voice echoed up into the crack. A low groan came from above them and black dust filtered down through the rocks.

'No speaking!' whispered Shia.

They rode on, emerging at last on a wide ledge overlooking a bowl-shaped crater. More than a hundred tents were pitched there. Belash touched heels to his horse and galloped down the slope.

'I think we're home,' said Senta.

From this high vantage point Angel could see the vastness of the steppes beyond the mountains, brown and arid, great folds across the land, rippling hills, humped-back ridges, as far as the eye could see. It was a hard, dry land and yet, as the sun dipped below the storm clouds, Angel saw in the steppes a relentless beauty that spoke to his warrior's heart. It was the beauty of a sword-blade, strong and unyielding. There were no fields or meadows, no silver streams. Even the hills were sharp and unwelcoming. And the voice of the land whispered to him.

Be strong or die, it said.

The mountains reared around him like a jagged black crown, the tents of the Nadir seeming fragile, almost insubstantial against the eternal power of the rocks on which they stood.

Angel shivered. Senta was right.

They were home.

*

Altharin was angry. He had been angry since the Emperor had given him this command. Where was the glory in wiping out vermin? Where was the advancement? Within days the main body of the army would be filing through Sathuli lands to invade the Drenai, sweeping across the Sentran Plain, meeting the Drenai sword to sword, lance to lance.

But no. Not for Altharin. He gazed up at the looming black peaks and wrapped his fur-lined cloak more tightly about his long, lean frame.

What a place!

Basaltic rocks, jagged and sharp. No horses could ride here – the lava beds cut their hooves to ribbons. And men on foot had to make long, lung-bursting climbs before reaching the enemy. He glanced to his left where the hospital tents had been erected. Eighty-seven dead so far, in five miserable days.

Turning he strolled back to his own tent, where an iron brazier glowed with hot coals. Loosening his cloak he cast it over a canvas-backed chair. His manservant, Becca, bowed low.

'Mulled wine, sir?'

'No. Send for Powis.' The man scurried from the tent.

Altharin had suspected this assignment would not be as easy as the Emperor believed. Surround and exterminate a few hundred Nadir, then rejoin the main army at the southern camp. Altharin shook his head. The first attack had gone well. The Green Monkeys had sat and watched as the Gothir lancers rode in, and only when the killing began did they recognise that death was upon them. But when the scouts reached the camp of the Wolves they found it deserted, the tracks leading off into these cursed mountains.

Altharin sighed. Tomorrow the Brotherhood would arrive, and his every move would be watched and reported back, his actions questioned, his strategies derided. I cannot win here, he thought.

The tent-flap opened and Powis ducked into the interior. 'You called for me, sir?'

Altharin nodded. 'You have gathered the reports?'

'Not quite all of them, sir,' answered the young man. 'Bernas is with the surgeons. He has a nasty wound to his face and shoulder. And Gallis is still on the peak, trying to force a path through from the north.'

'What have you learned from the others?'

'Well, sir, we have found only three routes through to the interior. All are defended by archers and swordsmen. The first is narrow and the men can move only two abreast. This makes them easy targets, not just for arrows, but rocks hurled from above. The second is some three hundred paces north. It is fairly wide, but the Nadir have moved rocks and boulders across it, making a rough, but effective wall. We lost fourteen men there this morning. The last route is the one Gallis is trying to force. He has three hundred men with him. I don't know yet what success he has enjoyed.'

'Numbers?' snapped Altharin.

'Twenty-one killed today, slightly more than forty wounded.'

'Enemy losses?'

'Difficult to say, sir.' The young man shrugged. 'Men tend to exaggerate such matters. They claim to have killed a hundred Nadir. I would guess the figure is less than half, perhaps a quarter of that.'

The manservant, Becca, ducked inside the tent and bowed. 'The Lord Gallis is returning, sir.'

'Send him to me,' ordered Altharin.

Moments later a tall, wide-shouldered man entered. He was around forty years of age, dark-eyed and black-bearded. His face was streaked with sweat and smeared with black, volcanic dust. His grey cloak was slashed and grime-covered, and there were several dents in his embossed iron breastplate.

'Make your report, Cousin,' said Altharin.

Gallis cleared his throat, removed his white plumed iron helm, and moved to the folding table on which sat a wine jug and several goblets of copper and silver. 'With your permission?' he croaked.

'Of course.'

The officer filled a goblet and drained it at a single swallow. 'The cursed dust is everywhere,' he said. He took a deep breath. 'We lost forty-four men. The pass is narrow at the base, flaring out above. We forced our way some two hundred paces towards their camp.' He rubbed at his eyes, smearing black ash across his brow. 'Resistance was strong, but I thought we would get through.' He shook his head. 'Then, at the narrowest point, the renegades struck.'

'Renegades?' queried Altharin.

'Aye, Cousin. Drenai or Gothir traitors. Two swordsmen, unbelievably skilful. Behind them, above and to the right, was a young woman with a bow. She was dressed in black. Every arrow found its mark. Between her and the swordsmen I lost fifteen men in that one place. And high above us, on both sides, the Nadir sent rocks and boulders down upon us. I ordered the men to pull back, to prepare for a second thrust. Then Jarvik lost his temper and ran at the swordsmen, challenging them. I tried to stop him.' Gallis shrugged.

'They killed him?'

'Yes, Cousin. But I wish they had shot him. As it was one of the swordsmen, the ugliest fellow I've ever seen, stepped out and accepted his challenge.'

'You're not telling me he defeated Jarvik in single combat?'

'That's exactly what I *am* saying, Cousin. Jarvik cut him, but the man was unstoppable.'

'I can't believe it!' said Powis, stepping forward. 'Jarvik won the Silver Sabre contest last spring.'

'Believe it, boy,' snapped Gallis. Turning to Altharin the officer shook his head once more. 'No one was in a mood to continue the attack after that. I left a hundred men to hold the position and brought the rest back.'

Altharin swore, then moved to a second folding table on which maps were spread. 'This is largely unexplored territory,' he said, 'but we do know there are few sources of food within the mountains – especially in winter.

204

Normally we would starve them out, but that is not what the Emperor has ordered. Suggestions, gentlemen?'

Gallis shrugged. 'We have the numbers to eventually wear them down. We must just keep attacking on all three fronts. Eventually we must break through.'

'How many will we lose?' asked Altharin.

'Hundreds,' admitted Gallis.

'And how will that look back in Gulgothir? The Emperor sees this as a short, punitive raid. And we all know who arrives tomorrow.'

'Send the Brotherhood in when they get here,' said Gallis. 'Let's see how far their sorcery will carry them.'

'I have no control over the Brotherhood, more's the pity. What I do know, however, is that our reputations and our futures are in the balance here.'

'I agree with that, Cousin. I'll order the attacks to continue throughout the night.'

*

'Stop grumbling,' said Senta, as the curved needle once more pricked under the flesh of Angel's shoulder, bringing together the flaps of the wound.

'You are enjoying this, you bastard!' retorted Angel.

'How cruel!' Senta chuckled. 'But fancy letting a Gothir farmboy fool you with a riposte counter.'

'He was good, damn you!'

'He moved with all the grace of a sick cow. You should be ashamed of yourself, old man.' Senta completed the last of ten stitches, and bit off the twine. 'There. Better than new.'

Angel glanced down at the puckered wound. 'You should have been a seamstress,' he muttered.

'Just one of my many talents,' replied Senta, rising and moving out of the cave and staring down over the mountainside. From the cave mouth he could hear the distant screams of wounded men, the echoing clash of war. The stars were bright in a clear sky and a cold wind was hissing over the peaks and crags. 'We can't hold this place,' he said, as Angel moved alongside him.

'We're doing well enough so far.'

205

Senta nodded. 'There are too many of them, Angel. And the Nadir are relying on the wall across the centre pass. Once the soldiers breach that . . .' He spread his hands.

Two Nadir women made their way across the open ground bearing bowls of clotted cheese. They stopped before the Drenai warriors, eyes averted, and laid the bowls on the ground before them, departing as silently as they had come.

'Really welcome here, aren't we?' observed Senta.

Angel shrugged. There were more than a hundred tents dotted around the giant crater and from the high cave the two men could see Nadir children playing in the moonlight, running and sending up clouds of black, volcanic dust. To the left a line of women were moving into the deep caves carrying wooden buckets, gathering water from artesian wells deep below the mountains.

'Where tomorrow?' asked Angel, sitting down with his back to the rocks.

'The wall, I think,' said Senta. 'The other two passes are easily defended. They'll come at the wall.' A shadow moved to the right. Senta chuckled. 'He's back, Angel.'

The gladiator swore and glanced around. A small boy of around nine years of age was squatting on his haunches watching them. 'Go away!' roared Angel, but the child ignored him. 'I hate the way he just stares,' snapped Angel. The boy was thin, almost skeletal, his clothes threadbare. He wore an old goatskin tunic from which most of the hair had long since vanished, and a pair of dark leggings, torn at the knees and frayed at the waist. His eyes were slanted and black, and they stared unblinkingly at the two men. Angel tried to ignore him. Lifting the bowl of cheese he dipped his fingers into the congealed mass and ate. 'Horse droppings would taste better than this,' he said.

'It is an acquired taste,' agreed Senta.

'Damned if I can eat it.' He swung to the boy. 'You want some?' He did not move. Angel offered him the bowl. The child licked his lips, but remained where he was. Angel shook his head. 'What does he want?' he asked, placing the bowl on the ground.

'I've no idea – but he's obviously fascinated by you. He followed you today, mimicking your walk. Quite funny, really. I hadn't noticed it before, but you move like a sailor. You know, rolling gait.'

'Any more of my habits you'd like to criticise?'

'Too many to mention.'

Angel stood and stretched. The child immediately imitated him. 'Stop that!' said Angel, leaning forward, hands on hips. The tiny figure adopted the same stance. Senta's laughter pealed out. 'I'm going to get some sleep,' said Angel, turning his back on the boy and re-entering the cave.

Senta remained where he was, listening to the faint sounds of battle. The boy edged closer and snatched the bowl, backing away to the shadows to eat. For a while Senta dozed, then he heard movement on the mountainside. He was instantly awake. Belash climbed to the cave mouth.

'They have pulled back,' he said, squatting down beside the swordsman. 'No more now until the dawn, I think.' Senta glanced to where the boy had been, but only the empty bowl remained. 'We killed many,' said Belash, with grim satisfaction.

'Not enough. There must be more than three thousand of them.'

'Many more,' agreed Belash. 'And others are coming. It will take time to kill them all.'

'Ever the optimist.'

'You think we cannot win? You do not understand the Nadir. We are born to fight.'

'I have no doubts concerning the skills of your people, Belash. But this place is ultimately indefensible. How many fighters can you muster?'

'This morning there were three hundred and seventy . . . three,' he said, at last.

'And tonight?'

'We lost maybe fifteen.'

'Wounded?'

'Another thirty . . . but some of these can fight again.'

'How many altogether – during the last four days?'

Belash nodded glumly. 'I understand what you are saying. We can hold for maybe eight . . . ten more days. But we will kill many before then.'

'That's hardly the point, my friend. We must have a secondary line of defence. Further into the mountains perhaps.'

'There is nowhere.'

'When we rode down here I saw a valley to the west. Where does it lead?'

'We cannot go there. It is a place of evil and death. I would sooner die here, cleanly and with honour.'

'Fine sentiments, I'm sure, Belash. But I'd as soon not die anywhere quite yet.'

'You do not have to stay,' pointed out Belash.

'True,' agreed Senta, 'but, as my father so often points out, stupidity does tend to run in our family.'

*

High above the mountains, linked to the spirit of Kesa Khan, Miriel floated beneath the stars. Below her, on the moonlit plain were the tents of the Gothir, erected in five lines of twenty, neat and rectangular, evenly spaced. To the south were a score of picket lines where the horses were tethered, and to the east a latrine pit, exactly thirty feet long. One hundred camp fires were burning brightly, and sentries patrolled the camp's perimeter.

'A methodical people,' pulsed the voice of Kesa Khan. 'They call themselves civilised because they can build tall castles and pitch their tents with geometrical precision, but from here you can see the reality. Ants build in the same way. Are they civilised?'

Miriel said nothing. From this great height she could see both the tiny camp of the Nadir and the might of the Gothir attackers. It was dispiriting. Kesa Khan's laughter rippled out. 'Never concern yourself with despair, Miriel. It is always the weapon of the enemy. Look at them! Even from here you can feel their vanity.'

'How can we defeat them?'

'How can we not?' he countered. 'There are millions of us, and but a few of them. When the Uniter comes they will be swept away like grass-seeds.'

'I meant *now*.'

'Ah, the impatience of youth! Let us see what there is to be seen.'

The stars spun and Miriel found herself looking down at a small campfire in a shallow cave on a mountainside. She saw Waylander sitting hunched before the flames, the hound, Scar, stretched out beside him. Waylander looked tired and she sensed his thoughts. He had been hunted, but had eluded the trackers, killing several. He was clear of Sathuli lands now, and was thinking about stealing a horse from a Gothir town some three leagues to the north.

'A strong man,' said Kesa Khan. 'The Dragon Shadow.'

'He is weary,' said Miriel, wishing she could reach out and hug the lonely man by the campfire.

The scene shifted to a city of stone set in the mountains, and a deep dungeon where a large man was chained to a dank, wet wall. 'You treacherous cur, Galen,' said the prisoner.

A tall, thin warrior in the red cloak of a Drenai lancer stepped forward, taking hold of the prisoner's hair and wrenching back the head. 'Enjoy your insults, you whoreson! Your day is over, and harsh words are all you have now. Yet they will avail you nothing: tomorrow you travel in chains to Gulgothir.'

'I'll come for you, you bastard!' swore the prisoner. 'They won't hold me!' The thin warrior laughed, then bunched his fist and struck the helpless man three times in the face, splitting his lip. Blood flowed to his chin and his one pale eye focused on the red-cloaked soldier. 'I suppose you'll tell Asten we were betrayed, but you managed to escape?'

'Yes. Then, when the time is right, I'll kill the peasant. And the Brotherhood will rule in Drenan. How does that make you feel?'

'It should be an interesting meeting. I'd like to be there to see you telling Asten how I was captured.'

'Oh, I shall tell it well. I shall speak of your enormous bravery, and how you were slain. It will bring a tear to his eye.'

'Rot in hell!' said the prisoner.

Miriel felt the close presence of Kesa Khan and the old shaman's voice whispered into her mind. 'You know who this is?'

'No.'

'You are gazing upon Karnak the One-Eyed, Lord Protector of the Drenai. He does not look mighty now, chained in a Sathuli dungeon. Can you feel his emotions?'

Miriel concentrated, and the warm rush of Karnak's anger swept over her. 'Yes. I can feel it. He is picturing his tormentor being killed by a soldier with red hair.'

'Yes. But there is something else to consider, girl. There is no despair in Karnak, yes? Only anger and the burning desire for revenge. His conceit is colossal, but so is his strength. He has no fear of the chains, or the enemies around him. Already he is planning, building his hopes. Such a man can never be discounted.'

'He is a prisoner, unarmed and helpless. What can he do?' asked Miriel.

'Let us return to the mountains. I am tiring. And tomorrow the real enemy will show himself. We must be ready to face the evil they will unleash.' All light faded in an instant and Miriel opened the eyes of her body and sat up. The fire in the cave had burned low. Kesa Khan added wood to the dying flames and stretched, the bones of his back creaking and cracking. 'Aya! Age is no blessing,' he said.

'What is this evil you spoke of?' asked Miriel.

'In a moment, in a moment! I am old, child, and the transition from spirit to flesh takes a little time. Let me gather my thoughts. Talk to me!'

She looked at the wizened old man. 'What do you wish me to talk about?'

'Anything!' he snapped. 'Life, love, dreams. Tell me which of the two men you wish to bed!'

Miriel reddened. 'Such thoughts are not for idle chatter,' she scolded.

210

He cackled and fixed her with a piercing gaze. 'Foolish girl! You cannot make up your mind. The young one is witty and handsome, but you know his love is fickle. The older one is like the oak, powerful and enduring, but you feel his lovemaking would lack excitement.'

'If you already know my thoughts, why ask me?'

'It entertains me. Would you like my advice?'

'No.'

'Good. I like a woman who can think for herself.' He sniffed and reached for one of the many clay pots beside the fire, dipping his finger into the contents and scooping a pale grey powder into his mouth. He closed his eyes and sighed. 'Yes . . . yes . . .' He took a deep breath and opened his eyes. Miriel leaned forward. His pupils had all but disappeared and the irises had changed from dark dark brown to pale blue. 'I am Kesa Khan,' he whispered, his voice lighter, friendlier. 'And I am Lao Shin, the spirit of the mountains. And I am Wu Deyang, the Traveller. I am He Who Sees All.'

'The powder is narcotic?' asked Miriel softly.

'Of course. It opens the window of worlds. Now listen to me, Drenai girl. You are brave, of that there is no question. But tomorrow the dead will walk again. Do you have the heart to face them?'

She licked her lips. 'I am here to help you,' she answered.

'Excellent. No false bravado. I will show you how to armour yourself. I will teach you to summon weapons as you need them. But the greatest weapon you possess is the courage in your heart. Let us hope that the Dragon Shadow has taught you well, for if he has not you will bed neither of those fine warriors. Your soul will wander the Grey Paths for eternity.'

'He taught me well,' said Miriel.

'We shall see.'

*

With the hound loping off ahead Waylander moved on to the boulder-strewn plain. There were few trees here, and the land sloped gently downward towards a white stone

211

village by a river bank. A horse pasture was fenced off at the north of the village and to the south sheep grazed on the last of the autumn grass. It was a small settlement, built without walls, evidence of the longstanding agreement between Gothir and Sathuli. There were no raids here. It struck Waylander as strange that the Gothir could treat the Sathuli so well and the Nadir so badly. Both were nomadic tribes which had moved slowly down from the north and east. Both were warrior races, who worshipped different gods from the Gothir, and yet they were perceived as opposites. The Sathuli, in Gothir tales, were proud, intelligent and honourable. The Nadir, on the other hand, were seen as base, treacherous and cunning. All his adult life Waylander had moved among the tribes and could find no evidence to support the Gothir view.

Save, perhaps, for the sheer numbers of Nadir who roamed the steppes. The Sathuli posed no threat, whereas the Nadir, in their millions, were a future enemy to be feared.

He shrugged away such considerations and looked for the hound. It was nowhere to be seen. He stopped and scanned the slopes. There were many boulders and the dog was probably scratching at a rabbit burrow. Waylander smiled and walked on. It was cold, the weak sunshine unable to counter the biting wind. He pulled his fur-lined cloak more tightly around his shoulders.

The Sathuli would remember the chase as they sang the Songs of Passing over the hunters who would not return. He thought back to the boy who had first tried to ambush him, and was pleased that he had not killed him. As to the others, well, they had made their choices and he regretted their deaths not at all.

He could see people moving in the village below, a shepherd with a long crook striding up the hill, a dog at his side, several women at the main well, drawing buckets of cool water, children playing by the horse pasture fence. It was a peaceful scene.

He strode on, the path winding down between two huge boulders that jutted from the earth of the mountainside. In the distance a horse whinnied. He paused. The sound had come from the east. He turned and gazed up at the thin stand of trees on the slope. There were bushes growing there and he could not see a horse. Flicking back his cloak he lifted his crossbow, stringing it and sliding two bolts into place. There should be nothing to fear now, he chided himself. The Sathuli were unlikely to venture so far north. But he waited.

Where was Scar?

Moving forward more cautiously he approached the boulders. A figure stepped into sight, green cloak fluttering in the breeze, a bent bow in his hands. Waylander threw himself to the right as the arrow leapt from the string, slicing past his face. He struck the ground on his shoulder, the impact making his hand contract, loosing the bolts on the crossbow, which hammered into the soft earth of the slope. Rolling to his feet he drew his sabre.

The man in the green cloak hurled aside his bow, drawing his own blade. 'This is how it should be, sword to sword,' he said, smiling.

Waylander pulled free the thongs that held his cloak in place, allowing it to drop to the earth. 'You would be Morak,' he said softly.

'How gratifying to be recognised,' answered the swordsman, angling himself towards the waiting Waylander. 'I understand you are not at your best with a sabre, therefore I will give you a short lesson before killing you.'

Waylander leapt to the attack. Morak blocked and countered. The ringing of steel on steel echoed on the mountainside, the two sabres shining in the sunlight. Morak, in perfect balance fended off every attack, his blade licking out to open a shallow cut on Waylander's cheek. Waylander swayed back and sent a vicious slashing blow towards Morak's belly. The green-clad swordsman neatly sidestepped.

'I'd say you were better than average,' he told Waylander. 'Your balance is good, but you are a little stiff in the lower back. It affects the lunge.'

Waylander's hand snapped forward, a black-bladed

throwing knife flashing towards Morak's throat. The assassin's sabre swept up, deflecting the knife which clattered against one of the boulders. 'Very good,' said Morak. 'But you are dealing with a master now, Waylander.'

'Where is my dog?'

'Your dog? How touching! You stand at the point of death and you are concerned for a flea-bitten hound? I killed it, of course.'

Waylander said nothing. Backing away to more level ground he watched the swordsman follow. Morak was smiling now, but the smile did not reach the gleaming green eyes. 'I shall kill you with a remarkable lack of speed,' he said. 'A few cuts here and there. As the blood runs so your strength will fail. Do you think you will beg me for life?'

'I would doubt it,' said Waylander.

'All men beg, you know. Even the strongest. It depends only upon where the knife enters.' Morak leapt. Waylander's sabre parried the thrust, the blades clashing again and again. A second small cut appeared on Waylander's forearm. Morak laughed. 'There is no panic in you – not yet. I like that. What happened to that daughter of yours? By Heavens I'll yet enjoy her. Long legs, firm flesh. I'll make her squeal. Then I'll open her up from neck to belly!'

Waylander edged back and said nothing.

'Good! Good! I can't make you angry. That's rare! I shall enjoy finding your breaking point, Waylander. Will it come when I cut off your fingers? Or will it be when your manhood is sizzling on a fire?'

He lunged again, the blade slicing the leather of Waylander's tunic shirt just above the left hip. Waylander hurled himself forward, hammering his shoulder into the assassin's face. Morak fell awkwardly, but rolled to his feet before Waylander could bring his sword to bear. The blades clashed again. Waylander aimed a thrust at Morak's head, but the swordsman swayed aside, blocking the lunge and sending a riposte that flashed past

Waylander's neck. Waylander backed away towards the boulders. Morak attacked, forcing his opponent further down the trail. Both men were sweating freely, despite the cold.

'You are game,' said Morak. 'I did not expect you to prove this resilient.'

Waylander lunged. Morak parried, then attacked in a bewildering series of thrusts and cuts that Waylander fought desperately to counter. Twice Morak's sabre pierced the upper chest of Waylander's tunic, the blade being turned aside by the chain-mail shoulder-guard. But the older man was tiring now, and Morak knew it. He stepped back. 'Would you like a little time to get your breath?' he asked, with a mocking grin.

'How did you find me?' said Waylander, grateful for the respite.

'I have friends among the Sathuli. After our . . . unfortunate . . . encounter back in the mountains I came here, seeking more warriors. I was with the Lord Sathuli when news of the hunt came in. The Lord Sathuli is most anxious to see you dead. He feels your journey across his lands is an insult to tribal pride. He would have sent more men – but he has other matters on his mind at the moment. Instead he paid me. By the way, would you like to know who hired the Guild to hunt you?'

'I already know,' Waylander told him.

'Oh, how disappointing. Still, I am by nature a kind-hearted man, so I will at least give you a little good news before I kill you. Even as we speak the Lord Protector of the Drenai lies chained in a Sathuli dungeon, ready to be delivered to the Emperor of the Gothir.'

'That's impossible!'

'Not at all. He was persuaded to meet with the Lord Sathuli, in a bid to prevent Gothir troops crossing tribal lands. He travelled with a small party of loyal soldiers and one, rather disloyal, officer. His men were slaughtered and Karnak taken alive. I saw him myself. It was quite comical. Unusual man – offered me a fortune to help him escape.'

'He obviously doesn't know you too well,' said Waylander.

'On the contrary, I have worked for him before – many times. He paid me to kill Egel.'

'I don't believe it!'

'Yes, you do – I can see it in your eyes. Ah well, recovered your breath? Good. Then let us see some blood!' Morak advanced, his blade lancing out. Waylander blocked, but was forced back, past the jutting boulders. Morak laughed. 'The lesson is now over,' he said. 'Time for the enjoyment to begin.'

A dark shadow moved behind him and Waylander saw the hound, Scar, pulling himself painfully forward on his front paws, his back legs limp and useless. An arrow had pierced his ribs and blood was dribbling from the huge jaws. Waylander edged to the left. Morak moved right. He had not seen the dying hound. Waylander leapt forward, sending a wild cut towards Morak's face. The assassin moved back a step – and Scar's huge jaws snapped shut on his right calf, the fangs sinking through skin, flesh and sinew. Morak screamed in pain. Waylander stepped in and rammed his sabre into the assassin's belly, ripping it up through the lungs.

'That's for the old man you tortured!' hissed Waylander. Twisting the blade he tore it free, disembowelling the swordsman. 'And that's for my dog!'

Morak fell to his knees. 'No!' he moaned. Then toppled sideways to the earth.

Casting aside his sword Waylander knelt by the hound, stroking its head. There was nothing he could do to save the beast. The arrow had pierced its spine. But he sat with it, cradling the huge head in his lap, speaking softly, his voice soothing, until the juddering breathing slowed and finally stopped.

Then he stood, gathered his crossbow, and walked to the stand of trees where Morak had hidden his horse.

14

The wall was rough-built, but bound with a mortar composed of the volcanic black dust of the mountains. Once tamped down and doused with water it set to the hardness of granite. From the south the enemy faced a structure ten feet high, but on the defensive side there was a rampart which allowed the defenders to lean out and send volley after volley of arrows into the ranks of the attackers, then duck down out of sight of any enemy archers.

So far the wall had held. In several places the Gothir had rolled boulders to the foot of it trying to find a way of scaling the defence and later, the front ranks had carried crudely-built ladders. Others used ropes with iron hooks to gain purchase, but the defenders fought with tribal ferocity, hacking and killing all who reached the top.

Once the Gothir had almost formed a fighting wedge, six men forcing their way on to the rampart, but Angel, Senta and Belash had charged into them – and the Gothir warriors died within moments. Again and again the Gothir charged, wave after wave, seeking to overwhelm the Nadir by sheer force of numbers. It had not succeeded.

Yet.

But now something had changed and each defender felt the stirrings of a terrible fear. Angel noticed it first – a coldness in the pit of the belly. His hands began to tremble. The Nadir warrior alongside him dropped his sword, a low, keening moan coming from his lips. Angel glanced at Senta. The swordsman was leaning on the wall and staring out over the narrows of the pass. The Gothir had fallen back, but instead of regrouping they had retreated out of sight. At first the fifty Nadir warriors manning the rough-built wall had jeered and shouted. But now an uncomfortable silence settled on the defenders.

Angel shivered. The black walls of the mountains

loomed around him, and he felt as if he were standing inside the gaping jaws of an enormous monster. The trembling worsened. He tried to sheath his sword, but it clattered against the scabbard. He swore and laid the blade against the wall.

Three Nadir warriors turned and ran back up the pass, leaving their weapons behind them. The voice of Belash roared out. The fleeing men halted and turned, sheepishly. But the fear was growing.

Angel made his way to Senta's side. His legs felt they had no strength, and he leaned on the wall for support. 'What the devil is happening?' he asked Senta. The other man, his face pale, his eyes wide, did not reply. Movement came from the mouth of the pass. Angel swung his head and saw a line of black-cloaked, black-armoured men moving towards the wall.

'The Knights of Blood!' whispered Senta, his voice shaking.

A Nadir beside him cried out and fell back, his bladder loosening, urine soaking his leggings. Angel saw Belash sheath his sword and snatch a bow from a warrior's hand. Notching an arrow the stocky Nadir climbed to the top of the wall and drew back on the string. Angel heard him groan – and cry out. Then Belash slowly began to turn.

Angel hurled himself at Senta, dragging him back just as the arrow was loosed. It flashed past them, ricocheting from a rock and plunging into the shoulder of a crouching warrior.

Silently the Knights of Blood advanced.

The Nadir seemed powerless to stop them. Angel scrambled to his feet and took up his sword. The trembling was now so great he knew he would not be able to use it. The defenders began to stream back from the wall – even Belash.

A tiny man in ragged clothes moved into sight, Miriel beside him. He was wizened and ancient, but Angel felt a sudden surge of elation, cutting through the fear, firing his blood. The Nadir paused in their flight. The little shaman

218

ran to the wall, climbing nimbly to the top. The Knights of Blood were less than twenty paces from the wall.

Kesa Khan raised his hands and flashes of blue fire leapt from palm to palm. Angel felt all fear lifting from him; anger replaced it. The shaman's hands swept out, bony fingers pointing at the marching, black-cloaked warriors. Blue fire lanced into the line, rippling over breastplates and helms. The man at the centre of the line stumbled. Blue fire became red as his hair burst into flames. Cloaks and leggings blazed – and the advancing line broke, men beating at the tongues of flame licking at their clothing.

The Nadir defenders returned to the wall, taking up bow and spear and sending shaft after shaft into the milling men.

The Knights of Blood broke and ran.

The little Nadir leapt down from the wall and walked away without a word.

Miriel approached Angel. 'You should sit down. Your face is the colour of snow.'

'I've never known such a fear,' he admitted.

'But you didn't run,' she pointed out.

Ignoring the compliment he gazed after the Nadir shaman. 'I take it that was Kesa Khan. He doesn't waste a lot of time on conversation, does he?'

She smiled. 'He's a tough old man, but he's exhausted. That spell will have weakened him more than you could possibly know.'

Senta joined them. 'We can't hold this place,' he said. 'They almost broke through this morning, twice. Only the Source knows how we held them off.'

A cry went up from one of the defenders. Senta swung to see hundreds of Gothir warriors charging into the pass. Drawing his swords he ran back to the wall.

'He's right,' said Angel. 'Talk to the old man! We must find another place.' Then he too ran to join the defenders.

*

Bodalen followed the torch-carrying Gracus deep into the bowels of the castle, through endless corridors and down stairways of metal. Everything was twisted, unnatural, and

219

a low humming filled the air, causing Bodalen's head to pound.

Behind the tall Drenai came the other eight Brotherhood warriors, grim silent men. The ninth had taken the horses into the mountains, and now all hope of fleeing this sorcerous place was gone from Bodalen.

Down, down they journeyed, through five levels, the humming growing ever more loud. The walls of the castle were no longer of stone, but sleek, shining metal, bulging and cracked in places. Beyond the cracks were wires of copper and iron, gold and silver, wound together, braided.

Bodalen hated the castle, and feared the secrets it might contain. But even through his cowardice his fascination grew. On one level there was a set of steel doors, which Gracus and two other men forced open. Within was a small room. There was no furniture, but one wall carried a small ornament, like a carving table, twelve round stones set in brass, each stone bearing a symbol that Bodalen could not decipher.

There was little of interest save for the ornament and the warriors moved on, seeking stairs.

At last they came to a great hall that was lit as if by sunlight, bright and cheerful. Yet there were no windows, and Bodalen knew they were hundreds of feet below ground. Gracus dropped the spluttering torch to the metal floor and gazed around him. There were tables and chairs, all of metal, and huge iron cabinets, ornately decorated with bright gems that sparkled, the light dancing from them.

Panels of opaque glass were set all around the hall, and these glowed with white light. Gracus drew his sword and struck one of them, which shattered, spilling fragments to the hall floor. Beyond the panel was a long, gleaming cylinder. A second warrior strode forward, thrusting his sword into it. There was a flash and the knight was lifted from his feet and hurled twenty feet across the floor. Half the lights in the hall dimmed and died.

Gracus ran to the fallen man, kneeling beside him. 'Dead,' he said, rising and turning to the others. 'Touch nothing. We will await the master. The spells are mightier than we can understand.'

Bodalen, the humming so loud it made him nauseous, moved across the hall to an open doorway. Beyond it he saw a huge crystal, some three feet in circumference, floating between two golden bowls. Tiny bolts of lightning flickered and shone all around it as it spun. Bodalen stepped into the room. The walls here were all of gold, save for the far wall, which had been partly stripped, exposing carved blocks of granite, twisted far beyond their original squares.

But it was not the crystal, nor the walls of gold that caused the breath to catch in his throat.

'Gracus!' he shouted. The Brotherhood knight entered the room – and gazed down at the immense skeleton stretched out by the far wall.

'What in the name of Hell is it?' whispered Bodalen.

Gracus shook his head. 'Hell is where it came from,' he answered, kneeling beside the two skulls, his fingers tracing the twin lines of vertebrae leading to the massive shoulders. The beast, whatever it was, had boasted three arms, one of which sprouted from below the enormous ribs. One of the knights tried to lift the thigh bone, but the rotted sinew held it in place.

'I cannot even get my hands around this bone,' said the man. 'The creature must have been twelve feet tall, maybe more.'

Bodalen glanced back at the doorway, which was no more than three feet wide and six feet tall. 'How did it get in here?' he asked. Gracus moved to the doorway. There were great tears in the metal around the frame, exposing the stone beneath.

'I don't know how it got in,' said Gracus softly, 'but it tore its fingers to the bone trying to get out. There must be another entrance. Hidden.'

For some time they searched the walls, seeking a disguised doorway. But there was nothing. Bodalen felt a great weariness settling on him and his headache worsened. He started for the doorway, but his legs gave way and he slumped to the floor. Fatigue overwhelmed him, and he saw Gracus stumble to his knees before the spinning crystal.

'We must . . . get out,' said Bodalen, trying to drag himself across the gleaming golden floor. But his eyes closed and he fell into a deep, and at first dreamless, sleep.

Awareness came to him slowly. He could see a cottage, built by a stream, a cornfield beyond it, blue mountains, hazy in the distance behind it. There was a man walking behind a team of oxen. He was ploughing a field.

Father.

No, not Father. Father is Karnak. He never ploughed a field in his life.

Father.

Confusion flowed over him like a fog, swirling, unreal. He looked up at the sun, but there was no sun, just a spinning crystal high in the sky, humming like a thousand bees.

The man with the plough turned towards him. 'Don't spend your day lazing, Gracus!' he said.

Gracus? I'm not Gracus. I am dreaming. That's it! A dream. Wake up!

He felt himself rising from sleep, felt the awareness of flesh and muscle. He tried to move his arm, but it seemed lodged, trapped. He opened his eyes. Gracus was lying beside him. Close beside him. He must be lying on my arm, thought Bodalen. He tried to roll, but Gracus moved with him, his head lolling, his mouth open. Bodalen struggled to rise. He felt an unaccustomed weight on his right side and swung his head. There was another man lying there.

And he had no head.

I am lying on his head, thought Bodalen, panic gripping him. He surged up. The body on the right rose with him. Bodalen screamed. The headless body was part of him, the shoulders bonded to Bodalen's flesh.

Sweet Heaven! Calm down, he told himself. This is still a dream. Just a dream.

His left arm had disappeared, embedded into and merging with Gracus' shoulder. He tried to pull it clear, but

222

the limp body of the Brotherhood knight merely moved closer. Their legs touched – and bonded.

The crystal continued to spin.

Across the room Bodalen saw the bodies of the other knights, melding together, twisting as if involved in some silent, unnatural orgy. And between them, lying still on the golden floor, was the huge skeleton.

Bodalen screamed again.

And passed out.

*

It awoke with no memory, but stretched its huge muscles and rolled to its belly, its three legs levering it upright, its two heads striking the golden ceiling. Rage suffused the beast, and one of the heads roared in anger. The other remained silent, grey eyes blinking at the light from the crystal.

Two other beasts were still asleep.

The crystal spun, blue lights dancing between the golden bowls.

The beast shuffled towards it, reaching out with its three great arms. A massive finger touched the flickering blue fire. Pain swept along the immense limbs, burning the creature. Both heads roared now. One arm swept out, striking the crystal, dislodging it, sending it hurtling towards the far wall. The blue flames died.

And all the lights dimmed and faded.

The near-darkness was comfortable, reassuring. The beast slumped down to its haunches. It was hungry. The smell of burnt meat came from the hall beyond. It moved to the doorway, and saw a small dead creature lying on the floor. The corpse was part-clothed in hide and metal. The meat was still fresh and the beast's hunger swelled. It tried to move forward but its great bulk could not pass through the doorway. Rearing up, it began to tear at the exposed blocks above the metal frame. The other beasts joined it, adding their strength.

And slowly the great rocks began to crack and give.

*

Kesa Khan opened his eyes and smiled. Miriel was watching him, saw the gleam of triumph in his eyes. 'We can move now,' he said, with a dry laugh. 'The way is made smooth.'

'But you said there was nowhere else!'

'There wasn't. Now there is. It is a fortress – very old. It is called Kar-Barzac. Tomorrow we will make the journey.'

'There is much that you are not telling me,' pointed out Miriel.

'There is much you do not need to know. Rest, Miriel, you will need your strength. Go – sit with your friends. Leave me. I will call you when the time comes.' Miriel wanted to question him further, but the little man had once more closed his eyes and sat, arms folded before the small fire.

She rose and wandered out into the night. Senta was asleep when she reached the small cave, but Angel was sitting under the stars, listening to the distant sounds of battle coming from the pass. A small boy was close by him. Miriel smiled. The two figures were in an identical position some twenty feet apart, Angel and the child both sitting cross-legged. The gladiator was sharpening his sword with a whetstone, the boy, holding a piece of wood, copying him.

'I see you have made a friend,' said Miriel. Angel grunted something inaudible. Miriel sat beside him. 'Who is he?'

'How should I know? He never speaks. He just mimics.'

Miriel's Talent reached out, then drew back. 'He's totally deaf,' she said. 'An orphan.'

Angel sighed. 'I didn't need to know that,' he said, sheathing his sword. The ragged child slid his stick into his belt.

Miriel reached out and stroked the gladiator's face. 'You are a good man, Angel. It means you have no real skill when it comes to harbouring hate.'

He caught her wrist and held to it. 'You shouldn't be touching me,' he said softly. 'The man for you is in there. Young. Handsome. With a disgusting lack of scars.'

224

'I will choose my own man when the time comes,' she told him. 'I am not some Drenai noblewoman whose marriage brings an alliance between warring factions. Nor do I have to concern myself with a dowry. I will marry a man I like, a man I respect.'

'You didn't mention love,' he pointed out.

'I have heard great talk of it, Angel, but I don't know what it is. I love my father. I love you. I loved my sister and my mother. One word. Different feelings. Are we talking of lust?'

'Partly,' he agreed. 'And there's nothing wrong with that, though many would have us believe otherwise. But it is more than that. I had an affair with a dark-haired woman once. Unbelievable. In bed she could raise more passion in me than any of my wives. But I didn't stay with her. I didn't love her, you see. I adored her. But I didn't love her.'

'There's that word again!' chided Miriel.

He chuckled. 'I know. It's just a short way of describing someone who is your friend, bed-mate, sister, aye even mother sometimes. Someone who will arouse your passion and your admiration and your respect. Someone, who when the whole world turns against you, is still standing by your side. You look for someone like that, Miriel.' He released her hand and looked away.

She leaned in close. 'What about you, Angel? Would you be a friend, a lover, a brother and a father?'

He turned his scarred features towards her. 'Aye, I would.' He hesitated and she sensed his indecision. At last he smiled and, taking her hand, kissed it. 'My boots are older than you, Miriel. And you may think it makes no difference now, but it does. You need a man who can grow with you, not grow senile on you.' He took a deep breath. 'It's hard to admit this, you know.'

'You are not old,' she admonished him.

'Don't you like Senta?' he countered.

She looked away. 'I find him . . . exciting . . . frightening.'

'That's good,' he said. 'That's how life should be. Me,

225

I'm like an old armchair. Comfortable. A girl like you needs more than that. Give him a chance. There's a lot of good in him.'

'Why do you like him so much?'

He grinned. 'I knew his mother,' he said. 'A long time ago. Before he was born.'

'You mean. . . ?'

'I have no idea, but he could be. He certainly doesn't take after the husband. But that's between you and me now! Understand?'

'And yet you would have fought him back at the cabin?'

He nodded, his face solemn. 'I wouldn't have won. He's very good. The best I've ever seen.' Suddenly she laughed. 'What's so amusing?' he asked.

'He wasn't going to try to kill you. I read that in his thoughts. He was looking to disarm or wound you.'

'That would have been a bad mistake.'

She looked into his eyes and her smile faded. 'But you might have been killing your own son!'

'I know. Not very uplifting, is it? But I am a warrior, Miriel, and when swords are drawn there is no emotion. Merely survival or death.' He glanced at the Nadir boy, who was sleeping now against a rock, his head resting on his stick-thin arms, his knees drawn up to his belly. Rising silently, Angel moved across to the lad, covering him with his cloak. Then he returned to Miriel. 'What is the old man planning?'

'I don't know, but we will be moving – tomorrow. To an old fortress in the mountains.'

'That is good news. We cannot hold here for much longer. You should get some sleep.'

'I can't. He will need me soon.'

'For what?'

'For when the dead walk,' she answered.

*

Kesa Khan sat by his fire, his ancient body shivering as the night winds fanned the flames. He was beyond tiredness

226

now, a mortal weariness settling on him. It was all so complex, so many lines of destiny to be drawn together. Why, he wondered idly, had this not come to pass when he was young and in full strength? Why now, when he was old and weary and ready for the grave? The gods were indeed capricious at best.

Plans, ideas, strategies flowed through his mind. And each was dependent upon another for success. The journey of a thousand leagues begins with a single step, he told himself. Concentrate only on the step before you.

The demons would come, and with them the souls of the dead. How best to combat them? The Drenai woman was strong, stronger than she knew, but she alone could not guarantee success. Closing his eyes he mentally summoned Miriel. The time was close.

He reached for the clay pot and the grey powder, but his hand drew back. He had taken too much already. Ah, but the gods do love a reckless man! Dipping his finger into the powder he scooped a small amount to his mouth. His heart began to beat erratically, and he felt strength flowing into his limbs. The fire burned yellow, then gold, then purple, and the shadows on the walls became dancers, spinning and turning.

The Drenai woman entered the cave. My, but she was ugly, he thought. Too tall and stringy. Even in his youth he could not have found her attractive. The Drenai warrior with the scarred face moved in behind her. Kesa Khan's dark eyes focused on the man. 'This is no place for those with no power,' he said.

'I told him that,' said Miriel, seating herself opposite the shaman, 'but he came anyway.'

'She said there would be demons and the undead. Can they be slain with a sword?' asked Angel.

'No,' answered the shaman.

'With bare hands, then?'

'No.'

'How then will Miriel fight them?'

'With her courage and her Talent.'

227

'Then I shall stand beside her. No one has yet doubted my courage.'

'You are needed here, to man the wall, to stop the human enemy. It would be the worst folly to allow you to enter the Void. It would be a waste.'

'You do not control my life,' roared Angel. 'I am here because of her. If she dies I leave. I care nothing for you lice-infested barbarians. You understand? So if she is in danger – I go with her.'

Kesa Khan's eyes became hooded and wary as he gazed on the towering Drenai. How I hate them, he thought. Their casual arrogance, their monumental condescension. Lifting his eyes he met Angel's pale gaze, and Kesa Khan allowed his hatred to transmit to the warrior. Angel smiled and nodded slowly. Kesa Khan rose. 'As you wish, Hard-to-Kill. You will journey with the woman.'

'Good,' said the gladiator, sitting beside Miriel.

'No,' she said. 'This is not wise. If I am to fight then I cannot look after Angel.'

'I need no looking after!' he protested.

'Be quiet!' she snapped. 'You have no conception of the journey – or the perils, or what is needed even to protect yourself. You will be like a babe in arms. And I will have no time to suckle you!'

He reddened and pushed himself to his feet. Kesa Khan stepped forward. 'No, no!' he said. 'I think you misjudge the situation, Miriel, as did I at first. The Void is a deadly place, but a man with courage is not to be lightly dismissed. I will send you both. And I will arm Hard-to-Kill with weapons he understands.'

'Where will you be?'

'Here. Waiting. But I will be linked to you.'

'But this is where the demons will come, surely?'

'No. They will not be hunting me. Did you not realise? That is why I needed you. They will be seeking out your father. Zhu Chao knows he is a terrible danger to him. He has tried to kill him in this world, and failed. Now he will seek to lure his soul into the Void. He must be protected.'

'He also has no Talent,' said Miriel, fear rising.

'There you are wrong,' whispered Kesa Khan. 'He has the greatest talent of all. He knows how to survive.'

15

Kasai and his men had been hunting for more than three hours when they saw the southerner on the giant red stallion. Kasai reined in his hill pony. It was a fine beast, fourteen hands tall, but the southerner's horse was sixteen hands, maybe more. Kasai's cousin Chulai reined in alongside him. 'Do we kill him?' he asked.

'Wait,' ordered Kasai, studying the approaching rider. The man was dressed in black, a dark fur-lined cloak slung across his shoulders. There was dried blood on his face. The rider saw them and angled his horse towards the waiting group. Kasai saw no sign of fear in the man.

'Fine horse,' said Kasai, as the man pulled back on the reins.

'Better than the man I killed to get him,' said the rider, his dark eyes scanning the group. He seemed amused, which angered Kasai.

'It is a horse worth killing for,' he said pointedly, hand on his sword-hilt.

'True,' agreed the rider. 'But the question you must ask yourself is, whether he is worth dying for.'

'We are five, you are one.'

'Wrong. One and one. You and I. For when the action begins I will kill you within the first heartbeat.' The words were spoken with a quiet certainty that swept over Kasai's confidence like a winter wind.

'You dismiss my brothers so easily?' he said, trying to re-establish the fact that they outnumbered the southerner.

The rider laughed and swung his gaze over the other men. 'I never dismiss any Nadir lightly. I've fought too many in the past. Now it seems you have two choices; you can fight, or we can ride to your camp and eat.'

'Let us kill him,' said Chulai, slipping into the Nadir tongue.

'It will be the last move you make, dung-brain,' said the rider, in perfect Nadir.

Chulai half-drew his sword, but Kasai ordered him back. 'How do you know our tongue?' he enquired.

'Do we eat or fight?' countered the man.

'We eat. We offer you the hospitality of the tent. Now, how do you know our tongue?'

'I have travelled among the Nadir for many years, both as friend and enemy. My name is Waylander, though I have other names among the people of the tents.'

Kasai nodded. 'I have heard of you, Oxskull – you are a mighty warrior. Follow me, and you will have the food you desire.' Kasai wheeled his pony and galloped towards the north. Chulai cast a murderous glance at the Drenai and then followed.

Two hours later they were seated around a burning brazier within a tall, goatskin tent. Waylander was sitting cross-legged upon a rug, Kasai before him. Both men had dined from a communal bowl of curdled cheese and shared a clay goblet of strong spirit.

'What brings you to the steppes, Oxskull?'

'I seek Kesa Khan of the Wolves.'

Kasai nodded. 'His death has been long overdue.'

Waylander chuckled. 'I am not here to kill him, but to help him survive.'

'It cannot be true!'

'I assure you that it is. My daughter and my friends are with him now – or so I hope.'

Kasai was amazed. 'Why? What are the Wolves to you? We still talk of Kesa Khan's magic and the werebeasts he sent to kill you. Why would you help *him*?'

'The enemy of my enemy is my friend,' answered Waylander. 'There is a man who serves the Emperor. He is the enemy I wish to see slain.'

'Zhu Chao! May the gods curse his soul until the stars burn out! Aye, a good enemy, that one. But you are too late to help the Wolves. The Gothir have already begun their attack upon the mountain stronghold. There is no way through.'

'I will find a way.'

Kasai nodded and drained the last of the spirit, refilling the goblet from a jug beside him. He offered it to Waylander, who drank sparingly. 'My people are the Tall Spears. We are enemies of the Wolves. Lifelong – and before that. But I do not want to see the Gothir destroy them. I wish to be the man who drives a blade into Anshi Chen. I wish to cut the head from Belash. I wish to drag out the heart of Kesa Khan. Such pleasures are not for some round-eyed, stone-dwelling pig to enjoy.'

'How many men do you have here?'

'Fighting men? Six hundred.'

'Perhaps you should consider aiding the Wolves.'

'Pah! My tongue would turn black and all my ancestors turn their backs upon me when I entered the Vale of Rest. No, I shall not aid them, but I will aid you. I will give you food and, if you wish, a guide. There are other routes into the Mountains.'

'I thank you, Kasai.'

'It is nothing. If you do find Kesa Khan, tell him why I helped you.'

'I'll do that. Tell me, do you dream of the day the Uniter will come?'

'Of course, what Nadir does not?'

'How do you see him?'

'He will be of the Tall Spears, that is certain.'

'And how will he unite the Nadir?'

Kasai smiled. 'Well, first he will obliterate the Wolves, and all other treacherous tribes.'

'Suppose the Uniter is not of the Tall Spears. Suppose he is of the Wolves?'

'Impossible.'

'He'll need to be a rare man,' said Waylander.

'Let's drink to that,' said Kasai, passing the goblet.

*

Wrapped in his cloak, his head resting on his saddle, Waylander lay on the rug, listening to the night winds howling outside the tent. On the far side of the brazier

Kasai was sleeping, his two wives on either side of him, his children close by. Waylander was tired, but sleep would not come. Rolling on to his back he gazed up at the smoke drifting through the hole in the tent roof, watching the wind swirl it away. He could see three stars, high in the night sky. He closed his eyes.

And remembered the day he had fought to protect the Armour of Bronze. The Nadir had come for him, but these he had slain. Then the last of the wolf-beasts had stalked him. Two bolts through the brain had finally ended the terror. Wounded and alone he had dragged himself from the cave – only to face the Knights of the Brotherhood. These he could not defeat, but Durmast the giant, treacherous Durmast, had arrived to save him, giving his life for a man he had planned to betray.

Waylander sighed. So many dead. Durmast, Gellan, Danyal, Krylla . . . And always the wars – conquest and battle, defeat and despair. Where does it end, he thought. With the grave? Or do the battles go on?

Kasai was snoring now. Waylander heard him grunt as one of his wives nudged him. Opening his eyes he gazed across the tent. The brazier was burning low, a soft red glow filling the interior. Kasai had a family. He had made a gift to the future. He was loved.

Waylander turned to his side, facing away from the Nadir leader. Once more he tried for sleep, but this time he saw Dardalion, tied to the tree, his flesh sliced and bleeding, the men around him laughing and mocking.

That was the day Waylander's world had changed. He had rescued the priest, then been drawn into the eternal battle, Light against Dark, Harmony against Chaos. And he had met Danyal. He groaned and rolled again, his body weary, muscles aching.

Stop dwelling on the past, he told himself. Think about tomorrow. Just tomorrow. He would find a way into the Mountains of the Moon. He would stand beside Miriel and Angel and do that which he did best. He would fight.

He would kill.

Sleep took him by surprise, and his soul drifted into darkness.

*

The walls were clammy, the corridor dark and claustrophobic. Waylander blinked and tried to remember how he had come here. It was so hard to concentrate. Was he looking for something? Someone?

There were no doors or windows, just this endless tunnel. Cold water was soaking through his boots as he waded on.

I am lost, he thought.

There was no source of light, and yet he could see.

Stairs. Must look for stairs. Fear touched him, but he suppressed it ruthlessly. Stay calm! Think! He moved on. Something white caught his eye on the far wall. There was an alcove there. Splashing across the streaming water he saw a skeleton, rusty chains holding it to the wall. The ligaments and tendons had not yet rotted and the thing was intact, save for the left leg, which had parted at the knee. Something moved within the ribcage and Waylander saw two rats had made a nest there.

'Welcome,' said a voice. Waylander stepped back in shock. The head was no longer a skull but a handsome face, framed in golden hair. It smiled at him. Waylander's heart was beating wildly and he reached for his crossbow. Only then did he realise he was weaponless. 'Welcome to my home,' said the handsome head.

'I am dreaming!'

'Perhaps,' agreed the head. A rat pushed its way through the gaping ribcage and sprang to a nearby shelf of stone.

'Where is this place?' asked Waylander.

The head laughed, the sound echoing away into the tunnel. 'Well, let us think . . . Does it look to you like paradise?'

'No.'

'Then it must be somewhere else. But one mustn't complain, must one? It is pleasant to have a visitor after so long. The rats are company, of course, but their conversation is rather limited.'

'How do I get out of here?'

The head smiled, and Waylander saw the pale eyes widen, a gleam of triumph showing there. Waylander spun. A sword lunged for his throat. Swaying aside he slammed his fist into a face out of nightmare. His assailant fell back into the water, but rose swiftly. He looked like a man, save that his skin was scaled, his eyes huge and set, like a fish, on either side of his head. He had no nose, merely slits in the skin of his face, and his mouth was shaped like an inverted V, lipless and rimmed with fangs.

The creature leapt forward. Waylander reached out, his fingers curling around one of the skeleton's ribs, and snapping it clear. The sword slashed down. Waylander sidestepped the blow and rammed the broken rib into the creature's chest. Dropping the sword it let out a terrible howl. And disappeared.

Waylander scooped up the sword and swung back to the skeleton. The handsome head was no longer visible. The rotting skull sagged against the vertebrae and toppled into the murky water.

Sword in hand Waylander moved on, every sense alert.

The tunnel widened and he saw an arch of stone and a path leading to a stairwell. An old man was sitting on the first stair. His robes were old and covered in mildew and mould. In his hands was a sphere of transparent crystal, a white light shining at the centre.

Waylander approached him.

'This is your soul,' said the old man, holding up the crystal. 'If I drop it, or break it, or crush it, you will never leave here. You will wander these tunnels for eternity. Go back the way you have come.'

'I wish to climb those stairs, old man. Step aside.'

'One step towards me and your soul perishes!' warned the old man, holding the crystal high. Waylander sprang forward, his sword smashing through the crystal, sending glittering shards to the water. The old man fell back. 'How did you know?' he moaned.

'My soul is my own,' answered Waylander. The old man vanished.

And the stairs beckoned.

Waylander edged forward. The stairwell walls shimmered with a faintly green light, the stairs glistening as if oiled. He took a long deep breath then ventured on to the first step. Then the second. Arms swept out from the walls, hooked fingers and talons reaching for him. The sword slashed down, hacking through a scaled wrist. Fingers grabbed at his black leather tunic. Tearing himself free he forced his way up the stairwell, the sword-blade hacking a path through the writhing, questing limbs.

At the top of the stairs was a square landing. There were two doors, one edged with gold and part-open, the other guarded by a huge three-headed serpent, whose coils rose up around the frame. The part-open door showed a shaft of sunlight, warm and welcoming, beckoning the man. Waylander ignored it, his eyes fixed to the serpent. Its mouths were cavernous, each showing twin fangs more than a foot long. Venom dripped from them, splashing to the stone of the landing, bubbling and hissing.

A figure in a robe of light appeared at the part-open door. 'Come this way. Quickly!' said the figure, a friendly-faced man with white hair and kindly blue eyes. 'Come to the light!' Waylander moved towards him, as if to comply, but once close enough he reached out, pulling the man forward by his robes, then hurling him at the serpent. Two of the heads darted forward, the first closing on the man's shoulder, the second sinking its fangs into his leg. The victim's screams filled the air.

As Waylander leapt past the struggling man the third head lunged down. Waylander's sword smote it in the eye. Black blood bubbled from the wound and the head withdrew. Throwing his shoulder against the door Waylander felt the wood give way, and he fell into a wide hall. Rolling to his feet he saw a man waiting for him, sword in hand.

It was Morak.

'No dying dog to save you now!' said the dead assassin.

'I don't need help for the likes of you,' Waylander told him. 'You were nothing then. You are less than nothing now.'

Morak's face twisted and he ran to the attack. Waylander sidestepped, parried the lunge then sent a riposte that almost tore Morak's head from his neck. The assassin staggered then righted himself, his head hanging at an obscene angle.

'How do you kill a dead man?' he mocked. Morak attacked again. Waylander parried and once more chopped at the gashed neck. The head fell to the floor, but the body continued its assault. Waylander blocked two thrusts, slashing his blade into the already open ribcage. It did not even slow the headless opponent. Laughter came from the air. 'Are you beginning to know fear?' Morak's voice echoed in the hall, the air filled with screaming obscenities.

Ducking under a wild cut Waylander ran to the head, lifting it by the hair. Spinning round he hurled it towards the doorway. It bounced and rolled through the gap. A serpent lunged, the great mouth snapping shut. The screams stopped instantly.

The headless body collapsed.

Waylander whirled, awaiting the next attack.

'How did you know which door to take?' asked another voice. Waylander searched for the source of the sound, but could see no one.

'It was not difficult,' he answered, holding his blade at the ready.

'Yes, I can see that. The sunlight and the white robe was a little too obvious. I won't make that mistake again. I must say Morak was a disappointment. He gave you a much greater battle while alive.'

'He had more to fight for,' said Waylander. 'Who are you? Show yourself!'

'Of course, how impolite of me.' A figure shimmered into being on the far side of the hall, a tall man wearing purple robes. His hair was waxed flat to his skull, save for two braided sideburns that hung to his slender shoulders. 'I am Zhu Chao.'

'I have heard the name.'

'Of course you have. Now, let us see what we can conjure for our pleasure. Something from your past, perhaps?' Zhu Chao extended his arm, pointing at a spot midway into the

237

hall. Black smoke swirled there, forming into a beast more than eight feet high. It had the head of a wolf, the body of a giant man. 'Such a shame you do not have your little bow with you,' said Zhu Chao.

Waylander backed away as the beast advanced, its blood-red eyes focused on its prey. A silver arrow lanced across the hall, spearing into the creature's neck. A second followed it, piercing the great chest. The beast slumped to its knees then fell headfirst to the flagstones.

Waylander spun. Miriel, bow in hand, Angel beside her, was standing by the doorway. Angel ran forward.

'Get back!' ordered Waylander, sword raised.

'What the Hell is the matter with you?' asked Angel.

'Nothing is as it seems in this place,' Waylander told him. 'And I'll not be fooled by a demon just because he looks like a friend.'

Miriel advanced. 'Judge by actions, Father,' she said. Waylander's crossbow materialised in his hand, a full bolt quiver appearing at his belt.

'How did you come here?' he asked, still wary.

'Kesa Khan sent us. Now we must get out of this place.'

Loading his crossbow, Waylander swung back to where Zhu Chao had been standing.

But the wizard had gone.

*

There were many doors on both sides of the hall. Miriel ran towards the nearest, but Waylander called her back.

'What is this place?' he asked her.

'It exists in the Void. The castle was created by Zhu Chao as a trap for you. We must get out, move beyond his power.' Once more she started for the door, but he grabbed her arm, his dark eyes showing his anger.

'Stop and think!' he snapped. 'This is *his* creation, so none of the doorways will lead to freedom. Beyond them is only more peril.'

'What do you suggest?' asked Angel. 'Do we just wait here?'

'Exactly. His powers are not inexhaustible. We stand, and we fight. Whatever comes we kill.'

'No,' insisted Miriel. 'You have no conception of what exists in the Void. Demons, monsters, spirits – creatures of colossal evil. Kesa Khan warned me of them.'

'If Zhu Chao had the power to conjure such creatures I would already be dead,' said Waylander softly. 'But whatever surprises he has for us are waiting beyond those doors. There or here. Those are our only choices. And here we have space. Tell me of the Void,' he ordered Miriel.

'It is a place of spirit,' she told him, 'of wandering. It is the Great Emptiness between what was and what is.'

'Nothing is real here?'

'Real and yet not real. Yes.'

'This crossbow is not ebony and steel?'

'No. It is a thing of spirit – *your* spirit. An extension of your will.'

'Then I need not load it?'

'I . . . don't know.'

Waylander levelled the bow and loosed the triggers. The bolts flashed across the hall, hammering into a black door. He gazed down at the weapon, the strings hanging slack. Then he raised it again. Instantly two bolts slashed through the air. 'Good,' he said. 'Now let them come. And I will have my knives.' A baldric appeared on his chest, three knives in sheaths hanging from it. His chain-mail shoulder-guard materialised, not black, but of shining silver. 'What of you, Angel?' he asked, with a wide grin. 'What do you desire?'

The gladiator smiled. 'Two golden swords and armour, encrusted with gems.'

'You shall have them!'

A golden helm appeared, a white-crested plume arcing back from brow to nape of neck. And a breastplate and greaves, glittering with rubies and diamonds. Two scabbarded swords shimmered into place at his side.

All the doors in the hall swept open and a host of shadow shapes swarmed towards the waiting warriors.

'I'll have light also!' yelled Waylander. The ceiling

disappeared and sunlight filled the hall, spearing through the dark horde, which vanished like mist in a morning breeze.

Then a black cloud formed above them, obliterating the light, and a cold voice hissed from all around them. 'You learn swiftly, Waylander, but you do not have the skill to oppose me.'

Even as the echoes died away nine knights in black armour appeared, long triangular shields upon their arms, black-bladed swords in their hands. Waylander spun and sent two bolts at the first. They thudded into the knight's shield. Miriel loosed a shaft, but this also was turned aside. And the knights advanced.

'What do we do?' whispered Angel, drawing both his swords.

Waylander aimed his crossbow above the advancing warriors and let fly. The bolt swept over the advancing men then turned, plunging into the back of the closest. 'Anything is possible here,' said Waylander. 'Let your mind loose!'

The knights charged, holding their shields before them. A white shield appeared on Waylander's arm, his crossbow becoming a sword of light. He leapt forward, crashing his shield into the first knight, hurling him back off-balance, then moved into the gap, slashing his blade to the left, cleaving it through the ribs of an advancing warrior.

Angel took two running steps then threw himself towards the ground, rolling into the charging knights. Three tumbled over him, their shields clattering to the flagstones. He reared up and killed the first two, one with a disembowelling lunge, the second with a reverse thrust. Miriel slew the third with an arrow through the eye.

Two knights converged on Miriel. Instantly her bow became a shining sabre. Ducking under a wild cut she leapt high, her foot hammering into the first man's chin. He was catapulted back. The second slashed his sword towards her face. She swayed and sent her sabre in a wicked slash that tore through the chain-mail at the knight's throat. He fell and she plunged her sword into his unprotected back.

The three remaining knights backed away. Angel ran at them. 'No!' bellowed Waylander. 'Let them go!'

Angel backed to where Waylander and Miriel were standing. 'I can't think of any magic,' he grumbled.

'You will need none,' said Waylander, pointing to the fading castle walls. 'It is over.'

Within a heartbeat they were standing on a wide grey road, the castle a memory.

'You risked your life for me, Miriel,' said Waylander, taking his daughter in his arms. 'You came into Hell for me. I'll never forget that, as long as I live.' Releasing her he turned to Angel. 'And you too my friend. How can I thank you?'

'You could start by letting Miriel take me away from here,' answered Angel, casting nervous glances at the slate-grey sky and the brooding hills.

Waylander laughed. 'So be it. How do we leave, Miriel?'

She moved alongside him and laid her hands over his eyes. 'Think of your body, and where it sleeps. Then relax, as if drifting to sleep. And we will see you in the mountains very soon.'

Reaching up he pulled clear her hands, holding to them. 'I won't be coming to the mountains,' he said softly.

'What do you mean?'

'I will just be another sword there. I must go where my talents can be used at their best.'

'Not Gulgothir?' she pleaded.

'Yes. Zhu Chao is the cause of all this. When he is dead maybe it will be over.'

'Oh Father, he is a wizard. And he will be guarded. Worse, he knows you will come – that is why he laid this trap for you. He will be waiting. How can you succeed?'

'He's Waylander the Slayer,' said Angel. 'How can he not?'

*

'What a fool!' cackled Kesa Khan, leaping to his feet and capering about the cave, his weariness forgotten. Miriel looked on in astonishment. Angel merely shook his head.

'To think,' continued the shaman, 'that he tried to kill Waylander by direct action. It is almost bliss! Like trying to choke a lion by forcing your head into its mouth. Bliss!'

'What are you talking about?' asked Miriel.

Kesa Khan sighed and settled down by the fire. 'You are his daughter and you do not see it? He is like a fire. Left to his own devices he burns down to low, glowing embers. But to attack him is to throw twigs and branches to the flames. Can you understand that? Look!' Kesa Khan waved his hand above the flames, which flattened into a mirror of fire. Within it they saw Waylander moving slowly through the Void tunnel, water drenching his boots. 'Here he was afraid, for there were no enemies, only darkness. He was lost. No memory. No weapons.' They watched the tiny figure reach the skeleton, saw the golden-haired head materialise. 'Now observe!' ordered Kesa Khan.

The scaled creature reared up behind Waylander, who snatched the rib and rammed it into the beast's chest. 'Now,' said the shaman, 'he has a sword. Now, he has a purpose. Enemies are all around him. His talents are focused. See how he moves, like a wolf.'

Silently they sat as the tiny figure destroyed the sphere and battled his way up the staircase of hands. 'This I loved,' cackled the shaman, as Waylander threw the white-robed priest into the jaws of the serpent. 'He knew, do you see? In the dark, surrounded by foes, he knew there was no succour. The doorway he chose was the guarded one. Oh, it is so perfect. He must have Nadir blood! And to summon sunshine into the Void! Beautiful. Perfect! Zhu Chao must be trembling now. By all the gods, I would be.'

'I do not know if he is trembling,' said Miriel, 'but I do know my father is riding for Gulgothir. And there will be no sunshine to summon there. Zhu Chao will surround himself with armed guards: he will be waiting.'

'As the gods will,' said Kesa Khan, with a wave of his hand. The fire flared once more. 'Tomorrow we must move the women and children to Kar-Barzac. I have sent a message to Anshi Chen. He will leave a small rearguard to hold the passes. Fifty men will remain here until dark to defend the wall. It should be enough.'

'What about my father?' insisted Miriel.

'His fate is in the hands of the gods,' answered Kesa Khan. 'He will live or die. There is nothing we can do.'

'Zhu Chao will use magic to locate him,' said Miriel. 'Can you shield him?'

'No, I do not have the power. There are deadly beasts in the valley of Kar-Barzac. I need all my strength to send them into the mountains, clearing the path for my people to the fortress.'

'Then what chance will my father have?'

'That we will see. Do not underestimate him.'

'There must be something we can do!'

'Yes, yes. We fight on. We make Zhu Chao concentrate his energies on Kar-Barzac. That is what he wants. His dreams lie in that old castle.'

'Why?' asked Angel.

'The Elders built it. They cast great spells there, creating living demons known as Joinings to fight their wars. Beasts merged with men: the magic was colossal. So great that it ultimately destroyed them, but in Kar-Barzac the magic lived on, radiating out. You will see. The valley is twisted by it, deformed trees, carnivorous sheep and goats. I even saw a rabbit there with fangs. Nothing could live in that valley without being corrupted, twisted out of shape. Even the castle is now a monstrosity, the granite blocks re-shaped as if they were wet clay.'

'Then how the Hell can we go there?' said Angel.

Kesa Khan smiled, and his dark eyes gleamed. 'Someone was kind enough to stop the magic,' he said. He looked away from them, staring into the fire.

'What is it you are not telling us?' asked Miriel.

'A great deal,' admitted the shaman. 'But there is much you do not need to know. Our enemies reached Kar-Barzac before us. They removed the source of magic – aye, and died for it. Now it is safe. We shall defend its walls, and there the line of the Uniter will be continued.'

243

'How long can we hold this fortress?' enquired Angel.

'We shall see,' answered Kesa Khan, 'but for now I need to drive the beasts from the valley. Leave me.'

16

Zhu Chao's image floated before Altharin as the General stood in his tent, his aide Powis beside him, the albino Brotherhood captain, Innicas, to his left.

'You have failed your Emperor,' said Zhu Chao. 'He set you a simple task and you have behaved like an incompetent. A few Nadir to kill and you baulk at the test.'

'Those few Nadir,' said Altharin coldly, 'have boxed themselves behind three narrow passes. I have lost more than two hundred men trying to force a way through them, and your famed Brotherhood have enjoyed no more success than I. One old man broke their attack.'

'You dare to criticise the Brotherhood?' hissed Zhu Chao. 'You are worse than incompetent. You are a traitor!'

'I serve the Emperor – not you, you puffed up . . .' He groaned and sagged into the arms of Powis, a long-handled knife jutting from his ribs.

Eyes wide with shock, Powis took the dying general in his arms, lowering him to the floor. He looked up at the white-haired figure of Innicas. 'You have killed him!' he whispered.

Altharin tried to speak, but blood bubbled from his lips and his head sagged back. Innicas leaned down and dragged the knife clear, wiping it clean on the dead General's tunic of silk. Powis rose, hands trembling.

'Do nothing rash, boy!' said the image of Zhu Chao. 'The order for his death came from the Emperor himself. Go and fetch Gallis. Tell him the Emperor has promoted him.'

Powis stepped back then gazed down at the corpse upon the floor. 'Do it now!' ordered Innicas.

Powis stumbled back and ran from the tent.

'There is another pass, Lord, thirty miles to the north,' said Innicas.

'Take one hundred men – the best we have. The Nadir

will try to reach Kar-Barzac. Catch them in the valley. They will be stretched thin, some already at the fortress, others trying to fight a rearguard. The women and children will be in a column on open ground. Destroy them! We'll see how well the Nadir fight when there is nothing left to fight for.'

'As you order it, Lord, so will it be,' said Innicas, bowing.

'Have you reached Gracus and the others?'

'No, Lord. But Zamon is waiting in the mountains with their horses. He said they arrived safely. They are planning to move below ground. Perhaps the magic of Kar-Barzac prevents communication.'

'They are there – that is what matters,' said Zhu Chao. 'All is as we planned it. The Ventrians have landed in the south. The Drenai, without Karnak, have fallen back in disorder. Our own troops are waiting to sweep down on to the Sentran Plain. But much of what we need for future control lies in Kar-Barzac. Do not fail me, Innicas!'

'You may rely on me, my lord.'

'Let it be so.'

*

The Gothir, dragging and carrying their wounded with them, fell back as the sun drifted low behind the mountains. Senta slumped to the ground, Belash beside him. 'I hate to admit it, but I'm getting tired,' said the swordsman.

'I also,' admitted Belash. The Nadir leaned his head back against the black rock of the wall. 'The attacks were more fierce today.' He rubbed his tired eyes. 'We will fall back in two hours.'

'How far is it to this fortress?'

'We will be in the valley by the dawn,' said Belash glumly.

'You don't sound too enthusiastic, my friend.'

'It is a place of much evil.' Belash opened the pouch at his side and removed the bones, which he held pressed between his palms. He sighed. 'I think Belash will die there,' he said.

'What are those things?' asked Senta, seeking to change the subject.

'The right hand of my father. He was killed, a long time ago now, and still I am no closer to avenging him.'

'What happened?'

'He had ponies to sell and rode to the market at Namib. A long way. He went with my brother and Anshi Chen. Only Anshi survived the attack. He was behind the herd, and when the raiders struck, Anshi fled.'

'That's why there is such anger between you? Because he was a coward?'

'He is no coward!' snapped Belash. 'There were too many of the raiders, and it would have been stupid to fight. No, Anshi and I loved the same woman. She chose him. But he is a fine chieftain, may my tongue turn black for admitting it. I tried to track the raiders. I found my father's body, took these bones and buried the rest. But the tracks were too old. Anshi watched as my father was struck down. He saw the man who dealt the death blow; he described him to me. I have lived since then in the hope of finding him – a white-haired warrior, with eyes the colour of blood.'

'There's still time,' said Senta.

'Maybe.' Belash levered himself to his feet, and wandered away along the wall, speaking to the defenders, kneeling beside the wounded and the dying.

Senta stretched himself out, lying back with his head on his hands, watching the stars appear in the darkening sky. The air was fresh and cool, the bonded rocks below his back feeling almost soft. He closed his eyes. When he opened them again Miriel was beside him. He smiled, 'I fell asleep,' he said. 'But I dreamt of you.'

'Something lascivious, I have no doubt.'

He sat up and stretched. 'No. We were sitting in a field by a stream, beneath the branches of a willow. We were holding hands. Like this.' Reaching out he took her hand, raising it to his lips.

'You never give in, do you?' she said, pulling back from his touch.

'Never! Why don't you kiss me, beauty? Just the once. To see if you like it.'

'No.'

'You cut me to the bone.'

'I think you'll survive.'

'You are frightened, aren't you? Frightened of giving. Frightened of living. I heard you with Angel last night, offering yourself to him. It was a mistake, beauty, and Angel was right to say no. Insane, but right. What is it you fear?'

'I don't want to talk about this,' said Miriel, making to rise. Reaching out he lightly touched her arm.

'Talk to me,' he said softly.

'Why?' she whispered.

'Because I care.'

She sank back and for a while, said nothing. He did not press her, but sat beside her in silence. At last she spoke. 'If you love someone you open all the doors into your heart. You let them in. When they die you have no defences. I saw my father's pain when . . . when Mother was killed. I don't want that pain. Ever.'

'You can't avoid it, Miriel. No one can. We are like the seasons – we grow in spring, mature in summer, fade in the autumn and die in the winter. But it is foolish to say, "It is springtime but I will grow no flowers for they must fade." What is life without love? Perpetual winter. Cold and snow. It's not for you, beauty. Trust me.'

His hand stroked her hair and he leaned in close, his lips brushing her cheek. Slowly she turned her head and his mouth touched hers.

An arrow sailed over the wall, and the sound of pounding feet echoed in the pass.

'The Gothir have immaculate timing,' he said, rising up and drawing his sword.

*

Angel was uneasy as he stood on the rim of the valley, looking out over the moonlit grassland and the gentle hills. In the distance he could see the turrets and walls of Kar-

Barzac, close to a wide flat lake the colour of old iron. Nadir women and children were moving down into the valley in a long, shuffling line, many of them dragging carts piled high with their possessions. Angel switched his gaze to the rearing mountains that circled the valley, scanning the twisted peaks. This was all open ground, and he thought of the defenders manning the three passes, and prayed the rearguard would hold. For if the Gothir forced their way through any one pass . . .

He closed his mind to the pictures of carnage.

Most of the Nadir warriors had ridden ahead to the fortress, the majority of those remaining defending the passes. Only thirty men rode with the women and children, shepherding them towards Kar-Barzac. Angel swung into the saddle and rode down the hill, his mood lifting as he saw the mute Nadir boy marching beside an overloaded cart, Angel's cloak upon his scrawny shoulders and in his right hand a length of wood, shaped like a sword. The cloak was dragging in the dust. Angel rode alongside the boy and leaned down, lifting him in the air and perching him on the saddle behind him. The boy grinned and waved his wooden sword in the air.

Touching heels to the gelding Angel galloped the horse towards the front of the line where Belash rode beside the Nadir war chief, Anshi Chen. The two warriors were deep in conversation. Anshi looked up as Angel approached. He was a stocky man, running to fat, and his dark eyes showed only hostility as the Drenai reined in.

'We are moving too slowly,' said Angel. 'It will be dawn soon.'

Belash nodded. 'I agree, but many are old. They can move no faster.'

'They could if they left those carts behind.'

Anshi Chen sniffed loudly, then hawked and spat. 'Their possessions are their lives,' he said. 'You would not understand that, Drenai, for yours is a land of plenty. But each of those carts carries far more than you see. A lantern of bronze may be just a light in the dark to you, but it might have been made by a great-grandfather a century ago, and prized ever since. Every item has a value far greater than you can comprehend. Leaving them behind would be a knife in the soul to any family here.'

'It is not a knife in the soul that concerns me,' said Angel. 'It is a knife in the back. But this is your war.' Swinging the horse's head he rode back along the line.

There were more than three hundred people filing on to the valley floor, and he guessed it would be another two hours before the last of them reached the fortress. He thought of Senta and Miriel back at the wall, and Waylander on his lonely journey to Gulgothir.

The stars were fading now, the sky lightening.

And his unease grew.

*

The white-haired Innicas moved back from the shelter of the boulder to where his brother knights waited. 'Now,' he told them. 'The moment is here.' Gathering the reins of his black stallion he vaulted into the saddle, drawing the black sword from the scabbard at his side. One hundred warriors mounted their horses and waited for his order. Innicas closed his eyes, seeking the Communion of Blood. He felt the flowing of the souls, tasted their anger and their need, their bitterness and their desires. 'Let not one Nadir live,' he whispered. 'All dead. Gifts to the Lord of All Desires. Let there be pain. Let there be fear and anguish. Let there be despair!' The souls of his knights fluttered in his mind like black moths, circling the dark light of his hatred. 'What do we need?' he asked them.

'Blood and death,' came the reply, hissing in his mind like a host of snakes.

'Blood and death,' he agreed. 'Now let the spell grow. Let fear flow out over our enemies like a flood, a raging torrent to drown their courage.'

Like an invisible mist the spell rolled out, drifting over rock and shale, down on to the valley, swelling, growing.

The one hundred Knights of Blood ended the communion and rode from their hiding-place, fanning out into a fighting line, swords at the ready.

*

Angel felt the cold touch of fear, his mind leaping back to the day at the cabin when the Brotherhood had first appeared. Dragging on the reins he swung the horse to face the south, and saw the enemy silhouetted against the sky, their black cloaks flowing in the breeze, their swords raised high. Belash saw them at the same time, and shouted to Anshi Chen.

As the spell of fear rolled over them women and children began to wail and run, scattering across the valley. Some threw themselves to the ground, covering their heads with their hands. Others merely stood, frozen in terror. Shia was walking in the centre of the column when the spell struck. With trembling hands she lifted her bow from her shoulder and clumsily notched an arrow to the string.

Angel felt the mute boy's arms tighten around him. Swinging in the saddle he lifted the child, lowering him to the ground beside a hand-drawn cart. The child looked up at him, his eyes wide and fearful. Angel drew his sword and forced a smile. The child pulled his stick from his belt and waved it in the air.

'Good lad!' said Angel.

The thirty Nadir outriders galloped their mounts to where Belash and Anshi Chen were waiting. Angel joined them. 'Their spell of fear will not hold once the killing starts!' said Angel. 'Trust me!'

'There are too many of them,' muttered Anshi Chen, his voice trembling.

'There'll be less before long,' snarled Angel. 'Follow me!' Kicking his horse into a gallop he charged at the black line.

The Brotherhood swept forward, and the thunder of hoofbeats echoed in the valley like the drums of doom. Anger swept through Angel. Behind him were women and children and if, as was most likely, the Brotherhood did break through he did not want to be alive to see the slaughter. He did not glance back to see if the Nadir were with him. He did not care. Battle fever was strong upon him.

251

The black line came closer, and Angel angled his horse towards their centre. Belash came galloping alongside, screaming a Nadir war cry.

Three horsemen closed on Angel. Ducking under one wild cut he slashed his sword into the helm of a second knight. The man was catapulted from the saddle. Belash's horse went down, but the Nadir leapt clear and rolled to his feet. A sword-blade glanced from his shoulder. He leapt and dragged the rider from the saddle, plunging his own blade deep into the man's belly.

The small wedge of Nadir riders was surrounded now, and the wings of the Brotherhood line, some forty men, swept on towards the women and children.

Shia watched them come, fear surging inside her, and drew back on her bowstring. Her first shaft pierced the neck of the leading horse. It fell and rolled, hurling its rider clear, but bringing down two following horses. Other knights swerved to avoid colliding with the fallen. A second shaft sank into the neck of a knight. He swayed in the saddle for a moment, before toppling to the ground.

Shia notched a third arrow – then heard the thunder of hooves from behind her! So close! Spinning she saw a score of riders in silver armour, white cloaks fluttering behind them. They galloped through the refugee line and bore down on the Brotherhood. Shia could not believe what she was seeing. Like silver ghosts they had come from nowhere, and in their wake the spell of fear vanished, like ice under sunlight.

On the far side of the field Angel cut his way clear of the mass and saw the white knights hammer into the Brotherhood. Exultant now he turned again and drove his mount back into the mêlée. Swords clashed all around him, but he was oblivious to danger. His horse went down and he hit the ground hard, a hoof clipping his temple. Losing his grip on his sword Angel rolled. A blade slashed down at him, but he ducked under it, then hurled his weight at the rider's horse. Off-balance the beast fell, tipping the knight to the earth. Angel scrambled across the fallen horse. The knight was struggling to rise when Angel's boot cracked into his helm. The chinstrap ripped and the helm fell clear. The knight tried in vain to stab his attacker, but Angel's fist smashed into his face, spinning him round. Angel's hands closed on his throat like bands of iron. Dropping his sword the knight grabbed at the fingers. But all strength fled from him.

Angel dropped the corpse and gathered up the knight's sword.

Anshi Chen hacked his blade towards the neck of an attacker, but the man part-blocked the blow, the sword striking the side of the helm and dislodging the visor. As it came clear, hanging from the helm like a broken wing, Anshi recognised the albino face. 'Belash!' he cried. 'It is him, Belash!'

Innicas' sword swept out, the blade plunging into Anshi's belly. Belash, hearing the cry, swung and saw Innicas deliver the death blow. All reason fled from the Nadir, and he let out a terrible scream of hate. A horse reared alongside him. Belash leapt at the rider, dragging him from the saddle. Not stopping to slay the man Belash took hold of the pommel and vaulted to the beast's back. Innicas saw him, felt his rage, and quickly scanned the battle line.

The Brotherhood were broken.

Panic rose in his heart. With a savage kick he pushed his horse into a gallop and rode for the south and the hidden pass. Belash set after him, leaning low over the stallion's neck, cutting down wind resistance. Innicas, in full armour, was the heavier man and his stallion tired as it pounded up the hillside. Innicas glanced back. The Nadir was closing.

The knight's stallion, almost at the point of exhaustion, stumbled upon the shale and half-fell. Innicas jumped clear. Belash bore down upon him. The shoulder of Belash's stallion cannoned into the knight, punching him from his feet. Dragging on the reins Belash leapt lightly to the shale.

'You killed my father,' he said. 'Now you will serve him for eternity.'

Innicas, sword in hand, gazed upon the stocky Nadir. The man had no armour, and carried only a short sabre.

The albino's courage returned. 'You cannot stand against me, vermin!' he sneered. 'I'll cut you into pieces.'

Belash attacked, but Innicas' sword blocked the blow and a murderous riposte saw the black blade bury itself in Belash's side, cleaving under the ribs. With the last of his strength Belash dropped his sword and drew his curved dagger. Innicas wrenched at his blade, trying to drag it clear. Belash reached out, his left hand clawing at Innicas' helm, fingers hooking around the broken visor. Innicas felt himself being drawn into a deadly embrace. 'No!' he shouted. Belash's knife plunged into Innicas' left eye, piercing him to the brain. Both men fell.

Innicas twitched and was still. Belash, with trembling hands, opened the blood-drenched pouch at his side, tipping the fingerbones on to the chest of the dead knight. 'Father,' he whispered, blood bubbling from his lips. 'Father . . .'

*

In his panic Innicas had misread the battle. Despite being surprised by the arrival of the white knights, the Brotherhood still had the advantage of numbers. Only seven of the Nadir warriors remained now and, despite being joined by the twenty white-cloaked knights, they were outnumbered by more than two to one.

Angel, bleeding from several wounds, could feel the battle was ready to turn against the Brotherhood. Their leader had fled, and the arrival of the white knights had stunned them. But the enemy could yet win, he knew.

Not while I live, he thought.

A sword slashed past his face, the flat of the blade slamming against his chin. He went down and struggled to rise. Hooves pounded on the earth all around him. Rearing up he pushed a booted foot from the stirrups and propelled the rider to the ground. Taking hold of the pommel he tried to mount the horse, but it reared, throwing him to the ground once more.

With a curse Angel gathered up his fallen sword. A blade lashed down. Angel blocked the blow and, as the rider rode

254

past him, reached up and grabbed the man's cloak, hauling him from the saddle. The knight hit the ground hard. The point of Angel's sword slid between visor and helm and with all his weight Angel drove the weapon deep into the man's skull. The blade snapped. Angel swore.

There was a fallen sword close by. Dodging between the milling horses Angel reached for it, but a rearing hoof smashed into his head and he fell face down on to the grass.

*

He awoke to silence and a terrible pounding in his skull.

'I always seem to be stitching your wounds,' said Senta.

Angel blinked and tried to focus on the ceiling above him. It was twisted at a crazy angle, and the window below it was canted absurdly. 'There's something wrong with my eyes,' he muttered.

'No. It's this place – Kar-Barzac. Nothing is as it should be here. Kesa Khan says it has been corrupted over the centuries by sorcery.'

Angel struggled to sit, but his head swam and he fell back. 'What happened?' he groaned.

'I arrived to save you.'

'Single-handed, I suppose.'

'Close. We waited until just after midnight then, when the Gothir had fallen back for the fifth time, we ran for our horses. There were only thirty of us left, but it was enough to send the Brotherhood fleeing from the field.'

'I don't remember that,' said Angel. 'In fact, my thoughts are hazy. I seem to recall ghosts riding to our rescue, in white armour.'

'Priests,' said Senta. 'Source priests.'

'In armour?'

'An unusual Order,' said Senta. 'They call themselves the Thirty, although there are only eleven of them now. They are led by an Abbot named Dardalion.'

'He was at Purdol. He helped Karnak. Get me up!'

'You should lie back. You've lost a lot of blood.'

'Thank you for your concern, Mother. Now help me up, damn you!'

'As you wish, old fool.' Senta's hand slid under Angel's shoulder, levering him to a sitting position. Nausea gripped him but he swallowed it down and sucked in a deep breath. 'I thought we were finished. Where's Miriel?'

'She's safe. She's with Dardalion and Kesa Khan.'

'And the Gothir?'

'Camped all around us, Angel. They've been reinforced. Must be seven, eight thousand men in the valley.'

'Wonderful. Is there any good news?'

'None that I can think of, but you do have a visitor. Charming little fellow. He's sitting in the hallway now – I'll send him to you in a while. I found him sitting by what we thought was your body. He was crying. Very touching it was. Brought a tear to my eye, I can tell you.' Angel swore. Senta chuckled. 'I knew you weren't dead, Angel. You're too stubborn to die.'

'How many did we lose?'

Senta's smile faded. 'Belash is dead, and Anshi Chen. There are some three hundred warriors left, but many of those are youngsters, untried. I don't think we can hold this place for long.'

'They've not attacked yet?'

'No. They're busy chopping down trees, making scaling ladders and the like.'

Angel lay back and closed his eyes. 'Just let them give me a day or two. Then I'll be ready. I'm a fast healer, Senta.'

'In that case we'll try not to start the war without you.'

*

Senta found Miriel on the inner rampart, leaning on the twisted wall and staring out over the camp-fires of the enemy. Nadir warriors were standing close by, sharpening their weapons. The swordsman moved past the Nadir and halted beside the tall mountain girl. 'Angel's fine,' he said. 'A few minor cuts and a large lump on that thick skull. I sometimes think if the world ended in fire and flood he would walk out of the cinders with singed hair and wet boots.'

256

She smiled. 'He does appear so wonderfully indestructible.'

'Come and see what I have found,' said Senta, walking away to a set of stairs which led down to a narrow corridor and a large suite of rooms. The windows were distorted, shaped now like open, screaming mouths, and the walls were crooked. But the large bedchamber was empty and in its centre was a golden four-post bed, beautifully proportioned, rectangular and solid. There were pillows of silk and a coverlet filled with goose down.

'How could such a bed survive when a fortress of stone is corrupted?' she asked.

The swordsman shrugged. 'There are other objects of gold that are apparently not affected by the sorcery. I found two goblets downstairs, exquisitely carved.'

She moved towards the bed, then angled away to the first of the three windows. From here the valley could be seen. 'There's another column of cavalry moving down,' she told him.

'I don't care about the cavalry,' he said.

She swung towards him, her back to the window, her face blushing crimson. 'You think I will let you bed me?'

'I think you should seriously consider it,' he told her, with a wide smile.

'I don't love you, Senta.'

'You don't know that yet,' he said reasonably. 'Here's where you can find out.'

'You think love springs from the loins?'

He laughed aloud. 'Mine always has – until now.' He shook his head, the smile fading. 'You are frightened, beauty. Frightened to live. Well, here we are, trapped in a decrepit fortress, our futures measured in days. This is no time to be frightened of life. You owe me a kiss, at least. The Gothir stole the last one.'

'One kiss is all you will have,' she promised, moving forward.

He opened his arms to her and she stepped inside. Reaching up he pushed his fingers into her long dark hair, easing it back from her face, stroking the high cheekbones, his hand curling round to the nape of her neck. He could feel his heart pounding as he kissed her brow and her cheek. She tilted her head, her lips brushing against his skin. Their lips met, and he felt her body pressing against him. Her mouth tasted sweet, warm, and his passion soared. But he made no move to pull her to the bed. Instead he ran his hands down her back, halting at the slender waist, feeling the curve of her hips. And he kissed her neck and shoulder, revelling in the scent of her skin.

She was wearing a black leather tunic, laced at the front with slender thongs. Slowly he moved his right hand to her breast, his fingers hooking to the first knot.

'No,' she said, moving back from him. Swallowing his disappointment he took a deep breath. She smiled. 'I'll do it.' Unfastening the knife-belt at her waist she lifted the tunic over her head, and stood before him naked. His eyes drank her in, the long sun-bronzed legs, the flat belly, the high, full breasts.

'You're a vision, beauty. No question of it.'

He stepped towards her, but she stopped him. 'What about you?' she asked. 'Do I not get a chance to admire?'

'Every chance,' he told her, pulling free his shirt and unhooking his belt. He almost stumbled as he struggled to remove his leggings, and her laughter was infectious.

'You'd think you'd never removed leggings before,' she said.

Reaching out he took her arm and gently pulled her to the bed. A cloud of dust rose as they fell upon it, causing him to cough. 'Such romance,' she giggled. He joined in her laughter and they lay quietly together for a few moments, staring into each other's eyes. His right hand stroked the skin of her shoulder and arm, moving down until his forearm brushed across her nipple. She closed her eyes and slid in towards him. The hand moved on, over the flat belly and on to the thigh. Her legs were closed, but now she parted them. He kissed her again. Her arm hooked around his neck, pulling him into a fierce embrace.

'Gently, beauty,' he whispered. 'There is no need for

haste. Nothing beautiful is ever crafted at speed. And I want this first time to be special.'

She moaned as his palm pressed gently against her pubic mound, and for some time he slowly caressed her. Her breathing quickened, her body moving into spasm. She cried out, again and again. Finally he rose above her, lifting her long legs over his hips and guiding himself into her. He kissed her again, then drove into her, releasing the self-imposed chains of his own passion.

He tried to keep his movements slow, but his needs were greater than his wish to make the moment last, and when Miriel cried out again, in a series of rhythmic, almost primal groans, he succumbed at last. His body spasmed, his arms pulling her into a tight embrace. Then he moaned and lay still. He sighed and his body relaxed as he lay upon her, feeling his own heartbeat and hers together, pounding against the warm skin of his chest.

'Oh,' she whispered. 'Was that love?'

'By all the gods I hope so, beauty,' he answered her, rolling to his back. 'For nothing else in my life has given me so much pleasure.'

Raising herself on her elbow she gazed down at his face. 'It was . . . wonderful. Let's do it again!'

'In a while, Miriel,' he answered.

'How long?'

He chuckled and drew her into his embrace. 'Not long. I promise you!'

17

Dardalion opened his eyes, his spirit returning to the flesh, feeling the weight of his body and the silver armour upon it. It was cold in the room, despite the log fire burning in the hearth.

'They will not attack today – and perhaps not tomorrow,' he told Kesa Khan. 'Their General Gannis is a careful man. He has sent work parties to the woods to cut trees and make scaling ladders. He intends one great attack which will swamp us.'

The little Nadir shaman nodded. 'We will hold them for one, maybe two assaults. After that . . .' He spread his hands.

Dardalion rose from the gold lacquered chair and moved to the fire, extending his hands to the flames, enjoying the sudden warmth. 'What I do not understand – and neither does the Gothir General – is why the Emperor has chosen this course. The coming Uniter will not be stopped. It is written that the Nadir will rise. There is nothing he can do to change the future. Nothing.'

'It is not the Emperor, but Zhu Chao who seeks our destruction,' said Kesa Khan, with a dry laugh. 'Twin needs spur him on: his hatred for the Wolves, and his desire for absolute power.'

'Why does he hate you so?'

Kesa Khan's eyes glittered and his smile was cruel. 'Many years ago he came to me, seeking to understand the nature of magic. He is a Chiatze, and he was studying the Dark Arts and the origins of the Knights of Blood. I turned him away. He had the wit, but not the courage.'

'And for this he hates you?'

'No, not just for this. He crept back to my cave, and I caught him trying to steal . . .' the shaman's eyes were hooded now '. . . objects of value. My guards took him.

They wanted to kill him, but I decided to be merciful. I merely cut something from him, gave him a wound to remember me by. He still had his life, but he would never sire life. You understand?'

'Only too well,' answered Dardalion coldly.

'Do not judge me, priest,' snapped Kesa Khan.

'It is not for me to judge. You planted the seed of his hatred, and now you are gathering the harvest.'

'Pah, it is not that simple,' said the shaman. 'He was always a creature of evil. I should have killed him. But his hatred I can bear. This fortress, and what it contains, is the second of his desires. There is more powerful sorcery here than has been seen in the world for ten millennia. Zhu Chao wants it . . . needs it. Once upon a distant time the Elders here performed miracles. They learned how to merge flesh. A man who had lost a leg could grow a new one. Organs riddled with cancer could be replaced, without use of a knife. Bodies could be regenerated, rejuvenated. Here was the secret of immortality. The force was contained within a giant crystal, encased in a covering of pure gold. It radiated power, and only gold and to a lesser extent lead, could imprison it. You saw the valley?'

'Yes,' said Dardalion. 'Nature perverted.'

'Fifty years ago, a group of robbers came to this place. They found the Crystal Chamber and stripped the gold from its walls, removing the covering from the crystal itself.' He laughed. 'It was not a wise action.'

'What happened to them? Why did they not steal the crystal?'

'The power they unleashed killed them. The Elders knew how to control it, to focus the forces. Without their skill it has become merely a corrupting, violent, haphazard sorcery.'

'I sense no power emanating from here,' said Dardalion.

'No. Zhu Chao sent men here. They removed the crystal from its setting. It sits now upon a golden floor some two hundred feet below us.'

'Did these men also die?'

'I think you could call it a kind of death.'

261

Dardalion felt cold as he looked into the shaman's malevolent eyes. 'What is it that you are not telling me, Kesa Khan? What secret strategies have yet to be unveiled?'

'Do not be impatient, priest. All will be revealed. Everything is in a delicate state of balance. We cannot win here by might or guile – we must rely on the intangibles. Your friend Waylander, for example. He now hunts Zhu Chao, but can he enter his palace, fight his way through a hundred guards and overcome the sorcery at Zhu Chao's command? Who knows? Can we hold here? And if not, can we find a way to escape? Or should we use the power of the crystal?'

'You know the answer to the last question, shaman – no. Else you would have come here years ago. No one knows what destroyed the Elders, save that there are areas of great desolation where once were mighty cities. Everything we know of them speaks of corruption and greed, enormous evils and terrible weapons. Even the wickedness within you recoils at their misdeeds. Is it not so?'

Kesa Khan nodded. 'I have walked the paths of time, priest. I know what destroyed them. And yes, I wish to see no return to their foul ways. They raped the land and lived like kings while fouling the rivers and lakes, the forests – aye, even the air they breathed. They knew everything and understood nothing. And they were destroyed for it.'

'But their legacy lives on here,' said Dardalion softly.

'And in other secret places, yet to be found.'

Dardalion knelt by the fire, adding several logs to the blaze. 'Whatever else, we must destroy the crystal. Zhu Chao must not possess it.'

Kesa Khan nodded. 'When the time comes we will seek it out.'

'Why not now?'

'Trust me, Dardalion. I am far older than you, and I have walked paths that would burn your soul to ashes. Now is not the time.'

'What would you have me do?'

'Find a quiet place and send out your spirit to seek

Waylander. Cloak him – as you did once before – protect him from the sorcery of Zhu Chao. Give him his chance to kill the beast.'

*

On the highest tower Vishna sat upon the ramparts, Ekodas beside him. The forked bearded Gothir nobleman sighed. 'My brothers could be down there,' he said.

'Let us pray that is not the case,' said Ekodas.

'I think we were wrong,' said Vishna softly, 'and you were right. This is no way to serve the Source. I killed two men in that charge yesterday. I know they were evil, I felt it radiating from them, but I was lessened by the deed. I can no longer believe the Source wishes us to kill.'

Reaching out, Ekodas laid a hand upon his friend's shoulder. 'I do not know what the Source requires, Vishna. I only know that yesterday we protected a column of women and children. I do not regret that, but I regret bitterly that it was necessary to kill.'

'But why are we here?' cried Vishna. 'To ensure the birth of a child who will ultimately destroy all that my family have spent generations building? It is madness!'

Ekodas shrugged. 'Let us hope there is some greater purpose. But I believe it will be enough to thwart the Brotherhood.'

Vishna shook his head. 'There are only eleven of us left. You think we can achieve some great victory?'

'Perhaps. Why don't you seek out Dardalion? Pray together. It will help.'

'No, it won't. Not this time, brother,' said Vishna sadly. 'I have followed him all my adult life, and I have known the great joy of comradeship – with him, with you all. I never doubted until now. But this is a problem I must solve alone.'

'For what it is worth, my friend, I think it is better to be unsure. It seems to me that most of the problems of this world have been caused by men who were too sure; men who always knew what was right. The Brotherhood chose a path of pain and suffering. Not their own, of course. They

263

rode into that valley to butcher women and babes. Remember that!'

Vishna nodded. 'You are probably right, Ekodas. But what when one of my brothers climbs this wall, sword in hand. What do I do? He is obeying the orders of his Emperor, as all good soldiers must. Do I kill him? Do I hurl him to his death?'

'I don't know,' admitted Ekodas. 'But there are enough real perils facing us, without creating more.'

'I wish to be alone, my friend. Do not be insulted, I beseech you.'

'I am not insulted, Vishna. May your deliberations bring you peace.' Turning, Ekodas ducked under the crumbling lintel and descended the undulating stairs. He came out into a narrow corridor leading to a long hall. Within it fat Merlon was helping the Nadir women to prepare food for the warriors. Ekodas saw Shia kneading dough close by. She looked up and smiled at him.

'How are you, lady?' he asked.

'I am well, prayer-man. Your arrival was a surprise most pleasant.'

'I did not think we would be in time. We first journeyed west into Vagria and then south in order to avoid the besiegers. The ride was long.'

'And now you are here. With me.'

'I was sorry to hear of your brother's death,' he said swiftly, as she rose from the table.

'Why? Did you know him?'

'No. But it must have caused you pain. For that I am sorry.'

Leaving the table she moved in close to him. 'There is a little pain, but it is my own. Yet I am also proud, for the man he slew was the same knight who killed our father. That is a blessing for which I thank the gods. But Belash is now in the Hall of Heroes. He has many beautiful maidens around him, and his cup is full of fine wine. Rich meats are cooking, and he has a hundred ponies to ride when he wishes. My pain is only that I will not see him again. But I am happy for him.'

Ekodas could think of no reply, so he bowed and backed away. 'You look like a man now,' said Shia approvingly. 'And you fight like a warrior. I watched you kill three and maim a fourth.'

He winced and walked swiftly from the hall. But she followed him out on to the lower rampart above the courtyard. The stars were bright and he drew in several deep, cool breaths.

'Did I insult you?' she asked.

'No. It is . . . just . . . that I do not like to kill. It does not please me to hear that I maimed a man.'

'Do not concern yourself. I cut his throat.'

'That is hardly an uplifting thought.'

'They are our enemies,' she said, speaking as if to a simpleton. 'What else would you do with them?'

'I have no answers, Shia. Only questions that no one can answer.'

'I could answer them,' she assured him brightly.

He sat back on the rampart wall and looked into her moonlit face. 'You are so confident. Why is that?'

'I know what I know, Ekodas. Ask me one of your questions.'

'I hate to kill, I know that. So why, during yesterday's battle, did I feel exultant with each sword-stroke?'

'I thought your questions would be hard,' she chided. 'Spirit and Flesh, Ekodas. The spirit is immortal. It loves the Light, it worships beauty, of thought and deed. And it has Eternity to enjoy, Time to contemplate. But the Flesh is Dark. For the Flesh knows it has not long to live. Against the time of the Spirit the life of the Flesh is like a lightning flash. So it has little time to know pleasure, to taste the richness of life; lust, greed, gain. It wants to experience everything, and it cares for nothing save existence. What you felt was the surging joy of the Flesh. Nothing more. And certainly nothing to cause you self-loathing.' She chuckled, a rich, throaty sound that touched him like fire in the blood.

'What is so amusing?'

'You should feel sorry for the part of you that is Flesh,

265

Ekodas. For what do you offer him in his brief existence? Rich food? No. Strong wines? Dances? Lust in the firelight?' She laughed again. 'No wonder he takes such pleasure from combat, eh?'

'You are a provocative woman,' he scolded.

'Thank you. Do I arouse you?'

'Yes.'

'But you fight it?'

'I must. It is the way I have chosen to live.'

'Do you believe the Spirit is eternal?'

'Of course.'

'Then do not be selfish, Ekodas. Does the Flesh not deserve a day in the sun? Look at my lips. Are they not full and pleasing? And is my body not firm where it should be, and yet soft where it needs to be?'

His throat was dry, and he realised she had moved in very close. He stood and reached out, holding her at arms' length. 'Why do you torment me, lady? You know that I cannot give you what you desire.'

'Would you if you could?'

'Yes,' he admitted.

'We have our own priests,' she said. 'Kesa Khan is one. He also forbears from lovemaking, but it is a choice. He does not condemn it as wrong. Do you believe the gods created us?'

'The Source, yes.'

'And did they . . . He, if you like . . . not create men and women to desire one another?'

'I know where this is leading, but let me say this: there are many ways to serve the Source. Some men marry and beget children. Others choose different paths. What you said about the Flesh has great merit, but in subjugating the desires of the Flesh the Spirit becomes stronger. I can, in my Spirit form, fly through the air. I can read minds. I can heal the sick, removing cancerous growths. You understand? I can do these things because the Source has blessed me. And because I abstain from earthly pleasures.'

'Have you ever had a woman?' she countered.

'No.'

'How does your Source feel about killing?'

He smiled ruefully. 'His priests are pledged to love all living things, and harm none.'

'So you have chosen to break one of His commandments?'

'I believe that we have.'

'Is lovemaking a greater sin than killing?'

'Of course not.'

'And you still have your Talents?'

'Yes, I do.'

'Think on that, Ekodas,' she said, with a sweet smile. Then, spinning on her heel she returned to the hall.

*

The deaths of Belash and Anshi Chen created a void in the battle leadership of the Nadir, and the mood in the fortress was sullen and fatalistic. Nadir wars were fought on horseback on the open steppes and despite the transient security offered by the warped citadel, they were ill at ease manning the crooked battlements of Kar-Barzac.

They viewed the silver knights with disquiet, and rarely spoke to Senta or Miriel. But Angel was different. His transparent hostility towards them made him a force they could understand and feel at ease with. No patronising comments, no condescension. Mutual dislike and respect became the twin ties that allowed the remaining warriors to form a bond with the former gladiator.

He organised them into defence groups along the main wall, ordering them to gather rocks and broken masonry for hurling down on an advancing enemy. He chose leaders, issued orders, and lifted their spirits with casual insults and coarse humour. And his open contempt for the Gothir soldiers helped the tribesmen to overcome their own fears.

As the sun rose on the third day of the siege he gathered a small group of leaders around him and squatted down among them on the battlements. 'Now none of you beggars have ever seen a siege, so let me make it plain for you. They will carry forward stripped tree trunks as scaling ladders and lean them against the walls. Then they will climb the broken branches. Do not make the mistake of trying to push the ladders *away* from the wall. The weight of wood and armed men will make that impossible. Slide them left or right. Use the butt-end of your spears, or loop ropes over the top of the trunks. Unbalance them. Now we have around three hundred men to defend these walls, but we need a reserve force, ready to run and block any gaps that appear in the line. You, Subai!' he said, pointing to a short, wide-shouldered tribesman with a jagged scar on his right cheek. 'Pick forty men and hold back from the battle. Wait in the courtyard, watching the battlements. If our line breaks anywhere, reinforce it.'

'It will be as you order,' grunted the tribesman.

'Make sure it is, or I'll rip out your arm and beat you to death with the wet end.' The warriors smiled. Angel rose. 'Now, follow me to the gate.' The gates themselves had long since rotted, but the Nadir had managed to lower the portcullis, almost two tons of rusted iron, to block the entrance. Carts and wagons had been overturned at the base and thirty bowmen stood by. Angel moved to the archway. 'They will attempt to lift the portcullis. They will fail, for it is wedged above. But it is badly rusted and they will bring up saws and hammers to force an opening. You, what's your name again?'

'How many times must you ask, Ugly One?' countered the Nadir, a hook-nosed, swarthy man, taller than the average tribesman. Angel guessed he was a half-breed.

'All you beggars look alike to me,' said Angel. 'So tell me again.'

'Orsa Khan.'

'Well, Orsa Khan, I want you to command this defence. When they break through – as they will eventually – set fire to the carts. And hold them back to allow the men on the walls to retreat to the keep.'

'They will not break through while I live,' promised Orsa.

'That's the spirit, boy!' said Angel. 'Now, are there any questions?'

'What else do we need to ask?' put in Borsai, a young warrior of sixteen, still beardless. 'They come, we kill them until they go away. Is that not so?'

'Sounds a good strategy to me,' agreed Angel. 'Now, when some of them reach the ramparts – as they will – don't stab for their heads. Slash your blades at their hands as they reach for a hold. They'll be wearing gauntlets, but good iron will cut through those. Then, when they fall, they'll probably take two or three others with them. And that's a fair drop, my boys. They won't get up again.'

Leaving the warriors to their duties, Angel toured the walls. According to the Thirty, the Gothir would attack first by the main gate of the southern wall, a direct frontal assault to overwhelm the defenders. Therefore they had concentrated their manpower here, leaving only fifty warriors spread thin around the other walls. Angel had wanted to arm some of the younger women, but the Nadir would have none of the plan. War was for men, he was told. He did not argue. They would change their minds soon enough.

Striding across the courtyard he saw Senta and Miriel walking out towards him. Anger touched him then, for he could see by their closeness, the way she leaned in to him, that they had become lovers. The knowledge tasted of bile in his mouth, but he forced a smile. 'Going to be a cold day,' he said, indicating the gathering snow clouds above the mountains.

'I dare say the Gothir will warm it up for us,' Senta pointed out, draping his arm around Miriel's shoulder. She smiled, and leaned in to kiss his cheek.

Angel looked at them, the tall mountain girl, her smile radiant, and the handsome swordsman, golden-haired and young, dressed now in a buckskin shirt beneath a breast-plate of glittering iron, and tan leggings of polished leather. Angel felt old as he watched them, the weight of his years and his disappointments hanging upon him like chains of lead. His own leather tunic was ragged and torn, his leggings filthy, and the pain of his wounds was only marginally less than the pain in his heart.

He moved away from them towards the keep, aware that they had not noticed his departure. He saw the mute child sitting on the keep steps, his wooden sword thrust into his belt. Angel grinned and clapped his hands. The boy copied him and rose smiling.

'You want some food, boy?' he said, lifting his fingers to his mouth and mimicking the act of chewing. The boy nodded and Angel led the way up to the main hall, where cook fires were burning in the hearths. A fat knight, wearing a leather apron, was stirring soup. He glanced at the child.

'He needs some weight on those bones,' he said, smiling and ruffling the boy's hair.

'Not as much as you're carrying, brother,' said Angel.

'It is a curious fact,' said the knight, 'but I only have to look at a honeycake and I feel the weight pile on.' Sitting the boy at the table he ladled soup into a bowl and watched with undisguised pleasure as the child enjoyed it. 'You should ask Ekodas to look at the boy,' said the knight softly. 'He has a real gift for healing. The child was not always deaf, you know. It faded slowly when he was a baby. And there is little wrong with his vocal chords. It is just that hearing no sound he makes no sound.'

'How do you know all this?' asked Angel.

'It is a talent fat people have, thin man.' He chuckled. 'My name is Merlon.'

'Angel,' responded the former gladiator, extending his hand. He was surprised to feel the strength in Merlon's grip, and he swiftly reappraised the priest. 'I think you're carrying a lot more muscle than fat,' he said.

'I have been blessed with a physique as strong as my appetite,' the other replied.

The child ate three bowls of the soup and half a loaf of bread while Angel sat and talked with the huge warrior priest. Shia approached them and sat on the bench seat alongside Angel.

'I told you they would not let us fight,' she said, anger showing in her eyes.

Angel grinned. 'That you did. But things will change, if

270

not tomorrow, then the day after – as soon as they try an attack from all four sides. We have not the numbers of men to stop them. Make sure the women gather all the surplus . . . weapons.'

'By surplus you mean the weapons of our dead?'

'Exactly,' he admitted. 'And not just weapons, breast-plates, helms, arm-guards. Anything to protect.'

At that moment a young woman ran into the hall. 'They are coming! They are coming!' she shouted.

'So it begins,' said Merlon, removing the leather apron and striding across the hall to where his breastplate, helm and sword were laid by the hearth.

*

Miriel stood to the left of the wall, almost at the corner, a crazily-angled turret leaning out above her. Her mouth was dry as she saw the Gothir line surge forward, and she ceased to notice the biting winter wind.

Twenty trees had been cut down and stripped of branches, and these were carried forward by heavily-armed men. Behind them marched two thousand foot-soldiers, shortswords and shields held at the ready. Miriel glanced to her right. At the centre of the ramparts stood Angel, grim and powerful, his sword still sheathed. Further along was Senta, a wide grin on his face, his eyes gleaming with the thrill of the coming battle. She shivered, but not with the cold.

More than a thousand men carried the tree trunks, and the pounding of their feet on the hard valley floor was like a roll of thunder. Two Nadir beside Miriel hefted large rocks, laying them on the battlement. Archers sent shafts down into the charging ranks, but wounds were few among the armoured men, though Miriel saw a handful of soldiers reel back or fall as iron points lanced into unprotected thighs and arms.

The first trunk was raised and fell against the battlement with a booming thud. A Nadir hurled a rope over the top and began to pull.

'Wait until there are men on it!' bellowed Angel.

More trees crashed against the wall. A section of battlement gave way and a Nadir was hurled screaming to the courtyard forty feet below. Miriel swung and saw the man struggle to rise, but his leg was smashed. Several women ran forward, lifting the injured man and carrying him into the keep.

Notching an arrow to her bow Miriel leaned out over the wall. Thousands of men were swarming up the ladders, using the stubs of sawn-off branches for hand and footholds. Sighting her bow she sent an arrow through the temple of a soldier who had almost reached the top. He sagged back, and fell into the man behind him, dislodging him.

Angel hefted a large boulder and hurled it over the wall. It struck an attacker on his upraised shield, smashing the man's arm and shoulder. Amazingly he managed to hold on to the branch, but the boulder hit the man below on the helm, sweeping him from the tree. Stones and rocks rained down on the attackers, but still they came on, a score of men reaching the battlements.

Senta leapt forward, spearing his blade through the throat of the first man to reach the ramparts. Miriel dropped her bow and gathered up the trailing rope the Nadir had looped over the first trunk. 'Help me!' she shouted at the nearest warriors. Three men turned at her cry and ran to her aid. Together they hauled on the rope and, just as the first Gothir appeared, they succeeded in moving the ladder a foot to the right. Top-heavy now, the wood groaned – and slid sideways. A Gothir soldier jumped for the battlement, but lost his footing and fell screaming to the valley floor. The tree collided with a second ladder and, for a moment only, was held. Then both began to move.

'Let go the rope,' shouted Miriel, as the overburdened ladder fell away. The rope hissed and cracked like a whip as it was dragged over the battlements. The falling ladders struck a third, which was also dislodged from the wall. Miriel ran along the battlements to where Senta stood. 'The scaling ladders are too close together,' she shouted.

'Move that one and you'll bring down three, maybe four more.'

He looked to where she was pointing and nodded. Ropes had been placed along the wall and he lifted one, shaking out the loop. While the Nadir battled to keep the Gothir from the battlements Senta hurled a loop over the closest ladder and started to pull. It would not budge. Miriel joined him – but to no avail. Angel saw them and sent four men to assist.

Gothir warriors were scrambling over the battlements now, and one of them threw himself at Senta. The swordsman saw the blow almost too late, but let go the rope and lashed out with his foot, kicking the oncoming warrior in the knee. The man fell. Drawing his sword Senta sent a crashing blow to the soldier's helm. The Gothir struggled to rise. Senta ran in and shoulder-charged him, hurling him from the ramparts to the courtyard below.

Miriel and the others were still trying to pull the tree clear, but it was wedged into one of the crenellations of the battlement wall. Angel picked up a fallen axe, ducked under the rope and delivered a thunderous blow to the crumbling stone of the battlement. Twice more he struck. The granite shifted. Dropping to his haunches he lifted his feet and kicked out. The granite blocks fell away. The tree slid clear, struck the next crenellation – and snapped.

The rope-wielders were thrown back – Miriel, still holding the rope, tumbling from the ramparts. As the tree snapped Angel saw Miriel fall and dived for the snaking rope. The hemp tore the flesh from his fingers and Miriel's falling weight hauled him to the edge of the rampart. But he held on, regardless of pain or the peril of the drop. Just as he was being pulled over the edge a Nadir warrior threw himself across the fallen gladiator. Then Senta grabbed Angel's legs.

Miriel was dangling fifteen feet below the rampart. With the rope now steady she climbed and hooked her foot over the stone. A Nadir hauled her to safety. Angel climbed wearily to his feet, blood dripping from his torn palms.

The dislodged tree had toppled seven more, killing more

than a hundred soldiers. Fearful of a similar fate the remaining Gothir warriors scrambled down to safety and retreated out of arrow range. Gleefully the Nadir sent all the trunks crashing to the earth. Subai, leaving the reserve force, climbed to the battlements, turned his back to the Gothir and, dropping his leggings, exposed his buttocks to the enemy. The Nadir howled with delight.

Orsa Khan, the tall half-breed, lifted his sword high above his head and shouted a Nadir refrain. It was picked up along the line until all the defenders were screaming it at the uncomprehending Gothir.

'What are they saying?' asked Angel.

'It is the last verse of the battle song of the Wolves,' said Senta. 'I can't make it rhyme in translation, but it goes like this.

> *Nadir we,*
> *Youth born.*
> *Axe-wielders,*
> *Victors still.'*

'You don't see too many axes among them,' complained Angel.

'Ever the poet,' said Senta, laughing. 'Now go and get those hands bandaged. You're dripping blood everywhere.'

18

The passing of the years, and with them the fading of his powers, was a source of intense irritation to Kesa Khan. As a young man in his physical prime, he had sought to master the arcane arts, to command demons, to walk the paths of mist, scouring the past, exploring the future. But when young, though strong enough, his skills were not honed to the perfection needed for such missions of the spirit. Now that his mind burned with power, his aged frame could not support his desires.

Even while acknowledging the manifest unfairness of life he found himself chuckling at the absurdity of existence.

He banked up his fire, not in the hearth, but in an ancient brazier he had set upon the stone floor at the centre of the small room high in the keep-tower. His precious clay pots were set around it, and from one of them he took a handful of green powder which he sprinkled on to the dancing flames. Instantly an image formed of Waylander entering the great gates of Gulgothir. He was disguised as a Sathuli trader in flowing robes of grey wool and a burnoose, bound with braided black horsehair. His back was bent under a huge pack, and he shuffled like an old man, crippled with the rheumatism. Kesa Khan smiled.

'You will not fool Zhu Chao, but no other will recognise you,' he said. The scene faded before he was ready. Kesa Khan cursed softly, and thought of the crystal lying on the golden floor below the castle. With it you could be young again he told himself. You could bide through the centuries, assisting the Uniter.

'Pah,' he said aloud. 'Were that the case would I not have seen myself in one of the futures? Do not delude yourself, old man. Death approaches. You have done all that you can for the future of your people. You have no cause to regret. No cause at all.'

'Not many can say that,' came the voice of Dardalion.

'Not many have lived as single-mindedly as I,' answered Kesa Khan. He glanced towards the doorway in which the Abbot was standing. 'Come in, priest. There is a draught, and my bones are not as young as they were.'

There was no furniture in the room and Dardalion sat cross-legged upon the rug. 'To what do I owe the pleasure of your company?' asked the old shaman.

'You are a devious man, Kesa Khan, and I lack your guile. But I do not lack powers of my own. I, too, have walked the paths of mist since last we spoke. I, too, have seen the Uniter you dream of.'

The shaman's eyes glittered with malice. 'You have seen but one? There are hundreds.'

'No,' said Dardalion. 'There are thousands. A vast spider's web of possible futures. But most of them did not interest me. I followed the path that leads from Kar-Barzac, and the child to be conceived here. A girl. A beautiful girl, who will wed a young warlord. Their son will be mighty, their grandson mightier still.'

Kesa Khan shivered. 'You saw all this in a single day? It has taken me fifty years.'

'I had fifty years less to travel.'

'What else did you see?'

'What is there that you wish to know?' countered the Drenai.

Kesa Khan bit his lip, and said nothing for a moment. 'I know it all,' he lied, shrugging his shoulders. 'There is nothing new. Have you located Waylander?'

'Yes. He has entered Gulgothir in disguise. Two of my priests are watching him, seeking to divert any search spells.'

Kesa Khan nodded. 'It is almost time to retrieve the crystal,' he said, transferring his gaze to the flickering fire.

'It should be destroyed,' advised Dardalion.

'As you wish. You will need to send one of your men – a priest who is unlikely to be corrupted by its power. You have such a man?'

'Corrupted?'

'Aye. Even in its dormant state it exerts great influence, firing the senses like strong drink that removes inhibition. The man you send must have great control over his . . . passions, shall we say? Any weakness he has will be multiplied a hundred times. I will send no Nadir on such a quest.'

'As you well know there is one among my priests with the strength to overcome such evil,' said Dardalion. He leaned in close to the wizened shaman. 'But tell me, Kesa Khan, what else is down there?'

'Have you not used your great powers to find out?' countered the wizened Nadir, unable to keep a sneer from disfiguring his face.

'No spirit can penetrate the lower levels. There is a force there many times stronger than I have encountered before. But you know all this, old man, and more. I do not ask for your gratitude – it is meaningless to me. We are not here for you. But I would ask for a little honesty.'

'Ask all you like, Drenai. I owe you nothing! You want the crystal – then seek it out.'

Dardalion sighed. 'Very well, I shall do just that. But I will not send Ekodas into the Pit. I shall go myself.'

'The crystal will destroy you!'

'Perhaps.'

'You are a fool, Dardalion. Ekodas is many times stronger than you. You know this.'

The Abbot smiled. 'Yes, I know.' The smile faded and his eyes hardened. 'And now the time for pretence is over. You need Ekodas. Without him your dreams are dust. I have seen the future, Kesa Khan. I have seen more than you know. Everything here is in a state of delicate balance. One wrong strategy and your hopes will die.'

The shaman relaxed, and added fuel to the flames in the brazier. 'We are not so different, you and I. Very well, I will tell you all that you desire to know. But it must be Ekodas who destroys the evil. You agree?'

'Let us talk, and then I will decide.'

'That is acceptable, Drenai.' Kesa Khan took a deep breath. 'Ask your questions.'

'What perils wait in the lower levels?'

The shaman shrugged. 'How would I know? As you say, no spirit power can enter there.'

'Who would you send with Ekodas?' asked Dardalion softly.

'The Drenai woman and her lover.'

Dardalion caught the gleam in the shaman's eyes. 'You are transparent in your hate, Kesa Khan. You need us now, but you want us all dead, eventually. Especially the woman. Why is that?'

'Pah, she is of no consequence!'

'And still the lies flow,' snapped Dardalion. 'But we will talk again, Kesa Khan.'

'You will send Ekodas?'

Dardalion remained silent for a moment. Then he nodded. 'But not,' he said, 'for the reasons you believe.'

The Abbot stood and left the room. The shaman fought down his anger, and remained sitting cross-legged before the fire. How much more did the Drenai know? What had he said of the Uniter? Kesa Khan summoned the words from memory: *'A vast spider's web of possible futures. But most of them did not interest me. I followed the path that leads from Kar-Barzac, and the child to be conceived here. A girl. A beautiful girl, who will wed a young warlord. Their son will be mighty, their grandson mightier still.'*

Did he know the identity of the young warlord? Where he might be found? Kesa Khan cursed softly, and wished he had the strength to walk the paths of mist once more. But he could feel his heart beating within the cage of his ribs, fluttering weakly like a dying sparrow. His dark eyes narrowed. He had no choice. He must go on with his plans. Let the Drenai destroy the crystal – it was not important to the future of the Nadir. What *was* vital was that Ekodas should journey to the chamber, and with him the woman, Miriel.

The merest moment of regret touched him then. She was a strong woman, proud and caring.

It was, he admitted, a shame she had to die.

*

Angel looked down at the perfectly-healed skin of his torn palms, then up into the face of the young priest. 'There is no mark,' he said. 'No scab or scar!'

The young man smiled wearily. 'I merely accelerated your own healing processes. I have also removed a small growth from one of your lungs.'

'A cancer?' whispered Angel, fear rising in his throat.

'Yes, but it is gone.'

'I felt no pain from it.'

'Nor would you until it was much larger.'

'You saved my life, then? By all the gods, priest, I don't know what to say. My name is Angel.' He thrust out his newly-healed hand.

The priest took it. 'Ekodas. How goes it on the wall?'

'We're holding them. They'll not try scaling the battlements again. Next time it will be the portcullis.'

Ekodas nodded. 'You are correct. But it will not be until tomorrow. Get some rest, Angel. You are no longer a young man and your body is very tired.' The priest glanced over Angel's shoulder. 'The boy is with you?' he asked.

Angel looked round. The deaf child was standing close, Angel's green cloak draped over his shoulders. 'Yes. Your large friend –Merlon? – suggested I ask you to look at him. He's deaf.'

'I am very weary. My powers are not inexhaustible.'

'Another time, then,' said Angel, rising.

'No,' insisted Ekodas. 'Let us at least examine him.'

Angel waved the boy to him, but he shied away when the priest reached out. Ekodas closed his eyes. The child immediately slumped into Angel's arms, deeply asleep. 'What did you do?'

'He will come to no harm, Angel. He will merely sleep until I wake him.' Ekodas placed his open palms over the child's ears and stood, stock still, for several minutes. At last he stepped back and sat down opposite the gladiator. 'He had a severe infection when very young. It was not treated, and spread through the bones around the ears. This damaged the eardrums, making them incapable of relaying vibrations to the brain. You understand?'

279

'Not a word of it,' admitted Angel. 'But can you heal him?'

'I have already done so,' said Ekodas. 'But you must stay with him for a while. He will be frightened. Every noise will be new to him.'

Angel watched the young priest move away across the hall. The boy stirred in his arms. His eyes opened.

'Feel better?' asked Angel. The boy stiffened, his eyes flaring with shock. Angel grinned and tapped his own ear. 'You can hear now.' A woman moved past them, behind the child. He swivelled and stared at her feet as they padded across the stone floor. Angel touched the boy on the arm, gaining his attention, then began to rhythmically tap at the table at which they sat, making small drumming sounds. The child scrambled from his lap and ran from the hall.

'What a great teacher you are,' muttered Angel. Weariness flooded him and he rose and walked through the hall, finding a small unoccupied room in a corridor beyond it. There was no furniture here, but Angel lay down on the stone floor, his head pillowed on his arm.

And he slept without dreams.

Miriel woke him and he sat up. She had brought him a bowl of weak broth and a chunk of bread. 'How are your hands?' she asked him.

'Healed,' he told her, turning them palms upwards. 'By one of the priests – Ekodas. He has a rare Talent.'

She nodded. 'I have just met him.' He took the soup and began to eat. Miriel sat silently beside him. She seemed preoccupied, and continually tugged at a long lock of hair by her temple.

'What is wrong?'

'Nothing.'

'Lying doesn't suit you, Miriel. Are we not friends?'

She nodded, but did not meet his eyes. 'I feel ashamed,' she said, her voice barely above a whisper. 'People are dying here. Every day. And yet I have never been happier. Even on the wall, when the Gothir were advancing I felt alive in a way I have never known before. I could smell the air – so sweet and cold. And with Senta . . .' She blushed and looked away.

'I know,' he told her. 'I have been in love.'

'It seems so stupid, but a part of me doesn't want this to end. Do you know what I mean?'

'Everything ends,' he said, with a sigh. 'In a curious way it is what makes life so beautiful. I knew an artist once, who could craft flowers from glass – fabulous items. But one night, as we were drinking in a small tavern, he told me he had never once fashioned anything with the beauty of a genuine rose. And he knew he never would. For the secret of its beauty is that it must die.'

'I don't want it to die. Ever.'

He laughed. 'I know that feeling, girl. But Shemak's balls! You're young – not yet twenty. Draw every ounce of pleasure you can from life, savour it, hold it on your tongue. But don't waste time with thoughts of loss. My first wife was a harridan. I adored her, and we fought like tigers. When she died I was bereft but, given the chance, I would not go back and live differently. The years with her were golden.'

She smiled at him sheepishly. 'I don't want the pain my father suffered. I know that sounds pathetic.'

'There's nothing pathetic about it. Where is the man himself?'

'Gathering torches.'

'For what?'

'Kesa Khan has asked me to lead Ekodas through the lower levels. We are to seek out a crystal.'

'I'll come with you.'

'No,' she said firmly as he started to rise. 'Ekodas says you are more tired than you will admit. You don't need a walk in the dark.'

'There could be danger,' he objected.

'Kesa Khan says not. Now you rest. We'll be back within a couple of hours.'

*

For the merchant, Matze Chai, sleep was a joy to be treasured. Each night, no matter what pressures his ventures loaded upon him, he would sleep undisturbed for exactly four hours. It was Matze Chai's belief that it was this blissful rest that kept his mind sharp while dealing with treacherous Gothir tradesmen and wily nobles.

So it was with some surprise that when he was awakened by his manservant, Luo, he noticed the dawn was still some way off, and that the night stars could still be seen through the balcony window.

'I am sorry, master,' whispered Luo, bobbing and bowing in the moonlight, 'but there is a man to see you.'

Matze Chai absorbed this information, and much more. No ordinary man could have prevailed upon Luo to disturb his rest. Nor would anyone of Matze's acquaintance leave the servant in such a state of fear.

He sat up and removed the net of silk that covered his waxed and gleaming hair. 'Light a lantern or two, Luo,' he said softly.

'Yes, master. I am sorry, master. But he was insistent that you should be awakened.'

'Of course. Think no more of it. You did exactly the right thing. Fetch me a comb.' Luo lit two lanterns, placing them on the desk beside the bed. Then he brought a bronze mirror and an ivory comb. Matze Chai tilted his head and Luo carefully combed his master's long beard, parting it at the centre and braiding it expertly. 'Where did you leave this man?' he asked.

'In the library, master. He asked for some water.'

'Ah, water!' Matze Chai smiled. 'I will dress myself. Be a good fellow and go to my study. In the third cabinet from the garden window you will find, wrapped I believe in red vellum and tied with blue twine, a set of parchments and scrolls. Bring them to the library as soon as you can.'

'Should I summon the guard, master?'

'For what purpose?' inquired Matze Chai. 'Are we in danger?'

'He is a rough and violent man. I know these things.'

'The world is full of rough and violent men. And yet I am

still rich and safe. Do not concern yourself, Luo. Merely do as I have bid you.'

'Yes, master. Red vellum. Third cabinet from the window.'

'Tied with blue twine,' reminded Matze Chai. Luo bowed and backed from the room. Matze Chai stretched and rose, moving to his wardrobe and selecting an open-fronted robe of shimmering purple, which he belted to his waist with a golden sash. In slippers of softest velvet he moved down the curving staircase into the long, richly-carpeted hall and across into the library.

His guest was seated upon a silk-covered couch. He had discarded a filthy Sathuli robe and burnoose and his clothes of black leather were travel-stained and dusty. A small black cross-bow lay beside him.

'Welcome to my home, Dakeyras,' said Matze Chai, with a wide smile.

The man smiled back. 'I'd say you were investing my money well – judging from the antiquities I see around me.'

'Your wealth is safe and growing apace,' Matze told him. He sat down on the couch opposite the newcomer, having first lifted the foul-smelling Sathuli robe between index finger and thumb and dropping it to the floor. 'I take it you are travelling in disguise.'

'Sometimes it is advisable,' admitted his guest.

Luo appeared, carrying the scrolls and ledgers. 'Put them on the table,' said Matze. 'Oh . . . and remove these items,' he added, touching the robes with the toe of his velvet slipper. 'Prepare a hot scented bath in the lower guest-room. Send for Ru Lai and tell her there is a guest who will require a hot-oil massage.'

'Yes, master,' answered Luo, gathering up the Sathuli robes and backing from the room.

'Now, Dakeyras, would you like to examine the accounts?'

The man smiled. 'Ever one step ahead, Matze. How did you know it was me?'

'A midnight guest who frightens Luo and asks for a

glass of water? Who else would it be? I understand there is a price on your head once more. Who have you offended now?'

'Just about everyone. But Karnak set the price.'

'Then it should please you to know he is currently languishing in the dungeons of Gulgothir.'

'So I understand. What other news is there?'

'The price of silk is up. And spices. You have investments in both.'

'I didn't mean the markets, Matze. What news from Drenai?'

'The Ventrians have had some success. They stormed Skeln but were pushed back at Erekban. But without Karnak they are set to lose the war. At present there is a cessation of hostilities. The Ventrians are holding the ground they have taken, and a Gothir force is camped in the Delnoch mountains. The fighting has ceased temporarily. No one knows why.'

'I could hazard a guess,' said the newcomer. 'There are Brotherhood knights in all three camps. I think there is a deeper game being played.'

Matze nodded. 'You could be right, Dakeyras. Zhu Chao has become more powerful in these last few months: only yesterday a decree from the Emperor was published bearing the royal seal, but Zhu Chao's signature. Worrying times. Still, that should not affect business. Now how can I help you?'

'I have an enemy in Gulgothir who desires my death.'

'Then kill him and be done with it.'

'I intend to. But I will need information.'

'Everything is available in Gulgothir, my friend. You know that. Who is this . . . unwise person?'

'A countryman of yours, Matze Chai. We have already spoken of him. He has a palace here and is close to the Emperor.'

Matze Chai licked his lips nervously. 'I do hope this is merely a bad jest.' The newcomer shook his head. 'You realise his home is guarded by men and demons, and that his powers are very great. He could even now be watching us.'

284

'Aye, he could. But there's nothing I can do about that.'

'What do you need?'

'I need a plan of the palace, and an estimate of the numbers of guards and their placements.'

Matze sighed. 'You are asking a great deal, my friend. If I aid you and you are captured – and confess – then my life would be forfeit.'

'Indeed it would.'

'Twenty-five thousand Raq,' said Matze Chai.

'Drenai or Gothir?' countered the newcomer.

'Gothir. The Drenai Raq has suffered in recent months.'

'That is close to the sum I have invested with you.'

'No, my friend, that is *exactly* the sum you have invested with me.'

'Your friendship carries a high price, Matze Chai.'

'I know of a man who was once a member of the Brotherhood, but he became overly addicted to Lorassium. He is a former captain of Zhu Chao's guard. And there are two others who once served the man we speak of and will be helpful with information as to his habits.'

'Send for them in the morning,' said Waylander, rising. 'And now I shall take the bath – and the massage. Oh, one small point. Before I visited you I went to another merchant who invests for me. I left him with sealed instructions. If I do not collect them tomorrow by noon he will open them and act upon the contents.'

'I take it,' said Matze, with a tight smile, 'we are talking about a contract for my death?'

'I have always liked you, Matze. You have a sharp mind.'

'This speaks of a certain lack of trust,' said Matze Chai, aggrieved.

'I trust you with my money, my friend. Let that be sufficient.'

*

The Gothir attacked three times in the night, twice trying to scale the walls but the third time launching their assault on the portcullis. The Nadir sent volley after volley of arrows into the attackers, but to little effect. Hundreds of soldiers clustered around the portcullis making a wall of shields against the rusted iron, while other men hacked and sawed at the metal bars.

Orsa Khan, the tall half-breed, threw lantern-oil over the barricade of carts and wagons and set fire to the base. Thick black smoke swirled around the gateway, and the attackers were driven back. On the walls Dardalion and the last of the Thirty battled alongside Nadir warriors, repelling assaults.

By dawn the last of the attacks had ceased and Dardalion made his way back through the hall, leaving Vishna and the others on the ramparts. He tried to commune with Ekodas, but could not break through the wall of power emanating from below the castle. He found Kesa Khan alone in his high room, the old shaman standing by the crooked window staring out over the valley.

'Three more days is all we have,' said Dardalion.

Kesa Khan shrugged. 'Much can happen in three days, Drenai.'

Dardalion unbuckled his silver breastplate, pulling it clear. Removing his helm he sat down on the rug by the glowing brazier.

Kesa Khan joined him. 'You are tired, priest.'

'I am,' admitted Dardalion. 'The paths of the future drained me.'

'As they have me on many occasions. But it was worth it to see the days of Ulric.'

'Ulric?'

'The Uniter,' said Kesa Khan.

'Ah yes, the First Uniter. I am afraid I spent little time observing him. I was more interested in the Second. An unusual man, don't you think? Despite his mixed blood and his torn loyalties he still drew the Nadir together and accomplished all that Ulric failed to do.'

Kesa Khan said nothing for a moment. 'Can you show me this man?'

Dardalion's eyes narrowed. 'But you have seen him, surely? He is the Uniter you spoke of.'

'No, he is not.'

Dardalion sighed. 'Take my hand, Kesa Khan, and share my memories.' The shaman reached out, gripping hard to Dardalion's palm. He shuddered, and his mind swam. Dardalion summoned his concentration, and together they witnessed the rise of Ulric Khan, the merging of the tribes, the great hordes sweeping across the steppes, the sacking of Gulgothir and the first siege of Dros Delnoch.

They watched the Earl of Bronze turn back the Nadir host, and saw the signing of the peace treaty, and the honouring of the terms; the marriage between the Earl's son and one of Ulric's daughters, and the birth of the child, Tenaka Khan, the Prince of Shadows, the King Beyond the Gate.

Dardalion felt Kesa Khan's pride swell, followed immediately by a sense of despair. The separation was swift, and brought a groan from the Drenai. He opened his eyes and saw the fear on Kesa Khan's face. 'What is it? What is wrong?'

'The woman, Miriel. From her will come the line of men leading to this Earl of Bronze?'

'Yes – I thought you understood that? You knew that a child would be conceived here.'

'But not to her, Drenai! I did not know about her! The line of Ulric begins here also.'

'So?'

Kesa Khan's breathing was shallow, his face distorted. 'I . . . I believed Ulric was the Uniter. And that Miriel's descendants would seek to thwart him. I . . she . . .'

'Out with it, man!'

'There are beasts guarding the crystal. There were three, but their hunger was great and they turned upon one another. Now there is only one. They were men sent by Zhu Chao to kill me. Karnak's son, Bodalen, was one of them. The crystal merged them.'

'You could breach the power all along! What treachery is this?' stormed Dardalion.

'The girl will die down there. It is written!' The shaman's face was pale and stricken. 'I have destroyed the line of the Uniter.'

'Not yet,' said Dardalion, surging to his feet.

Kesa Khan lunged out, grabbing the priest's arm. 'You don't understand! I have made a pact with Shemak. She will die. Nothing can alter it now.'

Dardalion tore himself clear of Kesa Khan's grip. 'Nothing is inalterable. And no demon will hold sway over me!'

'If I could change it I would,' wailed Kesa Khan. 'The Uniter is everything to me! But there must be a death. You cannot stop it!'

Dardalion ran from the room, down the winding stair to the hall, and on to the deep stairwell leading to the subterranean chambers. Just as he was entering the darkness Vishna pulsed to him from the ramparts. 'The Brotherhood are attacking, brother. We need you!'

'I cannot!'

'Without you we are lost! The castle will fall!'

Dardalion reeled back from the doorway, his mind whirling. Hundreds of women and children would be slain if he deserted his post. Yet if he did not, then Miriel was doomed. He fell to his knees in the doorway, desperately seeking the path of prayer, but his mind was lost in thoughts of the coming chaos. A hand touched his shoulder. He looked up. It was the scarred, ugly gladiator.

'Are you ill?' asked the man. Dardalion rose and took a deep breath. Then he told all to Angel. The man's face was grim as he listened. 'A death, you say? But not necessarily Miriel's?'

'I don't know. But I am needed on the wall. I cannot go to her.'

'I can,' said Angel, drawing his sword.

19

Zhu Chao stood on the balcony, leaning on the gilded rail and staring at the battlements of his palace. There were no vulgar crenellations here, but sweeping flutes and curves as befitted a Chiatze nobleman. The gardens below were filled with fragrant flowers and trees, with elaborate walkways curving around ponds and artificial streams. It was a place of quiet, tranquil beauty.

Yet it was still strong. Twenty men, armed with bow and sword, walked the four walls, while four others – keen-eyed and watchful – manned the mock towers at each corner. The gates were barred, and six savage hounds patrolled the gardens. He could see one of them now, lying on all fours beside an ornate path. Its black fur made it almost invisible.

I am safe, thought Zhu Chao. Nothing can harm me.

Why then am I so afraid?

He shivered and drew his sheepskin-lined robe of purple wool more closely about his slender frame.

Kar-Barzac was becoming a disaster. Kesa Khan still lived, and the Nadir were defending the walls like men possessed. Innicas was dead, the Brotherhood all but destroyed. And Galen had been inexplicably murdered upon his return to the Drenai forces. He had walked into the tent of General Asten, and told the man about the tragic betrayal that had seen the death of Karnak. Asten had listened quietly, then stood and approached the Brotherhood warrior. Suddenly he reached out, grabbing Galen by the hair and wrenching back his head. A knife-blade flashed. Blood gouted from Galen's throat. Zhu Chao had seen it all, the dying warrior falling to the floor, the stocky General looming above him.

Zhu Chao shivered. It was all going wrong.

And where was Waylander?

Three times he had cast the search spell. Three times it

had failed. But tonight all will be made well, he assured himself. Midwinter's Eve, and the great sacrifice. Power will flow into me, the gift of Chaos will be mine. Then I shall *demand* Kesa Khan's death. Tomorrow the Ventrian King will be dead. His troops will turn to the Brotherhood for leadership, as will the Drenai soldiers. Galen was not the only loyal knight among them. Asten would die, as the Emperor would die.

Three empires become one.

Not for me the petty titles of King or Emperor. With the crystal in my hands I shall be the Divine Zhu Chao, Lord of All, King of Kings. The thought pleased him. He glanced at the nearest wall, watching the soldiers marching along the parapet. Strong men. Faithful. Loyal. I am safe, he told himself once more.

He glanced up at the mock tower to the left. The soldier there was sitting with his back to the outside. Sleeping! Irritation flared. Zhu Chao pulsed a command to him, but the man did not move. The sorceror mentally summoned Casta, the Captain of the Guard.

'Yes, Lord,' came the response.

'The guard on the eastern tower. Have him brought to the courtyard and flogged. He is sleeping.'

'At once, Lord.'

Safe? How safe can I be with men such as these guarding me? 'And Casta!'

'Yes, Lord.'

'After he is flogged, cut his throat.' Turning on his heel Zhu Chao returned to his apartments, his good mood in tatters. He felt the need of wine, but held back. Tonight the sacrifice must be conducted without error. He thought of Karnak in chains, the curved sacrificial knife slowly slicing into the Drenai's chest. His mood brightened.

This is my last day as the servant of others, he thought. From tomorrow's dawn I shall be the Lord of Three Empires.

No, not until the crystal is in your power. For only then will you know immortality. Only then will you be whole again. A muscle at his jaw twitched and he saw again the unholy fire and the sharp little dagger in Kesa Khan's hand. Hate suffused him, and shame rose like acid in his throat.

'You will watch your people die, Kesa Khan,' he hissed. 'Every man, woman and babe. And you will know who is to blame. That is the price for what you stole from me!'

His memories echoed the remembered pain, and the months of terrible suffering that followed the mutilation. But the crystal would change everything. The Third Grimoire told of it. An ancient knight had been carried into the chamber, his arm cut away by a weapon of light. They had laid him upon a bed, and unleashed the power of the crystal. Within two days a new arm had sprouted from the severed limb.

But better even than this, according to the Fourth Grimoire, leaders of the Elder Races had been transformed by the crystal, their aging bodies made young again. Zhu Chao's throat was dry, and this time he succumbed to a small goblet of wine.

'Lord! Lord!' pulsed Casta, fear radiating in his spirit voice.

'What is it?'

'The sentry is dead, Lord! A crossbow bolt through the heart. And there is the mark of a grappling hook on the turret.'

'He's here!' screamed Zhu Chao, aloud. 'Waylander is here!'

'I cannot hear you, Lord,' pulsed Casta.

Zhu Chao fought for calm. 'Get the men from the walls. Search the gardens. Find the assassin!'

*

The oil-dipped torch sent crazed shadows across the rippled walls of the stairwell, and black smoke swirled in Angel's nostrils as he descended the stairs. There was a fear in him greater than any he had experienced. It was a fear of death. Not his own – that he was prepared for. But his terror grew as he considered Miriel and the monster, her young body broken, her dead eyes staring up, seeing nothing.

Angel swallowed hard, and moved on. He could not afford the security of stealth, but blundered on down the stairs, ever down. Dardalion had said the crystal chamber was on the sixth level, but the beast could be anywhere. Angel hawked and spat, vainly trying to dampen his dry mouth. And he prayed to any god that might be listening, Dark or Light, or any shade in between.

Let her live!

Take me instead. I've had a life, a good life. He missed a step and stumbled against the wall, sparks showering down from the torch, burning his bare forearm. 'Concentrate, you fool!' he told himself, his words echoing along the silent corridors.

Where now, he wondered as the stairwell joined a long, flat hallway. There was a dim light here, glowing from panels in the walls. He gazed around him. Everything was made of metal – walls, ceiling, floor. Shining and rust-free, the metal everywhere was crumpled and ripped, as if it had no more strength than rotted linen.

Angel shivered. The corridors were damp and cold and his muscles ached with it. Ekodas had pointed out how tired he was, and he felt it now. His limbs seemed leaden, his energy waning. Drawing in a deep breath he thought of Miriel and pushed on.

A large, arched doorway loomed before him. He entered it, sword raised. A movement sounded from behind. He swung, his sword arcing down. At the last moment he dragged the blade aside – just missing the child dressed in his own cloak of green. 'Shemak's balls, boy! I could have killed you!'

The boy shrank back against the doorway, his lip trembling, his eyes wide and frightened. Angel sheathed his sword and forced a smile. 'Followed me, did you?' he said, reaching out and drawing the child to him. 'Ah well, no harm done, eh?'

He knelt down beside the boy. 'You take the torch,' he said, holding it out for the lad. In truth he no longer needed its light, for the panels cast an eerie glow over the hall. There were metal beds here and rotted mattresses. Angel stood and drew his sword once more. Signalling to the boy he moved out into the corridor, seeking stairs.

Despite the danger he was pleased the boy was with him. The silence and the endless corridors were unnerving him. 'Stay close,' whispered the man. 'Old Angel will look after you.'

Not understanding, the boy nodded and grinned up at the gladiator.

*

'Have you the faintest idea of where we are?' Senta asked Ekodas, as the silver-armoured priest rounded yet another bend in the labyrinth of corridors on the seventh level.

'I think we are close,' said Ekodas, his face eerily pale in the faint yellow light.

Senta saw that he was sweating heavily. 'Are you all right, priest?'

'I can feel the crystal. It is making me nauseous.'

Senta turned to Miriel. 'You do take me to some romantic places,' he said, putting his arm around her and kissing her cheek. 'Volcanic caves, sorcerous castles, and now a trip in the dark a hundred miles below the earth.'

'No more than three hundred feet,' said Ekodas.

'Allow for poetic overstatement,' snapped Senta.

Miriel laughed. 'You needn't have come,' she chided.

'And miss this?' he cried, in mock astonishment. 'What sort of a man refuses a walk in the dark with a beautiful woman?'

'And a priest,' she pointed out.

'That is a flaw, I grant you!'

'Be silent!' hissed Ekodas. Genuinely surprised, Senta was about to fire back an angry reply when he saw that Ekodas was listening intently, his dark eyes narrowing to scan the gloom at the end of the corridor.

'What is it?' whispered Miriel.

'I thought I heard something – like breathing. I don't know, perhaps I imagined it.'

'It is unlikely there'd be anything living down here,' said Miriel. 'There is no food source.'

'I cannot use my Talent here,' said Ekodas, wiping sweat from his face. 'I feel so . . . so limited. Like a man suddenly blind.'

'Happily you do not need your Talent,' said Senta, still irritated by the priest's outburst. 'This is hardly the most . . .' He halted in mid-sentence, for now he could also hear stentorian breathing. Silently he drew his sword.

'It could be a trick of the earth,' whispered Miriel. 'You know, like wind whistling through a crack in the rocks.'

'There's not usually a great deal of wind at this depth,' said Senta.

They moved cautiously on, until they came to a long room, filled with metal cabinets. Most of the glowing panels had ceased to operate, but two still cast pale light across the iron floor. Miriel saw an object lying beneath an overturned table. 'Senta,' she said softly. 'Over there!'

The swordsman crossed the room and knelt. He rose swiftly and backed to where Ekodas and Miriel were standing. 'It's a human leg,' he said. 'Or what's left of it. And believe me, you don't want to know the size of the bite-marks.'

'Kesa Khan said there was no danger,' put in Miriel.

'Perhaps he didn't know,' volunteered Ekodas. 'The crystal is through that doorway. Let me find and destroy it, then we'll leave as fast as we can.'

'If we disappeared in a flash of magic it wouldn't be fast enough,' Senta told him. The priest did not smile, but moved on through what was left of the doorway. 'Look at that,' Senta told Miriel. 'The stone of the wall around the door has been torn out. You know, call me boring if you like, but at this moment I'd like to be sitting in that cabin of yours, with my feet out towards the fire, waiting for you to bring me a goblet of mulled wine.' The lightness of tone could not disguise the fear in his voice, and when Ekodas cried out, apparently in pain, Senta almost dropped his sword.

Miriel was the first to the doorway.

'Get back!' shouted Ekodas. 'Stay beyond the walls. The power is too much for you to bear!'

Senta caught Miriel by the arm and hauled her back. 'You know, beauty, I don't mind telling you that I am frightened. Not for the first time, but I've never known anything like this.'

'And me,' she agreed.

A shuffling sound came from the other end of the hall.

'I have a bad feeling about this,' whispered Senta.

And the creature moved into sight. It was colossal, almost twelve feet high, and Senta gazed in horror at the beast's two heads. Both were grotesque, with only vestigial traces of humanity; the mouths wide, almost as long as his forearm, the teeth crooked and sharp. Miriel drew her sword and backed away. 'Whatever you have to do, Ekodas, do it now!' she shouted.

The creature leaned forward, part-supporting its weight on two huge arms, its three legs drawn up beneath its bloated belly. It looked to Senta like a giant white spider crouching before them. One of the heads lolled to the left, eyes opening, fastening on Miriel. A groan came from its grotesque lips, deep and full of torment. The mouth on the other head opened and a piercing scream echoed in the hall. The creature tensed and shuffled crablike towards them, groaning and screaming.

Miriel edged to the left, Senta to the right.

The beast ignored the swordsman and charged at the girl, scattering tables and chairs. The speed was not great, but its huge bulk seemed to fill the room.

Senta ran at it, hurling himself at its broad back. One of the four arms clubbed at him, smashing his ribs. He staggered and almost fell. But the creature was rearing up above Miriel. She slashed her sword across a huge forearm, slicing deep into the flesh. Then Senta attacked again, plunging his own blade into the great belly.

A fist clubbed him again and he was sent spinning to the floor, his sword torn from his grasp. He saw Miriel dive beneath the creature's grasp and roll to her feet. Senta tried to rise, but a piercing pain clove into his side, and he knew several of his ribs were broken.

'Ekodas! For the sake of all that's holy help us!'

Ekodas knelt in the golden chamber, the crystal held in his hands, his thoughts far away. The doors of his mind were all open now, and the noises from beyond the chamber held no meaning for him. His life unfolded before the eyes of memory, wasted and filled with ridiculous fears. The sanctuary of the temple now seemed more of a grey prison, holding him from the riches of life. He gazed down at the many facets of the crystal, seeing himself reflected a hundred times, and he felt the strength of his soul expanding within the frail flesh of his body.

In an instant he could see not only the battle in the hall outside, but also the grim fighting on the walls far above. And more than this he saw the man Waylander moving silently along the darkened corridors of Zhu Chao's palace.

He laughed then. What did it matter?

And he saw Shia, standing beside the tall Orsa Khan, and the hole in the portcullis gate through which Gothir soldiers were scrambling. Meaningless, he thought, though he felt a shaft of irritation that he would no longer have the opportunity of enjoying her body, his enhanced memory recalling again the smell of her skin and her hair.

'Ekodas! For the sake of all that's holy help us!'

For all that's holy! What an amusing thought. Just like the temple, the Source was created by men as a prison for the soul, to prevent stronger men from enjoying the fruits of their power. I am free of such baggage, he thought.

Dardalion had said the crystal was evil. Such nonsense. It was beautiful, perfect. And what was evil, save a name given by weak men to a force they could neither comprehend nor control?

'Now you understand,' whispered a voice in his mind. Ekodas closed his eyes, and saw Zhu Chao, sitting at a desk in a small study.

'Yes, I understand,' Ekodas told him.

'Bring me the crystal, and we shall know such power, such joy!'

'Why should I not keep it for myself?'

Zhu Chao laughed. 'The Brotherhood is already in place, Ekodas. Ready to rule. Even with the crystal it would take you years to reach such a position of power.'

'There is truth in that,' agreed Ekodas. 'It will be as you say.'

'Good. Now show me the battle, my brother.'

Ekodas stood and, the crystal in his hands, walked to the doorway. Beyond it he saw Miriel dive to the floor and roll as the beast lunged for her. Senta, one hand clutching his ribs, had drawn a dagger and was stumbling forward to the attack.

Foolish man. Like trying to kill a whale with a needle.

The injured warrior plunged his dagger into the beast's back. The beast half-turned, and a mighty fist crashed into Senta's neck. He crumpled to the floor without a sound. Miriel saw him fall. And screamed, the sound full of fury. Hurling herself forward she thrust her blade into one of the open mouths, plunging it up into what should have been a brain.

Ekodas chuckled. There was no brain there, he knew. It was situated – if brain it could be called – between the heads, in the enormous lump of the shoulders.

The beast caught hold of Miriel, lifting her from her feet. Ekodas found himself wondering whether it would tear her apart, or merely bite her head from her shoulders.

'Such confusion in the beast's mind,' said Zhu Chao. 'Part of it is still Bodalen. It recognises the girl, the twin of a maid he killed by accident. See it hesitate! And can you feel the rising anger from the souls that were once of the Brotherhood?'

'I can,' admitted Ekodas. 'Hunger, desire, bafflement. Amusing, is it not?'

A figure moved in the background.

'More entertainment,' whispered the voice of Zhu Chao. 'Sadly I cannot retain the spell, and must miss the inevitable conclusion. We will share the memory in Gulgothir.'

The sorceror faded from Ekodas, and the young priest

returned his attention to the gladiator who had entered the hall.

You shouldn't have come, he thought. You are too weary for such an adventure.

*

Angel had heard the awful screams and was already running as he entered the hall. He saw Senta stretched out, unconscious on the floor and witnessed the monster lunge down, grabbing Miriel and dragging her into the air.

Reversing his sword, holding it now like a dagger, Angel angled his run, leaping first to a metal table and then launching himself at the beast's bloated back. He landed knees first and plunged his sword deep in the creature's flesh, driving it down with all of his weight. The monster reared up and swung. Angel was thrown clear. It still held Miriel in one huge hand, but now it turned on Angel. Half-stunned he rolled to his feet and staggered.

The boy carrying the torch ran forward, thrusting the burning brand at the beast. One of its many arms thrashed out, but the boy was nimble enough to duck and run back. Angel, his pale eyes glittering with battle fury, saw the beast charge again. Instead of running away, he hurled himself at the grotesque colossus, his hand reaching out for Senta's sword, where it jutted from the swaying belly. Massive fingers caught at Angel's left shoulder, just as his own hand curled around the sword-hilt. The beast lifted him high, the movement tearing the sword free of its prison of flesh. Blood gouted from the wound. Angel smashed the blade into the brow of the second head, splitting the skull.

The creature dropped Miriel, as pain from the awful injury flared through it. Angel struck again. And again. Another hand grabbed Angel's leg, drawing him towards the gaping mouth and the sabre-long fangs.

*

Miriel swung to see Ekodas, holding tightly to the crystal and leaning on the door-frame watching the drama.

Running to him she pulled his sword from its scabbard and returned to the fray.

'Between the shoulders,' said Ekodas, conversationally. 'That's where the brain is located. Can you see the hump there?'

Holding the broadsword two-handed, Miriel sent a powerful cut into the beast's leg, just above the knee. Blood spurted from the wound and the creature staggered back, one hand releasing its hold on Angel's leg. The former gladiator hacked his own sword into the arm holding him. The great fingers spasmed, and he fell to the floor. Blood was pouring from the monster, gushing from both heads, and numerous wounds to the body.

Still it came on. Miriel saw Angel backing away, and knew he was trying to draw it away from her. But now Miriel felt the power of the crystal, enhancing her Talent, filling her with rage. Images flooded her mind, radiating from the beast. Confusion, anger, hunger.

But one image flickered above the rest. Miriel saw Krylla running through the woods, a tall wide-shouldered man pursuing her.

Bodalen.

And she knew. Locked within this loathsome beast was the man who murdered her sister.

A huge arm swept down towards her. Ducking under the clumsy lunge she ran to the left – then charged in at the beast, leaping high, her foot coming down on one massive knee joint. Using this as a foothold she propelled herself up on to its back. A hand reached for her, but she threw herself forward. Reversing the sword she stood high on the beast's shoulders. 'Die!' she screamed. The blade lanced down through the bulging hump. As it pierced the skin the sword seemed to accelerate, for there was no muscle beneath to hold it back, and the skin split like an overripe melon, brains gushing out.

The beast reared one last time, dislodging Miriel. Then it swayed and fell.

Angel ran to where Miriel had fallen, reaching out and helping her to her feet. 'Thank the Source! You're alive!'

He put his arm around her, but she stiffened and he saw her staring towards the still form of Senta. Breaking clear of his embrace she ran to the fallen swordsman, turning him to his back. Senta groaned and opened his eyes. He saw Angel and tried to smile.

'You're wounded again,' he whispered. Angel could feel the blood trickling from torn skin on the side of his face.

Angel knelt by his side, noting the blood at the corners of his mouth, and the unnatural stillness of his limbs. Gently he reached out, squeezing the man's fingers. There was no answering grip.

'Let me help you up,' said Miriel, dragging on his left arm.

'Leave him, girl!' said Angel, his voice soft. Miriel slowly let the arm down.

'Not much of a place to end one's days in, eh, Angel?' said Senta. He coughed and blood sprayed from his handsome mouth, staining his chin. 'Still, I guess I couldn't . . . be . . . in better company.'

Angel swung towards Ekodas. 'Can you do anything, priest?'

'Nothing. His neck is broken, and his spine in two places. And his ribs have pierced a lung.' The priest's tone was light, almost disinterested.

Angel returned his attention to the dying swordsman. 'Fancy letting a creature like that kill you,' he said gruffly. 'You ought to be ashamed of yourself.'

'I am.' He smiled and closed his eyes. 'There's no pain. It's very peaceful really.' His eyes flared open, and fear was in his voice. 'You'll carry me out, won't you? Don't want to spend eternity down here. I'd like to be able . . . to feel the sun . . . you know?'

'I'll carry you myself.'

'Miriel . . .!'

'I'm here,' she said, her voice trembling.

'I'm . . . sorry . . . I had such . . .' His eyes closed again. And he was gone.

'*Senta!*' she shouted. 'Don't do this! Get up. Walk!' Standing she dragged on his arm.

Angel rose and grabbed her. 'Let him go, princess. Let him go!'

'I can't!'

He drew her into a tight embrace. 'It's over,' he said softly. 'He's not here any more.'

Miriel pulled away from him, her face set, eyes gleaming. Spinning on her heel she walked to the dead beast, dragging her sword clear. Then she turned on Ekodas. 'You bastard! You stood by and did nothing. He would be alive but for you.'

'Perhaps,' he agreed. 'Perhaps not.'

'Now you die,' said Miriel, suddenly running forward. Ekodas raised his hand. Miriel groaned and halted so suddenly it seemed she had run into an invisible wall.

'Calm yourself,' said Ekodas. 'I didn't kill him.'

'Destroy the crystal, priest,' said Angel, 'before it destroys you.'

Ekodas smiled. 'You don't understand. No one would who had not felt its power.'

'I can feel it,' said Angel. 'At least I would guess it is the crystal that is filling me with the desire to kill you.'

'Yes, that is probably true. On a lesser mind the crystal would have that kind of effect. I should draw back. Return to the fortress.'

'No,' said Angel. 'You were sent here by those who trusted you. They believed only you had the strength to resist the . . . thing. They were wrong, weren't they? It's overpowered you.'

'Nonsense. It has merely enhanced my considerable Talents.'

'So be it. We'll wait for you at the fortress,' said Angel, with a deep sigh. He stepped forward. 'One small point, though . . .'

'Yes?'

Angel leaned back, and kicked out and up, his boot hitting the crystal, sending it spinning from the priest's hand. Ekodas tried to punch out, but the warrior rolled away from the blow and swung his elbow into the priest's face. Ekodas staggered. Angel sent a thundering left cross

301

that cannoned into his opponent's chin. Ekodas hit the floor face-first – and did not move.

Miriel, freed from whatever spell Ekodas had cast, moved towards the still body.

'Leave him be, child,' said Angel. 'He was not responsible.' Moving to the crystal Angel felt its power reaching out to him, with promises of strength, immortality and fame. Angel reeled back. 'Give me the sword,' he told Miriel. Taking the hilt in both hands he smote the crystal with one terrible blow.

It exploded into bright, glittering fragments, and a great rush of cool air filled the hall.

Ignoring the fallen priest Angel walked wearily back to Senta's body and lifted it, letting the head fall against his shoulder.

'Let's take him back to the sunlight,' he said.

20

Zhu Chao was trembling, sweat trickling down his cheeks. He struggled for calm, but his pulse was racing and he could feel the erratic hammering of his heart.

He cannot reach you, he told himself. He is one man. I have many men. And there are the dogs. Yes, yes, the dogs. They will sniff him out! He sat down at his desk and stared at the open doorway, where the two guards waited, swords drawn.

The hounds had been shipped from Chiatze, formidable beasts with huge jaws and powerful shoulders. Hunting dogs, they had been known to drag down bears. They would rend him, tear the flesh from his bones!

The sorceror poured himself a goblet of wine, his trembling causing him to spill the liquid over several parchments lying on the oak-topped desk. He didn't care. Nothing mattered now, save that he lived through this fear-filled night.

'Lord!' pulsed Casta.

'Yes?'

'One of the dogs is dead. The others are sleeping. We found the remains of fresh meat by one of them. I think he poisoned them. Lord! Can you hear me?'

Zhu Chao was stunned, and felt his reasoning swept away on a tide of panic.

'Lord! Lord!' pulsed Casta. But Zhu Chao could not respond. 'I've ordered all the men into the main palace grounds,' continued Casta. 'And we've sealed the ground floor, and I have men guarding all three stairways.'

The sorceror drained his wine and poured a second goblet. The spirit steadied his failing courage. 'Good,' he pulsed. He stood –and swayed, catching hold of the side of the desk. Too much wine, he realised, and drunk too swiftly. Never mind. It would pass. He took several deep breaths, and felt his strength return.

Swiftly he crossed the room and stepped into the corridor. The two guards snapped to attention. 'Follow me,' he ordered, and marched towards the stairwell leading to the dungeon chambers. He made one man walk before him on the stairs, the other following sword in hand. At the foot of the stairwell they emerged into a torch-lit corridor. Three men were playing dice at the far table. They sprang to their feet as Zhu Chao stepped into the light.

'Bring the prisoners to the Inner Sanctum,' he said.

'Lord!' pulsed Casta, his voice triumphant.

'Speak!'

'He is dead. One of the guards found him scaling the roof. They fought, and the assassin was killed and hurled to the stones below.'

'Yes!' roared Zhu Chao, his fist sweeping up into the air. 'Bring his body to me. I will consign it to Hell!' Oh, how sweet life felt at that moment, the words in his mind singing like a nightingale: *Waylander is dead. Waylander is dead!*

Leaving the men he entered a small room at the end of the corridor, locking the door behind him. From a hiding place beneath a desk of oak he removed the Fifth Grimoire and studied the ninth chapter. Closing his eyes he spoke the words of power and found himself floating above the walls of Kar-Barzac. But there was no way past the pulsating force that radiated from below the fortress. Then, as suddenly as sunshine following a storm, the power faded and died. Zhu Chao was stunned. Swiftly he sent his spirit questing into the labyrinth below the citadel and found the priest Ekodas nursing the crystal. He could feel the surging of the man's Talent, his growing ambition, his burgeoning desires.

He spoke to the priest, sensing a kindred spirit, and when Ekodas said he would bring the crystal to Gulgothir, Zhu Chao knew he spoke the absolute truth. He fought hard to keep his triumph from Ekodas, and returned to his palace.

Waylander was dead. The crystal was his. And in a few short moments the souls of kings would be dedicated to Shemak.

And the son of a shoemaker would be the Lord of the Earth!

*

The Gothir forces had fallen back again, but the defenders manning the walls were fewer now, and desperately weary. Dardalion moved among the Thirty, pausing only at the body of fat Merlon. He had died at the ruined gateway, hurling himself into the mass of warriors surging through the ruptured portcullis. Orsa Khan and a score of Nadir warriors had joined him, and together they had forced back the attackers. But, just as the Gothir retreated to their camp, Merlon had slumped to the ground, bleeding from many wounds.

He died within moments. Dardalion knelt by the body. 'You were a good man, my friend,' he said softly. 'May the Source greet you.'

From the corner of his eye he saw Angel emerge from the hall, carrying the body of the swordsman, Senta. Dardalion sighed and stood. Miriel came next, a small boy beside her. The Abbot walked across to them, and waited silently as Angel laid down the body of his friend. In the presence of the silver-armoured Abbot the small boy eased back and vanished into the hall.

'Where is Ekodas?' Dardalion asked at last.

'He's alive,' said Angel. 'And the crystal is destroyed.'

'The Source be praised! I was not sure that even Ekodas would have the strength.'

He saw Miriel about to speak, but Angel cut in swiftly. 'It was a creation of great evil,' he said.

Ekodas appeared in the doorway, blinking in the fading light. Dardalion ran to him. 'You did it, my son. I am proud of you.' He reached out to embrace the priest, but Ekodas brushed him away.

'I did nothing – save let a man die,' he whispered. 'Leave me, Dardalion.' The priest stumbled away.

The Abbot swung back to Miriel. 'Tell me all,' he said. Miriel sighed and related the story of the fight with the monster, and the death of Senta. Her voice was low and spiritless, her eyes distant. Dardalion felt her pain and her sorrow.

'I am so sorry, my child. So terribly sorry.'

'People die in wars all the time,' she said tonelessly. As if in a dream she walked away towards the battlements.

Angel covered Senta with his cloak then stood. 'I'd like to kill Kesa Khan,' he hissed.

'It would achieve nothing,' replied Dardalion. 'Go with Miriel. She is fey now, and could come to harm.'

'Not while I live,' said Angel. 'But tell me, Abbot, what is it for? Why did he die down there? Please tell me it was worth something. And I don't want to hear about Uniters.'

'I cannot answer all your questions. Would that I could. But no man can know where his steps will ultimately lead, nor the results of his actions. But I will tell you this, and I will trust you to keep it in your heart and not speak of it to any living soul. There she is, sitting on the battlements. What do you see?'

Angel looked up and saw Miriel bathed in the fiery light of dusk. 'I see a beautiful woman, tough and yet gentle, strong and yet caring. What do you think I should see?'

'What I see,' whispered Dardalion. 'A young woman carrying the seed of future greatness. Even now it is growing within her, tiny, a mere spark of life, created from love. But that spark could one day, if we survive here, give birth to a flame.'

'She is pregnant.'

'Yes. Senta's son.'

'He didn't know,' said Angel, staring down at the cloak-shrouded corpse on the stones.

'But you know, Angel. You know now that she has something to live for. But she will need help. There are few men strong enough to take on the burden of another man's child.'

'That is no worry to me, Abbot. I love her.'

'Then go to her, my son. Sit with her. Share her grief.'

Angel nodded and moved away. Dardalion strode into the hall. The boy was sitting at a bench table, staring down at his hands. Dardalion sat opposite him. Their eyes met and Dardalion smiled. The boy returned it.

Kesa Khan entered the hall from the stairwell leading to the upper floors. He saw Dardalion and crossed to the table. 'I saw her on the battlements,' he said. 'I am . . . happy that she survived.'

'Her lover did not,' said Dardalion.

The shaman shrugged. 'It is not important.'

Dardalion bit back an angry reply, and shifted his gaze to the boy. 'I have something for you, Kesa Khan,' he said, still staring at the black-eyed child.

'Yes?'

'The young warlord who will wed the daughter of Shia.'

'You know where to find him?'

'You are sitting beside him,' said Dardalion, rising.

'He is a mute. Worthless!'

'By all that's holy, shaman, I do despise you!' roared Dardalion. Fighting for calm he leaned forward. 'He had an infection of the ear that made him deaf. Without being able to hear he never learned to speak. Ekodas healed him. Now all he needs is time, patience, and something that is a little beyond you, I think – love!' Without another word Dardalion spun on his heel and strode from the hall.

Vishna met him in the courtyard. 'They are massing again. We'll be hard pressed to hold them.'

*

Waylander crouched down on the roof, watching the men gathering round the body below. The guard had almost surprised him, but the man had been slow to bring his sword to bear, and a black-handled throwing-knife had sliced into his throat, ending his indecision – and his life. Swiftly Waylander had stripped the man, then he removed his own jerkin and leggings and dressed the corpse.

The dead man was a little shorter than Waylander, but the black breastplate and full-faced helm fitted well, though the dark woollen leggings rode high on the calf. This discrepancy was covered by the man's knee-length boots. They were tight, but the leather was soft and pliable, and the fit caused Waylander little discomfort.

Leaning out over the parapet he had seen the guards in the courtyard below. Drawing the dead man's sword and holding his own blade in his right hand he shouted. 'He's here! On the roof!' Out of sight of the men below he clashed the two swords together, the discordant noise ringing above the palace. Then he clove his own blade three times into the dead man's face, smashing the bones and disfiguring the features. Laying aside the swords he had then hauled the corpse to the parapet and sent the body plummeting to the ground.

He waited several minutes, and watched as the soldiers below carried the body inside the palace. Then he put on the full-faced helm, gathered his second rope and ran to the rear of the roof, leaning out and scanning the windows below. According to the information supplied by Matze Chai there was a stairwell at the corner of the building, winding down to the lower levels.

Looping his rope over a jutting pillar he climbed to the wall and abseiled down, past two windows, halting by a third. It was open, and no light showed within. Hooking his foot over the sill he climbed inside. It was a sleeping chamber with a narrow bed. There were no blankets or sheets upon it, and he took it to be an unused guest-room. Hiding his loaded crossbow within the folds of the dead man's black cloak he stepped out into the corridor. The stairs were to his right and he made for them. He heard sounds of footfalls on the stairs and kept moving. Two knights rounded a bend and climbed towards him.

'Who was it who killed the assassin?' the first asked him.

Waylander shrugged. 'Not me, more's the pity,' he said, continuing on his way.

'Well, who else is up there?' continued the first man, grabbing Waylander's shoulder. The assassin turned, the crossbow coming up.

'No one,' he said – and loosed a bolt which hammered into the man's open mouth and up into the brain. The second knight tried to run, but Waylander shot again, the bolt plunging into the back of the man's neck. He fell to the stairs and was still.

Reloading the crossbow with his last two bolts the assassin moved on.

*

As his chains were unlocked Karnak tensed, but a knife-blade touched his throat, and he knew his struggles would be useless. The huge Drenai general glared at the men holding his arms. 'By all the gods I'll remember your faces,' he told his captors.

One of them laughed. 'You won't have long to remember them,' he said.

They dragged him out of the dungeon and along the torch-lit corridor. He saw Zhu Chao standing by a door-way. 'A pox on you, you yellow-faced bastard!' he shouted.

The Chiatze did not reply, but stood aside as Karnak was led into the Inner Sanctum. A pentagram had been chalked on the stone floor, and gold wires had been stretched between candle-holders of stained iron, forming a six-pointed star above the chalk. Karnak was hauled to a wall, where once more he was shackled by the wrists. He saw another prisoner already there, a tall, slender man, his bearing regal despite the bruises and cuts to his face.

'I know you,' whispered Karnak.

The man nodded. 'I am the fool who trusted Zhu Chao.'

'You are the Emperor.'

'I was,' replied the man sourly. He sighed. 'The serpent enters . . .'

Karnak swung his head to see the purple-robed figure of Zhu Chao approach them.

'Tonight, gentlemen, you will witness the supreme gift of power.' His slanted eyes glowed as he spoke and the faintest trace of a smile showed at his thin-lipped mouth. 'I do appreciate that you will not share my pleasure, even though you will be instrumental in supplying it.' Leaning forward he laid a hand on Karnak's massive chest. 'You see, I will begin by cutting out your heart and laying it upon the golden altar. This gift will summon the servant of the

309

Lord Shemak.' He turned to the Emperor. 'That is where you enter the proceedings. You I will deliver whole, and the demon will devour you.'

'Do as you please, wizard,' snapped the Emperor. 'But do not bore me any longer.'

'I assure *Your Highness* you will not remain bored for long.' Three men entered the room, carrying a blood-drenched body. Zhu Chao swung round. 'Ah,' he said. 'My supposed nemesis. Bring it here!'

The knights carried it forward and laid the corpse on the floor. Zhu Chao smiled. 'See how puny he looks in death, his face sheared away by the sharp sword of a valiant knight? See how . . .' He faltered, his eyes staring at the right hand of the corpse. The third finger was missing, an old wound covered in a white scar. Zhu Chao knelt and lifted the man's right hand. Upon the signet finger was a ring of red gold, shaped like a coiled serpent. 'You fools!' hissed Zhu Chao. 'This is Onfel! Look, see the ring!' Zhu Chao scrambled to his feet, his composure lost. 'Waylander is alive! He is in the palace. Get out! All of you! Find him!'

The knights ran from the room. Zhu Chao pushed shut the door, and dropped a heavy lock-bar into place.

Karnak's laughter boomed out. 'He'll kill you, sorceror. You are dead!'

'Shut your stinking mouth!' screamed Zhu Chao.

'How can you make me? With what will you threaten me?' asked the giant Drenai. 'Death? I don't think so. I know this man who hunts you. I know what he is capable of. By the bones of Missael, I had men hunting him myself. The best assassins, the finest swordsmen. Yet still he lives.'

'Not for long,' said the sorceror. A slow, cruel smile curved his thin lips. 'Ah yes! You hired assassins – to protect your beloved Bodalen. He told me of it only recently.'

'You have seen my son?'

'Seen him? Oh, I saw a lot of him, my dear Karnak. He was mine, you see. He fed me all your plans, in return for a promise that when I had killed you he would rule the Drenai.'

'You lying whoreson!' stormed Karnak.

'Not so. Ask your fellow guest, the late Emperor. He has no reason to lie. He will die alongside you. Bodalen was weak, spineless, and ultimately of little use to me.' Zhu Chao laughed, a high shrill sound that echoed in the chamber. 'Even when he had the strength of ten he had difficulty completing his task. Poor, stupid, dead Bodalen.'

'Dead?' whispered Karnak.

'Dead,' repeated Zhu Chao. 'I sent him to an enchanted fortress. You would not like to see what he became. Therefore I shall show you.'

The sorceror closed his eyes and Karnak's mind reeled. He found himself staring into a dimly-lit chamber, where a creature out of nightmare was battling against a young woman and the gladiator, Senta. He watched Senta struck down, and saw a second arena warrior – Angel – leap to the attack. The scene faded.

'I would like to be able to show you more, but sadly I had to leave,' said Zhu Chao, his words ripe with malice. 'But the monster was Bodalen – and several other of my men, merged by magic.'

'I do not believe you,' said Karnak.

'I thought you might not. So, for your edification, Drenai, here is another scene I took from Kar-Barzac.'

The vision shimmered again, and Karnak groaned as he saw Bodalen and the other warriors falling asleep in the crystal chamber, the bodies beginning to writhe, and merge . . .

'No!' he screamed, and wrenched savagely at the chains which held him.

'I do so enjoy your pain, Drenai,' said Zhu Chao. 'And here is a second source of agony for you. Tomorrow Galen will kill your friend Asten, and the Drenai will come, as the Gothir already have, under the rule of the Brotherhood. As indeed will Ventria. Three empires under one Lord. Myself.'

'You are forgetting Waylander,' snarled Karnak. 'By all the gods, I would give my soul to be alive at the moment he kills you.'

311

'Before the night is over my powers will be so great that no blade will be able to cut me. Then I will welcome this . . . Drenai savage!'

'Welcome him now,' came a cold voice from the other side of the room.

Zhu Chao spun, dark eyes narrowing as he peered into the shadows by the door. A knight stepped from behind a pillar, and lifted clear the full-faced helm he wore.

'You can't be here!' whispered Zhu Chao. 'You can't!'

'I came in with the men carrying the body. So good of you to lock the others out.'

The assassin stepped closer, crossbow raised. Zhu Chao ran to his left and leapt over the golden wires, making for the centre of the pentagram. Waylander loosed a bolt that flashed for the sorceror's neck, but Zhu Chao swung at the last instant, his hand coming up. The bolt pierced his wrist – and he screamed in pain. Waylander took aim. But the sorceror ducked behind the altar of gold and began to chant.

Black smoke oozed around the altar, swirling up to form a massive figure, with hair and eyes of green flame. Waylander sent a crossbow bolt into the huge chest, but it passed through and clattered against the far wall.

Zhu Chao rose and stood before the creature of smoke and fire. 'Now what will you do, little man!' he jeered at Waylander. 'What pitiful weapons can you bring to bear?' The assassin said nothing. He had no more bolts, and dropped the crossbow, drawing his sabre. 'Lord Shemak!' screamed Zhu Chao. 'I call for this man's death!'

The figure with eyes of flame spread its massive arms, and a voice like distant thunder rumbled in the room. 'You do not command me, human. You ask for favours, and you pay for them with blood. Where is the payment?'

'There!' said Zhu Chao, pointing to the chained men.

'They still live,' said the demon. 'The ritual is incomplete.'

'I will deliver their strength to you, Lord, I swear it! But first, I beg you, give me the life of the assassin, Waylander.'

312

'It would please me more to see you slay him,' said the demon. 'Shall I give you the strength?'

'Yes! Yes!'

'As you wish!'

Zhu Chao suddenly screamed in pain, his head arcing back. His body twisted and grew, stretching, swelling. His robes fell away as new muscles formed, huge and knotted. His body spasmed and a series of terrible groans came from the deformed throat. Nose and chin stretched out, and sleek velvet fur burst through his skin, covering the now colossal eight-foot frame. His mouth opened to reveal long fangs, and his fingers, treble-jointed now, boasted talons.

The creature that had been Zhu Chao stumbled forward, dislodging the delicate golden wires, scattering the black candlesticks.

Against the wall Karnak tore at his chains, using all of his mighty strength. Two of the links stretched, but did not give. Again and again the Drenai threw his weight against them.

Waylander backed away from the beast, and the smoke-demon's laughter filled the room.

Outside the Sanctum the remaining Knights of Blood were hammering on the door, calling out for their master. Waylander ran back to where he had discarded his helm. Slipping it over his head he lifted the bar on the door – and stepped aside. The door burst open, three knights tumbling inside, one falling to his knees directly before the awesome beast. The man screamed and tried to rise. The beast's talons tore into him, lifting the knight into the air, the deadly fangs ripping open his throat. Blood sprayed across the altar.

The other knights stood transfixed.

'It killed the master!' yelled Waylander. 'Use your swords!'

But the knights turned and fled. The beast leapt at Waylander. Ducking under the sweep of its talons the assassin sent a slashing cut to the creature's belly, but the blade merely sliced the surface of the skin. Waylander dived and rolled to his feet.

313

Karnak, with one last effort, snapped the right-hand chain, then turned and used both hands to rip loose the left. Spinning on his heel he swung the chains around above his head and charged the monster. The iron links hit the beast on the throat, whipping around the neck. It turned and reared high, dragging Karnak from his feet. Waylander darted forward and plunged his sword into the open belly, driving it home with all his weight and strength.

A great howl went up – and a taloned arm flashed down, opening the flesh of Waylander's shoulder. He fell back. Karnak dragged back on the chain, which tightened around the beast's throat. It tried to turn and rend its attacker but Karnak, despite his great bulk, moved nimbly, keeping the chain taut. Waylander ran to the fallen knight, retrieving the man's sword. Holding the blade double-handed, the assassin advanced once more, lifting the sword high and cleaving it down on the elongated skull. The blade bounced clear on the first stroke, but twice more Waylander struck. The bone of the skull parted on the third blow, the sword wedging deep into the beast's cranium. It sank to all fours, blood gushing from its mouth, talons scratching at the stone.

And died.

The smoke-demon was silent for a moment. 'You offer me good sport, Waylander,' he said softly. 'But then you always have. I think you always will.'

The smoke billowed and faded – and the demon vanished.

Karnak unwound the chain from the dead beast's throat and crossed to Waylander. 'Good to see you, old lad,' he said, with a wide smile.

'The men you sent are all dead,' said Waylander coldly. 'Now only you remain.'

Karnak nodded. 'I was trying to protect my son. No excuses. He's . . . dead. You're alive. Let that be an end to it.'

'I choose my own endings,' said Waylander, moving past the giant Drenai to where the Emperor stood, still chained to the wall. 'It has always been said that you are a man of honour,' Waylander told him.

314

'It is a source of pride to me,' said the Emperor.

'Good. You see I have two choices, Majesty. I can kill you, or I can let you go. But there is a price for the latter.'

'Name it, and if it is within my power you may have it.'

'I want the attack on the Nadir Wolves stopped; the army ordered back.'

'What are the Nadir to you?'

'Less than nothing. But my daughter is with them.'

The Emperor nodded. 'It will be as you say, Waylander. Is there nothing you want for yourself?'

The assassin smiled wearily. 'Nothing any man can give me,' he said.

*

Angel pushed the table on to the stairs, up-ending it to block the view of the enemy archers on the landing above, then sank to his haunches and stared around the hall.

The Gothir had forced the portcullis gate on the eleventh day of the siege, the defenders falling back to the transient safety of the keep. The older women and children hid in the lower levels of the fortress while, as Angel had predicted, the younger women now joined the men in the defence of the citadel.

Only eighty-five men remained, and these were desperately tired as the siege reached the thirteenth day. The barricades at the keep-gate were holding, but the Gothir had scaled the outside walls, climbing in through undefended windows, and were now in control of all the upper levels, occasionally attacking down the narrow stairwells, but more often merely loosing shafts into the packed hall below.

An arrow thudded into the upturned table. 'I know you're there, arse-face!' yelled Angel.

Miriel joined him. She had lost weight, the skin of her face taut and fleshless, her eyes gleaming unnaturally. Since Senta's death she had fought as one possessed with a lust for death. Angel had been hard-pressed to defend her, and had taken two minor cuts, one to the shoulder, the other to the forearm, hurling himself into the path of warriors closing in on her.

'We're finished here,' she said. 'The barricade will not hold them for long.'

He shrugged. There was no need to reply. The point was all too obviously correct, and Angel could sense the mood of grim resignation among the Nadir. Miriel sat beside him, resting her head on his shoulder. He curled his arm around her. 'I loved him, Angel,' she said, her voice barely above a whisper. 'I should have told him, but I didn't know until he was gone.'

'That makes you feel guilty? That you didn't say the words?'

'Yes. He deserved more. And it's so hard to accept that he's . . .' She swallowed hard, unable to give sound to the word. Forcing a smile she brightened, briefly. 'He had such a zest for life, didn't he? And always so witty. Nothing grey about Senta, was there?'

'Nothing grey,' he agreed. 'He lived his life to the full. He fought, loved . . .'

'. . . and died.' She said it swiftly, and fought to hold back the tears.

'Yes, he died. Shemak's balls, we all die.' Angel sighed, then smiled. 'For myself I've no regrets. I've had a full life. But it grieves me to know that . . . you're here with me now. Everything is ahead of you – or it should be.'

She took his hand. 'We'll be together in the Void. Who knows what adventures await. And maybe he's there . . . waiting!'

Another arrow thudded into the table, then Angel heard the sound of boots upon the stairs. Surging to his feet he drew his sword. As the Gothir swarmed down Angel wrenched the table aside and leapt to meet them, Miriel just behind him.

Angel killed two, Miriel a third and the Gothir fell back. An archer loomed at the top of the stairs. Miriel hurled a knife which lanced into his shoulder, and he dived from sight. Angel backed away and wedged the table across the stairwell. 'Well,' he said, with a wide grin, 'we're not finished yet.'

Striding across the hall he saw the priest Ekodas, kneeling beside the stricken Dardalion. The Abbot was still sleeping and Angel paused. 'How is he?' he asked.

'Dying,' replied Ekodas.

'I thought you had healed the wound.'

'I did, but his heart has given out. It is almost ruptured and the valves are thinner than papyrus.' It was the first time the two men had spoken since the battle against the beast. Ekodas glanced up, then stood before the former gladiator. 'I am sorry for what happened,' he said. 'I . . . I . . . '

'It was the crystal,' put in Angel, swiftly. 'I know. It had a similar effect on me.'

'Yet you destroyed it.'

'I never had it in my hands. Don't torture yourself, priest.'

'Priest no longer. I am not worthy.'

'I'm no judge, Ekodas, but we all have weaknesses. We're made that way.'

The slender priest shook his head. 'That is generous of you. But I watched as your friend died – and I made a pact with evil. Zhu Chao came to me in that chamber. He seemed like . . . like a brother of the soul. And for that short time I had such vile dreams. I never realised there was so much . . . darkness inside me. I will walk another path now.' He shrugged. 'The crystal didn't change me, you see. It merely opened my eyes to what I am.'

Dardalion stirred. 'Ekodas!' The young priest knelt by the Abbot, taking his hand. Angel moved away towards the barricade.

'I am here, my friend,' said Ekodas.

'It . . . was all . . . done in faith, my son. And I can feel the others waiting for me. Summon the living for me.'

'There is only Vishna.'

'Ah. Fetch him then.'

'Dardalion, I . . . '

'You wish to be . . . released from your vows. I know.

317

The woman, Shia.' Dardalion's eyes closed and a spasm of pain twisted his features. 'You are free, Ekodas. Free to wed, free to live . . . free to be.'

'I am sorry, Father.'

'You have nothing to be . . . sorry for. I sent you down there. I knew your destiny, Ekodas. From the moment she came to the temple there was a bond between you. Know peace, Ekodas . . . and . . . the joys of love.' He smiled weakly. 'You have done your duty by me, and by the others. Now . . . fetch Vishna, for time is short.'

Ekodas sent out a pulse and the tall forked-bearded warrior came running from the far side of the hall to kneel beside the dying Abbot. 'I can speak no more,' whispered Dardalion. 'Join me in communion.'

Vishna closed his eyes, and Ekodas knew their two spirits were now united. He made no attempt to join the communion, and waited patiently for it to end. He was holding Dardalion's hand when the Abbot died. Vishna jerked and groaned, then opened his dark eyes.

'What did he say?' asked Ekodas, releasing the hand.

'If we survive I am to travel to Ventria and found a new temple. The Thirty will live on. I am sorry that you will not be accompanying me.'

'I cannot, Vishna. It's gone from me. And, truth to tell, I don't want it back.'

Vishna stood. 'You know, just as he died, and flew from me, I felt the presence of the others – Merlon, Palista, Magnic. All waiting for him. It was wonderful. Truly wonderful.'

Ekodas gazed down on Dardalion's dead face, perfectly still and serene. 'Farewell, Father,' he whispered.

The silence beyond the keep was broken by the sound of distant trumpets.

'The Source be praised,' said Vishna.

'What is it?'

'That is the Gothir signal for withdrawal.' He sat down and closed his eyes, his spirit flying from the keep. Moments later he returned. 'A messenger has come from the Emperor. The siege is lifted. It is over, Ekodas! We live!'

318

At the barricade Angel peered into the courtyard. The Gothir were withdrawing in order, silently and in ranks of three. Angel sheathed his sword and turned to the defenders. 'I think you have won, my lads!' he shouted.

Orsa Khan leapt to the barricade and watched the departing soldiers. Swinging to Angel he threw his arms around the gladiator and kissed both his scarred cheeks. The other remaining Nadir surged forward, pulling Angel down and hoisting him to their shoulders, and a great cheer went up.

Watching the scene Miriel smiled, but the smile faded as she gazed around the hall. The dead were lying everywhere. Kesa Khan emerged from the lower stair, leading women and children back to the light. The old shaman approached her.

'Your father has slain Zhu Chao,' he said, but he did not meet her gaze. 'You have won for us, Miriel.'

'At great cost,' she told him.

'Yes, the price was not insignificant.' The small boy who had followed Angel was beside the shaman, and Kesa Khan reached out and patted his head. 'Still we have a future,' said the old man. 'Without you we could have been dust in the mountains. I wish joy for you.'

Miriel took a deep, slow breath. 'I can't believe it is over.'

'Over? No. Only this battle. There will be others.'

'Not for me.'

'For you also. I have walked the futures, Miriel. You are a child of battle. You will remain so.'

'We shall see,' she said, turning away from him to see Angel striding towards her. She looked up into his scarred, ravaged face, and the twinkling grey eyes. 'It looks as though we've a little time left after all,' she said.

'It certainly seems that way,' he agreed. Reaching down Angel hoisted the young Nadir boy to his shoulder. The child giggled happily and waved his wooden sword in the air.

'You're good with children,' said Miriel. 'He adores you.'

319

'He's a courageous pup. He followed me down into the depths, and then charged the beast with a burning brand. Did you see him?'

'No.'

Angel turned to Kesa Khan. 'Who will look after him?' he asked.

'I shall. As a son,' answered the shaman.

'Good. I may visit now and again. I'll hold you to that.' Lifting the boy down he watched as Kesa Khan led him away. The boy glanced back and waved his sword. Angel chuckled. 'What now?' he asked Miriel.

'I'm pregnant,' she said, looking into his pale eyes.

'I know. Dardalion told me.'

'It frightens me.'

'You? The Battle Queen of Kar-Barzac? I don't believe it.'

'I don't have any right to ask, but . . .'

'Don't say it, girl. There's no need. Old Angel will be there. He'll always be there. In any way that you want him.'

*

The walls of Dros Delnoch reared high into the southern sky as Waylander drew rein. Karnak heeled his mount alongside the black-clad assassin. 'The war beckons,' he said.

'I'm sure you'll conquer, General. It's what you're good at.'

Karnak laughed. 'I expect I shall.' Then his smile faded. 'What of you, Waylander? How does it stand between us?'

The assassin shrugged. 'Whatever is said here will not change a jot of what is bound to follow. I know you, Karnak, I always did. You live for power, and your memory is long. Your son is dead –you'll not forget that. And after a while you'll come to blame me – or mine – for his passing. And I too have my memories. We are enemies, you and I. We will remain so.'

The Drenai leader gave a thin smile. 'You do not think highly of me. I can't say as I blame you, but you are wrong. I *am* willing to forget the past. You saved my life – and in so

320

doing you have probably saved the Drenai from destruction. That's what I shall remember.'

'Perhaps,' said Waylander, swinging his horse's head and riding towards the Mountains of the Moon.

Epilogue

Karnak returned to Dros Delnoch, gathered the forces there and led them against the Ventrians, smashing their army in two decisive battles at Erekban and Lentrum.

In the two years that followed Karnak took to brooding about the fear of assassination, becoming convinced that Waylander would one day seek him out and slay him. Against the advice of Asten he once more contacted the Guild, increasing the price on the assassin's head.

A veritable army of searchers was despatched, but no news of Waylander surfaced in Drenan.

Until one day three of the best hunters returned, bearing a rotting head, wrapped in canvas, and a small ebony and steel, double-bladed crossbow. Stripped of flesh, the skull and the crossbow were exhibited in the Museum at Drenan, under the inscription, cast in bronze: *Waylander the Slayer, the man who killed the King.*

One winter's day, three years later, and five after the siege of Kar-Barzac, the crossbow was stolen. In the same week, as Karnak marched at the head of the annual Victory Parade, a young woman with long dark hair stepped from the crowd. In her right hand was the stolen bow.

People in the crowd saw her speak to the Drenai leader just before she killed him, two bolts plunging into his chest. A rider, leading a second horse, galloped on to the Avenue of Kings, and the woman vaulted to the saddle just as Karnak's guards were rushing to apprehend her.

The two assassins made their escape, and many were the theories surrounding the murder: they were hired by the son of the Ventrian King, the battle monarch whose body was thrown in a mass grave after the defeat at Erekban. Or she was one of Karnak's mistresses, furious after he discarded her for a younger, prettier girl. Some in

322

the crowd swore they recognised the male rider as Angel, a former gladiator. None knew the woman.

Karnak was given a state funeral. Two thousand soldiers marched behind the wagon bearing his body. Crowds lined the Avenue of Kings, and many were the tears shed for the man described on his tombstone as '*this greatest of Drenai heroes*'.

The skull of Waylander was sold eight years later. It was bought at auction by the Gothir merchant Matze Chai, acting on behalf of one of his clients, a mysterious noble who lived in a palace in the Gothir city of Namib. When asked why a foreigner should pay such a vast amount for the skull of a Drenai assassin, Matze Chai smiled and spread his elegant hands.

'But you must know?' insisted the curator of the museum.

'I assure you that I do not.'

'But the price . . . It is colossal!'

'My client is a very rich man. He has invested with me for many years.'

'Was he a friend to this Waylander?'

'I gather they were close,' admitted Matze Chai.

'But what will he do with the skull? Display it?'

'I doubt it. He told me he intends to bury it.'

'Why?' asked the man, astonished. 'Forty thousand Raq just to bury it?'

'He is a man who likes to choose his own endings,' said Matze Chai.